THE FIRST
PROTECTORS

786.21

THE FIRST
PROTECTORS

A Novel

V I C T O R   G O D I N E Z

TALOS PRESS

Talos Press books may be purchased in bulk at special discounts for sales promotion, corporate gifts, fund-raising, or educational purposes. Special editions can also be created to specifications. For details, contact the Special Sales Department, Talos Press, 307 West 36th Street, 11th Floor, New York, NY 10018 or info@skyhorsepublishing.com.

Talos Press is an imprint of Skyhorse Publishing, Inc.®, a Delaware corporation.

Visit our website at www.talospress.com.

10 9 8 7 6 5 4 3 2 1

Library of Congress Cataloging-in-Publication Data is available on file.

Cover artwork by Amir Zand, amirzandartist.com
Cover design by Mona Lin

Print ISBN: 978-1-945863-35-6
Ebook ISBN 978-1-945863-36-3

Printed in the United States of America

For Sarah, Thomas, Elizabeth, and Eleanor

battered spaceship blinked into existence on the far side of the sun. A burst of blue erupted from the tail of the pockmarked ship and launched it toward Earth on the opposite side of the yellow star, 130 million miles away. Moments later, a second craft, elegant, like a droplet of silver, blinked in just behind the first intruder and darted off, riding a wake of fierce yellow.

The two visitors opened fire on each other. Trading incandescent red and green volleys, the two ships sliced through the solar system at nearly one-third the speed of light. Occasionally the shots intersected, creating brief electric explosions, silent in the vacuum, but nearly bright enough to outshine the nearby star.

The first ship, with the blue tail, was large, bulbous, ugly. A blob of discordant corners with bulges and edges seemingly carved by a blind maniac; it was scarred and scorched from previous battles.

The second machine was smooth, sleek, tapered, and unblemished, an arrowhead with a point that seemed sharp enough to divorce a water molecule into hydrogen and oxygen. It slipped through the void on a golden trail.

But as war machines, the ships were equals. Guns fired and probed for weakness from each side, colliding against staccato batteries of defensive energy. The ships plunged through the gateway of a solar flare that had arced from the stellar surface. They burst through the arch, trailing twin contrails of superheated gas, with the waterfall of weaponry continuing to pour from each fighter.

The crafts rocketed through the solar system.

Mercury, a blasted rock with no atmosphere, was bombarded by stray fire, carving fresh, molten craters. The ships raced on around Venus. The yellow clouds of sulfuric acid absorbed the wayward artillery, the blossoms of light quickly swallowed up by the poisonous fumes. Now the fighters plunged toward the blue Earth.

The second, sleeker ship launched a small auxiliary craft from its underbelly, which vanished and reappeared ahead of the first, hulking craft. The drone unfolded a scaffold of guns and fired. The battered ship momentarily evaded the new attack, changing course and turning toward the night side of the living planet. Then as the North American continent came into view beneath the fighters, one shot, then two, slipped through the defenses. Chunks of the misshapen craft disintegrated in a flash of flame and light.

The damaged ship jettisoned the ruined sections, but the wounds were lethal. More crashing than flying, the smoking ship made one last stab at the planet, fending off its still-firing pursuer as it burned into the atmosphere.

I

Ben Shepherd struggled up the hill, alone but for his jabber-mouthed demons. He glanced down at his small campsite. It seemed to have barely receded in the last hour.

A dying fire. An old tent. A pickup truck with more miles on it than Rand McNally. Home, or close enough.

You'll never make it. You're weak. Just lie down and die.

He was only about 75 feet above the desert floor but gulping for air like an asthmatic running a marathon. Finish line nowhere in sight. Sweat poked at his eyes, and his damaged right leg whined as he forced it to churn through the cold sand and pebbles.

Give up. The only thing in front of you is more pain.

The clear, cool night air swallowed his wheezed breaths as he inched up the slope. The stars rained down their billion-year-old photons on his back. A scrawny coyote loped by the bottom of the hill, sniffed, and jogged on.

Ben paused, his ragged panting the only sound for miles. Sweat trickled through his unkempt beard, making it itch. Most Special Forces guys grew their hair and beards long, partly to blend in with the local populations they moved through. It was also a thumb in the eye to high-and-tight regular military that looked on SpecOps with a mixture of disdain and envy. But Ben had to admit that his hair and beard had migrated past "special operations chic," through "unemployed," and were well on their way to "homeless." So what. He had more immediate concerns. For example, he was no longer sure if the warm liquid trickling down his leg was sweat or blood.

"Or maybe you just pissed yourself," he muttered. *That would certainly complete my transformation into shambling derelict,* he thought. *And talking to myself is just the icing on the cake.*

He wiped his brow with his shirt sleeve and ran his hand through his shaggy black hair in frustration. Once as fit as an Olympic decathlete, the long recovery had sapped his strength and endurance. His still-damaged leg had made it impossible to get any kind of serious exercise for weeks. He wasn't fat, exactly, although his flat stomach now sagged just a bit, to his disgust. His arms and shoulders were still strong, but he'd spent too much time recently on his back or his ass. His legs shivered under a strain that, six months ago, they would have borne without complaint.

Most of the other wounds had healed. The shrapnel buried in his right arm had been fished out, save for a sliver curled near the bone, too close to the nerves for surgeons to dig out. He had a laminated doctor's note to present at airport metal detectors. The spray of hot metal that had grazed the side of his head had left an impressive claw mark ("Like Wolverine took a swipe at you," his friend and teammate Eddie Dworsky had joked during Ben's initial treatment in Germany) and had come within a fraction of an inch of blinding him. Just scars now, though. Mementos. Like photos from a foreign vacation where you couldn't quite remember which cathedral that was in the background.

But the leg. The leg was still a mess. Less of a mess than it had been in the hospitals. Definitely less of a mess than when Ben had been sprawled in a swampy marsh just south of Karachi, with a terrorist who smelled like a goat's asshole in his left hand and a ruined HK416 assault rifle in his right. The mess was gone. Covered, at least, with scar tissue, unless he really had torn something again. The tired soldier leaned against a boulder on the hillside in the desert.

Everything had gone right. Right . . . until it went wrong.

Satellite surveillance and thermal scans and human informants could only eliminate so much risk. You couldn't predict the path of every rocket-propelled grenade. All things considered, his team had been lucky to escape at all. Just depended how you defined "lucky." Three dead friends seemed well outside that definition. Ben struggled to push the memories away. Like the voices, they refused to go, like querulous drunks ignoring last call.

—

The initial stages of the assault had gone exactly as planned.

Gliding across the dark water under cover of night, the two Special Operations Craft-Riverine gunboats slipped through the shallow mangrove swamps outside the Pakistani coastal city of Karachi. The city itself was a disorganized hellhole of some 15 million people. Ruined shacks built on top of ruined shacks, the streets choked with garbage and human waste. Telephone and electrical poles spiderwebbed with homemade wiring used to steal service leaned precariously out into the streets and over homes. Kids played soccer around zigzagging cars and scooters, and the tantalizing aroma of grilled meat from shawarma vendors mingled with the stench of open latrines.

Ben had done business there before. So had most of his teammates. Tonight, though, they were heading south of the city.

Each SOC-R boat was loaded with an eight-man fire team of Navy SEALs based out of Dam Neck, Virginia, home to the Naval Special Warfare Development Group. Piloting each ship were four Special Warfare Combatant-craft Crewmen based out of Stennis, Mississippi. A midnight run a long way from home. That was the job, and they were good at it.

The 33-foot boats were weapons, too. Ben's craft, SOC-R 1, was decked out with twin GAU-17/A six-barrel miniguns on the forward mounts, M240B light machine guns at the mid-mounts, and a thunderous aft-mounted M2HB .50 caliber heavy machine gun capable of vaporizing a rhino at 2,000 yards. SOC-R 2 was nearly identical, but with 40mm grenade launchers instead of machine guns at the port and starboard, about halfway down the hull. It was enough firepower to turn a city block into rubble and then grind the rubble to dust.

For now, though, silence was golden. The water jet propulsion system kept the boats free of the roots and rocks just inches below the surface (too shallow for a submersible insertion), and newly installed electric motors whispered softer than the ocean breeze. The original 440-horsepower diesel engines were there if needed, ready to drop back down into the water at the flip of a switch. Everyone on the team had chuckled when Ben had pointed out that they now drove hybrids to the office.

After twenty-three minutes of navigating the winding littoral maze, a spark of campfire appeared on one of the tiny, temporary islands scattered in the mangroves. The island was the shape of a lima bean and about the size of a football field. It came and went at the pleasure of the tides and storms.

Months of scouting and surveillance had brought Ben and his team to this backwater.

Asir flitted through this part of the world like a rumor of a ghost. The CIA had never before been able to calculate his location in real time; they were always weeks or months behind. He set his bombs or, worse, trained more bomb-makers, and disappeared into the shadows. A paid informant had finally paid off, and the terrorist had been traced to this spit of land.

Ben had no qualms about the nature of the men he hunted. They were terrorists. The sentiment back home that the US needed to pull back, stay home, power down the drones, and retreat into its fortress was wishful thinking. A fantasy. He'd picked up too many shredded body parts and catalogued too many mass graves to think of the men he hunted as anything but evil. They weren't cowards. They'd stand and fight when cornered, and Ben and his men had been in some knock-down slugfests that had only ended when every man on the other side had stopped breathing. Physical courage or not, they were a scourge. Every member of Ben's team was itching to finally bring Asir in.

The reports said Asir would spend the night on this slice of sand and vines before moving on in the morning. Ben's team stationed in the region had received just a 30-minute briefing after being transported out to the nearest Navy ship via V-22 tilt rotor aircraft. That had been plenty of time, though. They all knew Asir's face.

The SEALs lowered their night-vision goggles into place with a soft click as their craft approached the island. They could see six fighters huddled around the fire. Ben scanned the tangled greenery with the thermal detection technology of his goggles to check for additional targets loitering out of visible range, then toggled to live surveillance video being beamed from an RQ-170 Sentinel drone 20,000 feet above. The same video was visible on a six-inch flexible OLED screen on his wrist, but that screen turned off during insertion. Too bright. Six fighters it was. He gave a thumbs-up to his teammates, who were all doing similar surveillance. Thumbs-up back.

Thirty seconds to landfall.

The firelight from the camp was dim enough that both gunboats could land at the opposite end of the beach without being seen. The boats eased onto the sand with a sigh, and the SEALs slithered off, rifles raised with sound-suppressors and laser sights attached. The infrared laser beams, invisible to the naked eye, were clear through the SEALs' eyepieces. The sharp lines cut through the warm air toward the target. They could easily have killed Asir from here, but orders were to take him alive.

The sixteen commandos crept forward on the thin slice of sand. They were more exposed on the beach, but the marshy interior was a slow, noisy slog under even the best of conditions; landing on the opposite side of the island had been ruled out almost as soon as it was suggested.

Asir was easy to pick out among the five other ragged fighters with AK-47s scattered at their feet. He was taller, with a shorter beard. The smell of cooking fish wafted from the fire, and the men laughed at something Asir said as he waved his hands in the air.

Ten feet to the edge of the light and attack. Ben gripped his rifle tight.

Five feet.

Half a dozen flares shot into the sky from the mangrove forest and surrounding swamp. Automatic weapons fire burst from the tree line and Asir bolted into the jungle as his remaining men dove for their guns.

Trap, Ben's mind registered, even as his body reacted. He dropped one of the guards with a pair of shots. They only needed Asir alive. The other SEALs were also moving and firing. They cut down the remaining guards before they could open fire and then swiveled to the barrage coming from the jungle.

Ben, Dworsky, and the rest of his team peppered the forest with machine-gun fire and grenades, marching forward in trained unison into the sprung trap without a word. Hunkering on the open beach would be suicide, and retreating back to the boats would be failure. They caught only occasional glimpses of figures appearing and disappearing behind the roots and leaves, but Ben and his team knew from experience that the wall of lead they were dumping into the underbrush was having both a physical and psychological effect. They'd keep their heads down or they'd lose them. But Asir was running, and they didn't have much time before he slipped away again.

The gunboats roared as their pilots brought them online, their big diesel engines taking over, the need for stealth gone. Enemy boats were also coming to life on nearby islands, floodlights stabbing the darkness, searching for Ben's team, passengers firing wildly, hoping to get lucky.

In seconds, it was complete chaos.

"SOC-R 1, cover north," Ben barked into his headset. The boat zoomed off to the north side of the island, the direction in which Asir had fled. Its guns roared and belched as it sped off, and one of the enemy skiffs was torn apart like it had driven into an industrial shredder.

Ben and his squad fanned out into the dense jungle while the remaining SEALs doused the campfire with a quick scoop of sand and set up defensive positions against the incoming boats. It wasn't a long-term solution. They had minutes, maybe, before the makeshift armada of rickety dinghies and fishing vessels overwhelmed them. They had to find Asir, and fast. Ben's green vision was now teaming with incandescent activity.

The CIA and ONI—the Office of Naval Intelligence—had been scoping this island for almost two days. The terrorists must have taken cover before then, hiding under insulating blankets under the hot sun. In a corner of his mind, Ben admired the dedication. They were certainly patient and ruthless. They were still poorly trained, sloppy fighters, though, and that time crouched in the hot muck had probably slowed their reflexes further. The SEALs were efficient, calm, and deadly, picking off the terrorists as they popped up, conserving their ammo and anticipating each other's actions, the product of thousands of hours together on training grounds and battlefields.

Ben shoved through the vines and roots, his rifle sweeping with his gaze back and forth, knowing without looking that his men were doing the same.

The opposite side of the minuscule island was soon in sight and Ben knew he'd have to abandon the search. If Asir beat the SEALs to the water, the canals in many places were no more than 20 yards wide. He could be dog-paddling to freedom right now. All their training. All their million-dollar equipment. All for nothing.

Fuck.

His radio crackled in his ear.

"What do you think, boss?" Dworsky, a Master Chief Petty Officer, whispered.

"Fuck, that's what I think."

A patch of vines about five meters ahead swayed slightly against the breeze. Ben took two large steps forward, raising the butt of his rifle in stride. He brought it down on the jumble with a crunch, and a man's voice cried out. Ben swung his rifle on his back and drew a machete from a scabbard at his side. He sliced through the vines, reached in, and yanked out the bleeding, yelling Asir from the small bog in which he'd been trying to conceal his body heat.

He flipped Asir on his stomach, bound his wrists with plastic zip ties, yanked a strip of duct tape over his mouth, pulled a hood over his head, and lifted him to his feet. "All teams, Caliban is secure. Rally home."

Dworsky grinned in the darkness. Ben nodded back.

He sheathed his machete and swung his rifle back into his hand. There was no beach on the north side of the island from which to quickly board the gunboats, so the SEALs turned around and double-timed it back south.

A figure popped out from behind a tree, the barrel of an AK-47 rising. None of the Americans carried that weapon, so anyone toting it was an enemy.

Ben kicked Asir's legs out, dropping him to the ground. As he dropped to one knee, three 7.62mm bullets tore over his head. Asir squirmed, trying to scramble away. Ben lunged sideways, landing on the terrorist's back and pancaking him into the mud. Asir was stunned for a moment and Ben drew a bead on the fighter who had just ambushed him. The silenced rifle barked twice and the attacker fell dead. Ben reloaded, stood up, pulled his prisoner to his feet, and resumed their march to the beach.

The beach was a maelstrom, like the most violent rave party ever staged. The second fire team was already loaded on SOC-R 2 and was now pouring a wall of lead into the approaching enemy ships. The *pop-pop-pop* of small arms fire was punctuated by the concussive *boom* of grenades. Smoke swirled across the scorched and cratered sand. The explosives had also set off a few small fires in the trees, and two or three enemy boats were on fire as well. It was too wet for anything here to burn for long, but for the moment, it was hell on earth. The thermal goggles were useless now, and Ben yanked his up. More flares snapped into the air. Shadows leaped like dancing devils, spawned from gunpowder and phosphorus.

Ben dropped Asir again, knelt on his back, and from behind a tree snapped off several shots against incoming enemy boats. Almost impossible to think, to plan, in the chaos. Bullets whizzed and snapped through the trees. The flashing light from the explosions and fires was as confusing as it was illuminating. There wasn't much time left to get out of this. He had to get control of the situation, direct his men, if they had any hope of getting out alive.

Two other SEALs, Jimmy Bradford and Dexter Bryant, emerged from the thick tangle of vines about 20 feet to Ben's left.

"Jimmy, Dex, set up a position on the beach so we can exfil Caliban."

The two men obeyed without hesitation, sprinting to the cover of a pile of driftwood on the shore that the terrorists had been using as benches before the team had arrived. They fired as they moved, their rapid, controlled shots punching at the flurry of ships buzzing through the small bay.

Once they were in position and SOC-R 1 was heading toward the beach, Ben stood up, hoisted Asir, and stepped from the tree line. As he did, two enemy ships zoomed in. One of the ships held half a dozen men, all carrying AK-47 rifles. The other boat looked empty.

A flare shot up out of the full boat, and Ben was exposed in the white glare. The fighters spotted him and his hooded prisoner and immediately opened fire, trying to kill Asir rather than have him taken alive.

Bullets flicked at the sand around their feet. One round nicked Asir's shoulder and ripped out a chunk of blood and meat. The terrorist yelped and fell to the ground as Bradford and Bryant peppered the light skiff with lead. Ben struggled to get Asir back on his feet but his blood made him slippery and holding on to the thin, struggling man was like trying to wrestle an eel.

Bradford turned to yell something at Ben, and just then a bullet caught him directly in the mouth. He tumbled backward in a spray of teeth, blood, and bone. He was close enough that Ben could hear him still trying to gurgle whatever he had intended to shout, his mangled jaw seeming to move in multiple directions at once. Bryant was distracted for a moment, and three bullets slammed into his torso in a neat diagonal line. His body armor stopped the bullets, but the force spun him around and he went down on one knee.

Ben, still struggling with Asir, fired off three quick shots that he knew went wide. It took all his training not to abandon his prisoner and bolt out to the aid of his injured comrade. Another SEAL, Terry Smith, a bulldozer with biceps, had arrived back on the beach as SOC-R 1 was cutting apart the boat with the fighters who had shot Bradford and Bryant.

"Terry, get Jimmy and Dex on SOC-R 1," Ben yelled. "We're leaving now."

The big man moved without a sound toward his fallen comrades.

Ben glanced out at the seemingly empty enemy boat just in time to see a figure pop up from where it had been lying flat, out of sight. The man hoisted a long slender tube to his shoulder—a rocket-propelled grenade—and fired.

Even as the rocket was cutting through the air, the gunners on SOC-R 1 demolished the ship. Ben opened his mouth to scream a warning at Smith and tensed to jump away, but the hooded Asir stumbled into Ben, his legs wrapping around the American's ankles, knocking him toward the grenade.

The RPG smashed and detonated in the middle of the three men. Sand, shrapnel, and blood sprayed across the beach, and the concussive force knocked Ben's breath from his lungs. SOC-R 1 opened fire again, its mini-guns spinning a hellish whirlwind. Tens of thousands of rounds spun off into the night, chewing up the enemy fleet.

Ben's right eye had gone red and then blind with blood, and a dull ring was the only sound he heard, despite the ongoing fury around him. His entire face was slick with blood. How much belonged to him, Asir, or the other SEALs, he had no idea. *Spilled milk*, Ben thought blankly. No use crying over it. He tried to stand and fell back, his leg shredded and wet.

Through his one good eye he gazed at his useless rifle, flecked with metal shards, and wondered how much worse the damage to his leg would have been if he hadn't been holding the rifle along his side. There was surprisingly little pain but his muscles felt slow, almost drugged. The sand was red. Then black, as the light from the flares faded. Then red again. It was hypnotic. Black and red and back again. More boats were coming in, too many for the small SEAL craft.

But he hadn't let go of Asir, who seemed unharmed. Bradford, Bryant, and Smith were crumpled in a pile, twisted at inhuman angles and half buried in sand. Bone jutted from skin, and Ben wasn't sure whose it was. The three men had been in that spot on orders. On his orders. They'd done what they were told, and now they were jammed into this alien dirt in a sort of grotesque and instant funeral. The terrorist squirmed, nicked but still alive.

Bomber's luck. Bomber's luck.

There was too much blood seeping from his body to stay conscious much longer. Perhaps they'd all be buried on this black beach together. He blinked, weakening. Bullets flicked sand. A pair of enemy boats whirred toward the island.

The OLED touchscreen on his wrist was still intact. Maybe he still had enough strength for that. He tapped it with his finger, feeling the shrapnel in his right arm shred the muscle into ground beef. The RQ-170 Sentinel drone's surveillance screen switched to the attack screen of a pair of armed MQ-8B Fire Scout drones.

The bulbous, unmanned helicopters each sported a pair of Advanced Precision Kill Weapon System guided missiles. With blood now oozing across his face into his one good eye, Ben watched the thermal images of the approaching boats on his screen, then tapped each outline once. The last of his strength gone, he slumped back in the sand, waiting for whatever end would come. He'd hold down Asir as long as he could.

Searchlights stabbed outward from the boats toward the contingent of SEALs now firing in almost every direction. Ben heard the heavy machine guns on the enemy boats begin to rattle, kicking up sand in a furious march up the beach toward the Americans. Then the Fire Scouts were there, buzzing in over the trees and unleashing their missiles. They screamed through the air, each pair plowing into one of the boats, dismantling them in a staccato series of bone-rattling detonations that left temporary craters in the water.

His teammates appeared from the red haze, roughly grabbing Asir and Ben, lifting both into SOC-R 1. He watched dimly as Bradford, Bryant, and Smith were also dragged into the boat.

They left behind weapons, fragments of their gear, and dark streaks in the sand. Pieces of themselves. Leave no man behind—at least, not all of him. *I'm sorry.* Ben was embarrassed at the emptiness of the emotion even as it filled his mind.

I'm sorry.

The ships roared into the night, dodging and cutting and unloading their firepower, shattered fragments of enemy boats tossed in their wake. Machine guns chattering like rain.

Ben slumped down, staring at the hooded terrorist. On the other side of the boat, three dead soldiers, three dead friends. They'd trusted him and now their open but sightless eyes stared at him, seeming to ask what else they could do . . . as if they hadn't done enough. He couldn't stand to return their gaze, but was too weak to break it. Their bodies bounced with every wave, their heads nodding. *What else? What else?* The .50 cals pounded away, covering their escape with thunder and lightning. The ships finally emerged from the dense cluster of islands and sprinted for the open Arabian Sea and the amphibious assault ship USS *Wasp*.

The sun was coming up.

From far away, he heard Nick Parson, another teammate and longtime friend, calling his name, yelling at him to stay awake.

The three dead men finally flopped to the side, seeming to look back the way they'd come . . . at the black, churning water and distant fires still burning. At least they were in the boat. Not left behind. Not lost in the water, sinking beneath the waves. Not like long ago.

Ben closed his eyes.

2

The cold desert starlight was just enough to make out the black stain seeping through Ben's pant leg.

He was now sure it was blood leaking down his calf, soaking his jeans and squishing in his sock. Whatever. No stopping now. Just 30 feet to the summit. The voice had piped down. Apparently even his demons were exhausted.

The plan had been to just go halfway up the hill tonight, a small cigar to celebrate, and then back down. Build gradually, the docs had said. In fact, they'd recommended he stay at the rehab facility for another month. Let the nurses and physical therapists do their jobs. Screw that. The truth was, he couldn't stand to be around people anymore, much less someone trying to serve or help him. He hadn't done anything to deserve that. So he'd put in his retirement papers and checked himself out. A few weeks later, he was here in the desert, grinding. Tonight, he was going all the way to the top of this godforsaken hill. Or maybe it was morning now. Whatever. He'd smoke his stubby cigar at the top either way.

Progress was measured in inches. His strength was depleted, but his reservoir of patience was still dark and deep. With each step, his weak leg struggled more. Soon, it was step, drag, step, drag.

His right foot caught in a hidden crack in the dirt. It twisted and Ben bellowed. He crashed down, his foot popped loose, his leg ripped open, and a supernova of white agony filled his brain and pushed aside everything else.

A small avalanche of loose gravel, dirt, and rocks big enough to break bones carried his heavy frame in a wave down the way he had come over the last hour. It was like being in a storm at sea. At high enough speed, dirt and rock behaved like water, sloshing and rolling like whitewater rapids. He tumbled to a stop, instinctively feeling for the pistol and knife strapped to his hips even as he hovered on the brink of passing out.

After several minutes, the wildfire of pain in his leg faded to a smolder. Ben propped himself up on his left elbow. Sweat cooled, then chilled. He shivered and sat up. The dark, wet line of blood coating his right leg was cooling, turning clammy, and he let out a trembling sigh and brushed his hands. They were also scratched and bloody from his tumble down the slope. Ben leaned back on the palms of both hands, winced, and inhaled deeply, preparing to stand and bracing for the pain. He was going up that hill tonight if he had to pull himself by his teeth.

This had always been rough country but, in a way, it was also home.

The Comanche had once called this stretch of the southwest not just their land, but their empire. The most savage warriors of all the Native American tribes, the Comanche had, for a brief while before the American flood westward, controlled hundreds of thousands of square miles across Texas, Oklahoma, and New Mexico. For most of Native American history, the Comanche had been a small, primitive band, hunters and wanderers, rootless and powerless. Then the Spanish had come from the south. They brought horses. Originally bred for the arid deserts and steppes of Asia, these creatures were ideally suited to western edge of the New World. The Comanche, by some quirk of fate, were suited to the horses.

In raids and trades, the Comanche had acquired hundreds, then thousands of the beasts, adapting to this new technology at a lightning pace. By the late seventeenth century, a once modest tribe had transformed itself into the most effective light cavalry in the world. They rode to battle and, unlike their contemporaries, rode *in* battle, firing arrows and throwing spears from horseback.

It was a revolution in warfare, and they were as vicious as they were competent. They mercilessly slaughtered every man, while women and children were killed or abducted and forcibly assimilated into Comanche tribes. One of these captives, hauled across New Mexico on horseback in the dead of night on a September in 1841, had been Ben's great-great-great-grandmother.

A detachment of Texas Rangers had eventually rescued her, but not before she gave birth to a son from her Comanche captor. That son eventually moved to New York, far from the blood-soaked plains and canyons of his birth. But the blood in his veins could not be escaped. Indeed, that blood was now dripping out from Ben's hands and leg, back into his ancestral soil.

Whatever ancient connection he had to this place, it had no memory of him. In a way, the places you lived and toiled eventually became part of you. The house you grew up in, even the barracks and apartments where you lived for a few months or years, the events that occurred within those spaces gave those places meaning—for good or bad. You defined yourself, remembered yourself, as much for where you were as for what you'd done. And all the old familiar places had memories Ben wanted no part of. Out here, where he'd never been, there were no ghosts waiting for him. There were only the ones he brought with him.

He paused, staring at the stars, noticing them for the first time that night. Here in New Mexico, far from any city lights, far from everything, the panorama was overwhelming.

Every star in the galaxy seemed to be dumped overhead, a vast horde of glittering diamonds scattered across a royal cloak of purple and black. They twinkled and winked as their light bent through the atmosphere. It had been years since he'd been out at night with no job to do, no mission to accomplish. The night was like a black ocean, deep overhead, impenetrable and implacable.

For nearly his entire adult life, the night had been a cloak, a camouflage. Special Operations worked almost exclusively in the dark, relying on technology and training to hunt while their enemies slept; to be the thing that goes bump in the night.

He was comfortable when miserable. Most of his transitory girlfriends had noticed, too, and eventually left, even the ones Ben had hoped would stay. Crawling through sand and mud and leeches and snakes was the only time he felt, if not happy, at least fulfilling his purpose, doing what he thought he was meant to do. He'd camped immobile for 36 hours, sprawled over a sniper rifle, waiting for his target to make an inevitable split-second mistake. You could deal with physical discomfort and pain. This, here, now, in the desert, was worse. Helplessness. That was the word. Crippled and diminished. A lifetime spent sharpening body and mind, a blade on a whetstone. He felt chipped and dull now—physically and spiritually beyond repair.

So be it. The physical pain he could deal with. It meant he'd survived, if not won. What he regretted was the pain others had suffered on his behalf. That ache would always linger. He couldn't ask for that sacrifice, couldn't inflict that sacrifice, any longer. Time for someone else to lead the fight.

Still, the training embedded in his body wouldn't let him stop fighting. He punished himself in this oblivious expanse because he knew nothing else. There was no quit. There was also no desire to go back. There was just here. Even if the leg someday healed, became more than a useless stump, Ben couldn't stomach the thought of riding into war again with his countrymen, his brothers, beside him. No one else would ever die for him, because of him.

Ben picked up a small stone and flung it at the sky.

As it arced back down to the ground, he noticed a blue star that seemed to be blinking faster than its companions. Almost immediately, the blinking light grew in size as a steadier yellow pinpoint accompanied it.

These couldn't be stars. Satellites traveling overheard, maybe, or airplanes with collision-warning lights. In seconds, though, the lights had grown so fierce that Ben knew they had to be crashing. Maybe it was a meteor shower?

Idle curiosity turned sharper as the lights expanded, sinking toward Ben and now accompanied by what sounded like rolling thunder. What's more, each large light seemed to be ejecting separate trails of light, spraying beads of illumination. When the strings intersected, a boom shook the sky.

The two objects now plummeted toward Ben and his hill, a tangle of light and sound more wrenching than anything Ben had ever seen or heard over the skies of Iraq or Afghanistan. The lead object, the blue *thing*, was smoking and burning. It was being chased by the yellow thing. *Is that a . . . ship?* Ben had time to wonder as he tried to scoot backward from the looming crash.

At the last moment, the two lights screamed overhead, a cascade of fire and fury as the ground itself felt like it was about to split open. The shockwave threw Ben onto his back. He rolled over to watch the twin streaks as they crested the hill down which he had rolled just a few minutes before. One last explosion shook the night and then the light show was extinguished. Echoes rolled back and forth across the peaks for a few seconds, and then faded as well. In the silence and calm, the afterimages floating in his vision were Ben's only evidence of what had just happened.

He struggled to his feet, almost completely oblivious to his tortured leg. Hobbling the few feet to his battered blue Chevy, Ben wrenched the door open and hopped in. The key turned, the engine fired, and he stomped the gas, fishtailing briefly and then accelerating around the hill. A crown of fresh sweat had formed on his forehead. Before he had completely rounded the mound, he could already see a new glow, something burning. The crash site, where the two meteors had hit the ground. But as he made the last twist around a giant jutting rock, Ben saw there had been only one crash and slammed the brakes.

About a hundred yards or so out in a shallow gulch, the blue object had belly-flopped and split apart, leaving a deep furrow in the dirt. No way was this a meteorite. Tangled scraps of metallic debris were jumbled in the gulch and splashed up and over the sides. The fire was loud, as were the arcs of electricity stabbing out from fragments of what had to have been a hull. What had caused Ben to stomp the brakes, pushing through the yelp of protest from his damaged leg, was the perfect silver dart hovering a few feet above the rough shrubs and dirt of the New Mexican desert.

It was the size of tractor trailer, but coiled like a sports car. Faint wisps of yellow smoke or vapor drifted from the reflective surface and wandered off into the night sky. The flames from the crash reflected off the bottom of the silver ship, dancing with the mirrored starlight from above.

It was definitely a ship. An alien ship. There was nothing in the human arsenal, not even in the experimental programs Ben had occasionally observed, that could do what this huge machine was doing, hovering silently in midair.

Ben's mind, trained to react to anything, struggled to respond. He killed the engine, eased open the door, and slipped out of his truck. Maybe he was still lying in the sand at the foot of the hill, hallucinating through his pain. Or perhaps he had simply lost his mind. That seemed unlikely. His senses seemed to be working normally. His leg was still in tearing, burning agony. His nose detected the bitter scent of the fire. *That couldn't be how insanity worked, could it? Did a psychotic break have a smell?*

At some point, you just had to trust what your body was telling you. Whatever was unfolding right now in this quadrant of nowhere must be real, or else nothing was. He'd deal with the impossibility of it all later.

Instinctively, Ben edged toward a shadow behind a boulder a few feet to his left, his right hand drifting down to the SIG P226 pistol strapped to his thigh. He sensed, though, that if this were to turn into a shooting match, he was probably outgunned.

Seconds passed. A minute.

No frame of reference for how to act. No training exercise had prepared him. This felt like a surreal video game, but with no indicators pointing to the next objective. He was hiding behind a rock, looking at a machine from another planet, and had no idea what to do next.

Just as he was about to inch out, the silver ship hissed and a door opened. Or, rather, it melted out of the hull of the ship, like mercury, changing shape, flowing into the form of a ramp. A moment later, a figure emerged. Ben stretched to see. The flames on the other side of the craft made it hard to make out details, but the creature looked human enough, with two arms, legs, and a head. It moved lightly, with a glowing cable or stripe of some kind extending down its left arm from roughly the elbow to the hand. In its hand, attached to the glowing cable, the creature held a device about the size of a small flashlight.

Gun.

Ben leaned back into the shadow, only his left eye exposed. A tingle of familiarity coursed through his body. A gun was something he could understand, even if nothing else here made sense.

The figure either didn't notice or didn't care that Ben was there. It turned right toward the crash site, hopped off the side of the ramp the last foot or so to the ground, and climbed down into the gully where the first ship had died. The creature disappeared into the maelstrom.

Ben breathed.

Rocks crunched behind him.

He spun, pistol in hand.

Another creature lay sprawled against the stone. It was nothing like the first. This seven-foot figure was, by all appearances, a grasshopper that had drunk the growth potion from *Alice in Wonderland*. A sprawl of legs and arms covered in a green-brown exoskeleton, each ending in talons and hooks. A long torso, or thorax, at the top of which was a small head with bulbous eyes, two antennas, and a pair of clicking mandibles for a mouth. Whatever flimsy grasp on the situation Ben had started to develop instantly came loose.

The creature was clearly dying. Two of its four legs had been torn off at the "knees," and two gaping holes in its side pumped out green fluid. The creature wheezed. A raspy, rattling sound clattered from its mouth.

Ben held his gun and his gaze steady on the crumpled figure. The creature attempted to rise. The arms and legs fought for purchase, yet failed, collapsing back. It stared up at Ben. The mandibles opened as if to speak, but made only an unintelligible snapping sound and spat out more of the green ooze.

One skeletal arm lifted off the ground and beckoned Ben forward. Hesitating, he clenched his weapon, feeling the sweat running again down his body, the heat from the crash fire mingling with the frosty air.

There was no other human within at least 30 miles. That's why he was here. It was a place to settle his thoughts and rebuild his shattered body. He hadn't spoken to another human in weeks, living out of a tent, catching small prey, learning to shoot again, and trying not to think of a future beyond the next dawn. The wandering coyote had been his closest thing to a companion. Under the sun and the moon, Ben had left behind the rest of the world and it had been happy to return the favor. He'd brought a cellphone with a solar charger, but it was kept off and he'd quickly forgotten about the device. All had collapsed down into a black hole, the solitary man slipping over the event horizon, the gnawing pain in his leg the only tether to the past.

But for all that had been lost, Ben had gained some clarity. He thought he might spend the rest of his life in this desert, a prophet without a gospel. There was life here. It was hard land, but not barren. There was water in the rocks if you knew how to call it forth, and food if you knew how to hunt. Ben had given enough to the world. He had bled on almost every continent, sometimes nearly to death. Certainly many of his friends, too many, had bled out on those alien, enemy wastelands.

Out here, though, now, on this frigid patch of dirt that had been ancient when humans were learning to walk, this shattered creature on the ground was going to be a problem that could not be ignored. Ben sensed that everything was about to change, for everyone, regardless of whether he lived through the next few seconds. He tensed, then relaxed.

"Aw, *hell*," he whispered, and bent forward.

The wounded creature struck with impossible speed, a last gasp that was almost imperceptible to the human eye. One claw slapped the gun from Ben's hand, snapping several bones in his wrist like toothpicks, while another drove a spike into his right thigh. Ben looked down, stunned at the lightning attack. His right hand flopped uselessly, but that was the least of his concerns. The object jutting from his leg was the bigger issue.

About the size of a test tube, the silver cylinder was buried so deep that it had scraped bone. The exposed end of the object sank down. It was apparently some sort of plunger on a syringe, and Ben felt a liquid injection course through his leg muscle. The pain came like flood water breaking the banks, quickly followed by a second surge of rage.

Ben ripped the object from his leg with his left hand and hurled it into the darkness—along with a stream of his own blood—and with a single motion pulled his knife from the scabbard. The six-inch blade slammed down. No need. Even as the knife crunched into the chest of the insect creature, Ben could tell it was already dead or unconscious. The blow to his leg had been its last act.

Ben sagged against the boulder, knife abandoned and the devastation in his right leg now impossible to ignore. The light was fading as the fire seemed to be subsiding, concealing the wound, but the leg was all but useless. Raw agony was spreading slowly from the site, enough to make Ben gasp. Tendrils of flame seemed to be licking his nerves, radiating out.

The ravaged muscles quivered, then spasmed. He fell to the desert floor, his breath shoved from his lungs as he landed on his back.

The first creature walked around the boulder. It still had the gun.

Up close, Ben could see it was about six feet tall, with gray skin, a hairless head, and wide, thin eyes, but was otherwise remarkably human-looking. It wore black pants and a long-sleeve shirt, with a glimmer of silver lines running diagonally across the right breast. The silver lines blinked at a regular pace.

Not glancing at Ben, the humanoid creature aimed and fired its weapon at the insect creature. A burst of gold light flashed from the barrel and the insect creature's head disintegrated. A cremated puff floated away on a slight breeze. Now the humanoid creature turned toward Ben.

Bleeding, paralyzed, defeated, Ben couldn't move. He was back on the beach near Karachi. In a daze, he looked around for his shattered friends, and for a moment he thought he saw them, looking silently into his eyes. Then the vision passed and the dead disappeared.

The creature bent down, grabbed Ben by the neck with its free right hand, and lifted him to his feet as casually as a child picking a dandelion. The cold grasp was almost a relief against the fever flooding Ben's body. The creature, the *alien*, stared into his face, turning it this way and that, peering into his eyes. The creature then glanced around, down at the ground, searching. Whatever it was looking for, it didn't find it. The creature looked back at Ben and flicked his 210-pound body 30 feet through the air.

The alien was already heading off into the darkness as Ben crashed into a pile of rocks. The edge of a large stone met his head, and a cascade of stars swarmed his vision, blocking out their real-life counterparts overhead.

No matter. The sensation migrating from the injection site in his leg now commanded all of Ben's attention. The pain had transformed into something much more foreign. It felt like spiders were crawling up his veins, not just under his skin but deep inside his body. A snippet of a childhood nursery rhyme flitted through his brain: *It wiggled and jiggled and tickled inside her.*

An odd stretching and pulling sensation spread from inside the muscle, like knitting. Ben writhed, the foreign substance unfurling across his body. Convulsions ripped through him, and the muscles thrummed like guitar strings tuned to their breaking point. Whatever had been in the syringe, it was now seeping through his arteries and capillaries, like liquid metal, down into his cells and DNA. His arms and legs thrashed and his back arched off the desert floor.

Pinpoints of light exploded across Ben's vision, like fireworks in his brain. Green and blue, the scattered illumination quickly settled on the profiles of the rocks and mountains and flickering flames in his field of view. The lights coalesced into sharp outlines, perfectly marking the shapes and locations and features of landmarks that had moments ago been obscured in darkness. Then the contours were filled in and the rocks became fully visible, the starlight amplified a thousandfold.

He could see in the dark. Some 400 feet away, a striped scorpion scuttled out of its hole, and Ben could see the ridges running down the length of its back, even the coarse hairs coating its body and stinger. He could see them in the night, from a distance that even during the noonday sun would have required powerful binoculars and an inhumanly steady hand.

More than that, the digital outlines began spitting out odd, indecipherable text . . . alien script, which in moments resolved into English. There was data, reams of information about everything from the composition of the smoke drifting into the night—carbon dioxide, sulfur dioxide, hydrogen fluoride, an anarchist's cookbook of chemicals—to the weight and height of the rocks and shrubs that stretched out into the desert, to the distance of the stars and galaxies in the sky. The scorpion was a *Hadrurus arizonensis*. The data rushed in, an avalanche of information that no human mind could have wrestled down in the brief seconds in which it flashed across his vision.

As the deluge mounted, Ben could feel his mind expanding. The data vanished from before his eyes almost as quickly as it appeared, shuttled off to new warehouses in his brain. The perceptive explosion filled his brain and threatened to overflow. All his senses were flooded. He could hear the coyote running, now more than a mile distant, and he could almost taste the dirt rubbing against his palms and the blood drying on his brow.

The wounds on his body were closing, binding, healing, expunging grit and pebbles when necessary. He watched as the shrapnel in his arm, his Pakistani souvenir, poked up through the skin on his bicep, popped out, and fell to the ground. It left no exit wound. His leg, his mangled, doomed right leg, was healing, binding itself together at a supernatural rate, while the freshly broken bones in his wrist were pulled back in place and mended. The pain lessened, then stopped. With control returning to his limbs, Ben sat up and yanked up his pant leg. The feeble light from the fire didn't illuminate much of anything, so his new eyes found other sources. Starlight and moonlight was amplified. Now it looked like late afternoon. And what he could see was a miracle.

The deeply scarred and gouged flesh running down his calf was now coated in a lattice of what looked to be thick ropes of silver, almost like silk from a gargantuan spider. The quarter-inch-thick tendrils glistened and pulsed. They spread across the wound, welding together new muscle and ligaments and skin. The silver strings now spread across Ben's body, like chain mail. The lines then dissolved into a single sheen and melted down into the skin. The material didn't disappear completely, though, leaving the skin a vague shade of gray. Ben stood up, leaning gingerly on his right leg. No pain.

Not only was the pain gone, but he had an almost literal spring in his step. He bounced easily off the desert grit.

"Son of a *bitch*," he muttered.

He clenched and unclenched his hands, then turned them over, outlined in the firelight. A vague awareness of his new capabilities flickered across his mind. With a quick thought, his hands vanished, and he could now see the flames clearly through the space where his flesh had once been. The sleeves still hung in the air, but the hand was almost invisible, revealing just the faintest silhouette.

Whatever technology the insect alien had injected let him bend light around his body, rather than block and reflect it. Ben clasped his invisible hands together to feel the physical sensation and assure himself they were actually still there. Despite his heightened sense, it was hard to believe any of this was real.

With a second thought, Ben turned his entire body invisible. Another mental command and he could see in infrared, his body's heat signature exposed in the desert chill, a small blob against the hotter fire of the crash off in the gulch. One last command, and Ben felt his body grow cold, his pulse slow. He disappeared from his own infrared eyes, an invisible iceman.

He snapped back, his vision returning to the visible spectrum, deactivating the light bend system. Whatever was now inside his body driving these changes must be some form of nanotechnology, computers and machines at a molecular scale, paired intimately with his nerves and cells.

Ben wasn't an engineer, but he knew that no one on earth was close to creating the technology now embedded in his flesh. *Hell*, he thought, *I might be the most valuable thing on the planet right now.* He looked down at the dead insect creature. Whatever it was, it hadn't been attacking him. It had been upgrading him, arming him. Arming him against . . .

A soft step in the sand jarred Ben from his thoughts.

The other one was still out there.

His new senses tingled with the slight but steady stream of radio signals that fell even in places as remote as the New Mexican desert. Television and communication satellites orbiting the Earth, a commercial jet cruising at 32,000 feet. A much more intense storm of data swirled around the other alien, an encrypted cloud some 100 feet distant that was wirelessly tethered to the creature's ship. And the creature was coming back.

Ben wondered if he'd become a wireless beacon himself, if the humanoid creature had sensed his transformation and was returning for the kill. It must have been looking for the alien's exotic serum, hoping to find it still in the syringe. It probably hadn't taken long to find the empty vial, though. And if Ben's body was now blasting radio signals out into the night, it would be obvious where the contents had gone.

Ben's pistol was lost in the jumble of rocks and scrubs, the cold metal invisible even to his enhanced vision. His knife was still buried in the chest of the insect alien, but he left it there. This was about to turn into a shoot-out, and a blade would be about as effective as harsh language. If he was a warrior again, he needed a real weapon.

The other ship.

Ben spun and sprinted. The silver dart was about 50 meters away. Before the leg injury, he guessed he could probably have covered that distance in seven or eight seconds. Not world record speed, but faster than the average bear.

He felt his new muscles tense and explode. His feet flew, nanomachines in his blood delivering oxygen with inhuman efficiency, the reinforced tendons and ligaments and muscles unleashing torque that would have shredded any other man's body. He covered the distance in less than two seconds. Stunned at his own speed, he nearly sprinted past the gleaming craft, skidding to a stop.

Up the ramp, into the gloomy interior. The perfect dark was momentarily disorienting . . . until his electronic eyes came to life, automatically searching for a connection to the ship's network. Three horizontal blue lights appeared, and it took him a moment to realize they were only digital projections on his eyeballs, a sort of virtual reality display. The three lines were answered by three dots that appeared on the wall of the ship, real lights illuminating the interior of the vessel. Then the entire ship awoke in a symphony of light, instrument panels firing up and a seat rising up from the floor. A display resolved into a 360-degree exterior view of the desert. Ben sensed that, given just a minute or two, he could connect to all the ship's system and take full control. But he had seconds, not minutes. The alien, a few hundred meters away, was now sprinting in his direction.

In a blink, Ben searched the ship's inventory, and a panel slid open by the entrance ramp to reveal a weapon locker. One slot was empty, presumably missing the gun the alien had taken when he exited the craft. The second slot held a small black pistol that seemed to be only a grip and a barrel, without an obvious trigger. Ben grabbed the device. It, too, automatically activated, lighting up as three tentacles extended from the barrel, back over his right arm. They snaked around his forearm, clamped down, and dozens of small needles punctured his skin, anchoring the gun and establishing a physical connection with his high-tech body.

Ben swung around, mentally scanning the available options on the gun before selecting a large explosive charge. He burst back down the ramp, leaping sideways as he emerged, turning in midair and firing at the feet of the alien as it rounded a jumble of rocks at full sprint. The alien fired at the same time, a thin stream of targeted energy that grazed Ben's left arm as he tumbled backward. Ben's shot struck the ground a few feet to the right of the attacker and exploded. The creature was swatted backward in mid-stride, and the shock wave catapulted Ben into the gulch where the other ship had crashed.

His new reflexes saved him from smashing into the rocks, and he landed in a tense crouch, his weapon raised. The wound on his arm was already zippering shut.

The enemy had disappeared into the night. The cloud of radio signals had vanished, apparently shut down. Infrared scanning turned up nothing. Ben leaped a dozen feet out of the bottom of the gulch, landing lightly on a chunk of rock, his hands and feet finding almost invisible purchase. He bounded to another rock, searching the area just beyond the silver ship where his shot had landed. A smoking crater about six feet across was glazed in sand that had melted into glass.

The smoke shimmered for a fraction of a second. Without a thought, he jumped backward as a bolt of energy streaked through the air and destroyed the rock to which he'd been clinging. He came up firing, his gun and eyes communicating directly without interference from his brain. The tiny fractions of a second it took for electrical impulses to travel from retinas to brain to hand would simply have been too slow to survive this encounter.

He was something more than human now. While he had trained for years to make his instincts override conscious thought, biology was still a hard limit. That was no longer the case. The nanomachines buzzing through his cells and nerves had cut Ben's conscious brain out of the decision loop. A computer in the gun had taken over direct control of his nervous system, creating a priority data flow that left his brain a mere spectator.

I'm not a warrior, I'm a weapon . . . or maybe I'm both.

Ben sensed he could shut down the direct link and forcibly retake control of his body. He wouldn't survive five seconds in this firefight, but he had the option. Instead, he watched almost from a distance as his body became a self-guided missile. He dodged and spun and fired with the preternatural foresight of a fly sensing a swatter.

The other creature was just as gifted. The two fighters attacked and counterattacked across the desert. Fireballs rose in the night, pencil-thin beams of lethal energy snapped across the landscape, and booms echoed and rolled across the wasteland. The strobe light of battle flickered across the sand and rocks.

Everything was unfolding so quickly that Ben's thinking, conscious brain could barely keep up. Through the blur he could tell that he was slowly being boxed into a shallow canyon, too deep to jump out of—even with his new athleticism. He had explored this place some days before, dragging his throbbing leg through the narrow path out of sheer bull-headedness, determined not to turn around until he'd reached the impassable end. As painful as that return journey had been, he was currently in a much tougher spot. Having cornered his query in a cul de sac, the other creature could simply lob volleys of high-explosive rounds and either obliterate Ben or bury him under an avalanche of boulders.

In a brief lull, Ben disengaged the gun interface, retaking manual control of his body. He ripped his clothes off, threw them behind a jumble of rocks, dropped on his back, and went cold and invisible. The nanomachines in his body obeyed instantly, throwing his bodily functions into a near comatose state. His field of vision narrowed and darkened. He felt dizzy as blood flow in his body slowed to a trickle. He lay sprawled, his weapon extended, but now as lifeless as the dirt on which it rested. The data stream that had been flowing across his vision for the last 20 minutes dwindled to nothing, a small blinking red light indicating standby mode.

Two explosive rounds streaked over Ben's head, pummeling the tightening passageway that led into the back of the canyon. Dust and small rubble spattered on his naked body, but he didn't flinch. His nearly hibernating body wouldn't allow it.

For a few moments, there was nothing. Silence. Then the creature bounded into view, jumping from rock to rock—an impossible target. It landed a dozen feet in front of Ben, scanning the passage ahead. *Wait. Not yet.* Move now and not even his new body could save him.

The creature glanced around and seemed to stare directly at Ben.

Then it took two steps forward. Three. Four. It was now parallel with Ben. Six, seven paces . . . past his almost lifeless, invisible body.

The alien raised its arm to fire again into the canyon. Just as it fired, Ben sprang to life, his body and mind roaring into action as his eyes and gun reconnected like iron to a magnet. The creature sensed its mistake and began to turn, its weapon already spraying a wide purple beam.

Damn, it's fast. But so am I.

Ben fired a shotgun-like blast of incendiary pellets. They streaked outward at twelve times the speed of sound, zigzagging through the air, a cone of destruction that swallowed up the alien even as it shrieked one last radio signal back to its ship. The alien was torn apart, its body nearly vaporized. The boom of the final blast echoed down the canyon and washed back out to the desert like a sonic flash flood.

Ben stood up, surveying the wreckage. Only bits and pieces of the alien remained. Its gun was still intact, though, and still attached to the creature's severed arm. Ben picked it up, and the tentacles uncoiled from the arm and the gun went dark. He collected his tattered, bloodstained clothes.

A hundred yards away, the silver ship still gleamed in the moonlight, undisturbed by the recent battle.

Clutching the guns and severed arm, Ben headed back toward the landing site. In his mind, he tried to decipher the encoded transmission the alien had sent back to its ship in its last moment. Ben's upgraded brain had automatically recorded the stream and stored it for analysis even as his body was fighting for its life. Exactly how much of his body was still under his control? Was he a soldier or a puppet? Did he have full control of his own body or was he now some kind of . . . drone? Or a vessel for delivering a payload he couldn't understand? Ben could sense new clouds of data hovering at the back of his mind, alien information encoded bit by bit in the robotic dust inside his body. A problem for later, though.

For now, he felt the billions of tiny computers embedded in his body tune their combined processing power to unraveling the encryption on his enemy's last transmission. He continued back toward the ship and was now about 50 yards away. The ship had forwarded the transmission on to an unknown destination. Back home, presumably. The ship was now waiting for a reply. A small, spiky antenna had sprouted from the spine of the ship, and Ben's new internal radio detected an open channel. A squirming feeling in his gut, a familiar feeling in this unfamiliar body, a vague intuition of danger, made him stop.

Several things happened all at once.

Ben's network of nanobots cracked the encryption on the outgoing message—//**Mission failed. Voyager destroyed but payload delivered. Human integration complete.**//—Just as a reply arrived. //**Self-destruct. We are coming.**//

Tendrils of electricity thrust out into the night from the silver vessel, snapping and cracking like Lucifer's lash. The writhing bolts extended a hundred feet in every direction, then folded back in on themselves, forming a dazzling white cocoon around the ship. An electric hum filled the air, and rose to a whine. The sound and vibration seeped into Ben's body.

The ground and air, in a circle around the craft, were sucked inwards, as if the machine had become a black hole, but of the fiercest white. Ben, too, was tugged toward the roiling energy. The tug became a yank and his heels cut furrows in the dirt. He clutched a jagged boulder, the edges digging deep into his new skin. He felt the rock begin to vibrate, answering the screaming call of whatever it was that now coursed around the ship. He felt as if every cell was being summoned to the fury. Smaller rocks and other debris flew toward the pulsing ball and vaporized on contact. Just when Ben thought his anchor would be ripped from the ground and catapult him into the howling vortex, the ship exploded.

It was a massive, angry detonation, and it briefly lit up the valley with a midnight sunrise. The shockwave expanded, lifting Ben off his feet and hurtling him hundreds of feet back into the desert. Again, his new reflexes saved him from splattering against the ground. He dodged a storm of debris, boulders, while being pelted with smaller pebbles and rocks. He looked up just in time to avoid one last projectile, the mangled engine block of his own pickup truck, as it plummeted from the sky and crashed to the ground, disintegrating in a cloud of rust.

Ben stood up, wiping the grime from his brow as the last echoes reverberated and faded into the darkness. The desert was scraped clean 200 meters in every direction from ground zero of the explosion. Nothing remained of the ships, aliens, or battlefield to indicate what had happened.

Nothing but the two silver guns and the severed arm in Ben's hand.

"Well, and me," he said out loud. He looked from horizon to horizon with his new eyes. He was still alone. So he'd be walking back to the world, but now with two good legs.

He dug in his pocket and fished out his battered cigar. The click of a Zippo. He chewed the cigar around his mouth, savoring the smell, noting absently how his new nano companions eliminated the toxic elements from his lungs as soon as they arrived, and he wondered what the hell he'd gotten himself into. Prophet or not, he now had his gospel.

Time to head back to civilization and preach. So he started walking.

3

"**G**eneral Rickert."

"*Voice identity confirmed. You may proceed.*" Computer-generated voices had gotten so good that Tom Rickert could no longer tell the difference between the humans and the machines. The only reason he knew this one was a computer was because the engineers who had created it worked for him.

"Colonel Hale, sir. We have a preliminary delta report that has been escalated."

"Oh?"

"Yes, sir. Roughly 36 minutes ago, New Mexico, about 120 klicks northwest of Albuquerque."

"Sounds like the ass-end of the middle of nowhere."

"Yes, sir. Pretty much just rocks and rattlers out there, sir."

"Yeah, I bet. So what have you got? More than last time, I hope."

"Yes, sir. We picked up a pair of incoming blooms, one real faint, but the other was hot, really cooking. It only popped up about 80 klicks above the Earth's surface. For such a hot signature, the fact that we only picked it up at the last minute suggests it was damaged just before entry."

"You think it was a firefight?"

"That's what the analysts are saying, sir."

"Hmm. Or a big meteorite and a small one. Sure sounds like another false alarm."

Rickert hovered his finger over the disconnect button on his phone. This job was essentially an endless series of false alarms, and another one added to the list. Number 379, to be precise. Which Rickert certainly was—even if no one ever read his reports.

"That was our first thought, sir. But . . ."

"Yes?"

Rickert leaned forward. Out of the previous 378 calls just like this one, there'd never been a "but."

"But we happened to have a Janus satellite in the region. We weren't lucky enough to catch the objects' incoming flight path, but we did tune in the ground-facing sensors just in time for the landing. Sending it to you now over secure video link."

"Hold on, let me grab my tablet. Just a second."

"Got it, sir?"

"Yes, dammit, just cool your jets. Okay, here we go. Whoa, that's a helluva of an impact. So, zooming in, can't see anything through that smoke. Okay, clearing . . . wait, what the hell happened? Why'd the screen just go white?"

"We lost all imaging at that moment, sir."

"Did we have another bird nearby?"

"No, sir, we lost *all* imaging. Every surveillance satellite orbiting the planet went dark at precisely 21:07 hours. We couldn't see a thing anywhere on the globe for 23 minutes."

Rickert was quiet for a moment, absorbing the implication.

"Not a lot of meteors that can do that, huh?"

"No, sir. It was some kind of jamming signal that our techs can barely even begin to analyze."

"Hmm, okay, forget about that for the moment. What did you see when the satellite came back online?"

"The crash site had been wiped clean, sir. Flat as a chalkboard. Both heat signatures gone, although some of the civilian seismic listening stations in the area reported a substantial ground disturbance that was almost certainly an explosion—a big one—while we were blacked out. We're telling them it was an accidental ordinance drop during a test flight."

"Christ in a sidecar. So what really happened out there?"

"As near as we can figure, sir, we had two intruders, exchanging fire. One crashed, the other landed, there was some kind of ground skirmish, and then one of the ships self-destructed, obliterating both ships."

"So we've got no solid intel at all?"

"Not quite, sir. After the satellites came back online, we scoured the area and we found one faint heat signal. Optical view confirmed it was human, or least human-*looking*, and on foot, walking away from the blast site. He's been flickering on and off our scopes, real hard to track, but he seems to be making a straight line south to the highway, I-40."

"There was someone down there? A person? Who is it?"

"Not sure, sir. But we've already dispatched a pickup crew. We've got the 512th Rescue Squadron scrambling three Pave Hawk choppers with modified stealth from the 58th Special Operations Wing at Kirtland Air Force Base southeast of Albuquerque. They're hauling pretty hard and should be there in about eight minutes. I've got live video if you want to be hooked in."

Rickert leaned forward on his worn leather sofa in his small home outside of Washington, DC, depositing his barely sipped whiskey on last month's issue of *Scientific American*. Fifty-two years on this planet, thirty-one of them in the Army, and twelve assigned to this oddball unit that all his colleagues had assumed was punishment for a mission gone pear-shaped.

The 1st Stellar Expeditionary Force? What the hell did that even mean? Rickert hadn't tried to explain it—had been ordered not to, actually. Now he spent his days in a basement in a nondescript, suburban office park. It looked like any other semi-successful tech firm. There was a server room and a refrigerator stuffed with old sandwiches and abandoned cans of Diet Coke.

Some of the accoutrements might have raised an eyebrow, though. Anyone who looked closely at the bookshelf in Rickert's modest office might suspect this was something other than a third-rate computer networking company. Rickert had edged away from the battlefield—and his gut had edged away from his waist—as he immersed himself in astrophysics and psychology, diplomacy and molecular biology. Barely 5-foot-6, with bad eyes and salt-and-pepper hair, he was far more comfortable with a book in his hand now than at any time during his days in the field. He occasionally felt his department's top export was email and paperwork. Most of the day-to-day production was routine and predictable, punctuated only by the occasional false alarm. He'd stopped fretting about career advancement years ago. He could live with the routine, and he enjoyed the quiet research. The only thing to worry about was the day—this day—when the false alarms stopped being false.

Rickert shifted in his seat, sighed, and wished silently that he'd retired years ago. Still, he was curious.

"Push it through."

A window popped open on the tablet, and the pudgy general peered into the glowing screen displaying the inside of a helicopter soaring through the New Mexico night nearly 2,000 miles away.

●

Ben heard the helicopters at about the same time he detected their radio signals. His new internal computer informed him the three aircraft were 12 miles out, traveling close to their top speed of 195 knots, or about 220 miles per hour. They'd be on him in a little over three minutes. No need for a computer to tell him they were likely Pave Hawks from Kirtland, as it was the only air base close enough to get here this fast. Each bird would be loaded with a handful of Air Force combat search-and-rescue specialists. He could easily disguise himself from the choppers' sensors, or even disarm the airmen once they'd landed, if he wanted to. But that wasn't his goal.

He needed to be found.

So he kept walking.

Soon, the muffled sound of the spinning blades could be heard even with unaided hearing. The three aircrafts rumbled over a ridge, searchlights raking the desert floor. The lights pinpointed Ben. He stopped, set his cargo on the ground, and raised his hands as the vehicles touched down around him in a swirl of dust.

Eight airmen poured out of the helicopters, M-4 rifles raised, advancing on Ben. They slowed when they were within a few meters, noticing his gray skin and bare torso. He'd wrapped the two weapons and alien arm in his shirt. No sense alarming his "rescuers" more than necessary.

"Sir! I need you to come with us!" one of the airmen shouted over the roar of the turbines and the growling sand. The engines were throttled down just enough to let the wheels rest lightly on the hard-packed dirt so the choppers could lift off again the moment the passengers were back onboard.

"I know," Ben said. "I'm glad you boys showed up. Long walk to Kirtland."

The lieutenant—"Rodriguez," Ben read from the tag on his chest—was surprised only for a moment and hid it well. Ben noticed the small video camera fixed to the airman's helmet and sensed the radio signals flowing back to the helicopter's communications gear and on up to a satellite stationed miles above. Would the facial recognition software be able to tag him despite his gray skin? Probably.

Rodriguez stepped aside and motioned Ben to the helicopter. Ben picked up his bundle and tucked it under his arm and started walking. Rodriguez grabbed his arm.

"What's that, sir?"

"Two pistols and a severed arm."

Rodriguez moved to grab the package, but stopped and glanced sideways toward his headset, pressing it against his ear with his free hand, obviously receiving instructions over the radio from the officer watching the video feed. He stepped back and waved toward the helicopter.

"Please get onboard, sir."

Ben climbed in, and the airmen hopped on, too.

All three helicopters were back in the air within a minute of touching down.

Rodriguez handed Ben a computer tablet, sheathed in thick rubber to survive tough battlefield conditions. A jowly, tired, middle-aged face with a crew cut peered from the screen.

"Hello, sailor. I'm General Tom Rickert. Glad we found you."

"General, I've got something you need to see."

"Yeah, I think you do."

4

"**M**ore tests?"

"No, no more tests, Lieutenant," Rickert said as they walked down the hall, ignoring the fascinated stares from military and civilian personnel that were peeking out of their offices at the short, fat general and the tall, gray-skinned sailor. "Time to meet the big dogs."

"Ah, meetings. That, I know how to handle. Not much training, but plenty of on-the-job experience. And you can call me Ben, because I'm going to call you Tom."

"You're the first SpecOps guy I've ever worked with. Are they all as insubordinate as you?"

Ben returned Rickert's grin.

"Most people in your position would be wound up pretty tight, I'd think," Ben said.

"Well, I've been drinking heavily."

Ben sent over a larger grin, loosening up for the first time since before the crash.

"But seriously, a lot of these folks are still just trying to come to terms with what happened to you, what you represent," Rickert continued. "I've been gaming out these sorts of scenarios for years. It's still blowing my mind, though. Can't imagine what the rest of them are going through, going from zero to sixty like this."

"Well, they better get up to speed fast. There's no time to give them the sugarcoated version."

"Is there a sugarcoated version?"

"Sure. Still gonna taste like shit, though."

"Yeah, I figured. Here we are."

Rickert pressed his palm against a scanner next to a metal door. It slid open noiselessly, and Rickert walked in with Ben trailing behind.

The conference room was small, but packed. The 20-by-20 cell was blinding white, with a table in the middle and video cameras in all four upper corners. A mirror covered one wall, with three large LCD monitors hung on the others. A dozen men were crammed into the space, and a dozen gray, balding heads turned when Ben entered through the only door. Rickert waved Ben to an empty chair.

Rickert settled in his chair with a scrape and a clatter, leaning forward, elbows on the table. He didn't share his colleagues' exhaustion. He felt supercharged. His sleepy career had received an adrenaline injection, and he was hurtling through the days and nights with barely a chance to glance at the clock. He wasn't even sure what day it was. No matter. It was "after," and that's all that mattered now. After first contact. He and his team had predicted, back before anyone had cared, that this moment, if it ever came, would be the next big pivot on human calendars. BC, AD, and now FC. Assuming humanity survived the first moments of this new era. He had to remind himself his job wasn't over. It was just beginning.

Rickert plopped his tablet computer down on the conference room table, which lit up.

The table surface was an interactive touchscreen computer monitor. Rickert tapped a file on his tablet and twelve digital comets shot out from his tablet to the other machines resting on the table, delivering the meager data to the other scientists. He clicked a button on a small remote control to call the information up on the LCD screens around the room. Rickert thumbed the device with the casual assurance of a man who knew Power-Point as thoroughly as the laces on his shoes.

"That's the full analysis," Rickert said. "Well, as full as we've been able to do so far. Lt. Shepherd's physiology is somewhat . . . resistant to our techniques, as most of you know."

As Rickert walked through the details of the report, Ben remembered how his medical exams had seemed more slapstick than science.

Drawing blood, for example. Ben's skin automatically stiffened and hardened against assaults, and the only way they'd been able to pierce it was with a modified pneumatic nail gun. The nurse, a combat vet, had been sweating with effort by the time it was done. No sooner had the needle been inserted, though, than the nanobots in Ben's bloodstream had literally chewed it up and spit it out. The imaging tests hadn't gone much better, with the alphabet soup of MRI, CT, PET, and other scans revealing only that Ben's body was essentially impervious to everything from X-rays to gamma rays.

Roy Barnes, one of the techs, a jittery man with a comb-over like an ocean wave, became so frustrated that he cranked up the dial and bombarded Ben with enough radiation to cook a TV dinner, vicious curiosity overwhelming the hastily written testing guidelines. The nanobots in Ben's body had simply reformulated into a variety of molecules such as boron carbide to act as radiation shields, with other 'bots repairing any cell or DNA damage caused by stray radiation that made it through the initial defense.

Rickert had watched on a computer monitor as Ben sat quietly in the testing chamber, a tight grin on his face as the sensors in his body tracked the rising dosage. When the massive lead door finally swung open with a rush of air as the pressure equalized, Ben had stepped through in a blink, before anyone could react, and planted a gray finger in Barnes's chest.

"Try that again, buddy, and I'll drag you in there with me." The tech cowered and stammered as Ben walked back into the room.

The techs had also discovered that the nanorobots functioned as solar panels, resolving into silicon to become photovoltaic cells which turned light into energy. At one point, the lab techs had handed Ben a light bulb and he'd illuminated it with a thought and tiny surge of electricity. The lab guys, all with enough diplomas to wallpaper a skyscraper, had no clue how any of it worked.

But what they couldn't understand, the scientists could measure.

At one point, they had Ben climb onto a treadmill. He sprinted for 30 minutes at almost 50 miles per hour. When they started to get bored, he held his breath and galloped for another 15 minutes at top speed before slowing down, as the trillions of nanobots in his bloodstream took over as hyper-efficient red blood cells, transporting oxygen far more effectively than his original biological cells.

His vertical leap was enough to catapult Ben over a basketball backboard, and he could bench-press a Buick. His hyper-vision and ability to slow his pulse to nearly zero made him a record-breaking sniper, plunking a three-inch target three miles away with an MK 15 rifle, and his immune system tossed aside everything from mustard gas to weaponized bird flu.

Ben wasn't immortal. He did eventually have to come up for air, and the desert shootout three weeks earlier obviously meant he could be killed. Not easily. But it could be done.

Rickert glanced over at Ben, who was obviously bored. He was concerned that Ben didn't seem to grasp just how important these meetings were. If nothing else, they gave people a familiar environment in which to grapple with this absurd, impossible situation. Those sorts of lighthouses would be invaluable in the coming tempest.

The assembled scientists had already seen most of these reports, but they scanned through them again in the conference room. Rickert walked through, again, the details of the elusive radar signals and blinded satellites. Most of these men had been part of his original team, quietly tasked to prep for the unlikely event of an alien encounter. As jarring as the actual reality of it was, at least they'd been considering it intellectually for years. A few of the scientists in the room, though, had been drawn from unaffiliated research teams, and Rickert knew many of them were still unsure if this was some kind of joke or a grand psychological test. *If Shepherd hates meeting with the scientists, just wait until we start briefing the politicians*, he thought. For now, all the eggheads were quiet, bobbing their heads like bespectacled chickens as he ran down the latest test results.

"So we have some rough idea of his physical capabilities"—Rickert waved at Ben—"and it seems clear, based on Lt. Shepherd's report of the message he intercepted, that we're looking at some kind of imminent assault, agreed?"

The concept of an alien invasion still seemed ludicrous to Rickert, even though he'd spent a decade training for such an event. He couldn't imagine how this sounded to the other scientists, much less the tiny handful of military brass and the president listening in. Ben's gray skin would not be denied, though. It forced everyone in the room to acknowledge the impossible.

Rickert wondered, not for the first or last time, how the hell he'd ended up here.

He thought back to his recruitment for this role. When he and his peers had been suiting up to head to Afghanistan in late 2001, he'd been approached by a CIA spook and told he had been selected for a classified assignment. Rickert had assumed the dour, chain-smoking spy meant some kind of psy-ops mission, counter-intelligence against the Taliban and Al Qaeda. It was almost 20 minutes into the briefing before he started to figure out what he was really being asked to do.

He was being tasked with planning for an alien invasion.

Not that anyone ever said that out loud. Hiding behind jargon saved everyone the embarrassment of actually saying the words "alien invasion." He'd been ordered to "assemble a full-spectrum defensive and counter-offensive portfolio against a Type I to Type II Kardashev-scale opposing force."

The Kardashev scale was a theoretical ranking of the levels of technological sophistication a civilization could reach. Type I meant you were using and storing at least some of the energy from your local star. Type II meant you had reached the ability to use and store all of your star's energy. At Type III, you were harnessing the power of all the stars in your galaxy.

That certainly wasn't in the Taliban's wheelhouse. It had slowly dawned on Rickert that this assignment was about potential non-human opponents. It all seemed like a joke. But the assignment came with a promotion to brigadier general, and he got to pick his own team, so what the hell. *A star on my shoulder to stare at the stars*, was the joke he told to the few peers of his who had enough security clearance to hear it.

I guess the joke was on me, Rickert though as he forced himself to concentrate on the meeting at hand.

"The problem, obviously, is that we're extremely limited in being able to access the technology embedded in the lieutenant," Rickert said to the room of waiting faces. "We know what he can do, but we don't understand how he can do it, or if there's some larger, as-yet-untapped capability."

Ben felt his boredom curdling into frustration and anger. This meeting just seemed to drag on and on, and yet they were avoiding all the important questions.

He suspected he was far more than just a battleship with legs. But as instinctively as he had acted and reacted in battle with the other creature, Ben sensed those impulses were actually commands from the alien weapon. He hadn't been controlling events, he'd been controlled by them. The gun had been a key. It had opened a door into a dark room, and he wasn't sure where the light switch was or if it even existed.

Perhaps the insect alien had intended to point him to the light switch. Perhaps Ben could find it himself, stumbling through the dark, arms outstretched. Or maybe he'd march straight into a stairwell and go tumbling down.

Ben was also worried that he didn't have much time. The encounter in the desert had been merely a prelude. He was sure of that.

He interrupted Rickert's laundry list of test results.

"Look, I'll do the dog-and-pony show as long as necessary. But we're on a schedule. I can feel it. Someone or some*thing* is coming . . . and soon."

The mirror shimmered to life, doubling as a video screen. Everyone in the room turned to see the face of the president of the United States, Lawrence Lockerman, who'd been listening in silently. He'd been elected on a folksy vibe, but word had gotten around quickly after the election that he had plenty of hard-ass in him, as well. Ben noticed everyone in the conference room sat up a bit straighter, but he was too annoyed for deference. Besides, he was retired.

"And what would you suggest, Lieutenant?" the president asked without preamble, setting aside his briefing folder. "Lot of people around here think you're some kind of Trojan horse, think we should quarantine you. Maybe stash you on the International Space Station. That's not the way I'm leaning. I've seen your file. I know what you've been through, both in the last few weeks and in your previous career. I'm inclined to give you the benefit of the doubt. But I'm not hearing much in the way of actionable intelligence."

Lockerman leaned forward in his chair, like he was trying to crawl into the conference room through the TV screen.

"Now we've got your statement that you intercepted a last-second transmission saying more are on the way. What do we do? Even if we knew an entire alien armada was bearing down on us, what the hell do we do about it? Outfit some dinky satellites with a few nuclear missiles? Whatever technology we're facing will be so advanced I suspect our best weapons would be like throwing stones at a tank. So, again, what do we do?"

"Goddammit, I don't know!" Ben snapped.

He slapped his gray palm down on the computer table, which burst to life around his hand. Everyone else scooted their chairs back fast enough to leave skid marks in the linoleum. Even the president flinched.

Ben kept his palm on the table, and he watched as formulas and schematics and documents tumbled virtually out of his hand and spilled out across the surface of the tabletop computer. The files at first scattered haphazardly, but soon began to organize themselves into stacks and columns. Neat animated piles of data poured forth. What looked like images of circuits and spaceships and mathematical proofs arced across the touchscreen, blueprints, and instruction manuals.

Everyone leaned forward again.

At last, the avalanche of information came to a halt, the files moved to the background, and the table and the three screens in the room went black, then filled with stars. The lights in the room shut themselves off. The stars began to slide up the screens along the wall, as if the table were the canopy of a cockpit on a ship zooming straight down. Everyone in the room fought off a brief but intense bout of vertigo as the video accelerated, becoming a virtual reality display that sucked them into the scene. They weren't watching a video. They were living inside it.

●

A map of the Milky Way. Zoom in not far from the galactic center, a journey of 10,000 light years in a blink. A planet, like Earth but not Earth, orbiting a yellow star, like the Sun but not the Sun.

Volcanoes and magma, then cooling over a billion years, as land masses emerge, yielding oceans and mountains and ice.

Down to the surface, through the ocean, at the floor. Microscopic, simple organisms milling about. Flash forward, the organisms get larger and more bizarre, with teeth and claws.

Another 100 million years, and an explosion of plant and animal diversity, life everywhere.

Another billion years or so, and the first lobster-like creatures are venturing onto land, scuttling through rocks and tiny grasses.

A billion more, and the lobster creatures have morphed again, into what look like giant armored beetles and ants and scorpions and other arthropods armed with clubs and horns and fangs.

Earthquakes and meteors and ice ages take their toll. The giants die off, but a race of smaller grasshopper-like creatures begins to spread, gifted with unusually large brains and claws that have developed long, articulated fingers with each "hand" sporting multiple thumb-like appendages. These creatures eventually call themselves *brin*.

Fire, iron, cities, and flight. The planet is wrapped in a cocoon of digital information. A new age.

Then fair-looking visitors arrive in gleaming ships.

At first, these travelers, called *mrill*, bring tools and knowledge.

Then many more shiny ships arrive, with news of catastrophe on their home planet. The ambassadors are stranded, shipwrecked, on one of the few habitable islands in the black galactic ocean. The friendship withers, replaced by suspicion and resentment. The visitors retreat into their cruisers and battleships high above the planet's surface to think and plan. The brin build bunkers and fighter craft. Negotiations are over before they begin. Missiles and energy blasts and asteroids are hurled from above.

The defenders are numerous, studious, and desperate. The mrill, though, have kept some secrets back, some weapons in reserve. When the brin decline to surrender, when they refuse the terms and slaughter the emissaries, the mrill respond with swarms of nano death, tiny robots sprayed in the clouds that rain down and devour plants, animals, buildings, women, and children. The mrill program the nano invaders to spare the strongest warriors. The weakest are consumed in agony; cities and families disintegrate in puddles and dust. The strongest can only watch, powerless to repel this final assault as their world turns to ash. They beg for mercy.

In secret, brin scientists race to decode the nanotechnology. Billions are dead, destroyed. As a race, they're finished. Their best hope is slavery.

They finally figure it out. They infiltrate the mrill's communication network. The planet is mostly dead rock now, scorched beyond use in all but a few pockets, and the mrill must seek out a new home with inhabitants easier to subdue. Robotic probes have discovered another blue planet on the edge of the galaxy. It will take nearly a year to get there, even using star drives, but it is ripe for the plucking, populated by creatures even younger than the brin. Once affairs are concluded on this barren desert, the fleet will depart. The brin scientists record all this and present it to their leaders.

The brin leaders surrender. There is no time to reverse-engineer the mrill technology and regroup. This war is lost. The mrill silence their guns and fly down to the scarred planet for final negotiations. All surviving brin are ordered to assemble in the capital city, some 100,000 weary soldiers out of more than a billion that once thrived. They will all kneel. But first, they bury their newest bomb in the ancient catacombs under the plaza where the ceremony will take place. The mrill wear magnificent, superfluous, golden armor. It shines in the sun.

The bomb explodes, a second sun, melting the spectacular armor, its wearers and all in attendance. The brin are extinguished.

All but one. In the fire and smoke and confusion, a single ship launches from the opposite side of the exhausted planet and twinkles into hyperspace. The technology accesses the universe as a ball of tangled string. Instead of moving down the length of the string, a ship can hop to different points where the string touches and overlaps. Travel is not instantaneous, but it makes otherwise impossible travel distances merely inconvenient.

The jump is immediately noticed by the mrill, who surmise the ship's intent.

They dispatch a pursuer.

●

The video ended. The lights came back on. All the scientists sat in stunned silence. Ben looked around. Rickert was lost in thought. On the video screen, President Lockerman rubbed his forehead. No one spoke.

Ben thought of the friends he had, the friends he lost, and the friends he sent to their deaths. Just ghosts now. Shades that lingered, not angry, but simply lost. Ben thought maybe they wanted his blessing, an affirmation that they'd done enough for him, that they'd done right. He wasn't sure. Had he done right? Had he made the right calls? The question pulled him into ever-tighter knots.

He retreated further into his past. He thought of his childhood on the shores of the Pacific, and his father, the fisherman, in a red boat, motoring west at dawn, returning at shimmering dusk. When storms came through, Ben had waited by the radio, out on the pier, for the silhouette of the ship, named *Constance*, to rumble into view. As he'd gotten older, Ben had started accompanying the old man out to sea. Out into the storms. If you were lucky, you came home with the sun at your back. That fiery image pulled him to another world, the burnt planet and its inhabitants' dying hope for Earth, a planet they would never see. Ben had become a hermit in the desert, fleeing all death but his own. War had a will of its own, galloping across the galaxy to the end of the Earth. It would happily kill everyone. Or Ben sensed he could handpick a few sacrifices to placate the horseman. Save many souls at the cost of his own. He could feel that choice being prepared for him.

If there was a hell, Ben figured, it was a noose he had to endlessly drape around the necks of those who trusted him the most. So be it. He accepted his destiny.

He leaned in.

"We better get to work."

5

President Lockerman slumped back into his chair in the Treaty Room of the White House and looked around the tired faces of his civilian and military advisers.

He generally preferred working in this office; less dramatic and more comfortable for quiet thought than the Oval Office. It didn't feel comfortable now. It felt only cramped and old, a tomb for a world that didn't yet know that it was already dead. *This isn't what I campaigned on. This isn't what I was elected for.* He recognized the futility and petulance of the *Let this cup pass my lips* sentiment even as he thought it, and forced it down, slightly ashamed. Lockerman shrugged off his despair and sat up.

"Miranda, what do you think?"

Eight heads swiveled to face Miranda Hawthorne, Assistant to the President for Science and Technology, who was fiddling with her glasses.

Hawthorne had a fistful of degrees in everything from aerospace engineering to biomechanical engineering to theoretical mathematics to computer science from Stanford, MIT, and Carnegie Mellon. She had fifteen patents to her name and had launched two successful startup companies focused on cloud technology and internet security that had netted her nearly a billion dollars. She was by far the richest person in the room—not that you could tell it from her jeans and ratty sneakers.

Lockerman thought Hawthorne was not only the smartest person he had ever met, but probably the smartest he ever would meet . . . and she knew it. Talking to her was like talking to the bastard child of Einstein and a YouTube video comments section. *The benefit of "fuck you" money*, Lockerman thought.

It hadn't helped when she'd realized early in his administration that her position was largely ceremonial. Science advisers spent a lot more time judging high school science fairs than making policy. He knew she'd been thinking of quitting. Not anymore. For the last few weeks, she'd been in almost every meeting he'd been in, usually no more than a chair or two away. She was the only person who actually seemed to be enjoying this.

"Seriously? Y'all still don't get it?" Hawthorne said as she slid her black-framed glasses on. Seeing the distressed look on the president's face, she waved her hands in a semi-apologetic manner.

"Okay, look. Has anyone here heard of the Great Filter? The Fermi Paradox? The Drake Equation?"

Blank stares. Lockerman knew better than to guess, and the rest of the attendees took their lead from him.

"Okay, here, look."

She flipped open her notebook, clicked her pen, and started scribbling out an equation. The generals and other staff exchanged glances.

"Don't worry, guys. It's really not that complicated. Here."

Lockerman glanced at the sheet of paper she slid in front of him.

$$N=R*fpneflfifcL$$

"I don't even know how to say that out loud," he said. "Give us the abbreviated version."

She tapped the tip of the pen on the notebook and glanced up at the ceiling. Lockerman could tell she was trying to bite down on the obscenity dangling on the tip of her tongue. She finally gathered herself.

"That's the Drake Equation. It's a way of thinking about how many intelligent alien civilizations we should find in our galaxy, based on factors like rate of star formation, the fraction of stars with habitable planets, the likelihood of those planets to result in the formation of life, and so on. It's not a law of nature or even a testable hypothesis, really."

Hawthorne slid the piece of paper back and forth on the table between her hands, spun it absently, and rocked a bit in her chair. Lockerman wondered if her one-time investors had found her manic habits as annoying as his old generals did.

"But under some reasonable estimates, we would expect something like 100,000 advanced civilizations in our galaxy alone. And many of those should have been around for millions or even billions of years. Our solar system is pretty young, after all. Lots of old-fart solar systems banging around. Again, just an estimate, but not totally insane. Follow?"

"I . . ."

"I know what you're going to say. Yeah, it's full of variables that are more like wild-ass guesses, but still, good enough for government work, right? Anyway, the point is, unless life is literally unique to our planet, it should have occurred on lots of planets."

She looked around the room as if to confirm everyone was following, but plunged on before anyone could interrupt.

"But that raises another question: If intelligent aliens are out there in such huge numbers, why haven't we seen any evidence of them, before now? Where is everyone? That's the Fermi Paradox. Still with me?"

"Is this going somewhere useful, Miranda?" Lockerman said, rubbing his forehead. He noticed that Hawthorne's pulled-back red hair, with a blue-dyed streak on one side, was held in place with a simple rubber band. Whatever she spent her fortune on, it wasn't clothing and accessories.

She blinked, visibly swallowing her annoyance at the interruption.

"Useful? This is the only useful thing worth talking about right now. Anyway, Fermi Paradox. Where are all the aliens? There have been a few suggested explanations. Maybe all the intelligent aliens avoid humans because we're too stupid and not worth their time. Or we're like a nature preserve. Don't harass the primitives."

She grinned wolfishly at the room, heedless of the faces as stony as Easter Island statues.

"Or maybe life is plentiful, but intelligent civilizations are not. Maybe lots of planets are teeming with simple life, just pond scum and worms, or even moderately advanced civilizations like ours. Those are the *happy* possibilities."

She stopped spinning her notebook, as if it had suddenly gotten too heavy to move.

"The *unhappy* possibility is maybe there aren't many advanced civs bouncing from solar system to solar system because something wipes them out before they can make that leap."

"You're saying that most moderately advanced species go extinct before they can graduate to a level of technological sophistication that would allow them to guard against their own extinction?" asked General David Winston, chairman of the Joint Chiefs of Staff.

"Exactly! He gets it!"

Lockerman suspected she would have high-fived the gnarled soldier if he'd been sitting next to her.

"*This* idea is called the Great Filter. Again, not a law of nature, but an idea. There's something that shuts down alien civilizations before they get to the level where we'd see evidence of them all over the galaxy, such as radio signals. Now, the Great Filter is a scary concept when you think about it. Asteroids, gamma ray bursts, nuclear war, all these things could be the sort of endgame that squashes most civilizations before they get smart enough to prevent them. Or maybe there are civilizations that have made that leap but, once they do, they guard that privilege jealously."

"This is my tree house. No one else allowed in. You're talking about the mrill," Lockerman said.

"Yup. Maybe the Great Filter isn't some natural cataclysm or act of suicide. It's other alien civilizations, chopping down potential competitors. It's the mrill. Every time a prairie dog pokes its head up out of the ground, down comes the hawk. And we're the prairie dog."

The room went quiet.

Hawthorne sighed, exasperated, and flopped her hands in the air, sending the Drake Equation skimming across the polished oak.

"Don't you see, though? We have an ace in the hole. The brin. That's our safe passage through the Great Filter. Well, not safe. But it's *a* passage. We *have* to do what they suggest."

"So you think we should really start building all that machinery, all that stuff in the blueprints we just saw from the brin? That's a hell of a lot of blind faith, Miranda. I'm just not sure."

"Faith? What's that line about faith, from the Bible? 'The evidence of things not seen?' I think we've got the opposite of that. Plenty of evidence that I can see. You don't really think this guy Shepherd is some Chinese plot, do you?" Hawthorne glanced around the room, her tone a mix of amusement and disbelief.

Winston spoke up again.

"I think we're agreed on that front. But who's to say he's not some kind of trap, a Trojan horse? We build all this stuff, and it turns out it's a bomb of some kind, or some other weapon the . . . the mrill are using to kill us from a distance."

Lockerman realized the general was still struggling to acknowledge that they were talking about aliens. He could feel Hawthorne's contempt for the military man's denial, but Lockerman sympathized. He was what he'd been trained to be. They all were.

"Oh, come on," Hawthorne said. "If the mrill are advanced enough to fly here from across the galaxy, they're advanced enough to kill us without breaking a sweat. There's no reason to try and trick us. Would you devise some fiendish subterfuge, General, if your opponent was a herd of cattle and you had a fleet of stealth bombers and guided missiles at your command? Why bother?"

Lockerman sipped his coffee and leaned back. "But why us? Why pick a fight at all? Yeah, their homeworld is dead, and they want some place to crash, but why here? Even if we're a minor nuisance, why risk any kind of confrontation with us when they could pick any uninhabited planet in the galaxy? What's so special about Earth?"

Hawthorne took her glasses off again, working the stems in her hand. She thought for a moment.

"That's an interesting question. Not really relevant to the immediate situation, but interesting. Maybe medium-sized planets with liquid water, rocky landmasses, and oxygen-rich atmospheres at a pleasant distance from a stable star are rarer than we realize. Maybe there are multiple Great Filters, and the first one is just hitting the lottery with a planet like ours. This may be as good as it gets. "

Air Force General Tim Linton verbalized the dark thought that had been bubbling in Lockerman's mind.

"Even with Lt. Shepherd, we're in a hell of a jam here, aren't we? He's got some good tech, but we're outgunned here."

"Oh, absolutely," Hawthorne said without hesitation. "I'd put the odds of a global holocaust, extinction of the human species, at something like . . . 75 percent. Maybe a smidge higher."

A murmur ran through the room, almost a rumble. Lockerman grimaced like a man gripped with a stomach bug who had just spotted a REST-ROOMS—30 MILES sign.

"Hey, cheer up. Could be a lot worse," she added. "All in all, we've been pretty lucky. If this had happened fifty years ago, there's no way we could build all the stuff in Shepherd's blueprints. That said, I hope Congress has their check-writing hands limbered up. This is gonna get spendy."

This was the first piece of good news—well, *manageable* news—the president had heard all day. He was a lot more familiar with budget battles than space battles. He clicked open his own pen and pulled over Hawthorne's wayward sheet of paper.

"Hit me."

"Well, Mr. President," she said, her eyes going unfocused as she seemed to start doing calculations in her head, "we've got a hell of a lot of defensive satellites to build. Normally, you can put together a bird in about 18 months or so, at about $500 million a pop. We can probably push that timeframe down to a about month if we really haul ass. But, you know, like they say in IT: fast, cheap, reliable. Pick two. We need fast and reliable, so better start pumping out those treasury notes."

Lockerman scribbled furiously, then sipped his coffee and made a face at the cold liquid, pushing the cup away.

"We need fifty satellites, and I think we need to get them up as fast as we can build them. Who knows how long it will take the mrill to get their invasion ready. And to get these things in orbit quickly, you'll probably want several more launch facilities than what we've got today, maybe a dozen."

Hawthorne drummed her fingers on the table.

"I'd guess $100 billion for that part of the project alone, maybe more."

"Hell, Miranda, we spend more than that every year on interest payments on the national debt alone," Lockerman said, not looking up as he jotted down the figures.

"Yeah, and great job on that," she replied without looking back down.

Lockerman could sense the room getting annoyed at her tone, but he let it slide. Everyone's ego would have to wait.

"But this is just stage one," she continued. "Assume the satellites work, and repel the initial nano assault. Next, the mrill will send troops, or more likely drones, perhaps with control ships in orbit. I'll defer to General Winston on the shooting stuff."

"Mr. President, I think Ms. Hawthorne is correct on this," Winston said with a nod. "The science is above my head, but tactically, it's pretty straightforward. I'd guess they'll look to first cut off the chain of command of the global militaries of any size, and some kind of aerial bombardment with drones or manned vehicles makes sense. It's what we'd do. So that means they'll be targeting us, China, Russia, England, France, Japan, Germany, India, maybe a few others. But that raises another issue, sir."

"What's that, General?" Lockerman said, swallowing a sigh.

"Do we tell those countries, sir? Do we tell the world?"

Now Lockerman did sigh.

Hawthorne spoke up again, almost bouncing in her seat.

"Precisely! You won't be able to keep this secret for long. The satellite construction will be hard enough to keep a lid on. Then if you start building antiaircraft guns, sorry, antispacecraft guns and other defenses on the ground everywhere, the cat is gonna be out of the bag in about three seconds. And we're going to have to bring in most, if not all, of the other governments."

The president slowly rotated the piece of paper on the table with his fingertips. The numbers and equations and dollar figures filled the page, and seemed to turn to gibberish as Lockerman swiveled the paper upside down, then become legible again as he returned the sheet to its original orientation. Around and around. Sense to nonsense and back.

"We're going to need help from a lot of people to pull this off," he finally said. "We at least have to start putting feelers out there. At some point, this has to be a global effort. A lot of people are going to think we're full of shit. That we're making this up to hide some other agenda."

"That doesn't even go into the cost of building that second line of defense," Hawthorne interjected.

"And what's the ballpark on that, Miranda?"

"I don't know. A trillion, maybe?"

Lockerman was quiet this time as he wrote then number down, then circled it, then underlined it. He started to write again, then set the pen down. Skull and crossbones was probably pushing it.

"Plus you've got to worry about the total breakdown of society when people find out they're about to get melted by space aliens," Hawthorne added almost as an afterthought.

"Now, hold on," said Dan Henning, the president's chief of staff. "When the Japanese bombed Pearl Harbor, there wasn't panic. The country pulled together. Give people a common enemy and they'll fight it in common. Why would this be any different?"

Hawthorne shook her head.

"Totally different. Everyone had been debating possible war with the Germans and Japanese for years. The specifics of Pearl Harbor were a shock, but the *idea* of war wasn't. Plus, the mainland US was never really threatened. None of that applies here. Plus, you know, *aliens*."

Lockerman swiveled back to General Linton, whose Air Force was in charge of satellite surveillance.

"General, how many other countries saw what happened in New Mexico? What would their satellites have picked up? Have we intercepted any chatter on this?"

Linton tapped a button on his tablet, scanning the info he'd already memorized.

"Maybe the Russians, maybe the Chinese saw some of it. Probably mistook the landings for meteors, as we did initially, if they noticed it at all. No one else had satellites close enough to pick it up. As for the global satellite blackout that followed, everyone definitely noticed that. The Chinese think we or the Russians were testing some experimental equipment. Russians blame us or the Chinese. Satellite TV providers, GPS companies, those guys noticed it, too. We had NASA put out a press release blaming a small solar flare. Seems to be working," he said with a shrug. "A few astronomers are saying they didn't notice a flare, but that's not getting much press."

"What about amateur astronomers, university observatories, that sort of thing? Lots of people are looking at the sky all the time."

"True. The ships would have just looked like small meteors, though. The Russians and Chinese might suspect something was up, but not like they're going to publicly claim aliens landed in New Mexico."

Lockerman was quiet for a moment.

"We have a short window to decide if and how we go public. I think we do have to say something, soon." He nudged the cup and saucer with his finger, unsure how to proceed. "I don't think it will go over well. To your point, Miranda, there's no Pearl Harbor here. We haven't really even been attacked yet. We're going to tell people they have to reorder the entire global economy against an enemy only one man has ever seen in person. I'm not sure they're going to believe it. Shit, I'm not sure *I* believe it."

Lockerman picked up the sheet of paper, stood up, and looked out the window, down at the Jacqueline Kennedy Garden. The sun was out, and the tulips bowed in the breeze. Lockerman looked back into the Treaty Room, his gaze caught on the painting *The Peacemakers*. Lincoln, his legs crossed, his right elbow resting on his knee and his chin on his palm, listened eternally as Major General William Tecumseh Sherman spoke, while General-in-Chief Ulysses S. Grant and Rear Admiral David Dixon Porter looked on.

The meeting in 1865 aboard the steamer *River Queen* had occurred in the final days of the Civil War, both sides exhausted and bled dry. More than 600,000 dead, the most lethal war in American history. By one estimate, 10 percent of all Northern men between the ages of twenty and fifty-four were killed, and 30 percent of Southern men between eighteen and forty. Lockerman tried to imagine tens or hundreds of millions Americans killed in an invasion, but the numbers were too big and he waved the thought aside. The figures on the paper in his hand were startling enough. Perhaps future generations would study it in a museum and be equally astounded at how such simple math could contain so much horror.

The president turned to his assembled advisers, folding the piece of paper and slipping it into his pocket.

"All right, let's get this rolling. Eventually, we'll have to tell the whole world. But for now, let's start briefing the heads of state we trust and the ones we need to ramp up their satellite production lines."

Lockerman looked again at the painting. He wondered if Lincoln had any inkling before the war started of the butcher's bill he would have to sign to preserve the Union. The sharp corners of the folded notepaper in his pocket pressed against his thigh.

"God help us all."

6

Bert Goldberg sank into his creaky office chair. He wiggled the grimy mouse to wake his wheezing Dell and gobbled a bite of his bologna sandwich. Berta, his wife—"the other 'Bert'" as she liked to introduce herself with a meaty laugh—was out grocery shopping. He had to make some kind of progress on the job search if he wanted her to come home from the next shopping trip with more than bologna and macaroni.

He was already scrolling through job listings, but there weren't a lot of openings for fifty-two-year-old electrical engineers with a background in aeronautics. Satellites, specifically.

He sighed and opened another tab in his browser to compose an entry for his blog, "To the Moon, Alice!"

Goldberg wasn't much for gadgets, although he certainly understood them. Given a screwdriver and a few minutes by himself, he could disassemble and repair most everything, as his fingers just seemed to work on their own, gently prodding and turning. Most of the modern toys held little appeal for their own sake. He was more interested in how they worked than how he could use them. "If it ain't broke, what's the point?" he'd once explained to Berta. He did enjoy blogging, though. He'd developed a dependable audience of a few thousand readers who followed his musings on everything from space travel to medieval warfare.

Goldberg tapped at his keyboard. The old keys were getting squishy, and the letter "Q" often got stuck. Good thing he didn't need that one often. Currently, he was trying to coax something readable from a previous draft post about the maintenance needs for "solar sails," a theoretical propulsion system for interplanetary probes. No matter how many edits he made, though, he couldn't seem to fix it. A few years ago, he'd dreamed of retiring and devoting himself to his hobbies. As it turned out, a hobby was much more fun as a diversion than a devotion. Particularly when you had credit card bills piling up in your kitchen.

He tabbed back over to the job listings.

He popped the last bite of sandwich in his mouth and banged out a few keywords, expecting the usual "no listings." Instead, more than 100 openings spilled down the screen.

Whoa.

In the last 30 minutes, dozens and dozens of positions had opened up, all looking for experienced electrical engineers willing to relocate and begin work immediately. In addition to the old standbys—Thales Alenia Space, Boeing, Lockheed Martin, Loral, Astrium, JSC—dozens of manufacturers that had gotten out of the satellite game years ago were now advertising, too.

Bert and Berta had already agreed that if they had to relocate from Denver for his job hunt, they'd do it. Lockheed Martin Space Systems had a big presence in the area, but the satellite division had been cutting staff due to the watery economy. Commercial and government clients had all been cutting their orders in the last year or so.

But you wouldn't have known it from this job board. There were now openings from Colorado to California to France, Russia, Canada, the UK, Japan, and more. Goldberg backed out of his refined search and did a broader search across all job categories at satellite manufacturers. Thousands of listings filled the browser, page after page after page.

"What the hell . . ." He dipped into a bag of Fritos with his free hand. He smeared the chips into his mouth, dusted his hands, and fired off his résumé to every opening for which he was remotely qualified, more than thirty in all, then clicked back to his blog.

Goldberg deleted the limp entry he'd been composing and tapped out a new post about the surge in job postings. What was going on? He scanned the news headlines. Then a deeper search for any space- or communications-related news that would justify this overnight multi-billion-dollar surge. He'd already looked twice earlier in the day, and he came up empty again. He refreshed the job listings page, just to make sure it hadn't been some kind of glitch. Nope. This was beyond bizarre. It made no sense. This industry could crash fast, but recoveries were always slow, as clients were reluctant to make such expensive investments until demand was unmistakable.

He finished composing his blog post, hit "publish," and opened his email to look through last night's correspondence. All thirty-four of his job applications had already been answered. They'd all come through in the last twenty minutes, while he'd been writing the post. All were requesting phone interviews. Today. He slumped back. Could this be some kind of scam? Seemed unlikely. All the job openings had been cross-posted to the websites of the individual manufacturers. If it was a scam, then it involved some kind of global computer hack against a bunch of companies who employed some of the best security nerds in the biz.

Not a scam, but something was definitely . . . *wrong*.

A childhood memory burbled up, of his uncle describing how the US geared up for World War II after the Japanese attack. Literally overnight, the country mobilized. Factories trickling out small batches of cars and refrigerators for a sleepy economy were jolted to life in a war fever. Tanks and airplanes and millions and millions of bullets, artillery shells, and bombs poured out. By the time they'd pulled the bodies from the water, America was a different country.

Goldberg rocked back in his chair.

Mobilization.

He rolled the word around in his mind, turning it over like a broken radio, looking for the loose wire or busted transistor. Mobilize? But why? For what? Why would you crank up the global satellite industry? War seemed unlikely. Beyond the usual political squabbles, there wasn't any kind of global confrontation brewing that would lead to World War III.

All those listings going live at the same time meant something. Couldn't deny that. Whatever was happening was bigger than just one company winning a contract and opening its wallet. All these guys seemed to be responding to the same signal. Like they'd all just gotten huge checks and tight deadlines. But for what?

It must be some kind of natural disaster, then? Something to do with global warming? Hard to imagine all these new birds were just for one storm, as they took months or years to build and launch. And there were already a handful of weather-tracking satellites overhead, some of them a far sight more sophisticated than most people knew. The military funded a lot of the satellite industry, after all. Any US government satellite, even if officially built for the National Oceanic and Atmospheric Administration or some other civilian agency, eventually did double duty for the soldiers and the spies. It didn't bother him. Every other country did the same. Just a fact of life, and he had no problem keeping an eye on the assholes of the world. The bottom line was that the US and the rest of the world had more than enough super-fancy birds watching the clouds, the oceans, and the surface of the planet for any near-term needs.

So if they weren't looking down, these new birds must be looking . . . the other direction? Out into space?

Goldberg munched a few more chips. Steve, their aging lab, snored and whimpered at his master's feet as his paws twitched. Goldberg dropped a handful of chips absently and the dog slurped them up with barely a glance, crunching them quickly and then drifting back to sleep.

An asteroid? A collision of some kind? What else could it be? He could imagine the gaggle of astrophysicists rushing into a White House briefing room, armed with maps and photos and laptops and coffee.

He sat up, crumbs and larger chunks of food tumbling to the floor. Steve vacuumed those up, too.

If it really was an asteroid collision, Goldberg realized he probably knew some of the guys who would be in those meetings, NASA PhDs and other big brains. For those guys, unemployment was just something economists studied. Windbags, most of them. But a few of the scientists didn't mind talking to the grunts who actually machined and assembled their telescopes and rovers and antennas.

He rummaged through a drawer and removed a thick stack of business cards held together with a double-wrapped rubber band.

A few months ago, his wife had bought him a scanner he could use to copy the names and addresses to his computer, but the scanner was still in a box in a closet, gathering cobwebs.

"Dammit, Bert, get organized!" she had said, then laughed, when she was cleaning the closet last week.

He snapped the rubber band off and flung it aside. He thumbed through the stack, looking for the card he wanted, flipping the others back into the drawer.

"Where is it? Ah, Mark, there you are, you bastard."

Mark Norris. Goldberg laughed, looking at the officious font on the card. Norris was an old friend from high school who loved pranks almost as much as Goldberg. Goldberg had wound up at community college, while Norris had gone to MIT.

Still, they'd shared a fascination with rocketry and space travel and had built a dry ice launcher out of metal pipe one Saturday afternoon and launched glow sticks into the principal's swimming pool from a hundred yards away on a November night. Their friendship had survived distance and time. Norris now worked at Phoenix Aerospace, a startup company made up mostly of former NASA hardware engineers and software developers. A Silicon Valley billionaire was funding the startup, the latest trend among the nouveau riche. It had been months since Goldberg had talked to his old friend, and he wasn't sure what to expect.

He thumbed the keypad on his cordless phone—the cell phone hadn't been charged in days, and was currently serving as a drink coaster for a can of soda.

After nearly a dozen rings, he was about to hang up when a frazzled voice came on the line.

"Yeah? I mean, hello?"

"Mark, you son of a bitch, I nearly gave up. It's Bert. You fall asleep at your desk again?" he asked with a snort. It was a joke, as Norris was the most tireless man he had ever met. Most meth addicts probably got more shut-eye.

He expected a good-natured rejoinder, but Norris's voice came back with a strained intensity.

"Bert, hey, how's it going, man?" he said, more statement than question. "Listen, uh, I've got a lot on my plate right now, and . . ." He trailed off. Goldberg leaped into the opening.

"Yeah, that's kind of why I'm calling. Don't know if you heard, but Lockheed laid me off a few months ago, and so I've been job hunting and came across something weird today."

"Wait, what?" Norris's voice had gained an electric intensity. "Holy shit, Bert, look, uh, how'd you like to come by the office tomorrow and chat? Hell, look, forget the meeting, how'd you like a job? The pay is $110k, and we need you to start yesterday."

Goldberg leaned back in his chair, staring at the ceiling. A column of ants was marching along the plaster from the window frame. The exterminator had quoted them 200 bucks for the job. Not a chance. So now the Goldbergs had a few thousand roommates.

"Mark, what's going on? I just searched through all the job boards, and yesterday there wasn't squat and now there's openings from here to Beijing. I'll be honest, buddy, I was a little freaked out before I called you, and now I'm a little more freaked out."

Norris let out a deep breath.

"Bert, I can't really tell you anything right now. I barely *know* anything. But there's something big going down, and we've been told to bring everyone onboard immediately. I'm sure you'll have your pick of jobs by the end of the day, but I can offer you pretty much whatever you want right now. I'm serious, we'll fly you out here to Arizona tonight, first class, and put you to work first thing tomorrow. We're in a god-awful hurry."

"Is it an asteroid, Mark?" He swiveled to look out the window as he heard Berta's van huff and creak into the driveway.

"Honestly, I don't know. Maybe. Nothing makes sense right now. I think . . . look, let me hold the chatter. If you take the job, I can fill you in on what I do know when you get here. You'll need security clearance. Yours still current? Say the word and you'll have a boarding pass emailed to you within the next five minutes for your flight. You in?"

Berta was singing the climax of "Nessun Dorma" from *Turandot* as she came in the door, swinging grocery bags from her ponderous arms. She marched into the office bellowing the final "Vincerò!" but stopped when she saw her husband's tense face.

"Yeah, I'm in," he said.

"Excellent. I'll pick you up at the airport. No, scratch that, I'll send someone to get you. I don't think I'm going home tonight. Give Berta my love."

Norris hung up.

Goldberg gently deposited the phone back in its cradle.

"Well, don't keep me in suspense. These ice cream sandwiches are about to drip down my toes."

"Looks like I've got a job," he said.

"Congratulations and holy shit. Doing what?"

He was stunned, then laughed.

"I forgot to ask."

7

Harry Campos looked up for the bus, shielding his eyes against the glare of the Detroit sun. Nowhere in sight. Dammit.

He fished his phone out of his pocket. He was going to be late for work again. His old Toyota pickup had broken down last Sunday on the way home from bailing his brother, Manuel, out of jail, and of course the lazy bum hadn't even offered to chip in. So now he had to figure out how to come up with $600 to get the fuel pump fixed on top of the $300 bail. And the odds of the steel mill handing out bonuses right now was about as likely as PETA sponsoring a cockfight. So the cell phone might be the next thing to get cut off.

Campos had barely finished high school fourteen years ago, and college wasn't even a pipe dream. Well, maybe a bit of a dream. Science had always intrigued him, and he'd taken second place in the state science fair as a junior for a model rocket festooned with a variety of sensors. He'd measured wind speed, temperature, and humidity at nearly 9,000 feet, and he'd built the device himself out of scrap metal and other scavenged parts. It was still sitting on a shelf at his apartment. And he liked to read science news whenever he got a chance.

"To the Moon, Alice!" was terribly formatted for mobile screens (and Campos didn't have a clue what the title referred to), but this guy Goldberg had a sense of humor that a lot of science blogs didn't. So he squinted at his phone's four-inch screen beneath the cold light, zooming and rotating as much as possible to make the latest post readable.

Campos scanned through the entry on satellite jobs with interest, half thinking of applying. Goldberg was right. This was weird.

Campos manually copied and pasted the link into his Twitter app (he figured Goldberg probably didn't know Twitter from a Twizzler) and fired it off to his own small band of followers.

A rumble. He looked up. The bus was here. He turned his screen off with a thumb press and dug deep in his pocket for change.

●

President Lockerman looked down at the front page of the business section of the *LA Times*. It wasn't a huge article, modest placement, but there was enough info there for smart people to start asking questions. Some of them had already started. Lockerman sighed and looked around the room at his assembled advisers.

"Gentlemen, we're gonna have to pick up the pace. I don't think we have much time before this all blows open."

8

The hulking V-22 Osprey tiltrotor aircraft thumped from the Arizona sky down toward the landing pad of Phoenix Aerospace. Ben looked out the window at the swirl of sand kicked up by the twin rotors that had flipped from horizontal flight mode to vertical takeoff-and-landing mode. Dusty hills and small mountains ringed the desert valley. The city some 10 miles away was an artificial oasis in this wasteland, willed into existence and maintained only with constant labor. A green island in an ocean of sand.

It wouldn't take long for the desert to swallow all of this if mankind disappeared. Within a year or two, it would be mostly dunes. Within a decade, there'd be no sign humans had ever set foot there. Technology had enabled people to carve out this spot. Technology might now wipe it out.

All the sweat that had been poured out in the sand would evaporate in an instant.

"I love Phoenix," Rickert yelled over the cacophony. "Great golf courses."

Rickert had leaned over to speak to Ben, but it was merely habit. The roar of the engines made it impossible to hear except through a microphone and headset. Well, impossible for Rickert, anyway. Ben's internal computers filtered out the rumble of the Rolls-Royce engines so he could monitor any and all chatter on the alien frequencies bathing the planet. For now, all was quiet. But he knew it wouldn't last.

"I'll probably retire out here someday. Hot as hell, but like they say, it's a dry heat. You rake your sand, check your shoes for scorpions, and, you know, it's nice. You a golfer?"

Ben chuckled in spite of himself and relaxed a bit.

"No, sir, can't say that I am. Guess I never could figure out which striped shirt should go with my checkered pants."

Rickert grinned, and the Osprey touched down with a clunk.

The rear loading ramp descended with an electric whine, and the two soldiers walked into the desert furnace. On the tarmac, some 50 feet away, a pair of rumpled executives stood hunched over, sweating and clutching their ties against the swirling wind. Seeing Ben and Rickert, they started to approach, then looked at the rotors and stopped. Even though the blades were some 20 feet above the ground, the instinctual fear was strong enough that even trained pilots regularly hunched their shoulders.

Reaching the pair of Phoenix Aerospace managers, Rickert extended his hand and motioned toward the main building, a long, brown structure that blended in with the environment, indicating that they should all start walking. The execs were frozen, though, gawking at Ben's silver skin that almost glowed in the blazing sun.

"Appreciate you meeting us on such short notice, gentlemen," Rickert said. "As you can see, we're here with some unusual news. We understand you guys are the best there is, so we want to get your input as soon as possible on this project."

"Of . . . of course," one of the managers finally stammered, southern drawl unmistakable even in his agitation. "I'm Montgomery Winterton, CEO here at Phoenix—Monty is fine—and this is Bill Hemming, my chief operating officer. We, uh, I'd be happy to give you a little tour . . ."

"Later, perhaps," Rickert yelled as the V-22's engines spooled up again for takeoff. He finally persuaded the execs to start walking as the aircraft rose back into the air, ascending a few hundred feet, and then flying off as the rotors tilted back down into their horizontal flight position. It would come back to retrieve them later, but the harried crew had three other assignments before then.

"Afraid time is very short, and we've got a lot of ground we need to cover. Some of it will be hard for you to hear."

As they entered the main building past a pair of broad-shouldered security guards armed with automatic rifles, Winterton and Hemming exchanged sideways glances and swiped their entry badges on scanners on the doors. The guards stole glances, too.

Ben intercepted the brief short-range wireless signal from the badge scanner and absently decoded the data stream and stored it away. The doors opened with a *whoosh* and the four men stepped inside as the roar of the V-22 finally disappeared.

Inside, the group walked down a hallway, more badged doors, to an executive conference room on the second floor. The conference room had a massive window on the south wall overlooking the landing pad outside and an even larger window on the north wall looking down on the first floor where the research and development lab sat in the middle of the complex. In fact, the ground floor was actually a subterranean floor, dug down into the sand and rock. Even though the building appeared from the outside to be only two floors tall, the R&D lab actually was four floors deep. It kept the facility a bit cooler and minimized vibrations for the delicate work.

Technicians and engineers were bent over workbenches littered with laptops, microscopes, soldering irons, oscilloscopes, spectrum analyzers, and other tools and measuring equipment. In the middle of the floor sat a half-finished minivan-sized satellite, its guts splayed out. Teams of workers swarmed the machine.

As the visitors stared quietly down into the teeming space, Winterton took a deep breath and tried to regain his composure.

"Before we start, I guess you'd like to see what your first billion dollars has bought you. We're three weeks in, and I've never worked on a schedule like this before. It's insane. After 9/11, I thought I learned what 'rush job' meant. But this is something else."

Winterton looked over at Hemming, who was still gaping at Ben. The two execs had rehearsed their presentation as a tag-team, but the CEO realized he was going to have to fly this mission solo.

"You know, I had a little speech planned, where I was going to ask what the hell this is all about. But I think you're gonna tell me anyway, so let's skip the speech and have a drink, eh?"

Winterton pulled a small drink cart from beside his desk, pulled the cap from a bottle of whiskey, and poured four glasses. The gray-skinned guy smiled.

"Sir, I appreciate the hospitality and the curiosity. My name's Ben Shepherd. And that looks and smells like exceptional liquor. The general here will have to pass, I'm sure, as these are working hours for him. But technically, I'm retired. So don't mind if I do."

Ben shot the single-malt back with a snap, but Winterton could see that he held the liquid in his mouth a moment to savor the flavor. *So he isn't a total barbarian.*

Ben set the glass down. Rickert had indeed passed on the drink.

"It's pretty straightforward, really," Ben said. "An alien invasion is coming, and I'm the closest thing we have to Paul Revere. If we don't get this equipment online in a few months, we're all going to die."

Everyone went quiet. Winterton took a sip from his glass.

"So this is the part where I call BS, and you convince me. So convince me." Ben nodded and disappeared, leaving his clothes hanging in midair around his now-invisible body. Winterton dropped his glass. The invisible man struck like a cobra—an empty sleeve where an arm should have been darting out and seizing the glass before it could strike the ground. The glass floated in the air, and was then deposited on the table.

"Well, that's a sight."

"I planned a speech, as well," Ben said, his disembodied voice floating out from somewhere above his empty collar. "I think you'll want to hear mine."

●

Twenty minutes later, Winterton stood up from his desk and walked over to the window looking down on the manufacturing floor. "So we've got maybe a few weeks before the first wave arrives, huh? You know, I served in the first Gulf War. Desert Storm. Marine Corps, 1st Marine Division, 1st Battalion, 7th Marines, and we drove right into Kuwait City."

His gaze never left the activity in the R&D lab, like ants frantically repairing their hill that a child had poked with a stick.

"Supposedly it was a cakewalk, and I guess in retrospect it was. But we all thought it was the end of the world, and even as a first lieutenant, I about near soiled myself during our first combat encounter. Other guys actually did. You know what that's like?"

Ben nodded.

"Yep, I don't think I've ever met anyone who didn't get a bit weak in the bowels during their first firefight."

"No kidding. Never saw so much damn puke," Winterton added. "Turned out, it was just a couple terrified Iraqi regulars popping off with AK-47s from behind a blown-up tank. But hell, we thought it was the entire Republican Guard coming to chew us up, and we dropped enough ordnance on those two poor bastards that I'm surprised we didn't strike oil."

Winterton refilled his glass without breaking stride. He raised an eyebrow at Ben, who waved no.

"Point is, we were trained marines, with solid intel and overwhelming firepower, and we still acted like a bunch of high school football players walking into an NFL stadium for the first time. Now, you get over that first reaction pretty quick, but it takes a lot of training and some really bloody experience."

He sipped his glass, then shrugged and slugged the whole thing and set the empty glass back on the cart.

"So now here we are, and we're about to put everyone on Earth into the fight, from used car salesmen to proctologists, against a bunch of aliens with enough guns to turn our whole planet into a crater, and you're banking on anything other than total panic and chaos? How exactly do you think you're going to keep this from turning into a gigantic clusterfuck?"

Rickert spoke up.

"Maybe we can't. It's gonna be a hell of a situation, no doubt. But believe it or not, we do have some contingency plans on the shelf for events like this. And that's where you come in. We have to know: Can you build these machines in time?"

Winterton rubbed his forehead and turned to Hemming, who had been silent throughout the conversation. He finally seemed to be regathering his wits, though.

"Bill, you're the operations guru. What do you think?"

"Well, uh, you see, between fabrication and software development, we're, uh, looking at least, maybe, around 40,000, maybe 50,000 man hours, and then if you calculate . . ."

"But can it be done?" Rickert asked, with an edge of impatience.

Hemming, swallowed, looked around, and then found his courage.

"Well, yes. Just barely. But yes."

Rickert gave a tight grin.

"Good. Now let's go downstairs and we'll see if the lieutenant here can't take your prototype for a little test drive."

●

Ben, Rickert, Winterton, and Hemming first passed through an outer air-lock where a tornado of wind whipped off any loose grains of sand, dirt, hairs, or flakes of skin. Once the whirlwind had subsided, the next door slid open to a dressing room, where a dozen "bunny suits" hung on the wall. Rickert moved to grab one from a hook, but Winterton waved him off.

"Don't need 'em," he said. "Standard protocol normally, but the blueprints on this project made it clear that the hardware tolerances are high enough that basic compressed air decontamination is all that's needed. Freaked my staff out something fierce for the first week or so, but they're able to work a lot faster. Maybe even fast enough to get this thing built on schedule."

Rickert raised an eyebrow and glanced at Ben for confirmation, who shrugged.

For all the data he now carried within his expanded brain, for much of it he was only a middleman. He could no more understand or analyze the information stored inside him than a hard drive could understand the programs stored on its magnetic discs. Ben could, however, control and analyze his own body in stunning ways. He thought back to his two-man battle in the desert that had seemed to play on fast forward. Most of that had happened on autopilot. The source code was walled off. Waiting for a trigger, maybe. Even the data Ben *could* access wasn't always usable to him. The files were there and he could spit them out on command. If he had to actually assemble any of the machinery, though, he would be nearly useless.

He had begun to suspect that the brin had deliberately crippled his capabilities, giving him, in many cases, data but not knowledge. His concern over these roadblocks had only grown in the last few weeks. He hadn't told Rickert or anyone else, though. After all, what could they do? They were all at the mercy of an extinct alien race.

The technicians didn't even glance up when Winterton and his entourage walked in, the door sliding open and shut with a whoosh of air. The boss was normally down here several times a day, often carrying a tablet with a readout of technical specifications and progress reports. No one knew how to activate any of the machinery they were building or even what it really did, but the materials and construction blueprints were atomically precise. If the hourly readout deviated at all, Winterton was down on the floor, pushing everyone back on track. It was like building the Transcontinental Railroad with blindfolds on.

All the workers quietly prayed someone else was about to get his ass chewed out. They didn't bother to glance at the other visitors. Whoever else the boss had brought down would just be the latest in a procession of suits and uniforms demanding to inspect the product—whatever the product was. It was a satellite, everyone knew that. No one could figure out much more than that, though. It seemed to be a telescope or measuring device of some kind, with its array of sensors and probes. The processor at the heart of the machine was apparently a quantum computer, which in theory could crunch numbers far faster than any traditional digital computer. But no one on Earth had ever designed or built a quantum computer that did anything useful. They were science projects . . . until now.

Assuming this one *did* do anything useful. There was no "on" button. Like the sword in the stone, everyone in the building had taken turns, fiddling with hardware and software to unlock this mystery, to no avail. Not that they had a lot of time for tinkering, as the schedule demanded round-the-clock labor. Some of the staff had taken to sleeping in conference rooms and most hadn't shaved in days. The delivery pizza was usually lukewarm at best when it arrived, thanks to security and airlock delays. Everyone was grumpy as hell, heads down on their projects.

Winterton steered the group to a small cluster of engineers huddled over a workbench covered in laptops and other equipment. The handful of workers at this station were clustered around one portly comrade, who was rocking back and forth on his heels as he lectured the team.

". . . no, dammit, we can't ask them to reprogram the actuator module. It's all connected. If we swap out the software now, they tell me that every component must be reprogrammed. And for what? Because we missed our spec by a millimeter? Nope, we need to do it again and do it right. Plus . . ."

Winterton laid a hand on the excitable engineer's shoulder.

"Heya, Bert. How we doing?"

Goldberg turned his head.

"Oh, hi Mr. Winterton, fine, sir. Just working through some hiccups. We've got most of the software routines running to code, but just need to fine-tune the tracking programs and debug some of the targeting systems. Unfortunately, we've hit a snag with the actuators, but once we get the kinks worked out, we'll, uh, holy hell . . ." He trailed off, spotting Ben and his silver skin for the first time.

"Yeah, that," Winterton said. "We're going to talk about him in a minute. Right now, though, I need to know where the prototype stands. Are we a go for phase one testing?"

Goldberg swallowed a couple times and the other workers remained quiet. Winterton made a rolling motion with his finger. *C'mon, spit it out.*

"Yes, we're a go. But again, we still don't have any kind of control module or data uplink. We've got a car with no key to put in the ignition. Now, I had some thoughts about the initialization . . ."

Ben glanced over at the prototype satellite and, again, his vision flooded with data and he knew what to do. Every piece of electronics on the nearly finished satellite burst to life, and dozens of robotic limbs began flexing and retracting and extending as Ben established a wireless link to the machine. The workers in the room stumbled back in nearly synchronized shock.

A high-pitched whine soon rose over the roar of confusion and excitement. As the machine whirred and rotated and various parts locked into place, the whine became a scream and a bulb of red light blossomed on the tips of the various metallic stalks reaching up toward the roof.

Ben reached out mentally to the controls for the retractable roof, pinging a signal to the receiver on the wall, using the key card access code he'd intercepted and decrypted on the way into the building. The control panel blinked from red to green. The aluminum slats folded back like a geisha's fan, exposing the cerulean heaven above. The air in the room began to shimmer, then vibrate, as the sound waves splashed back and forth. The engineers, scientists, executives, soldiers, and guards cupped their ears, nearly deafened and paralyzed by the tidal wave of sound and fury. Only Ben stood still, undisturbed, awash in supersonic streams of data and diagnostics. Inside the machine, hydrogen gas was ionized, adding electrons to each atom of the gas. Negatively charged ions flooded an ion acceleration chamber.

When the roof had finished opening, Ben looked up, and with a flick of his brain fired the weapon, unleashing a massive negative electrical charge that repelled the negatively charged hydrogen ions and accelerated them to nearly the speed of light.

A searing javelin of red energy tore from the satellite, carving through the one unfortunate cloud hovering overhead. The electron particle beam burned for just a fraction of a moment, unleashing a petajoule of energy;

a 50-megaton nuclear explosion poured down a pathway no thicker than a drinking straw, then disappeared with a thunderclap that shook the room. The cloud was now a vaporous donut, blue sky visible through a seared hole in the fluffy white.

Silence for a second, then pandemonium. The engineers and other workers in the room hollered and clambered to their feet, surrounding but not quite daring to touch this quiet, gray, motionless figure who had obviously triggered the shot. Even Rickert gaped at Ben, who looked over at Rickert and gave a small shrug. He was still discovering his own capabilities. He hadn't known he could fire the weapon until he walked into the room and his vision and senses lit up with information and a subliminal, intuitive understanding of what to do next. Still much he didn't know. Worse, no way to know how much there still was to know. What was it the poet had said? I contain multitudes? At least he could intuit his own depths. Ben felt like he was staring down a dark mineshaft and maybe it extended 50 feet or 5,000 feet. Or maybe it had no end.

He had power he couldn't understand, and maybe not even fully control. Super soldier . . . or time bomb?

"That was interesting," Ben said, looking at Rickert.

"Think you can do it again?"

"Yes, sir, like flipping a light switch now. And I'd estimate a rate of fire between 35 and 40 shots per minute. If we can get these birds in the sky, we might have a chance."

By now, Winterton had all but lost control of the small crowd in the assembly room. He finally turned to the two soldiers and raised his hands in surrender. "Gentlemen, I'm going to let you field this one."

Rickert gestured toward the curious, nervous faces. "All yours, sailor."

9

General Dimitri Gretchenko gazed at Ben and Rickert as he methodically prepared his tea.

"Do you know what this is?" he asked, gesturing at the metal urn at his elbow. "It is called a samovar," he said without waiting for a reply, his thick accent emerging from beneath a bushy mustache.

"You boil the water in the urn using a metal heating rod that runs down the center of the device," the Russian continued. "In the old days, but not so long ago, fuel for the heating tube could be coal, oil, anything that burned. Now, of course, it is electric. But the process is same, yes? Heat the water, which then heats the *zavarka*, the water and tea leaves in the container here at the top. You pour a small amount of *zavarka* in the cup when it is hot, like so, then add the hot water from the samovar. More water or less, for weaker or stronger tea."

The old general stared intently at his American visitors as he completed the ritual. The white porcelain cup sat in a white saucer, unornamented. The dark, nearly black tea was hot, too hot to drink yet.

"It is a tradition, part of Russian life. Tsars, peasants, communists and capitalists, all drink tea in this way. A simple drink. But very important to Russians."

Steam curled out of the cup, unhurried. Outside, bitter wind howled through icy teeth.

"But tea did not come from Russia," Gretchencko said, folding his hands on the table in front of him and ignoring the steam and the storm. "In 1638, an envoy from Tsar Michael I to Altyn Khan, a Mongolian ruler, came back with these dried leaves, a strange gift. But it was not long before Russians saw the value of this new material and adopted tea as our own, a national drink. And you, Lt. Shepherd, are tea, a strange new thing from a very distant place."

Gretchenko finally lifted his cup and blew softly over the hot liquid, his eyes never leaving his visitors. He sipped, expressionless. "The only question is, are you a gift, or something else?"

Ben and Rickert said nothing. Ben slid his plain, porcelain cup containing the puddle of black *zavarka* under the small faucet at the base of the samovar and turned the metal key to release the hot water. When his cup was nearly full, he turned the key shut. The samovar was old, but the key moved silently, a machine well and long maintained. Ben waited a moment for the drink to cool, then lifted it to his lips.

"Excellent, sir. The finest I've ever had," Ben said.

"Of course it is," Gretchenko replied with a grin, his eyes still cold. "It is the first real tea you have ever tasted."

Ben could sense Rickert's impatience, but the process seemed important, almost sacramental. Ben knew this trip was as much diplomatic as military. Outside, a cold wind smacked anyone unfortunate enough to have to scuttle between buildings. It would be a bracing walk back to their airplane waiting on the tarmac of JSC Information Satellite Systems in Zheleznogorsk, central Russia. Ben had never been to Russia before. Every mental image he had of it certainly seemed to be validated here—except for this Russian general. He didn't seem to be an enemy, but not quite a friend, either. He was wary, which Ben could understand. Something seemed to be troubling him even more than the mrill invasion.

Rickert, who was bored by the tea ritual and yearned for coffee, cleared his throat.

"General, as you know, we have given you everything. The details of Lt. Shepherd's . . . encounter, the schematics, the initial test results, everything. Very few countries have received the details you have seen."

Rickert pointed to a thin, sleek laptop computer opened next to the antique samovar. A series of schematics and construction reports flashed across the LCD screen.

"Yes," Gretchenko said, "I have seen the data. But the data is not what interests me. Correction, the data is tremendously interesting. For my engineers, this is probably as close as they will ever come to a religious experience."

"So what's the issue?" Rickert asked.

"You have, what's the word, 'outsourced'? Yes, that is correct. You have outsourced this work to us, and to other governments, I presume. We will build your weapons. Guns more powerful than any I expected to see in my lifetime. And then we will turn them over to you. This is not a comfortable position for my government, for my nation, to be in."

"I understand," Rickert said.

"Do you?" Gretchenko replied, one eyebrow arching, the closest thing to emotion he'd shown since they'd met. "It is not so long since the Cold War, my friend, and there are many who remember when our missiles were pointed at each other. Some in my country preferred it that way. This new arrangement . . . they will say Russia surrendered without ever firing a shot. There will be problems."

"What are you saying?" Rickert asked.

Gretchenko smiled, but Ben thought he could read sadness in the Russian's face and voice. "It's been a long time since you Americans faced revolution and civil war. But not so for Russia. Blood flows easier, and hotter, than tea in some parts of the world."

A Russian captain entered the room and handed the general a phone. He glanced at the screen and stood up.

"I have ordered all production to full speed. My men will work night and day. We will have our machines ready in time, and I pray, yes, pray, even an old communist like me, that you will have the strength to protect our planet. But even in victory, not all things can be preserved. You may find this world much changed, even should you win the day. Go, now, and report back to your leaders, and I shall do the same."

●

"This isn't going to help matters," Ben said as they walked out on the airstrip.

Zheleznogorsk was a "closed town," locked down with strict travel restrictions, one of several in the always-suspicious motherland. Once an official state secret and devoted to producing weapons-grade plutonium for the Soviet Union's nuclear program, Zheleznogorsk was now largely a company town for JSC, which had developed the GLONASS navigation system, the

Russian answer to the US military's network of global positioning system satellites. Nearly thirty years after *Glasnost*, openness in the heart of Russia was still more rumor than reality.

So the town was self-contained, drab and plain, but well stocked for its 86,000 or so citizens. That included the twin runways on JSC's corporate campus, mammoth stretches of high-grade asphalt capable of launching and landing the hulking Tupolev Tu-160 and Tu-95 strategic bombers that had once been designed to drop nuclear bombs from Sacramento to Savannah. A Tu-160, which to Ben looked a bit like a weaponized Concorde passenger jet, was parked in one of the open hangers.

"If the Russian government crumbles in the middle of their construction effort, we're in a bad way," Ben said. "We're down to the bare minimum number of planned satellite launches as it is. Without the Russians, we're doomed. We have to share our info with the world, make it clear this isn't a hoax or a conspiracy to destabilize other governments."

It was January, six weeks after the first encounter in New Mexico, and it was late, cold, and dark. *This place redefines "dead of winter,"* Ben thought. But the stark, blunt JSC buildings hummed with activity and light. Ben's test fire demo had guaranteed that buzz wouldn't die down anytime soon. Ben ignored the slice of cold wind and dry snow across his face as he and Rickert walked to their waiting US Air Force cargo plane, a Boeing C-17 Globemaster III. Rickert was not as stoic, gasping at the frigid finger of winter that snaked down through his tightly fastened collar.

"I don't disagree. It just isn't my call," he said, nearly yelling over the wind. "The president has convened another advisory council meeting for Tuesday, so you'll get another chance to make your case."

Ben started to reply but stopped as a new information readout appeared before his eyes. The first satellites they'd built, small surveillance birds, had already been launched several weeks ago. These early warning systems detected the electromagnetic disturbances, or "cuts," as the scientists were calling them, created when alien spacecrafts traveled across interstellar distances. The data Ben was receiving indicated a small force of mrill spy satellites would soon enter the solar system. Unsure what intelligence the brin had shared with the humans, the mrill were treading carefully. Ben knew Earth wasn't ready. The mrill would soon realize that, and then the strike force would come.

Rickert noticed the look on Ben's face, the vacant expression as a new wave of digital information sprawled across his eyes.

"What is it?"

Ben at last blinked and refocused on Rickert.

"I don't think we have until Tuesday, sir. They're almost here."

The two Americans paused for a moment on the frozen runway of the Russian satellite maker. Then they ran for their waiting jet.

10

"This is crap."

President Lockerman frowned at the pile of papers on his desk in the Oval Office. Cameras went live in 30 minutes, and he'd rather dance nude for the networks than recite a word of the script laid out in front of him. The page was covered in red ink, but he was no closer to a useable document than he had been an hour ago when he started.

"'An epic hour, a critical moment?'" Lockerman said to the cluster of aides huddling on the other side of his desk. "Christ, guys, I'd be less embarrassed if I broke wind during a state dinner attended by the pope and my mother. We don't need Shakespeare. We just need to be clear. Terry, get this out of here and have the writers take another crack." Lockerman waved the sheaf of papers at his chief speechwriter, who grabbed them and went on his way, aides trailing in his wake.

Lockerman leaned back and rubbed his eyes. Hawthorne, his science adviser, sat on a nearby stool, shuffling through her own crop of paperwork. She had one pencil tucked behind her right ear, but appeared to have forgotten it was there, and was scribbling on the sheaf with another one, just about worn down to the nub.

She frowned, upgraded to a scowl, and wrote furiously. The taut tendons in her forearms made Lockerman wonder if she'd break the pencil. He knew she was looking at reports of the satellite production. Work was behind schedule and seemed likely to slow even more before it got better. Now she was thumbing through the pages, as if better numbers might show up somewhere in the footnotes.

"Dammit, Miranda, that bad?" Lockerman asked.

"It's fucking bad enough, man—I mean, uh, Mr. President."

"No, please, don't stand on ceremony, Miranda."

She ignored his jibe and the slightly horrified looks of the aides and assistants scuttling through the room.

"We're ass-deep in trying to run assembly lines for stuff that a few months ago was considered theoretical physics, at best. It's like we just fast-forwarded through a century of scientific research. It's insane. It's awesome, don't get me wrong. It's also totally nuts."

"You've got the blueprints. Just follow the specs."

Hawthorne shoved her glasses up on her forehead, pinched the bridge of her nose, and set the papers aside.

"Not that simple. It's like the Wright brothers land after their first flight, and you show up with the schematics for a 747 and tell them you want a fleet in a couple months."

"Are we going to get our fleet?"

"I . . . we'll have something. I *think* it will be enough. We'll need to rerun the algorithms for where we park them in orbit, how we overlap the fields of fire, all that stuff, if we end up with a smaller force than we'd planned. We'll be stretched thin, though."

"So where do we stand?"

Hawthorne took a deep breath. "We have fifteen satellites that will be ready to launch within the next four days. Another ten are likely to be completed within three weeks. Ten more within two months. That is short of the fifty originally called for. Like I said, I think we can make it work. People are asking questions, you know. Our assembly facilities are running hot, 24/7. It's the ultimate tech bubble. Too bad I didn't buy stock in the satellite industry before this mess happened."

"You and me both," Lockerman said.

He was surprised how quickly he had come to terms with the absurdity of this predicament. There was no clause in the Constitution, no Federalist Paper that gave any insight, any illumination of the path ahead. Budget disputes, international rivalries, political scandals. As excruciating as each could be, they all also had a sort of accepted ritual, a ceremonial formality where each participant knew their roles, even if the outcome was uncertain. They'd been done a thousand times before. Just play your part and get off the stage when it was time so the next bunch could take over. This, on the other hand, was wholly new. Like being the first ancient amphibian that found itself thrown ashore and needed to learn how to breathe, walk, and survive.

Not to say you didn't get a choice. There was always a choice. You could go forward or go back. Live or die. Often, forward meant death, too. Or you could just freeze in place, hope someone else came along to make your decision for you. But that's usually when a bigger predator gobbled you up. So it was time to go on TV and announce that a war of the worlds was imminent. The first shots had already been fired, and the second battle for Earth was only days away.

"Ten minutes to air, Mr. President," an assistant said. The makeup crew descended on Lockerman like a flock of pigeons as the technicians fiddled with the camera.

"Did you evacuate your family to the safe zone yet?" Lockerman asked Hawthorne.

"Don't have any. Only child. Parents died a few years ago. They were only children, too. You?"

"Sorry to hear that. And yeah, I sent Maggie and the kids off to Arizona last week. At least it's warmer there."

"Hmph."

Hawthorne wasn't much for small talk.

"Where the hell is Terry?" Lockerman asked. "That script might have been crap, but it sure beats the giant plate of nothing I've got in front me right now."

Terry Strazzinski bounded through the swarm, sweat stains groping at his armpits.

"Here, sir." Strazzinski handed over a stack of papers still warm from the printer.

Lockerman scanned through. Just a few pages of text, but maybe the most portentous words any president had ever had to speak. Thirty minutes later, he'd be down in the press room, talking to reporters. Everyone in the White House had agreed that it was best to air the speech first, let the reporters gather their wits, and then hold the Q&A. This was going to be a wild ride, and Lockerman wanted to keep the chaos to a minimum.

"Good enough," Lockerman said after scanning through the new script. "I can ad lib over some of this, but it works. Thanks, Terry."

He nodded at Strazzinski, who was nearly bug-eyed, having only learned the content of the speech an hour ago.

"Thank you, Mr. President. Good luck."

The speechwriter melted back into the throng, leaving the president alone at his desk. Lockerman settled in as the cameras came to life. Thirty seconds. He took a measured swallow of water from a bottle. Wouldn't do to choke now. Five seconds. Four, three, two, one . . .

●

My fellow Americans, good evening. I come to you tonight with urgent and difficult news. As hard as it may be to hear, we have irrefutable evidence that the United States of America, and indeed the entire world, is confronted with an imminent military threat. More than a military threat, an existential crisis. Once I've concluded my remarks, additional details will be available on the White House website and I'll be taking a few questions from media, but I want to give you the overview.

A little over a month ago, a retired officer in the United States military—I am not disclosing his name, rank, or branch of service for national security reasons—encountered in New Mexico what we are now confident was a hostile extraterrestrial being.

I am going to say that again.

He encountered a hostile, intelligent, technologically advanced creature that was not from this planet. There was a short confrontation between the retired officer and the creature, and the officer was able to defeat and kill the creature.

However, we believe this being was just the first of many to come, a forerunner for a global attack and invasion, an invasion against which we, the entire world, must now mobilize.

I understand that this sounds shocking, confusing, alarming, and perhaps even ridiculous or absurd. I can assure you this is not a hoax. This is not a conspiracy. And we are convinced, beyond a shadow of a doubt, that the threat is real and imminent. Preparations have already begun. What details we can share will be available on all federal government websites as soon as this address has concluded. We are also briefing all congressional representatives, and I urge them to conduct town halls and discussions as they deem appropriate with their constituents. Other presidents and heads of state around the world assisting in our defensive preparations already have the information I'm now sharing, and they agree that this is the only prudent course of action.

That said, I am fully aware that this is disturbing news. Every resource is being marshaled, and we are confident we can meet and repel the threat. The Department of Defense has existing plans for exactly this sort of contingency. Not because we had any warning this was coming—there is no government cover-up here, nor have previous administrations engaged in such a cover-up—but because we have the finest fighting force in the world that is dedicated to planning for every possible threat. And we are prepared. But I am aware that many will find this news disturbing and upsetting. That is understandable. What we cannot allow, though, is for our emotions to lead us into panic. I trust all Americans to rise to that challenge.

So while we are now on a wartime footing, similar to the state of readiness established by President Roosevelt after the bombing of Pearl Harbor in 1941, I am *not* declaring martial law. While you will see extensive and sustained activity of US military forces across the country, all civil law enforcement, civil law, and civil courts will remain operational. Local police and judges will continue to patrol our streets, enforce our laws, and protect our constitutionally guaranteed rights and freedoms. Our military forces are acting solely to prepare against the imminent attack, and are *not* authorized to make arrests, seize supplies without payment, or otherwise impede lawful activity except in cases where such activity interferes with the establishment or movement of vital military equipment. Schools will not be turned into barracks and I am not initiating a military draft.

Meanwhile, the Treasury secretary and his staff will be working with financial exchanges, banks, and other critical financial institutions to ensure our economy continues to function, that food, gas, medical supplies, and other vital material gets where it needs to go. We are Americans, and we are all in this together. I cannot emphasize that enough. Now, more than ever, we are all each other's keeper, and

I ask not just for your calm, but for your vigilance, your fortitude, and your compassion.

The president paused, unsure what to say or do next. This was the end of his prepared remarks. There was no more guidance or script. Whatever came next, he'd be operating alone, making it up as he went, with hundreds of millions of people living or dying as a result. Maybe nothing he was doing mattered and the mrill would wash over the world like the tide and all his words were as useless as spitting at the waves. Worse, maybe he was just pouring out fear and panic, and the world would die in agonizing, extended terror. Just shut up and let it end quickly.

He thought about Lincoln again, on that steamboat, at the end of the war that had drained the country and drained the man. He'd borne up through it all, though. Whatever weariness and despair had filled his body, he had seen it through. Do your part as long as you can, as well as you can, until it's someone else's turn.

Lockerman looked up at the camera.

My fellow Americans, my fellow citizens of the world, my friends, I don't know how this will end. I don't even know how this will begin. We're going to war. More accurately, war is coming to us. I know many of you will doubt everything I've said, and there will be anger and protests. I understand these sentiments. Nor will the road be any easier for those who do believe.

We're arming and preparing as best we could in the little time we've had. The evidence indicates we will soon face a vicious enemy, fully committed to exterminating us. We cannot depend on their mercy or their restraint. They are coming in search of a new home, and mean to take ours. This first fight will test our technology. The coming battles will test our spirit. For now, all you need to do is be safe, be strong, help your neighbors, and hold your children. There may come a time, soon, when the fight will not be overhead, but on the ground, among us, in our streets. There will be no front line, no home front, and we will not know where the next attack will fall. But I know this.

We will fight to the end, with hope and purpose. We are not empty-handed. We have tools, weapons, shields, our courage, and our love.

We will hold those to the end, come what may. I will be speaking with you regularly, telling you what I can, asking for what we need. Other leaders will be giving similar updates to their people. For now, for the next few hours, be strong and brave. We expect to engage the enemy before the day is through, and we will do everything we can to keep that fight above the planet and, if we cannot, assist those on the ground who are affected. Don't be afraid to help each other. We are all in this together and, God willing, we will all come out of this together. May God bless us all, may God bless the United States of America, may God bless all the people of the world.

II

The technicians clustered around Ben's ship like nursing piglets. Propulsion, navigation, weapons, life support, all the systems were still being finished even as the launch clock ticked over to T-minus 30 minutes. The smell of sweat and stale coffee filled the air in the cramped hangar. Ben and Rickert threaded their way through tangles of cable and around half a dozen workbenches with open laptops wired into the various ports on the black and gray spacecraft.

"You think this is going to work?" Rickert asked, dodging a shower of sparks.

"I'm getting a good signal on my scans, and all the completed systems are coming online. Once it gets up in the air, though? That I don't know."

Ben reached out to the dimpled surface of the machine, running his hands over the ridges and seams. The ship looked like a bubble perched on the open face of a flower. The cockpit was in the shiny silver sphere, while the petals that fanned out from the bubble were more crude-looking and mechanical. Like everything else in this effort, it was all foreign substance, an exotic recipe that the technicians had followed assiduously but blindly, mixing chemicals and molecules in combinations they'd never dreamed, using sub-atomic manufacturing processes they could barely understand. Would it work? Hell, they didn't even know *how* it would work. Assuming it did function as planned, Ben knew he could operate it. But if that made him an expert, then any idiot capable of using a telephone qualified as a network engineer, Ben thought. This ship was a black box, and Ben and Rickert both knew they were still flying blind.

The two men walked around the ship. At the rear of the ship (or *stern*, as Ben's Navy mind insisted), a small ramp extended from an opening in the hull. Inside, a simple chair was installed in a cockpit with no visible controls or displays. Rickert stopped, and Ben did too.

"You know, no one wants to send you up there. The tech guys still haven't made much progress reverse-engineering your nanomachines. You're the only version of you we have. You're the protector. Of everything. Without the technology in your cells, we're dead. If you die, we all die."

"Technology won't be enough," Ben said. "It's never enough."

"The hell do you mean by that?"

"Did you know a distant relative of mine was a Comanche Indian? The Comanche were . . . interesting. They were barely a tribe at all for most of their history. Just a group of people hunting together. But when they got their hands on Spanish horses, everything changed. Almost overnight, that single technological leap made them the preeminent power on the frontier. They mastered it in a way no one else did. Sioux, Apache, none of them could match up to the Comanche, and they killed everyone in their path. They were truly savages, and, one-on-one, unstoppable."

"I guess I never thought of horses as technology," Rickert said.

"Technology is anything that makes you better at what you do," Ben said with a shrug. "A stick or a cruise missile, it's all the same."

"So what stopped the Comanche and their new tech?"

Ben smiled. "The United States Army. Lots and lots of them. And the Americans eventually learned not to fight one-on-one."

Ben continued to examine the spacecraft, occasionally holding his palm over a panel to get a readout on the specific component. "Of course, we need the technology. I just don't know if it's gonna be enough. I heard that we're not giving other countries the full technical readout of the nanobots in my body, just the satellite blueprints. I think that's a mistake. We need help."

Rickert sighed. "Yeah, I know. Politics is alive and well, even at the end of the world. The president means well, or at least thinks he does. Showing too many of our cards might give someone else—the Chinese, maybe the Russians—a chance to figure out something we haven't, and then try to get leverage on us. At least that's the explanation I got."

Ben rolled his eyes, which Rickert pretended not to see. After all, he was still active duty and Lockerman was still commander in chief.

"So right now, you're all we've got," Rickert continued. "So be careful. As tough as it sounds, we're better off losing a city than losing you. You're the only thing we *can't* rebuild. If it comes down to making a stand or living to fight another day, we need you to do the smart thing."

This had been weighing on Ben for some time. Before he'd been turned into an human/alien hybrid and thrust into this interstellar war, he'd had no intention of ever going back to war, even if his leg had healed completely. Then this upgraded body had thrust him into a new mission. At first it seemed like he'd able to fight alone, suffer alone. A one-man army. That had been a cruel joke, though. He might fight alone. But if he failed, he'd kill everyone. Charging up a hill alone just gave you a better view of the entire world below that was depending on you.

The two men were quiet for a moment. Ben continued to examine his ship, but sensed Rickert's gaze on him.

"I read your file, you know," the general said.

"My DD 214?"

"No, not your discharge papers. Well, yes, those too. But your personal file."

"What personal file?"

"Almost as soon as this thing got rolling, the president had the FBI do a full background check on you."

"I guess I shouldn't be surprised."

"No, you shouldn't," Rickert said, shaking his head. He gestured around the buzzing facility. "I'm sure there's an FBI file on me now, too, and everyone else on this insane project."

Ben drew back a bit, folding his arms.

"So what did mine say? Document all my speeding tickets and late library books?"

"Yes, actually, but that wasn't what caught my eye. Your childhood. Your father."

"Doesn't seem relevant. That was a long time ago."

"Really? How could it not be relevant? Don't you—"

A technician scurried in, interrupting them without hesitation.

"Lt. Shepherd? We're ready for the preflight checklist."

Ben was grateful for the intrusion, cutting off the conversation Rickert had tried to start. The past was like an anvil crushing Ben's chest. The weight of the past and the weight of the future.

Ben nodded, and the technician stepped back. Rickert stuck his hand out. Ben shook it and tried to look confident, but the worry was etched on Rickert's face, permanent and impervious. Ben didn't know what else to say. Finally, Rickert gestured awkwardly to the ship, and Ben stepped up the ramp. The door melted back into the exterior with a sound like a small stream.

As the ramp closed, the interior of the ship filled with a soft glow and the constant chatter of data running across his vision thinned as the ship's systems asserted themselves. Ben ducked through the short passageway to the cockpit, scanning three-dimensional schematics popping up before his eyes that provided readouts on the ship's various systems. He settled into the black chair, pushing Rickert's concerns out of his mind. None of that mattered. Hadn't mattered in a long time. The squishy material molded to the thin, tight-fitting black flight suit covering his body, and when he laid his arms on the armrests, the leather-like material oozed around his frame.

It wasn't quite a full cocoon, but his body was all but merged with the seat. Dozens of microscopic sensors pierced his arms and the back of his head, creating a direct, physical link between the ship and his body and mind. It was just like the first fight in the desert. Machine and man merged into one weapon. With a mental command, Ben turned the silver cockpit bubble transparent from the inside, so he could see the cluster of technicians unplugging and packing up. Across the viewing screen, a map of the defensive satellites rotated into place. Ben zoomed out, and confirmed the mrill drones were still approaching from beyond the sun.

A technician walked up to the outside of the cockpit bubble, looking into the smooth sphere. He pressed his headset against his ear.

"Lt. Shepherd, we're ready to test your primary ignition system. Are you locked in?"

Ben nodded, then remembered the tech couldn't see him.

"Uh, yeah, affirmative, I'm good to test."

The notion of "testing" was mostly a farce, Ben thought. None of the equipment in the ship was actually testable by the computers and sensors at ground control. Ben was the tester . . . or the crash-test dummy. The techs could read the output, but they had no way of initializing or deactivating any of the onboard systems. If something went wrong, no one on the ground would know it until the ship exploded . . . or worse.

But protocol demanded testing. Checklists must be checked.

With a thought, Ben powered up the antigravity generator. It wasn't an actual propulsion system but rather generated antigravitons: particles that repelled the gravity-generating force of gravitons. At least, that's how the scientists *thought* the antigravity system worked. Rickert had pointed out that gravitons were merely theoretical, and perhaps even impossible in Einstein's framework of general relativity. And yet, when the antigravity drive was engaged, the ship floated like a leaf in the wind. Even though the craft weighed well over 50,000 pounds, with the antigrav engaged, a strong breeze was enough to nudge it forward.

The actual propulsion system was what the techs called a magnetoplasmadynamic, or MPD, thruster. Ben barely grasped the physics, but he'd been assured that the ionized lithium gas system, powered by a miniaturized 100-megawatt nuclear reactor, was revolutionary. It would change the world if they could save it first.

As cutting-edge as the ship was, though, Ben knew it was deficient in numerous ways. It was not the peak of brin technology. The problem was that mankind simply lacked the manufacturing capabilities to take advantage of the most cutting-edge designs in the brin portfolio. *They'd had to dumb it down for the primitive apes they were trying to save*, Ben thought. Hawthorne, President Lockerman's science adviser, had explained to Ben at one point that the problem was like asking a nineteenth-century watchmaker to build a smartphone.

"A watchmaker was one of the smartest engineers on the planet at the time," she'd said. "If you crammed him in a time machine, brought him into the present, and sat him down for a crash course in modern microelectronics, physics, radio, and all the other stuff that goes into a smartphone in the early twenty-first century, he'd get the basic concepts in a few days. But then kick his butt back to 1823 or whenever, and tell him to make you an iPhone, and he'd be totally lost."

Understanding a concept was vastly different from being able to put it to use. To do that, to put a functioning phone on a store shelf, you needed a multi-billion-dollar manufacturing plant. A series of them, for the processor, the screen, the memory chips, the cellular radio, and so on. Not to mention a wireless network to connect the phone to the internet, which was an industry unto itself. Money was only half the equation. Time was the other. Modern factories were the result of decades of labor, stretching from Henry Ford into the era of robotics. Technology was never created in a vacuum.

Ben thought he understood the dilemma better than Hawthorne realized. After all, his body had become exactly that sort of mysterious machine. SEAL training—hell, all military training—was iterative. You started with the basics: running, lifting, swimming, shooting. From there you graduated to more complex mapping, planning, infiltration, and so on. There was no eureka, no epiphany. Making a soldier was no different than making a computer. *Or making art, for that matter*, he thought. A marble sculpture was the result of a million tiny strokes, not a single hammer blow. Now everything was moving faster than it should have. Mankind was being thrust forward into the future on a rocket. Or a time machine.

Ben wondered if it was healthy for a civilization to lunge forward like this, fumbling with toys and tools it hadn't earned. Well, that would be a dilemma for the sociologists, assuming any survived.

Ben activated the antigravity field and the ship hummed.

Ben mentally toggled his mic back on. "Tower, this is Liberty-1, antigrav engaged, all systems reading nominal."

"Copy that, Liberty-1. Best we can tell, you're in the green. You're a go for maneuvers."

Ben shifted in his seat and smiled. "Thanks, tower. Let's kick the tires."

The techs and their equipment still were scattered around him on the ground of the massive hangar, although they had all been backed up 20 meters or so. But Ben wasn't going out. He was going up. He flicked the retractable overhead doors open with a mental command. Once they'd rumbled open, Ben sent the ship slowly up into the air. The scaffolding around the ship slipped away, then the cavernous vehicle assembly building itself dropped out of sight, sending the craft into the clear, warm air of Cape Canaveral. To the east, the glittering sea beckoned.

"Liberty-1, this is tower, looks like a beautiful day to fly. Godspeed, and good luck."

Ben took one last look around. The main launchpad a few hundred meters away buzzed with activity as workers prepped it for the next satellite launch. Everyone had to keep operating on the assumption the world wasn't going to end today, that other battles were yet to be fought. Work also kept despair at bay; idle hands made for idle thoughts. There were sporadic riots and protests, from New York to Nairobi. New cults and conspiracies bloomed with the sunrise, and terrorist attacks were spreading in the chaos. Most things still held, though. Enough people still got up in the morning and went to work to keep the world turning. The lights were still on in most places. Businesses were generally open. Shelves were mostly stocked, and gas prices had surged, but not exploded. For now, fear was held in check.

For some, this was the busiest they'd ever been. For those actively engaged in Earth's defense, the frenzy of work simply didn't leave any time for anxiety or despair. Indeed, for many of them, it was turning out to be a hell of a ride. The boundaries of technological possibility were being pushed back daily, thanks to the instructions and guidance from the brin, exposing new frontiers. For the scientists and engineers and programmers, it was like being present at the creation of a new universe.

The petals of the ship fanned out, the complex geometric shapes on their downward-facing surfaces glowing a faint blue. The base of the ship, the ring of petals, began to spin, like an upside down helicopter. Ben scanned his display.

Power output at 100 percent.

He turned the ship on its side, the cockpit bubble rotating independently of the base to keep him sitting up.

"Liberty-1, this is tower, what's your readout."

"Tower, Liberty-1, I feel like I'm flying a magic carpet. Too bad you guys didn't make this thing a convertible," Ben said. He sensed this levity might be the last for a while.

"Uh, copy that, Liberty-1, we'll work that into the Mark 2," the mission control team responded. "You're clear for orientation maneuvers, and we're looking at T-minus 15 minutes for orbital insertion. Go ahead and take it for a test drive."

During a normal NASA launch, flight control was turned over to mission control in Houston once the ship left the launch pad. But given the unusual circumstances, the senior staff at NASA had decided it was best to keep mission control in Florida, so they could keep direct visual contact with Ben as long as possible to closely monitor his test flight.

Ben did a long, slow turn toward the sea and opened the throttle to one percent. Liberty-1 rocketed toward the turquoise water, the antigravity system minimizing the crush of acceleration inside the ship. His airspeed indicator flashed. Within three seconds, he was traveling at more than 500 nautical miles per hour. The spinning metallic petals left an intricate, woven contrail of blue ionized gas that extended about 50 feet behind the ship. Flight tests on a new fighter jet normally took years, if not decades. Ben had 15 minutes at the controls of a ship that was the first and only of its kind. But the biologic-to-digital link between his body and the ship made flying the alien spacecraft as natural as breathing. Ben sent the ship soaring and diving, cutting low enough to the surface of the ocean to draw plumes of water spray in the air, then screamed into the sky, slicing through the handful of clouds. He slipped past the sound barrier like a cat burglar, leaving not so much as a sonic whisper.

"Engines and controls check, tower. Let's go to weapons," Ben said.

"Roger, Liberty-1, the targets are up and you're clear to engage."

Finding suitable dummy targets had been tough. Boats and airborne drones ended up being the best option, although everyone knew the mrill crafts were likely to be much faster and better armed. But there wasn't time to prepare anything more, so this would have to do.

Ben dove down toward the ocean surface, a dozen boats ranging in size from canoes to decommissioned cargo vessels popping up on his heads-up display. He scanned each target with the sensors embedded in the ship— now wired directly to his body. Faster than thought, he fired, blasting the ships apart in a mix of fire and steam.

Ben gained altitude, searching for the drones and balloons while dialing back the power output of the guns. Again, he tore through them effortlessly, anticipating each evasive maneuver as every shot found its mark.

In the control room, Rickert clutched an empty soda can as he watched Ben's flight on a monitor, spinning and rolling the can in his sweaty hands,

From a purely technical standpoint, it was a breathtaking performance playing out on the massive screens suspended on the wall above the control room. Rickert had never seen anything other than a hummingbird accelerate and maneuver like Liberty-1. He and his team had once envisioned something like this. They'd gamed out endless scenarios for what first contact with an alien intelligence might look like. Some had been peaceful, others less so. Most of the peaceful encounters had been straightforward. Any species that had the technology to reach Earth was necessarily more advanced, and if they were willing to be polite, then the only rational response was to be polite in return. Not everyone would be rational, of course, but that's why you wanted trained professionals handling that first encounter.

The scenarios involving hostile encounters were what kept everyone up at night. Most of them ended with lots of dead people. The only survivable scenarios for humanity involved some kind of third-party assistance, just as had occurred with the brin. If the mrill had shown up alone, mankind's fate would already be written.

The problem was that Rickert's team could only offer so much advice. In the case of a hostile encounter without outside aide, the scenario was always a loss. Eventually, Rickert and his team had suggested two courses of action to mitigate a worst-case scenario. The first was to digitally archive every human record—every scrap of DNA, every history book, every work of art—store it on dozens of automated spacecrafts, and launch them in every direction at the first sign of alien contact. Even if every last person on Earth was killed, at least a record of mankind had a chance to survive. Perhaps another, more peaceful alien civilization would one day intercept one of the ships and have advance warning of an impending attack and maybe even revive humanity via cloning.

The other recommended course was to begin colonizing Mars and the rest of the solar system as quickly as possible. Give mankind a place to retreat to, if need be. And accelerate the development of the technology that might one day allow a realistic defense of Earth.

All leadership saw was a line item in the defense budget that would start in the billions and likely climb into the trillions. The reports were filed and forgotten.

Rickert didn't blame them. He hadn't really believed any of this would ever happen. It had been an intellectual exercise, the ultimate dorm room bull session. He'd shrugged and gone back to work. Still, he was a bit pleased that his team had even predicted that something like the ship Ben was now flying would be required to even the odds against an invader—not that he nor anyone else had any idea how to build it.

And even if Lockheed or Boeing or the Chinese or anybody else could have created such a marvel, without the brin antigrav technology, any normal human pilot would have been pummeled into a slushy bag of splintered bones and battered brains after the first 30 g-force turn. Ben's body and mind had been remade, reinforced, and were married to a machine that danced like a heavily armed angel on the head of a pin. This was pretty much the best of all the worst-case scenarios. Even so, Rickert was a nervous wreck. Ben was literally their only hope against a far better equipped invader. In truth, Ben and his fighter were at best a delaying force.

If they could fend off the first wave of mrill, just long enough for mankind to build and equip an army of nano-powered warriors and ships, then humanity might just stand a chance.

If not, Rickert feared, every last person on the Earth would be dead before spring.

He barely noticed the excited chatter around him as the engineers and scientists drank in the data from Ben's first test flight. He had been right that the technology wouldn't be enough. Wars in the end always came down to people, and Rickert was still worried about that.

The old general pulled out his phone and opened the file with Ben's FBI background check, scrolling through it with flicks of his thumb. Like Rickert had said, it wasn't the military service history or Ben's personal life as an adult that bothered him. Back when Ben was eleven, he and his dad had gone out on their small fishing boat off the coast of Washington state to catch some skipjack and yellowfin tuna. They were supposed to return after three days. Instead, their boat had disappeared for two weeks after getting punched by a massive typhoon that had spun up out of nowhere. When another fishing vessel finally stumbled on the crippled *Constance*, Ben was the only person aboard. Eventually the investigators had determined that his father, William, had been swept out to sea by a particularly fierce wave that had nearly capsized the ship. It had taken days to get this story out of the nearly catatonic boy, though, and the report acknowledged that no one knew for sure how long Ben had been floating alone on the sea.

Rickert turned the phone off and stuck it in his pocket. It would have to wait. Whatever was going to happen in the next few minutes or hours was literally beyond his control.

Commander Miles Bennett, a veteran astronaut, was capsule communicator, or CAPCOM, on this mission, the person in charge of talking directly with the spacecraft. Rickert leaned over and tapped Bennett on the shoulder. "Commander, request to temporarily assume CAPCOM?"

"Of course, sir. Transferring comms to your headset," Bennett said. A green light lit up on Rickert's headset, alerting everyone in the room that he was now acting CAPCOM.

"Liberty-1, this is tower. We're showing a 100 percent kill count, and green lights across the board."

Ben smiled. "General Rickert? Who let you on the mic, sir?"

"Uh, affirmative, Liberty-1, I figured some adult supervision was in order. How are you feeling, lieutenant? Everything seem to be in working order?"

Ben ran through his diagnostic programs once more in the blink of an eye and verified everything looked solid. "Roger, tower, I'm showing all clear."

"No, that's not what I'm asking. How do *you* feel? How does the ship feel? We're about to send you on a solo hike into uncharted territory and I want to know if your walking boots fit."

Ben looked down through his feet, the vacation-perfect blue-green water slipping by at Mach 4. All was quiet inside the ship. He took a deep breath and looked up to the cerulean sky.

"I'm all laced up, sir."

Rickert felt the room around him go still, but kept his gaze fixed on the screen showing the ship, mankind's ungainly salvation. "All right then, sailor, let's go light a fire."

Ben nodded and, with a thought, sent Liberty-1-1 rocketing into the heavens, knowing that hell waited on the other side.

12

In an apartment building in Washington, DC, Arturo Vargas gathered his wife and two children around him and tapped an app on his smartphone. The TV was off, the lights were dark, the computer shut down. He could hear convoys of police and National Guard cars and armored vehicles rolling down his street every few minutes, but their lights were off and sirens quiet. There had been an initial surge of hoarding, but all the stores and shops had asked their customers to buy only what they needed. It was a polite request, and most had complied. Still, there was definitely a lot less bottled water on the shelves than normal. Vargas had turned off the lights and lamps because it seemed safer that way, for some reason, and the glow of the phone's screen filled the room.

". . . and if you're just joining us, we're in the midst of one of the most bizarre battlefield broadcasts any of us can remember. Within literally minutes we're expecting the first engagement in what governments around the world are insisting is an extraterrestrial invasion."

The normally unflappable newsman couldn't quite keep the excitement and fear out of his voice. Vargas held his son and daughter a little tighter, but they were too young to understand what was going on, He wasn't sure *he* understood what was going on. It was happening so fast: the president's speech, all the soldiers in the streets, now these spaceships supposedly flying overheard, somewhere above the planet. It felt like a dream . . . or a nightmare.

"But even as we've seen extraordinary preparations on behalf of the largest militaries and defense companies around the world, there has been little to no independent verification of the threat," the newscaster continued. "We literally do not know what is coming, and yet at any minute we expect to see *something* happening in the skies overhead. We're . . . we're, ah, getting no official video feed from any branch of the United States government, or from any other government on Earth, for that matter, but, true to its word, the federal government has not imposed martial law on the various research and amateur observatories around the country."

The newsman was visibly tense, hands curled in loose fists around sheets of paper, almost crumpling them into balls. Vargas had to admit he respected the guy for gutting it out, though. Some of the other stations had gone off the air entirely.

"So, on the right side of your screen, you're seeing a rotating live feed from some of the most powerful terrestrial telescopes. We don't know where the first shots will be fired. The anonymous pilot we've all heard about will be responding and reacting based on what he discovers. In the meantime, all we can do is watch and wait. With so much information being withheld, or perhaps unknown even to our leaders, the best we have is educated guesses on what we face and how we'll fight it."

He seems to finally be hitting his stride, Vargas thought. Maybe sticking to a routine during times of stress wasn't such a bad idea.

"To shed some light on these questions, we're joined by Dr. Melvin Lewis, who holds a PhD in molecular biology from Stanford University with a focus in astrobiology, and Dr. Anusha Chandrasekhar, professor of astrophysics at Princeton. Both guests are at home with their families and are joining us via video call. Dr. Lewis, first to you. Given what has been disclosed publicly and assuming it's all true, what is your assessment of the enemy force we're encountering tonight?"

"Well, Carl, again, assuming we have accurate data, we now can make several educated guesses. First, if the mrill race truly is looking at Earth for colonization purposes, then that's a small piece of good news."

"In what way?"

"If Earth is a hospitable environment for them, if our planet has a suitable atmosphere, gravity, and so forth, then their biology must be similar to our own. Probably carbon-based, likely requiring oxygen in some form, with their bodies likely composed substantially or largely of water. And more basically, if they need a place to live, then they must also be susceptible to injury and death in ways with which humans are familiar. They can be killed."

"I . . . hadn't thought about that."

"Of course. The bad news is that, if they can travel across the galaxy to Earth, then obviously they're much more advanced technologically than we are. They might have found ways to reduce or eliminate their biological weaknesses. In other words, they're going to be very hard to kill."

"And, uh, Dr. Chandrasekhar, that brings us to your area of expertise. What level of technology are we facing here?"

"It is all speculation at this point and, frankly, I still am reluctant to believe this story of extraterrestrial attack. What evidence have we been given? None. Nevertheless, if this is all true, I will not mince words. Mankind will almost certainly lose."

"Ah, uh, what, uh, on what do you base that?"

"The ability to travel between the stars in just weeks or months is a technology that is *at least* hundreds of years out of our reach. With an unlimited budget, we could not make a spaceship with human passengers that would reach even the nearest star in less than a thousand years using existing technology. And yet, this is the enemy we are supposedly facing. It would be like a Roman legion facing tanks and missiles. That's not a battle, it's a massacre."

The scientist's bluntness seemed to be melting down the façade the newscaster had briefly been able to construct.

"But, but, we've been told that the retired US military officer who received the alien injection . . ."

"Yes, we have one man. Facing an entire army. The odds are terribly long. Now, I must say goodbye. If this is real, I want to spend my last moments with my family."

"Uh, it appears we've lost Dr. Chandrasekhar and . . . wait, we're seeing some activity on the video feed from an observatory on the Canary Islands. Wow, look at that. Oh . . . oh my God."

Vargas pulled his family in tight.

13

Liberty-1 lunged at the upper atmosphere through the almost imperceptible tug of gravity. Ben focused on the tracking data displayed across the transparent cockpit, glowing outlines of major landmarks and skymarks flitting across his vision. Even with his super-focused senses, he still found a moment to marvel at the fact that he was now an astronaut, slipping from Earth's grasp. *Not bad for a kid who couldn't even fly a kite*, he thought.

Hundreds of miles below, the Pacific Northwest rolled into view; the deep blue ocean topped with cotton candy clouds off the emerald coast. With enough distance, it all looked calm, serene, even motionless. The only danger was up here. That wasn't true, though. It was an illusion. The illusion of distance. Down on the surface, the wind and water could grab you in an instant, pull you under, and smother you. Ben tried to shove the thoughts aside, but the alien technology in his body couldn't help with that. While his eyes fed him the tranquil scene from out here in space, his mind shoved jagged fragments of memory at him. The boat. The storm. An arm clutching the gunwale, fingers digging into the old, scarred wood, the rest of the body invisible over the side. A child pulling on the arm. Straining. Crying out and begging, the sounds lost in the locomotive roar of the wind. Rain like a machine gun. The boat sliding and rising on the waves. Cracks of lightning at turns distant and immediate.

Ben shook his head, trying to whip the invading memories from his brain. No time for the past. Focus on now. Too much at stake.

No one else gets hurt. He had the power now to save everyone.

He looked away from the rolling planet below and out to the stars. Half a dozen communication and several more combat satellites were outlined

96

in white and green. All the combat satellites were online, with every reactor showing 90 percent power output or better. In the distance, the crescent moon gave a Cheshire grin. Beyond that pockmarked ball, a few dozen mrill ships, outlined in red, were coming in, advancing under the indifferent gaze of a billion stars. They had cut into the solar system behind the sun, then navigated to arrive at Earth from behind the moon. According to the readout, these first ships were light reconnaissance and warfare drones with preprogrammed orders. Plenty of firepower, though, for an unprepared planet.

The brin research had said the mrill wouldn't attempt to bombard Earth with conventional weapons like antimatter bombs or asteroids or nuclear missiles. The goal, after all, was colonization. Hard to live on a molten, radioactive rock. Besides, the mrill liked to think of themselves as clever. During a ground battle with the brin for control of a minor city, the mrill had broken through the brin line, leaving hundreds of dead soldiers in their wake. Then the advance had ground to a halt, as the mrill had seemed to lose the initiative, digging in when they should have been advancing. With time to regroup, the brin had bombarded the mrill all night with heavy artillery, antimatter shells exploding in purple flame up and down their trenches. By morning, the mrill had retreated and withdrawn to their camps. The brin collected their dead, gathering their mangled bodies for ritual cremation. Six hours later, the corpses had been collected and gathered in a storage facility near the brin command center.

That's when the mrill had detonated the 143 bombs their engineers had buried in the bodies of the dead brin, vaporizing the command center and the two thousand or so soldiers resting nearby. The mrill then marched into the city without firing another shot, executing every survivor. It was a tactic that would never work again, but the mrill didn't care. The point had been made.

The sensors in Ben's ship couldn't detect what weapons the mrill scouts carried, but the brin had guessed (and Hawthorne had agreed) that a swarm of invisible nanobots was the most likely. Instead of indiscriminately melting every living thing on Earth, as the mrill had done with the brin, these tiny invaders would likely be programmed to rain down on major cities, then quietly devour any humans they fell upon. It was a weaponized version of the machines running through Ben's body. Scientists had speculated that, if the nanoclouds were successfully dispersed, they could probably eat their way through most of the human race in just about two weeks. When they were done multiplying and consuming, the nanobots would most likely shut down as the mrill fleet arrived to an empty planet, inert dust that would disappear in the wind. No muss, no fuss, no mess.

"Liberty-1, this is tower, what are you seeing?"

"We've got what looks like thirty-six bandits coming in behind the moon, just as we thought. Weapons scan inconclusive, so I'm assuming nanobot payload, with possible additional hardware. Range to targets is 49,000 kilometers and closing at a rate of 279,000 kilometers per hour. I don't think they've seen me yet. Battle satellites still in passive mode to avoid detection, but it's going to get lively in a minute."

Ben sent his ship blazing past the International Space Station, which had also been outfitted with a bristling array of weaponry, and on toward the moon. A skeleton crew was still on the ISS, the minimum human contingent needed to keep the station aloft. The drones could now see Ben's ship and began to slow, less than 20,000 kilometers from Earth. Both groups were still too far apart to attack each other with their ship-based guns. The battle satellites were much more powerful, though, and the mrill robot ships had yet to realize that Earth had its fists up.

Ben mentally selected the nearest satellite, orbiting a few hundred kilometers above South Africa, and it unfurled like a spider. Red lights winked on at the tips of its antennas as the hydrogen ionization chamber spooled up. This would be the first time any of these weapons would be fired in space. The brass was worried test shots would tip their hand to the mrill, not to mention terrify any humans who spotted the incandescent beams. In fact, even the remote test fire in Arizona had not gone unnoticed. A high school rocket team had set up camp not far from the Phoenix Aerospace base and was shooting video of their launch prep when the stream of fire had exploded into the sky. The video was crystal clear, at least until the sonic boom startled the cameraman, who dropped his phone. Before the feds even knew the video existed, it had three million views on YouTube.

Ben watched the ionization readout on his display quickly climb to 100 percent. Detecting the threat, the mrill drones began to scatter. Ben selected the nearest ship some 7,000 kilometers away, and the satellite, Pincer-7, rotated slightly. A surveillance satellite trained on the incoming ships pinged his display as a canister about the size of a football burst from an open panel on the mrill ship and streaked toward Earth. The video beamed directly to Ben's eyes was also transmitted down to the teams on the ground. Ben knew Rickert was seeing the same thing he was, but he had to make sure.

"Incoming projectile from mrill drone," Ben said, a little louder than he'd intended.

"Roger, Liberty-1, you are cleared to engage at your discretion."

Ben fired the satellite. The inner chamber of Pincer-7 glowed with a scarlet fury for a fraction of a second, then the molten beam scorched the vacuum and obliterated the drone in another fraction of a second. The ship disintegrated in a puff of flame, the shrapnel vaporized. As the satellite oriented to the next ship, Ben accelerated his ship to intercept the tumbling canister. Two more mrill drones ejected gray canisters and sent them hurtling toward the blue planet. Ben opened fire with his short-range cannons, green droplets of energy annihilating the ejected canisters while the red beams from the satellite targeted the mrill ships. The mrill drones responded with their own short-range weaponry, staccato blasts of blue that skittered through the dark, like poisonous centipedes.

Ben piloted his ship through the swarm. His conscious mind was, again, largely irrelevant, an observer and, if necessary, an arbiter. A big-picture guy. But for this ship-to-ship network, it was simply too slow to handle most of the decision making. So while his body dodged and parried with the mrill drones, Ben let his mind operate the defensive satellites. He picked his targets deliberately, aiming for the closet mrill ships, those preparing to dumping their genocidal payload on Earth. Red beams carved through the empty space, incinerating the mrill ships like paper airplanes gliding through the path of a flamethrower. Six, seven, eight mrill ships were torn apart. Nine, ten. But they kept coming, and now they were fanning out around the globe, probing for holes in the safety net, like wolves encircling a flock, making it harder for Ben to track and destroy each ship. There were huge gaps over portions of Asia and Europe, the result of too little time to build the necessary satellites.

The battle migrated above the Earth, from North to South America, across the Atlantic and up the west coast of Africa, then down the Middle East and across India. The main cannon on the International Space Station stabbed out into the vacuum, then a second time and a third. The drones measured the threat and attacked, swarming the ISS from every direction.

The short-range defensive weapons on the station fired, straining to repel the assault. Ben maneuvered closer to assist, but another handful of drones chased him off. He struggled to fight through the diversion, but even as he chopped through the drones, another group cut through the space station's defensive barrage. The cannons scattered across the gantries continued to fire, picking off mrill drones as fast as they could. There were just too many of them. One drone raked the massive solar panels on the port side while another blasted the Zvezda Service Module, which contained the station's life support systems. The pressurized compartment burst, spraying out metal, plastic, and oxygen.

"No!" Ben screamed, straining in his seat even as he blasted another drone.

The loss of Zvezda was an eventual death sentence for the three-man crew of Expedition 37, unless they were able to escape back to Earth in the Soyuz return ship. Huddled in the Tranquility module to keep the station operational and combat-ready, the three crewmembers, two American and one Chinese, had at most 30 minutes to live. The mrill had no intention of granting them even that long.

As Ben destroyed the last drone that had chased him off and turned to speed back to the ISS, a pair of mrill ships skimmed over the crippled space station and ejected a pair of glowing orbs that zoomed toward the structure. With his enhanced vision, Ben could see the faces of the three men peering out through the panoramic cupola viewing platform. They were bathed in the orange glow of the pulsing orbs. Ben fired as he turned, straining to intercept the incoming artillery, knowing he was already too late. The two glowing spheres clamped onto the metallic structure and exploded.

The ISS was transformed into superheated plasma in an instant, briefly as bright as the sun, but slowly enough that Ben's new eyes captured it all and burned the image into his brain.

A millisecond later the shock wave arrived, traveling at 12,000 miles per second. It was just enough time, just barely, for the spinning petals of Ben's ship to fold around his cockpit and lock in place, forming a protective cocoon. Then the blast enveloped the ship and ejected it away from Earth, toward the moon. Even with the antigravity technology, Ben was whipped about, his head slamming against his seat as various bits of electronics fizzled and sparked. His display shimmered and flickered as the spinning of the ship caused the sun, moon, and Earth to careen across his vision like a spinning top. Gamma radiation splattered over the ship, but a layer of tungsten in the cockpit and the boron carbide nano-shielding in Ben's body protected him from the vast majority of the damage. The rest could be repaired. Earth would be less lucky, Ben knew.

Even this miniaturized supernova would dump enough gamma rays on the exposed side of the planet to hurt a lot of people, maybe even kill them through short-term burns or long-term cancer. But the mrill didn't want to sear the Earth and turn it into a radioactive, roasted rock. If they had wanted that, they would have simply carpet-bombed the planet and left. These munitions were a show of force. Or, rather, a bit of chest-thumping. *Look on my works, ye mighty, and despair.* It was effective.

As his ship lurched off into the dark, kicking away from Earth like a pool ball scattered by the opening break, Ben's body felt frozen, immobile, useless. Even out here, in the black absence of gravity, he felt the weight of his responsibility, his guilt, pressing on his chest. He'd met the space station crew a few weeks ago, before their launch. The two Americans— Jeff Schweitzer and Greg Dent—were former Air Force pilots, while the Chinese crewman—Zhang Wei—had served as a nuclear engineer aboard China's first nuclear submarine. They were fighters and thinkers, and they knew they were volunteering for what was likely a one-way trip. Ben had thought of them as his personal responsibility, the only other people directly engaged in this first battle with the mrill, but without the benefit of his hyper-tuned physiology.

They had been exposed, like gunners in the ball turrets on the bellies of World War II–era bombers, dependent on the pilot to guide them through the flak and bring them home safe. And he had failed them. There weren't even any bodies to bury. He knew he would remember his failure, carry it like a cross, as long as he lived.

A panicked thought hit him even as his battle sense tried to shove these debilitating obsessions away. With these new nanomachines patrolling his body for disease and injury, just how long would he live if he didn't die in combat? A hundred years? Two hundred? Forever? It would be the universe's cruelest joke to make him immortal, powerful beyond human imagination, just so he could watch helplessly as everyone else died in agony.

For a moment, Ben considered letting his guard slip, letting the mrill drones finish their work and turn him to so many particles of heated vapor, to mingle in the dark with the atoms of those he'd already let down. The only thing that stopped him was the knowledge that, if he did, the result would only be more death, the death of all mankind. No.

Anger brought clarity. He felt the rage coursing through his veins as clearly as he had felt the initial nanobot injection on that cold New Mexico night. The anger overcame and transformed him, fresh armor and new will. His ship wasn't out of control, it just needed his guidance.

He found his bearings, found his targets, and fired.

The dozen or so remaining drones blew apart like piles of straw in a tornado, and he almost didn't notice how he screamed with triumph after each successful shot.

Ben dipped down closer to the planet to avoid intersecting a spray of antimatter fire, and a faint glow of heat enveloped Liberty-1 as it dipped down into the atmosphere, compressing the thin air, then thundering back out. The final handful of mrill ships broke off into two groups. Four of the ships accelerated toward Earth for a bombing run, while the rest converged on Ben. Ben zapped two of the attackers with satellite fire, then accelerated to maximum speed to catch up with the bombers, who were spreading out to drop their ordnance on different locations across the planet.

He destroyed two of the bombers, but the final two attack ships were closing on him from behind. Ben swiveled his craft around, now flying backward. He shredded his pursuers and their wreckage sank down toward the Indian Ocean. Only two bombers remained, both still armed with their nano payloads. The two mrill ships had finally identified the holes in the defensive grid and had split up to attack Europe and Asia.

I can make it. I can stop them. I can do this.

He repeated it like a mantra, a prayer. The ship hummed as he opened the throttle to the max, screaming down toward the planet. Warning lights flashed as he reentered the atmosphere with a rattling thud, but he shut them down with a thought. He was closing on the Asian attacker.

The drone spun and spat fire as Ben chased it from above. He dodged the first few shots, but one finally found its mark and tore through one of the petals on the propulsion system. The ship shuddered and started to veer off course before he was able to redirect power and stabilize. Ben poured everything he had at the enemy, his own ship starting to tear itself apart in an effort to destroy its quarry. His vessel rattled with every shot, green light like St. Elmo's fire enveloping man and machine. His targeting systems had been damaged, and his shots were missing and slamming down toward the surface of the planet. He could only hope they weren't hitting anyone below.

The mrill drone bobbed and weaved, popping diversionary flares and floating mines that exploded as Ben narrowed the distance between the two ships. Shrapnel pinged off the cockpit bubble, and Ben had to divert some of his computational power to targeting and shooting the explosive mines before they punched through his ship.

He had to finish this quickly, within seconds. The other bomber was still out there. The drone he was pursuing was now beelining for Shanghai and its 23-million-plus residents. Ben pulled closer, and the flares and mines dwindled, then stopped. Empty. Ben honed in for a final shot when the drone's canister bay opened. He retargeted his guns for the canister but, at that moment, a final mine popped out of the back of the drone. *Clever machine*, Ben had time to think as he squeezed off a round.

The canister was vaporized, but the mine exploded before he had time to turn his weapon to the drone. The blast ripped apart the sky and sent Ben's already damaged ship into a momentary tailspin. Warning lights and alarms flashed and screamed as he struggled to regain control. Sparks and fire and smoke began to fill the cockpit. Even as he spun through the air, he could see the drone he'd been pursuing reach Shanghai and open fire on the skyline. Ben brought his ship back under control and wrenched it back across the sky to chase down the mrill drone. There was a deep crack in his cockpit bubble, but it didn't seem to be spreading.

The drone had seemingly decided that even if it couldn't kill the entire population of Earth, it would take out as many of its inhabitants as it could. Tracer fire from defensive installations around the city illuminated the night, not that guns dependent on slow human computers had a chance to keep up. They couldn't see the way Ben could see, not with his speed and precision. The drone was now darting between buildings, down through the streets. The kill would have to happen close, like a knife to the gut. So be it. Ben accelerated and his radio crackled to life.

"Ben! Stop! Disengage! The other drone is making its bombing run still armed with its nano weapon!" he heard Rickert shout. "I repeat, disengage! Let the Chinese handle this one!"

"No, sir, they can't keep up with it," Ben snapped back. "Half the city will be destroyed before they can bring it down."

The desperation in Rickert's voice was unmistakable over the crystal-clear connection.

"No, dammit. There's no time! You have to let this one go and . . ."

Ben snapped off the radio link with a mental command. There was time. There had to be time.

The drone was destroying Shanghai's glittering financial district, a collection of exotic skyscrapers on a tongue of land surrounded on three sides by the Huangpu River. Glass and fire filled the night, as shot after shot pulverized the skyline. With his enhanced vision, Ben could see the chaos and death on the streets below. Razor-sharp glass tore pedestrians to crimson shreds, and chunks of concrete and steel struck the ground like bombs.

The drone spiraled up around the massive Shanghai World Financial Center, with Ben in close pursuit, firing wildly, his desperation outweighing his caution. The drone shot through the trapezoidal opening at the apex of the building, and Ben followed. Just as his balky targeting computer locked on for a final shot, the drone fired a rapid burst at the adjacent, pagoda-styled Jin Mao Tower. The blasts struck roughly 200 feet below the nearly 1,400-foot peak, shredding a dozen floors. The building shuddered and crinkled, then tipped over and plunged toward the ground. Ben turned toward the wreckage and opened fire, trying to pulverize it before it speared into the street. Only a couple shots found their mark before the spire drilled into the throng of cars and pedestrians. Debris burst outward, enveloping the fleeing crowd. Screams filled the air and, a moment later, Ben's voice joined the chorus.

In a froth of rage, he drove his ship down a corridor of skyscrapers, chasing after the automated drone. His own ship was barely holding together now, damaged portions flying off as alarms screamed for his attention. Guns and engines still working, at least. As he drew a bead on the fleeing ship, a turret on the enemy craft rotated backward and fired at the same instant as Ben. The two shots bypassed each other and then stabbed into each ship. The vessel tore apart around him, as shocking and painful as if his skin had been stripped from his muscles and bones.

The largest hunk of Liberty-1, with Ben still strapped inside, careened off the side of a building, gouging school bus–sized hunks of concrete. The antigravity device was torn open and vomited out a blue flame. The exotic blast sprayed across Ben's right arm and leg, searing his flesh. He howled in agony and in memory of agony from that shitty beach and hill in the desert. The ship bounced against a wall again, then finally crashed into the ground. The impact ripped the battered pilot from his seat and he flopped onto a tangled pile of steel rebar poking out of slabs of jagged concrete. He almost blacked out, but the nanobot medics in his body wouldn't allow it. Microscopic repair crews were already mobilizing, fanning out across his wounds.

His head felt as heavy as one of the concrete blocks he'd landed on. He seemed to be bleeding from somewhere just above his eyeline. Or maybe his head had landed in a puddle of his own blood? Or . . . he noticed the dusty form of a pair of legs deeper in the rubble. Then another. Dead. Obviously dead. He'd brought the building down on top of them. He'd killed them. Hadn't he? Why had he done that? He was supposed to protect people. But there was something else. Somewhere else he was supposed to be. His mind felt full of lazy bees, a sluggish and aimless buzz.

Some 50 yards away lay the shattered remnants of the alien drone.

Ben tried to stand, but something held him in place. He looked down and noticed he was impaled on three steel bars, poking like fingers from a concrete slab. He couldn't remember that happening. Blood. Blood everywhere. It had mixed with the dust and formed a black sludge. The rusty metal had reached into his left side, under his armpit, in his gut, and through his thigh. His side smoldered, but he felt no pain . . .

The nanobots at work.

They were trying to work, trying to fix him. They couldn't fix the people crushed in the wreckage, though, could they? No time to think about that. This mission wasn't over. Not yet. Maybe not ever.

A small crowd was now gathering around the crash sites. Even in their dazed, terrified state, a few of the onlookers already had their phones out to video the scene. Beyond the shocked and curious faces, Ben saw the wreckage of the drone twitch. Someone had to deal with that. *He* had to deal with that.

With a roar, he pushed up on his one good leg, the rough metal sawing through his body. With a last thrust, he toppled off the metal spikes, three gouts of blood shooting out of his wounds as he tumbled onto his back.

He gasped, the pain finally overwhelming his defenses, and the handful of smartphones was now a dozen, as sirens and gawkers both swarmed.

Then a piercing shriek of metal.

Ben, exhausted and bleeding, looked over as the mountain of debris that had been the alien drone bubbled up and then tumbled aside to reveal a gleaming white two-legged robot.

Three red eyes blinked on, expanded and contracted, then targeted. Gun barrels slid out from each arm where hands should have been, and the machine opened fire on the crowd in long, ripping bursts. The gold bolts punched through the shrieking masses, dismembering, vaporizing, and boiling the victims. Severed arms and legs landed with a sickening thump amid the larger bodies and burning vehicles.

Get up, sailor. GET. UP.

Ben staggered to his feet. The robot ignored him and marched off down the street, killing everyone in its path. Cars screeched to a halt before it, and the machine tore them apart with its guns, fireballs mushrooming into the night; the jagged, dancing light bouncing off the glittering glass and polished metal. The screams were everywhere, and were soon joined by sirens, as the Chinese military and Shanghai police, already on alert, rushed to the scene. Troops scrambled out of an armored personnel carrier and opened fire. The bullets pinged harmlessly off the juggernaut, and the spotless machine vaporized the dozen soldiers with a single sweep of fire. Police ducked behind their cars and attacked, also equally ineffective. The robot shrugged its right shoulder, and a bulky chunk of its upper arm detached and slid down to the weaponized forearm and attached itself to the gun. A red targeting laser flickered on and touched half a dozen police cars. Then the gun attachment spit out six missiles in quick succession, the firing chamber rotating with each launch. The rockets streaked through the air and shredded several cars, sending cops and bystanders flying.

Ben tried to run, to give chase, but his body was depleted. He felt his wounds mending, his broken ribs and pelvis and collar bone being knit together at a furious pace. The pain was a bulldozer, as shards of bone were literally dragged through muscle and forced back together. Charred skin was repaired, scar tissue sloughed off.

The energy expenditure was immense, a caloric furnace beyond anything the human body was designed to handle. Ben dropped to one knee as

his vision dimmed, his body shutting down as the energy demands overwhelmed the supply. The nanobot swarm in his body, sensing the danger,
diverted all their stored power, one milliwatt at a time, to maintaining
Ben's heartbeat, his brain functions, his respiratory system. The tornado of
wireless digital information Ben had become accustomed to vanished, and
the visual readout that played before his eyes shut down. He could feel his
superhuman strength and speed drain from his limbs as the nanomachines
repairing his wounds worked overtime. But even his unaided hearing was
enough to track the path of the marauding robot, as explosions and screams
of pain and terror continued to echo down the streets now clogged with
rubble and stranded cars.

He begged his body to move, but he was weaker than a newborn colt,
unable to even wobble to his feet. He fell and lay sprawled in a pile of
debris, small pieces of sharp concrete digging into his cheek. Conscious-
ness was slipping away. His body was killing itself to heal itself. He rolled
over with his last strength and stared straight up into the night sky. An
orange haze danced at the periphery of his vision, the city on fire, but he
could only look up. The buildings sparkled above the destruction. Beyond
them was only smoke and cloud. Then the obstructions cleared, for just
a moment, a whisper of wind, and a single star appeared. It shone, for a
moment, then disappeared again in the gray. His eyes rolled back and the
world went dark.

The nano swarm made one last attempt. The tiny machines coalesced
in his chest, near his heart, and bound themselves to each other, forming
complex molecular connections. They formed a sphere and, inside, a small
pellet made of deuterium and tritium. The surrounding nanobots pooled
their remaining energy into a single laser blast that superheated the pellet
and triggered a small, fierce explosion that blew off the outer layer of the
ball of exotic material. The intense pressure forced the core to generate
a self-sustaining reaction. Deep in Ben's body, nuclear fusion, the same
engine that powered the star he'd seen through the haze a moment before,
took off. The nanomachines absorbed the heat and transformed it into the
energy they needed to do their work and revive their host. It thrummed
through his body, an electric blast that surged across every nerve, cell, neu-
ron, and muscle fiber. He awoke like a shotgun blast, yelling out loud with
raw physical sensation as his vision exploded with data.

Every muscle arched and twitched, as if on the verge of releasing bolts of lightning.

All his senses burned like live wires. He could hear each grain of dust crunching beneath the feet of the stampeding mobs half a mile away just as clearly as the pattering heartbeat of a small mouse watching him with trembling eyes from a pile of trash at the end of the street. He could smell the computers and other plastics burning a thousand feet above him in the mangled Jin Mao Tower, and taste the smoke. It was too much, too much sensation. He forced the data flood back, channeling it. Now he could hear the merciless machine that was sweeping through the city, but he couldn't see it. It was moving quickly.

Ben darted to the wreckage of his ship. He swept chunks of the hull and engines aside, the debris flying like a dog digging for a bone. At last he found the weapons locker and opened it with a thought. The two pistols were damaged beyond immediate repair, so he grabbed a bulkier rifle. He'd probably need the extra firepower anyway. The tentacles wrapped around his arm as he ran off, leaping over bodies and past shell-shocked survivors. They needed help, but other people needed it more.

The robot had gone far in just a few minutes, tearing through the city. The landscape was unfamiliar, alien, but Ben's internal computer tapped into GPS systems and internet mapping services to give him an orientation. A three-dimensional map popped up and rotated in his vision. He was heading northeast on Mingzhuta Road toward the much larger Fenghe Road, a major highway. The robot had apparently turned southwest on Fenghe. Ben leaped over an abandoned car, then another. Now the street was crammed with burning, smoking vehicles and crying, screaming civilians trying to drag themselves to safety. He moved over and through the thick debris like water.

Sirens were blasting from every direction and confused soldiers and police tried to administer first aid while hunkering for cover, unsure where the attacker had gone and if it might return. Ben suppressed his urge to stop and help the wounded and dead. There was nothing he could do other than stop the machine up ahead. Ben reached Fenghe and turned right down the wide thoroughfare, the battle now unmistakably near. Tracer fire and rocket trails sliced down toward the street from helicopters and infantry surrounding the robot. The machine was undisturbed, picking off the relatively slow-moving targets with ease while dodging projectiles with even less effort. Blinding flashes of light erupted from the robot's position as the glistening machine marched through the street. Three streaks of blue artillery arced out of a cannon on the creature's back and screeched like bottle rockets into an adjacent street.

The explosion was catastrophic. A blue bubble of light washed over the city, followed by a shockwave that tossed men and vehicles like newspapers. The three attack helicopters slammed into a wall of buildings and detonated, pouring fire and wreckage on the streets below. The soldiers on the ground were nearly incinerated. Ben, though, responded in a fraction of a second, kneeling down as his skin hardened into armor. The blast washed over him and receded, and he kept moving, the rifle cradled in his arm. For a moment, everything was quiet. All the people in the immediate vicinity were dead, all the tanks and cars turned to twisted metal.

A pair of buildings collapsed, their structures twisted and weakened by the blast. The wreckage coughed up a cloud of dirt and debris between Ben and the robot just as their eyes met. Ben raised his rifle, already dodging as he fired, spraying the target area with a mix of focused and wide-area ordinance, shooting blind. The robot did the same, and the two enemies dissected the neighborhood. Ben tried to filter through the dust, cycling through infrared and other slices of the light spectrum. But the smoke and dust and flames and jagged wreckage made it nearly impossible to identify anything ahead. Without hesitating, Ben leaped forward, rolling and firing, terrified he might hit innocent civilians, more terrified that the machine would deliberately try to do so.

Out of the gloom, the enemy answered, lobbing rockets and grenades that exploded around Ben, showering him with debris, cutting into his flesh. The nanobots kept working, putting him back together again.

All the king's horses and all the king's men, Ben thought wildly.

As he darted through the battlefield, dodging and juking, he realized that the robot didn't seem to be moving much at all. Perhaps it was stymied by the choking dust and smoke, unable to process its next move with no clear path in any direction. Ben skidded to a stop at the edge of a shattered tank, its main cannon splintered with smoke pouring from the shredded cabin. The haze was now beginning to clear as the dust from the collapsed buildings was settling. Soon the view would be clear enough for the robot to resume its rampage. He fired off a few smoke grenades in what he assumed was the machine's direction, then bolted.

Just as he fled the tank, a yellow globe of pulsating light emerged from the gloom and struck the tank. The already crippled machine glowed white hot for a moment, melting and sinking down through the bubbling asphalt. Then it exploded, spewing molten pellets of steel. A handful of the slugs raked his right side, so hot and fast that they cauterized as they carved and then flew on out of his body.

Ben crashed to the ground, gasping at the agony.

He rolled, trying to regain his feet, his body slowed by the damage it had sustained. The nanos were working, but not fast enough. A crunch of footsteps and the robot emerged from the swirl. The three red eyes focused on the human, reading and studying him before the kill shot. His fingers scraped across the pavement, fumbling for his weapon. Even as his hand curled around the rifle, the electrical and biological circuits reconnecting, he knew it was too late, too slow.

A yellow glow formed deep in the barrel of the robot's gun.

A microsecond before the weapon fired, though, the robot raised its gaze. A pair of missiles slammed into the creature's chest, hurtling it back over the crest it had just crossed. A pair of Chengdu J-10 fighter jets screamed overhead, the roar of their engines ripping open the sky.

It was the most welcome sound Ben had ever heard. The two planes began to circle back for a second attack run, but he was already on his feet.

He staggered through the shattered street, firing and rolling and ducking. The robot was almost certainly still alive—was "alive" the right word for the robot? For Ben himself?—but now he had a chance. The confused tangle of wreckage where the robot had gone down lay at the feet of the Oriental Pearl radio and TV tower. The structure looked like a ladder with three legs arranged in a triangle, sort of a mini Eiffel Tower. Three additional legs held up a sphere about 300 feet off the ground, and then the three main legs extended up from there to another large sphere nearly 1,000 feet off the ground, like tomatoes on a kebab. A communications antenna was mounted on the last sphere.

His internal scanner showed the structure was deserted.

It was time to end this.

Chunks of concrete stirred in the crater a few dozen feet away. Ben poured a rocket barrage into the legs of the tower, like chopping a tree. The legs exploded, sending shards of steel, glass, and concrete hurtling in every direction. He kept firing, blasting the supports, and the building swayed. The deep crack of support cables snapping in the structure, the force of gravity taking over, millions of pounds of stored kinetic energy about to be unleashed.

He ran for the edge of the crater, sprinted up the side, and jumped as the tower began to collapse. The robot, distracted by the crumbling structure and still half buried in debris, now tried to turn back to its adversary, ripping apart its own trapped legs in the process. Too late. Ben unloaded everything he had on the machine. The robot popped like a can of beans left too long on a camp fire, fragments of armor and machinery and purple fluid spraying everywhere. Ben landed and stumbled on the other side of the crater, rolled and jumped, hoping he'd cleared the impact site of the plummeting tower.

It crashed like a thunderbolt, square on the robot—or whatever remained of it—driving the invader into the earth. The ground shook like an earthquake. Ben's internal radar detected an incoming clump of twisted metal and concrete. His body reacted before his brain could process the info, sending him twisting and falling back as the two-ton meteor sailed a fraction of an inch past his nose and then bounded harmlessly down the street. Now flat on his back, he wanted desperately to just stay there, to rest and heal.

He had to make sure, though.

The mangled cars in the crater and the pancaked tower had formed a single ball of unrecognizable debris coated in a uniform of dust and cloaked in smoke. The sirens and emergency lights were coming back. He had to make sure this was done before anyone else was back in harm's way.

Ben climbed down into the charred center of the crater, yanking aside rebar and hunks of concrete. It was in here somewhere. He could see the radio signals still emanating from the robot. It wasn't dead yet. Or . . . something else. The signal was changing. One last heave, and there it was, the thing's head. The three red eyes were already fading, blinking, drawing the final reserves of energy in for . . .

In a flash he decoded the mystery. With a savage jolt, Ben ripped the head free from the ruined metal carcass and turned north, running for the river. The eyes were almost dark now, but blinking faster. No time. He hurled the head toward the Huangpu River. It was almost a quarter mile away, a throw no human could make. He wasn't just human anymore, though.

The dirty, battered head streaked through the air, then pierced the water and sank. It burbled down, the eyes blinked one last time, and then it exploded. The detonation sent a small mushroom cloud of water up into the air, killing a few fish, maybe, but well away from any people.

Now it was over.

Ben sank down to the ground. He looked down at his arms and legs, a dozen minor scratches and deep cuts already healing before the blood on his mangled flight suit was even dry.

Then he remembered. With a thought, he reopened his radio link.

"General Rickert, you there? Come in."

For a moment, silence.

"Ben, you still alive? Thank God."

"General, did the defense grid catch the other drone?"

Silence again.

"Yes."

"But?"

"We lost Saint Petersburg."

"What? What do you mean we *lost* Saint Petersburg?"

"We're sending a team to pick you up."

14

"No, dammit, there's no time! You have to let this one go and take out the other ship. It's still armed. Ben, are you there? Ben?!"

Rickert squeezed the console in front of him. The massive monitors in the command center in Cape Canaveral had been blinking madly when tracking the initial wave of frenzied attackers, but now the action was distilled down to the last three ships: the two invaders and one defender. Rickert understood why Ben wouldn't, *couldn't*, disengage, but he also hated it. There was no time.

"Do we have a target? Where is this thing headed?"

The technicians didn't even look up, punching through simulations on their computer screens.

"We're running multiple potential tracks, sir," one of the radar techs finally said. "Could be anywhere from northern Europe to Siberia. Our satellite defense grid is weakest over that area and looks like the drones finally figured it out."

Rickert knew instantly that Russia was the target. It was their greatest point of vulnerability, in more ways than one. Gretchenko had warned them that Russia would be destabilized, and the headlines proved him right almost daily. Hardline communist and nationalist elements were agitating and conspiring. They were sending swarms of angry youths out into the streets to protest that this was all an American plot to undermine and overthrow Russia. Often, the protests turned to riots and looting, and the aging generals were happy with this, too. Old men moving young men like pawns, sacrificing them as they saw fit. Russia had always been a fertile field for conspiracy theories. Now the crackpot theories seemed indistinguishable from the truth. If the President of the United States could go on television and warn of an alien invasion, who was to say what was theory and what was fact? No tale was too outlandish to be dismissed as myth or madness anymore. So the agitators had seen an opening to power and were determined to squeeze through, even if their country burned behind them win the process. Rickert had seen the plans. Russia's manufacturing industry was critical to building the bulwark against the mrill. If the Russian government fell and was replaced by a more belligerent regime, the whole world would suffer.

A two-front war with Russia turned the tide of World War II. I wonder if it will do the same with World War III?

The team managing the fire control systems for the orbital satellites frantically plowed through calculations.

"Can we shoot it down ourselves?" Rickert asked. The cluster of colonels and lieutenants looked ashen and tired. One finally spoke up (Glen Cameron, Rickert remembered through the panicked fog clouding his mind).

"We'll try, sir, but our targeting computers are like molasses compared to the systems embedded in Lt. Shepherd. Our best hope is to strafe the approach vector and hope for a lucky shot."

Rickert wiped his forehead with the back of his hand as fear wriggled in his gut like a furry caterpillar.

"Fine, open it up. Everything we've got, both airborne and ground-based."

It would be damn funny if a plain old iron-and-gunpowder antiaircraft gun brought down the last alien drone, but at this point Rickert didn't care if a slingshot provided the killing blow. He opened a live video link on his tablet with General Sergey Parchomenko, head of the Russian Ministry of Defense, currently located in a bunker in Kazakhstan. The position was a military rank, but Parchomenko was a politician, having risen through the bureaucracy over nearly thirty years in office. He reported directly to the Russian president and oversaw the country's entire military machine. Rickert dreaded the conversation he was about to have, although all the leaders of the world had been briefed on its possibility. Over the video link he could see Parchomenko struggling to contain his despair. *Still, he's doing a damn better job than I would in his shoes.*

"General, I'm sure you can see on your screens the same data I'm seeing. The last drone is heading your way and looks to be approaching . . ." A tech handed Rickert a scribble on a slip of paper. ". . . Saint Petersburg. We're linking our targeting data with your systems, although we're having a much tougher time tracking the bogies without Lt. Shepherd's internal computers. We . . ."

Parchomenko cut him off. "Thank you, General. We're receiving your data. I must go." The video and audio feed stayed open, though, and the activity level in the background turned to a frenzy.

The caterpillar in Rickert's stomach begin to spin a cocoon.

On the screen, the icons for the remaining orbital weapons were blinking as they fired, their high-energy beams carving through the night, unable to keep up with the zigzagging drone. The streams of energy stabbed and jabbed at the machine like a man trying to catch a housefly with chopsticks. Who knew what kind of destruction they were causing on the ground below?

"General," Rickert yelled, louder than he'd intended. "The ship is coming in range of your surface-to-air systems."

No response.

"General?!"

●

Nearly 7,000 miles away, in a bunker that smelled of both ancient and fresh cigarettes, the Russian politician wished very much he had become a baker like his mother had wished. The family business. This business was much nastier.

"I know, dammit," Parchomenko growled, as the American general's pleading voice squeaked from the speakers on the handheld computer. He had regarded that machine as nearly magical just a few months ago, a piece of technical wizardry. That seemed likes ages now.

He took a drag on his cigarette to calm his nerves. The smoke drifted through the air, slipping through the throng of yelling, running soldiers. Military discipline was breaking down, close to a complete collapse. Who knew how much longer orders would be obeyed? A lot of things were about to fall apart. He had the data feed from the Americans, but knew it to be unreliable. The drone flitted on and off the display, skipping through radar detection. Parchomenko knew the approximate area the drone was in, but not precise coordinates. His soldiers would have to simply dump ordnance into that corner of the sky and hope for the best. Spray and pray, as the saying went. Kazakhstan was more than a thousand miles from Saint Petersburg, but Parchomenko was sweating nonetheless. He knew the stakes as well as the Americans did. What's more, his parents lived in Saint Petersburg and had refused to relocate to the countryside, even as Parchomenko had pleaded with them, begged them to abandon the city. All population centers would be targets. But they would not leave their home. Stubborn fools.

"Do you have the location? Then fire, damn you! Fire everything," Parchomenko growled at his control team.

They moved without looking up, some barking orders into their headsets while others activated computer-controlled defense systems outside the ancient city. The fixed defense systems were mostly missile batteries, as they had largely replaced machine guns over the last few decades due to their longer range and tracking capabilities. That very technology made them less useful now. It was nearly impossible to track the drone in the minute or so they had before it dropped its cargo, and the missiles simply would not fire without a lock. Traditional antiaircraft machine-gun fire were actually a better option for this scenario. Pull the trigger and off the slugs went. Dumb though the shells might be, at least they had a chance at a lucky shot.

The best weapon in the Russian arsenal for such a job wasn't on Russian soil. The *Admiral Kuznetsov* aircraft carrier, parked in the Baltic Sea just off the coast of the city, bristled with surface-to-air defense systems. Admiral of the Fleet Dmitri Tokmakov was stationed on the *Kuznetsov*, overseeing the entire Russian navy, depleted and rusty as it had become over the last thirty years. The *Kuznetsov* was the centerpiece of the Russian fleet, and it made sense for Tokmakov to be onboard during this engagement. Parchomenko suspected the ship would be a tomb for Tokmakov and the nearly 1,700 crew members. Nevertheless, the primary plan must be followed before the contingency plan was put into effect.

Parchomenko toggled through several live video feeds from the deck of the Kuznetsov, tuning in just in time to see the various weapons systems swivel to the west and tilt up to the sky. The most powerful was the Kashtan weapon system, a hulking 34,000-pound device outfitted with a pair of six-barrel, 30-mm rotary cannons. A single Kashtan could pour 9,000 rounds per minute into the sky, each slug traveling at roughly 2,800 feet per second. A wall of supersonic death. The *Kuznetsov* had eight Kashtan systems. Each combat module was linked to the command module, which tracked and identified airborne targets. But the guns could also be fired manually, without requiring an electronic target lock in case of damage to the radar system. It was one of the most lethal short-range weapons on the planet, and under any other circumstances, would have made the *Kuznetsov* just about untouchable by any airborne attacker. Against the alien drone, however, Parchomenko had no idea what to expect.

The last of the combat modules rumbled into place and they all opened fire. Even just coming through the speakers in the central command room in Kazakhstan the sound was deafening, a thunderous drum roll. Parchomenko couldn't imagine the cacophony aboard the ship. He glanced down at the radar screen. The drone disappeared from the screen for a moment, then reappeared to the east, still on a direct course for Saint Petersburg. The guns on the *Kuznetsov* struggled to adjust to the glimmering signal, belching out tracer rounds.

Three kilometers out.

Two kilometers.

The drone would launch its main weapon in just seconds.

The control room in the Kazakh bunker had finally gone quiet, all the staff huddled around the monitors, last-ditch orders and reports clutched in sweaty hands. On a frenzied hunch, Parchomenko tapped out a new command for one of the Kashtan emplacements, swiveling it southwest a few degrees and ordering it to fire into seemingly empty airspace. At the same moment, the drone vanished again. The radar was empty for an agonizing instant. Then the ship blipped back in at the very spot Parchomenko had filled with hundreds of thousands of rounds. On the video screen, a massive fireball erupted over the ocean as the shells found their mark.

"Yes!" Parchomenko screamed as the room erupted around him in cheers.

Then out of the cloud of smoke and fire streaked a tiny tongue of silver, so small as to be almost imperceptible, even on the high definition displays, a device no bigger than, say, a samovar of tea. Parchomenko felt his smile freeze on his face, like wet concrete poured into an industrial furnace.

The guns of the *Kuznetsov* opened up again, but the projectile was already past the warship, hurtling toward the city. The device burst in midair, several hundred feet directly over the dome of Saint Isaac's Cathedral.

"Did we hit it?" one of the crewmembers in the bunker yelled with near hysteria. "Did we hit it?"

No chance. Parchomenko knew what was happening, even without seeing the gray cloud that had blossomed and was now spreading and enveloping the golden dome and the surrounding areas.

He slumped into his chair and stared up at the screen. He felt more tired than he ever had in his entire life. An exhaustion no sleep could cure. The cameras and monitors, oblivious to despair, kept recording and displaying. The Russian could not look away, and the signal was so clear it was like he was perched on a roof of the ancient city. The electronics could not protect them, only torment them. A helpful gust of wind grabbed a corner of the gray cloud and dragged it toward Nevsky Avenue, the vital heart of the city. As the dust settled onto the church and ancient buildings, Parchomenko reached for a secure phone with a trembling hand.

Click. "Voice identification required."

"Sergey Parchomenko, 197–23."

"Please wait."

The dome seemed to be melting. The spectacular gold sheath was being eaten. Where the clouds caressed the sparkling metal, they left behind only the underlying stone, like meat dropped in corrosive acid. Now the stone was being gently but quickly dismantled, too. Each atom was repurposed, reconstructed, into more machines. An army of zombie soldiers biting and converting its helpless adversary. The city was consuming itself.

"Identification confirmed. Proceed."

"Directive 258."

"Authorization code required."

"MTL-7041."

"Hold for presidential verification."

The cloud had also settled onto the apartments and shops lining the famed Nevsky area, which had served as the backdrop for Dostoevsky's *Crime and Punishment.* Fancy bakeries and Western clothing stores lined the streets, coffee shops and cell phone stores. The bewildered pedestrians and disorganized soldiers and policemen stared up at the dark swarm, not certain what it was or how to respond. A tendril of the nanocloud curled around a segment of building housing a Burger King and a bank, which crumbled and slammed into a small group of onlookers. The bloodshed finally woke the people from their gaping wonder, and they stampeded in every direction.

None escaped.

Gray death swooped down on the shoulders of the whistling wind and cut a path through the screaming hordes. Every person touched by the maelstrom howled in agony for a brief moment before bursting in a cloud of gray machinery. Cars, shops, groceries, newspapers, and families were all devoured and transformed in moments.

"Verification denied."

"Goddammit, motherfucker! Emergency interrupt."

"Hold."

Entire sections of the city were now disintegrating, the tiny machines subtly directing micro currents of air into a tornado of destruction. The whirling dervish sucked in buildings, helicopters, buses, everything. Expanding outward, the surging storm left only bare, scraped earth behind.

"This is President . . ."

"Shut up, you imbecile. You must authorize the launch now. We have only a few minutes, seconds maybe, to contain this disaster. Everything depends on this. Do you hear me, you feeble communist cocksucker?"

"Now, General, I think . . ."

"No, you do not think! Are you watching this? Do you see? Now, dammit, now!"

"I, I . . . but this will be the end of us, General. Everything will fall."

"Of course it will! If we see each other again, it will be at the firing squad. But this must be done, or the whole world is eaten and *shit out*. Now do it!"

Click.

Parchomenko leaned back in his chair, but his body did not relax. He stared at the monitors showing Saint Petersburg. What was left of it, anyway. It was no longer recognizable as a place where prosperous, modern Russians could live.

It looked like a giant, gaping skull attached to a flopping body that did not yet realize it was dead. A swirling, pulsing tornado had consumed most of the city and was expanding outward at an impossible rate. A caravan of cars was trying to flee on one of the highways, Parchomenko saw, barreling around and in some cases over pedestrians running on the same road. The wind was faster than all of them. It cut the vehicles open, metal and blood spraying for a moment before being digested and repurposed into more machines to consume the next group. The enemy was advancing relentlessly in all directions, a march that would have been the envy of Napoleon or Hitler. Parchomenko calculated they had perhaps two minutes to contain the swarm before it spread beyond all control. He saw the red blinking phone on the control panel, the United States president calling. To hell with him. What was there to say? Parchomenko's gaze bounced back and forth between the monitor and his computer. His computer screen still said "Verification denied." He ticked off the seconds in his head, counting down to the end of the world—or at least this piece of it. If Russia didn't deal with this, Parchomenko knew the Americans, British, and French would. They would have no choice.

His hand drifted down almost of its own volition to the old Makarov pistol he'd taken to carrying on his hip since the alien attack had been revealed. It seemed an ostentation, a bit of costume drama at which his aides with actual battlefield experience rolled their eyes when they thought the boss wasn't looking. But Parchomenko had never been sentimental. There were difficult elements now wandering the streets at night in Russia, bands of bewildered, suspicious, terrified people. A strange frenzy had settled over the country, a barely contained panic.

He feared many of his fellow citizens had simply gone mad. The official statistics were massaged for public consumption, but everyone knew the murder rate had exploded. Dawn always brought fresh bodies now, like driftwood abandoned by the tide. The Makarov was protection. And escape. Parchomenko rested his hand on the smooth leather strap pulled over the butt of the gun, securing it in place.

"Verification confirmed," the robot intoned. "Fire Dome initiated."

Even without cameras, Parchomenko knew the chain of events those words had set in motion. He could almost see it in his head, clearer even than the images on the screens. Nearly a thousand miles from Saint Petersburg, in the North Sea off the coast of Norway, the Russian submarine *Alexander Nevsky* launched two Bulava missiles, ballistic nuclear projectiles each carrying six 150-kiloton warheads. The missiles appeared on one of the screens as white blips. Parchomenko watched on the screen as the two projectiles arced up to the edge of space, peaked, and began their descent.

The entire launch/descent phase had taken less than a minute. Saint Petersburg was well within range, and these were fast missiles. They released their individual warheads, which spread out to encircle the doomed city. The timing and location were critical. This had all been agreed in advance, the physicists and engineers from America, Russia, and other countries confirming that a ring of fire must be established to trap and burn any and all nano invaders. Should even one of the tiny warriors survive, the entire mission would fail. They *all* had to burn.

The warheads streaked downward. The twelve cones detonated five hundred feet above the ground, just as planned. Twelve sparks of light became twelve small suns. The blast waves preceded the heat. The raw power was enough to overcome the circular sway of the nanorobots, disrupting their intricate dance and forcing them toward what had once been the center of the city. The machines were whipped into a tight ball, a roiling mass, defanged. A nanosecond later came the fire and the city was wreathed in flames.

The periphery of the city, untouched by the alien swarm, was incinerated by the human weapons. Buildings were annihilated, along with everyone inside and outside of them. The ring of fire tightened like a noose, squeezing the city, choking alien and human alike. Six seconds after the initial detonations, the firestorm reached the center of the city. With no avenue of escape, the airborne gray invaders were burned, returned to the primordial carbon, hydrogen, and other basic elements of which the entire universe had been born. And so was everything else around them.

The city was pummeled, then cremated.

Saint Petersburg, once Petrograd, then Leningrad, birthplace of the Russian Revolution and the Soviet empire, site of the murder of the monk and mystic Grigori Yefimovich Rasputin, home to nearly five million Russians, was wiped from the map.

Parchomenko slumped in his chair. The room was quiet, funereal. There was nothing left to do. Not now. Maybe not ever. He watched the lumpy mushroom cloud push up into the sky, the only gravestone these dead would ever get. Parchomenko thought of his gun. He tapped a button on his console, and Rickert's haggard face appeared.

"Comrade, it is contained. You may alert your president. Your Superman apparently could not save us all. But it is done. Perhaps it was enough."

"Sergey, I . . ." With another tap, Rickert was gone.

Parchomenko lit another cigarette, ignoring the blinking light of incoming calls.

He inhaled deeply, filling his lungs and savoring the bitter sensation. He finally let it out, blowing a ring of smoke up to the ceiling. It looked not unlike the ring of smoke now crowning what had been Saint Petersburg. His parents, he realized, were almost certainly a microscopic part of that ring.

Ash to ash, dust to dust.

Parchomenko took another drag and closed his eyes. His hand dropped to his belt again.

15

It was a beautiful day.

Sunlight skipped across the snow on the peaks of the Rocky Mountains, white wisps of clouds sailing the deep blue sky like clipper ships bound for the New World. The granite mountains seemed eternal and fixed, but they too were travelers, drifting to the southwest aboard the North American geologic plate at the speed of about one centimeter per year. Everything was migrating. Whether molecule or moon, every element of the physical universe was in transit. Creation would not tolerate stasis. For now, it was a beautiful day. It would become something else eventually. Maybe still pleasing, maybe not. But undoubtedly different.

Ben stared out the window of the black SUV, not speaking, watching the road unfurl across the rugged landscape. He noted without interest through his tireless internal digital sensors that the truck's exhaust emissions were increasing. The catalytic converter was dying, although no one else, not even the SUV's onboard computer, was aware of it yet. The vehicle would almost certainly fail its next inspection.

The inconsequential malfunction nevertheless tugged at Ben's mind and he did not chase it away. Perhaps because it was an easier thought to deal with than the ones which had been haunting him the last few days. Fallout from the engagement had been severe and was still unfolding. Russia was now in a full-scale civil war, with elements of the army in open rebellion, joined by scattered yet numerous civilian elements. The government was in tatters, with the president in hiding and Parchomenko nowhere to be found and presumed dead. Gretchenko had taken command of what was left to command. That gave Ben some comfort, but he knew there was only so much the man could do. A series of confused tank battles outside

Moscow had left hundreds dead and no clear winner, while IEDs exploded at all hours in cities and military bases across the country. The Russian ambassador to the United States had first gone on CNN demanding the US surrender Ben as a war criminal, and then three hours later requested political asylum in the US. It was total chaos, and the entire Russian defense industry had shut down, including the half dozen facilities that had been building additional defense satellites.

The Chinese, on the other hand, had gone completely dark, which made the rest of the world even more nervous. Not a peep since Ben had been whisked out of the country aboard a Chinese military helicopter to the USS *Nimitz* aircraft carrier stationed 200 miles off the coast of China. Seeing a Ka-28 Helix chopper with a People's Liberation Army red star emblazoned on the fuselage land on their decks had certainly been a new experience for the crew of the *Nimitz*. But then, most everything over the past several months had been a new experience, and the sailors had only stopped what they were doing when they'd recognized the passenger who'd stepped from the aircraft.

It hadn't been Ben's first trip aboard *Nimitz*, as he and his SEALs had toiled anonymously on those previous trips, moving in silence and deploying at night. He felt like something completely different now, an object of fascination and fear. A celebrity or a pariah. Maybe both.

Then the Chinese helicopter had retreated to the mainland, and the official communications channels had been extinguished. Every nation was on some form of emergency footing. The obliteration of Saint Petersburg was still round-the-clock news. The fact that the initial battle was essentially a victory for the planet had gone largely unnoticed in the horror at the deaths in Russia and China. The headlines screamed that none were safe, that Ben was dead. Or maybe alive, but badly wounded. Or uninjured, but that he'd fled from battle and left the cities to their fate. Or he'd joined with the mrill.

Borders were shut. Weapons were pointed in every direction. Riots were spiraling out of control. Even in the US, where things were relatively calmer, the demonstrations were getting out of hand, with a ragtag collection of anarchists, conspiracy theorists, and environmentalists firebombing government buildings and other property. In one case, a masked group of thugs had blown up a dozen cell phone towers outside Seattle. After four members of the group were shot and killed by a local SWAT team, the remaining members insisted during interrogations that they had proof the cell towers were part of a human/alien conspiracy. Those sorts of flare-ups were increasing, getting more violent.

The Israelis had shut their borders and expelled all Arab residents, while Egypt had declared war on Israel. It was a meaningless declaration, as the Egyptians could barely contain the seething mass of their own terrified people. Nevertheless, Israel retaliated by bombing an Egyptian munitions factory that had actually been abandoned years before. Any way you looked at it, people seemed to be working on faulty intelligence these days, Ben thought. Panic lapped at the shores of most minds now, from government leaders to schoolchildren.

Oddly enough, the greatest threat was the most thoroughly ignored. News coverage of the space battle had been intense the first several hours. With only limited video footage from a few ground-based telescopes and even the leakiest government sources themselves unsure what had happened, there wasn't much to report. China had somehow managed to put an airtight lid on any and all amateur video shot during the battle of Shanghai. The lack of footage was only part of the explanation, though. The truth was that no one wanted to acknowledge such an inscrutable and mysterious threat was looming overhead. It was like receiving a diagnosis of end-stage cancer and wanting to shift the conversation to the weather or politics.

The technology involved was nearly incomprehensible to most people, but Ben thought the real reason for the scant conversation was that the threat itself was so primitive. This wasn't a skirmish over borders or economics, with diplomats drafting terms even as brigades deployed. This was a raw, fingers-to-throat tribal brawl for survival. Losing wouldn't mean peace treaties, occupations, and reparations. It would mean stacks of corpses. Mass graves. The world hadn't seen that in a long time. Not the "civilized" parts, anyway. Most people had forgotten what war, in its most basic form, really meant. Some would remember in time to stand up and fight, Ben thought (and hoped). But for over seven billion people, the dominant emotion now was a thrumming, barely contained panic. So people kept their heads down from the threat they could not understand and instead picked fights with their neighbors, friends, families, and colleagues.

The world was tearing itself apart. It was only a matter of time before someone—maybe India or Pakistan—was overcome with the fear and hysteria blowing in the wind and lobbed a nuclear bomb at an old enemy. The chain reaction would be swift, as everyone rushed to fight the foe they understood so they could ignore the invader they did not. Something had to change, or everything would fall apart.

Ben could almost taste his guilt and shame, like bile in the back of his throat. His failure with the drones was all-consuming. He endlessly replayed the feverish pursuit of the machine over China. He understood why he had done what he had done. Scarred by hundreds of missions where civilians and fellow soldiers died in droves before his eyes, he could no longer tolerate collateral damage; could not distinguish, in the heat of battle, between immediate action and the greater good. He couldn't take watching one more person die while begging for help. There were already too many faces that he saw when he closed his eyes at night. He knew he should have turned his ship around, left Shanghai to its fate, and pursued the other threat. One machine versus the nano bomb should have been an easy decision.

But he couldn't do it. To turn his back, to deliberately abandon the city, was intolerable. Even if he could rewind back to that moment, he wasn't sure he would have acted differently—*could* have acted differently. Between the nanobots in his cells and the guilt coursing through his soul, maybe he wasn't really in control of himself anymore. Forces beyond his grasp or even understanding seemed to be shoving him to and fro, a small ship in a big storm. Or maybe that was just a cheap dodge, unearned absolution. The hell of it was, he would almost certainly be faced with this situation again: two battles when he only had time for one. He would have to acknowledge defeat or send someone else to fight when he couldn't. That was the most terrifying possibility. Not just that someone else would die, but that Ben would have to *order* someone else to go die for him. There would be no escaping that responsibility, no pretending it was someone or something else's fault—not the machines in his blood or the scars on his mind. The deep dread of that seemingly inevitable future pressed down him, almost blacking out the cloudless sky.

Ahead, just a bit farther up the immaculate road under the beaming sun, was the Cheyenne Mountain Complex, the Cold War–era command center for NORAD, the North American Aerospace Defense Command. Designed to withstand as much as a 30-megaton nuclear blast, the aging underground compound had been repurposed and expanded to oversee America's space defense, dubbed Skywatch. President Lockerman was at Cheyenne, and he wanted to speak to Ben personally.

The convoy wound its way up Norad Road, and Ben watched as the famous semicircular entrance to the facility came into view. The massive tunnel looked like a gun barrel whose bottom half had been sawed off, then shoved into a rock. Rickert occasionally glanced over at Ben, but he also stayed quiet. His pinkie finger tapped against the side of his leg, a nervous tic Ben noticed he'd picked up recently and which he could barely suppress.

The lead vehicle of the six-car caravan stopped at the guard shack and the driver, a Secret Service agent, reached out with his ID badge and a small thumb drive. The beefy military policeman manning the gate snapped the thumb drive into his tablet and scanned the screen. The MP waved everyone out of their SUVs and to a narrow metal corridor that would take them from the main parking lot to the 50-foot asphalt road leading into the mountain itself. As each person stepped into the metal hallway, doors clanged shut at both ends and a pair of cameras did a 3D scan of the visitor, matching his height, weight, facial features, and retinal characteristics against a database. In addition to the MP scanning the visitor list, fifteen or so marines patrolled the grounds, while a pair of towers with snipers flanked the scanning corridor. Ben had been here years ago and knew this amped-up security was a recent addition. It would be effective at keeping human trespassers out, at least, he thought.

After they were all in, a marine drove up in an extended electric cart. Ben, Rickert, and four Secret Service agents climbed aboard, and the driver turned the cart around and steered it toward the yawning entrance. The portal swallowed the small vehicle and its passengers, and darkness enveloped the men.

Ben's eyes adjusted immediately. Beyond the opening, the two-lane road extended a couple hundred feet directly into the granite mountain. There, a massive steel door blocked their path.

At a station inside, a guard with the US Air Force 721st Mission Support Group watched on his monitor as the various video feeds were assembled into a single three-dimensional image. He could now rotate around the cart and its occupants like a camera floating through a video game, seeing any angle he wished. He scanned the visitors as the hidden sensors in the entryway sniffed for chemical, biological, or radiological material. They couldn't yet scan for the nano materials the mrill had used in their bombs, Ben realized with a quick glance through the compound's encrypted security bulletins. Not that it mattered. If the nano weapons had made it this far, they could easily gnaw their way through any conventional defenses. As the engineers in the facility had noted, if the visitors were carrying the nanomachines, the only way to destroy them would be incinerating them with nuclear weapons, as they had in Saint Petersburg.

And in fact, the entire mountain complex was now rigged with half a dozen nuclear bombs. Everyone inside the Cheyenne complex lived with the knowledge that they were surrounded by armed nukes that could go off at any moment if the security teams determined a nano invader was inside the structure. Given the speed with which the nano weapons could devour their targets, there were multiple guard locations throughout the multi-story facility, each with individual authorization to turn the key if needed. Ben figured these had to be the most loathed jobs in the complex. Probably the world.

The massive steel blast door rumbled open as the security screening was completed. The cart rolled forward before the three-foot-thick doors were even half open, and they began closing again as soon as the cart was through. They clanged shut and the cart stopped. As the eleven hydraulic pistons on the inside of the first door clanked into the locking mechanism embedded in the granite, a second blast door swung open. Once through that second line of defense, the cart came to a stop inside an empty, cavernous garage.

Ahead loomed the first of the fifteen three-story buildings carved into the mountain. On the white metal wall were painted the insignias of the main tenants of the Cheyenne complex: NORAD, US Northern Command, Air Force Space Command, and US Strategic Command. Inside that building was the main entrance to the facility, and the last security checkpoint for visitors entering the complex.

But that wasn't where Ben and his group were going.

To the right, against the granite wall, a cluster of metal junction boxes sat atop half a dozen or so gray metal conduits running into the main building. Rickert hopped off the cart and flipped open one of the junction boxes. He placed his palm on a flat black surface inside. Three amber lights lit up in succession as his prints were scanned, then a final green light as he was verified. A strobe light on the wall blinked twice as the only warning, then the granite wall receded half a dozen feet into the mountain, stone grinding on stone, and slid to the side. Rickert climbed back on the cart as LED lights inside the hidden chamber came on.

The driver turned and backed into the chamber and stopped as the granite door slid back into place. The moment it ground shut, the floor dropped and Ben realized it was actually an elevator. As the heads of the occupants sank below floor level, a metal plate slid in over them, sealing off the elevator shaft. Everything was built to defend against the most apocalyptic of attacks here, and usually the engineers had built two or three of everything. The backups had backups.

The elevator sank deep into the mountain. A hundred feet, two hundred, Ben measured. It was getting warmer inside the shaft. He noticed that Rickert was sweating. The postcard-perfect weather up above might as well have been on the other side of the planet. The elevator stopped and another door opened, releasing a rush of cool air. The cart whirred down the passageway about 300 feet or so and stopped in front of a metal door. This time everyone got off, although Rickert again was responsible for unlocking the door. Ben glanced at him. Rickert caught it and shrugged.

"Don't be that impressed. I'm sure the catering crew in the mess hall has access, too."

Despite everything, Ben suppressed a grin.

The door opened and Ben, Rickert, and two of the Secret Service agents filed through, while the other two took up positions outside the door.

The room on the other side was large and tall, although the overwhelming bulk of the mountain above still seemed to fill the air. The room was sparsely but elegantly furnished, with a long oval oak table ringed with silver and black chairs. Flat-screen monitors coated the walls, but were all off. At the head of the table, President Lockerman was sipping a glass of ice water while flipping through a thick binder as the usual assortment of generals and staff murmured among themselves.

The president set his glass down as the visitors entered and waved Rickert and Ben to sit. The Secret Service agents who had come in with Ben and Rickert drifted to the corners, joining half a dozen other agents already in the room. They didn't speak at all, but seemed to relax a bit, down deep in this fortress.

Behind the president was a closed metal door, which Ben assumed led to a communications center and perhaps living quarters of some sort. Hard to imagine sleeping down here, in this capsule under ten million tons of rock and dirt. This wasn't a shelter, but rather an impregnable tomb. He itched for the open desert of New Mexico, his former sanctuary, with moonlight and stars his only cover. Just run and keep running as his ancestors once had, no memory of the past, no thought of the future.

Lockerman held Ben in a long, steady gaze. Ben leaned back ever so slightly in his chair, his hands below the table, respectful but steady. Lockerman spoke at last.

"Tough piece of work out there. Russia, I mean. Well, all of it, actually, I guess."

Ben didn't speak, but finally broke eye contact with the president and stared at the table.

"I understand why you did what you did. And I don't know that you should have done differently, despite what everyone is saying. The Russians nearly had that ship. Honestly, it was a lucky shot that slipped through their defenses. And the drone in China, hell, it could have rampaged for hours and done just as much damage. No, that's not the problem. You might have made the right call. But you did it for the wrong reason."

"Sir?"

"You did it because you can't stand to see anyone die. But if you haven't figured it out yet, let me tell you: that's an indulgence. People are going to die one way or the other. Lots of them, in fact. Maybe every person in this room. Hell, most *likely* everyone in this room."

Lockerman snapped the binder shut and leaned forward.

"But that doesn't matter. Our job is not to save everyone. It's to survive. As a species. If you need to sell the lives of everyone in this mountain to keep the human race from going extinct, then that's your job. And if you had calculated the odds, figured the Russians were in a better spot to defend themselves than the Chinese were and had rolled the dice, I'd give you a damn Medal of Honor. But that's not what happened. And it cannot happen again."

Ben nodded. What else was there to say?

"We've all seen your bio. I don't know what kind of emotional toll that took, losing your dad like that. We never did get the exact details of what happened, but I've had about a dozen shrinks each give me their pet theories on your state of mind, repressed emotions, and whatever other crackpot diagnosis they can cook up. But one of them said something that stuck with me."

Ben struggled to keep his composure, the mountain-like stolidity he had adopted as they'd descended into the granite. He was glad that his new skin was unable to display the flush of anger and shame swirling inside. The president, at least, didn't seem to notice Ben's discomfort, but Rickert shifted awkwardly.

"It's a quote from Jung: 'Neurosis is always a substitute for legitimate suffering.' Took me awhile to wrap my head around that one. But I think I figured it out. I believe it means that our guilt, our humiliation, whatever we're embarrassed about or afraid of, bubbles up in quirky ways if we don't actually deal with the consequences of what we've done. Or failed to do. You're a hell of fighter. But you're dealing with some stuff. I don't know how to help you get through it. I don't think anyone does. But you're going to have to find your way through it before this is all over."

Ben blinked, all of his previous emotions now replaced by a thundercloud of confusion. He shook his head. Was the President of the United States really psychoanalyzing him right now? Surely they had more important things to worry about. He was about to say so when Lockerman beat him to it.

"Now, new business," he said as he slid the binder to the side.

"As much bad luck as we've had, we were due for some good, and we just got it. As you know, our best geneticists and molecular biologists have been trying to reverse-engineer the nano computers in your body without much success. And by 'without much,' I mean 'none.' We've quietly put out feelers to other labs and research centers around the world because, honestly, we're getting desperate. As much as we all appreciate what you're doing, we need more than one of you. But so far, zilch. After your . . . adventure in Shanghai, we received an inquiry from China, asking if they could send their top researcher to us. I don't know how familiar you are with Chinese politics, but sending aid to the US, no strings attached, as seems to be the case here, well . . . that's not generally how they operate. So we obviously said yes."

Lockerman pushed a button on his desk and leaned toward the embedded microphone.

"Dr. Ying? Could you join us?"

The door slid open and Ben was surprised when a Chinese woman walked in. He stood. Her black hair was pulled back in a ponytail, which rested on the collar of a white lab coat on top of military fatigues. The woman walked up to Ben and surprised him again by saluting. She held the pose. She was tall and nearly met his sightline. Ben raised an eyebrow and glanced over at the president, who waited, motionless.

Ben returned the salute and Dr. Ying Lai dropped her hand. She opened her mouth to speak and then paused, and Ben assumed she was casting for the few words of English she might know. She surprised him again when she spoke fluently.

"Thank you, Lieutenant, for what you did. While the Chinese president and his staff have asked me to formally extend their appreciation, I must be more personal. My family lives in Shanghai. They are alive, I suspect, because of you. And you have my eternal thanks."

Ben was, at last, flustered.

"I . . . yes, of course. I mean, you're welcome. It was nothing."

She cocked her head slightly.

"I assure you, it was not nothing. But I take your meaning. And I will convey your gracious response to everyone at home."

"Yes, please, uh, please do."

President Lockerman laughed. "Why don't we all sit down and get to business before the lieutenant literally melts into the floor."

Ben went to pull the doctor's chair out for her, but she had already slipped into the seat, catlike, despite the cumbersome clothes and boots.

Ben shuffled into his own seat, remotely amused at his own sudden clumsiness.

The president, though, was done with triviality.

"Dr. Ying Lai is a computer scientist and microbiologist with Peking University, and a colonel with the Chinese army. And while she's only been working with us for a few days, she's done some amazing work. Doctor?"

"Thank you, Mr. President," she said, nodding almost imperceptibly. "The work your team has done so far is extremely impressive, but I do believe we have made a significant advance in the last 48 hours. I'll forgo the details, but we've cracked the code on the machines in your body, Lieutenant."

"Really?" Ben said. "How?"

She smiled. "By realizing there is no code."

"I beg your pardon?"

"Well, it might be more precise to say that it is encoded, but we already have the key. You see, the nanomachines are programmed to adhere to the precise structure of your cells, your DNA. You and the machines are bound at the molecular level, likely for the rest of your life."

"When you say it like that, it sounds like a death sentence."

"Not at all. Indeed, I suspect you will, if you survive the war, be as close to immortal as any living thing can be. But the point is that the American research team quickly realized that the machines are custom-tailored for your specific genetic makeup. But how could that be possible? You had never met the brin before the night you were injected. There is no way they could have customized their technology to your body. So what you were injected with clearly had to adapt itself to you. It wasn't made for you. It was *remade* for you."

Ben shifted in his chair.

"But surely it can't be as easy as just injecting my blood into someone else and letting the machines reproduce."

She laughed, a straightforward Western laugh, not the girlish giggling Ben associated with most Chinese women he'd met. Who was this woman?

"No, it was not that easy. But almost. For the trick, it turned out, wasn't to reprogram the machines. No, all we had to do was turn them off and then let them reboot, if you will, in someone else."

"And how do you do that?" Ben said.

"EMP. Electromagnetic pulse."

"What? Like in a nuclear bomb?"

"Yes. The same effect, but we didn't use anything so crude. Using a modified Van de Graaff generator, we think we've finally been able to isolate the correct frequency to temporarily disable the nanomachines for re-injection."

"You *think*?"

"Well, we have not yet had a chance to test it. But I am confident it will function as needed."

"And if it doesn't?"

"If the machines are not properly recalibrated, then I presume the nano-bots will read their new host as in fact an enemy and destroy the subject."

"Why do I get the feeling you're sparing me the gory details?"

"Oh, I have no aversion to that. I suspect the unfortunate victim of a failed transfusion would be essentially devoured from the inside out by the hostile machines. It would be extremely"—she seemed to be searching for the right word—"unpleasant."

"So how do you know if you have it calibrated correctly?"

"We must test it on a volunteer."

"Jesus."

Ben turned to Rickert.

"What do you think?"

Rickert glanced at the president before responding, paused, then seemed to make a decision.

"I think it's a nasty piece of business. It's going to make a lot of countries very nervous to have a bunch of superpowered human soldiers running around that are basically one-man armies that can turn invisible. And if this tech falls into the wrong hands—ISIS, the KKK, whatever—we'll be dealing with a total nightmare. And I think we need to do it immediately."

Ben felt the old, familiar pressure on his chest, pressing on his heart, squeezing the breath from his lungs, at the thought that another human sacrifice would soon be called for.

Rickert saw Ben grimace and leaned forward.

"There's no time for anything else. We've lost a dozen satellites from the last battle," he said, ticking off the challenges on his fingers, "and while the Chinese production lines are coming online extremely fast, we're still going to have a hard time getting those defenses back up soon enough, assuming the mrill dispatched a full invasion force as soon as they realized the drone attack failed. But rebuilding the satellite net won't be enough. It was barely enough against what was, to be fair, a small strike force. If they come back with a full fleet of armed ships, the satellites will be overwhelmed. We need more manned defense ships like yours, mobile fighters and bombers that can engage the mrill in orbit and, if necessary, on the ground."

Lockerman waved at the seated generals and admirals.

"The Joint Chiefs and their advisers think the most likely scenario is a full invasion. While some targeted bombing is likely, the use of nuclear weapons or other weapons of mass destruction is unlikely. After all, they want to live here when we're gone. We're beachfront property, and nothing drives down home value like giant radioactive craters. So, what we're looking at is essentially an extraterrestrial D-Day. And we can't win that battle. We can't let the bulk of their infantry get on the ground. We have to take out as many of their landing ships as we can before they unload their troops. And to do that, we need our own fleet. And, so, we need volunteers."

"Volunteers? For what, a suicide mission?" Ben said.

"No, we've got something else in mind," the president replied.

The door opened and three men that Ben knew walked through the door. Eddie Dworsky, Nicholas Parson, and Diego Marquez. SEALs. His friends and fellow warriors.

Ben snorted.

"Damn. Any other surprise guests in that room?"

The men laughed and hugged, although Ben's friends were also fascinated by his new skin. They stared with the unabashed familiarity of men who'd hiked through hell together and had the devil's scalp to prove it.

"Look, I'll give you the *Reader's Digest* version later. But first tell me what you guys think you're doing here," Ben said.

Dworsky, the shortest person in the room and always the first with a joke, put on a look of mock outrage. "What, you think you're the only one who gets to kick some alien ass? We're all ready for a close encounter."

Ben's smile faded. "C'mon, guys, you can't be serious. The doctor here"— he waved toward Dr. Ying—"basically just told me we're looking for guinea pigs. If this doesn't work right, putting my blood in your body will be like pouring sugar in a gas tank, if sugar could actually turn your car into a puddle of goo."

Ying spoke up again.

"These men were carefully selected, Lieutenant," she said in a tone that indicated the debate was over before it had begun. "Your familiarity with them was a key consideration. My government initially insisted that Chinese soldiers be included in this mission as a condition of our aid, but I was able to convince them these men needed to be the first participants. Once the injection process is complete, I suspect you will have a sort of telepathic connection with any others like you. If that is indeed the case, it will be essential to have partners you know and trust, colleagues who are trained to act and think like you. No confusion . . . well, minimal confusion."

Ben shuffled his feet and looked over at Rickert.

"Look, these guys are the toughest bastards I know. But this, uh, transplant or infusion or whatever you want to call it sounds risky as hell. Shouldn't we test this on monkeys or rats or something first?"

Ying shook her head.

"Impossible."

"Why?"

"We tried it. It killed the monkey. The nanomachines seem to require a human host. And in the short time the test animal did survive, it was in a frenzy. The data feed seemed to simply overwhelm its brain."

Ben sighed.

"Dammit, guys, I—"

Marquez waved him off.

"Look, man, we're all volunteers. Have been for a long time. We can handle it. And if we can't, we're prepared for that, too. This is just another deployment. We understand the risks."

Marquez was the youngest of the group. He'd joined the team just a couple years ago, fresh out of training, eager to prove himself. Unlike most SpecOps fighters, he'd stuck with his boot-camp buzz cut, making him look even younger than his twenty-four years. He was a SEAL, though, and had saved Ben's life more than once, including one particularly hairy mission in Nigeria. *I owe all these guys my life. And this is how I'm supposed to repay them?*

Lockerman spoke again.

"Lieutenant, they aren't here to meet with your approval. This is an order. You've been recalled to active duty, effective immediately, and they never left. This is your team, and this is your mission. *My* team and Dr. Ying agree that this is the best course of action, the most likely to succeed. After all, it's the only shot we've got," he said as he jabbed his finger into the table. "We've got a few weeks, tops, before the mrill fleet arrives. We must get your men ready, and then train more. The four of you are a start, but that's all. We're going to need as many upgraded soldiers as we can churn out. So please accompany your team and Dr. Ying to the lab and let's get started. Thank you, that will be all."

Lockerman rose to leave, and the assembled generals and admirals did as well.

Dworsky stepped over to Ben's side and looked him up and down, taking in his gray skin and strained appearance.

"C'mon, bro," he said with a laugh. "Lighten up. All we have to do is save the world."

Ben chuckled at last.

"Yeah, and all *I* have to do is make sure your ass comes home in one piece."

16

Dworsky settled into the gurney as the technicians strapped down his tattooed arms and legs. The bed was inside a metal chamber, and the gleaming walls made it look like a giant oven. Which it was. If the nano injection went haywire and the machines looked to be any sort of danger to the facility, the room would be flooded with fire to destroy the bugs. Nothing would be left of Dworsky's body other than a fine gray ash.

"Hey, guys, I'm already inside a goddamn kiln. Do you think we could do without the restraints?"

Ben, standing beside Dworsky, shook his head.

"Nah, these aren't to stop you from escaping. They're for your protection. When I was injected, I almost had a seizure. And the machines were embryonic, designed to mold themselves to any host. What they're injecting into you is a bit more of a brute-force solution. The doctor tells me this could be considerably more . . . vigorous."

"Awesome," Dworsky said with a sigh.

"On the other hand, if this works, you won't need any help getting out of the restraints," Ben said. "You'll be able to tear out of them like toilet paper."

"Yeah, and first thing I'm gonna do is tear you a new asshole for not talking me out of this," Dworsky said.

Ben held his palms up. "Hey, I tried."

One of the technicians walked over. "We're ready, gentlemen. Lieutenant Shepherd, if you could step out of the room, we'll get started."

Ben tapped his fist on Dworsky's shirtless chest.

"You'll be fine. It feels weird at first, but you'll be fine."

"Hey, can you do me a favor? Reach in my pocket and hand me what's in there."

Ben snorted.

"No time for pocket pool, man."

"No, I'm serious."

Ben looked at him a moment, then reached in his pocket and pulled out a metal necklace, a pendant. On the pendant, a winged angel was thrusting a spear at a demon he was holding down with one foot.

Ben raised an eyebrow at his friend.

"Saint Michael the Archangel, patron saint of soldiers. SEALs too, I guess. That's Satan he's curb-stomping. Mike hasn't let me down yet."

Ben put the pendant in his friend's hand and Dworsky gripped it tightly. He took a deep breath. "Okay, I'm ready. See you on the other side."

A sleek metal door slid open, and Ben and the technician walked out. The door hissed shut.

A handful of techs, VIPs, and Dr. Ying were huddled around three big monitors. One showed a video feed of Dworsky strapped down, another showed his vital signs, and a third was a touchscreen control panel for the EMP generator and injection device. The nanomachines they'd withdrawn from Ben would be deactivated only for a few seconds, so the generator was actually located in the ceiling of the injection room. To protect any electronics outside the room from being fried in the process, the walls and ceiling were coated in a thick layer of lead. The lead even dulled Ben's heightened senses. It felt like a black hole in the otherwise frenetic galaxy swirling around him.

Dr. Ying tapped a few keys and leaned toward a microphone.

"Are you ready, Master Chief?"

Dworsky nodded. Then he smiled and laughed.

"I'm ready, Cortana."

"What?"

"You don't have an Xbox, Dr. Ying? You know, Master Chief? Savior of mankind against the Covenant alien invasion, side-by-side with Cortana, his AI companion? When I made chief, it was pretty much the highlight of my life. Well, until all this mess."

"We don't have time for video games, Master Chief."

Dworsky chuckled again.

"Yeah, I'm not expecting to get a lot of R&R anytime soon. Okay, let's do this."

Dr. Ying nodded to one of her assistants (the team was a nearly even mix of American and Chinese scientists) and he typed out the final sequence.

A low hum filled the room, although it was more of a roar to Ben's delicate ears. He could also feel a surge of energy gathering, despite the thick blanket of lead. A pulse of electricity swelled and rushed out. Immediately, a robotic arm unfolded out of the ceiling, like a scorpion's tail with a metal stinger. On Dworsky's chest, a red laser cross appeared. The arms of the cross shrank as the syringe approached, converging down to a dot just as the syringe reached his skin. Ben noted that Dworsky's heart rate was holding nearly perfectly steady. He wasn't surprised, although the techs were. SEALs were trained to control their emotions in stressful situations. What's more, the kind of men who *became* SEALs were naturally able to control their emotions in stressful situations. Even so, Ben could see that Dworsky was tensed, alert. It was as close to nervous as a SEAL would get.

The mechanical arm inserted the syringe into Dworsky's chest without hesitation, and Ben could see through a clear window on the side of the syringe as the thick green fluid disappeared down the barrel of the device.

Dworsky's body arched upward off the table, like a bow pulled back to launch an arrow. He didn't scream, but every muscle and tendon clenched. Ben felt odd as well. He was accustomed now to the constant stream of data that flowed across his vision, the rivulets of wireless signals he could literally see over every cellphone, computer, and other piece of technology. But something else was happening now. He felt, almost saw, a flicker of something probing at his mind, a tentative tendril of awareness reaching out. Ben knew immediately it was Dworsky being plugged in and connected as the nanobots meshed their technology with his biology.

"It's working," Ben said to the technicians in the room.

Most looked confused or didn't respond at all, but Dr. Ying stood up straight and turned away from the monitors. She stepped directly in front of Ben and looked into his eyes.

"You can feel him, can't you? His brain is establishing a connection with yours, yes?"

"You knew this would happen?"

"I suspected. Based on your reports, the true value of this technology is in the connections it creates between its users. An instant and constant link. An entire army or city or race wired together, able to move as one when needed, to share their knowledge immediately. Can you talk to him?"

Ben ignored her now. The sensation was more forceful, tinged with panic, as Eddie struggled to absorb the flood of information pouring into his brain. He was looking for something to steady himself. Ben instinctively responded, providing the anchor his friend needed.

I've got you, buddy. Just hang on. You'll stabilize in a few moments.

With a flick of his finger, Ben opened the locked door separating the observation room from the injection room. Eddie was sitting up now, the restraints in tatters, breathing hard, the muscles settling but his gaze unfocused. Ben knew exactly what he was going through. Not just because he had gone through it himself once before, but because he could literally feel it happening to his friend. It was a shared sensation that Ben would not have been able to fully explain. There was no human precedent for this moment. Ben could see through his own eyes, his own senses, but at the same moment he could also see himself through Eddie's eyes, could feel the already subsiding fear as it was replaced with curiosity and wonder, and could grasp the swirl of data and thought that was coalescing into new knowledge and insight. It was a new awareness of the world and all the secrets it contained, now laying itself bare to his augmented abilities. At the same time, Ben could feel Eddie swimming through his own mind, reading Ben's calm, seeing that indeed the flow of data was manageable. He could see and feel Ben's memories of his previous battles with the mrill and their drones, and all the battles he'd fought before then. Eddie felt Ben's horror at ordering his friends into battle, and truly appreciated for the first time the deep reluctance Ben had felt and still felt at leading this new war.

All that happened in an instant.

Now Ben watched as Eddie's skin turned gray, a silver sheen. The techs filed into the room, huddling and whispering. Dr. Ying, though, strode right up to Eddie and looked him over. She waved a device over his body—*radiation detector*, Ben and Eddie thought simultaneously—and set it down on the table, apparently satisfied.

"How do you feel, Master Chief?" she said.

"Weird. Great. I feel like him," Eddie said, nodding at Ben.

She flicked a glance between the two men, and nodded, apparently pleased with his response.

"Good. Master Chief, please accompany the researchers for full testing. We need to keep going. Time is short. Lieutenant, please bring in Chief Petty Officer Parson and then Petty Officer Marquez."

"Yes, ma'am."

Parson's experience was identical to Eddie's. Ben felt the energy surge, watched the injection arm unfold from the ceiling, and felt Nick's mind fumble for a handhold. This time, though, both Eddie and Ben reached out to steady Nick, like a pair of tugboats bringing a ship into port. Nick followed the techs out for his testing.

Marquez settled into the table.

"So, no sweat, huh?" he said.

Ben bumped fists with Marquez.

"Not a drop," Ben said. "In two minutes, you'll be a new man. Gonna feel like your brain turned inside out, but I'll be here and so will the rest of the team. It's hard to explain, but you'll know we're here."

"Cool. I always wanted to be a superhero."

Ben smiled. "Dude, you've already kicked more kinds of ass in your career than Batman ever did. Just relax. After this, the hard work starts."

"Will I still be . . . me?"

"What do you mean?"

Marquez looked up and down Ben's gray body.

"Yeah, that. Look, it's hard to describe what happens inside. But it's still me. I can see a lot more and, I dunno, sense a lot more. There's a . . . connection with the world."

Ben held out his arms, turning them over.

"Tell you the truth, the one part of me that's gone that I really miss are the scars."

"Yeah, chicks dig those."

"Well, yes. Doesn't get them to stick around long, though, does it? But what I really mean is that before all this, my body was a mess. But it was a reminder, you know? Where I'd been, what I'd done, what I . . . what I sacrificed. I can remember every scar, could draw them right now with my eyes closed. Sometimes I think I can still feel them. But they're gone."

Marquez looked at him quizzically.

"Look, you'll be fine," Ben said, snapping out of his reverie. "You think the ladies couldn't get enough of you, wait 'til they see the all-new you."

Marquez laughed.

"That's what I'm talking about. Let's roll."

The techs keyed in the commands and Ben felt the now-familiar surge of energy, like a mental vacuum sucking him in and then blasting him out as the electromagnetic pulse exploded invisibly through the nano material. He absently ran his hands over his forearms, his fingers gliding over the perfectly smooth, perfectly healed segments that had once been twisted chunks of scar tissue. He drifted inside his own memories as he waited for Marquez's mental link to open up.

Inside the mechanical arm in the transfusion chamber sat a small fragment of metal, a shaving left over from the frantic machining process. The fabricators in Boston had missed it during their harried inspection process before shipping the arm to Colorado. It was nestled in a safe spot, but each movement of the arm nudged the fleck of titanium toward the gears. This time, as the arm extended, the shaving tumbled into the gears and was swallowed by their teeth. Deep inside the small, intricate cogs, the shaving, a whisper of an ounce, congealed between two of the gears. For a moment, maybe a second, the arm froze, and then the mechanism ripped through the metal shaving and continued its plunge. Dr. Ying, examining a readout of Eddie's initial testing, didn't notice the pause. Ben was distracted, mentally communicating with his other teammates, each testing their new abilities and moving through a battery of tests. The technician in charge of the arm frowned, opened his mouth, closed it, and then opened it again and spoke just as the syringe pierced Marquez's skin. "Dr. Ying . . ."

"Yes?"

"I think there might have been a . . ."

Everyone froze at the sound of Marquez's scream.

On the video monitor they could see him thrashing in his restraints, every limb lunging in a different direction, the metal bands cutting into his skin. He was still screaming. Now his skin began to undulate, ridges and seams appearing and disappearing while the color of his skin cycled, chameleon-like, though gray, brown, and various shades of green.

While the screams pouring from his throat could be heard by everyone in the room, only Ben could hear the loudest cries, a mental shriek pouring out of Diego's mind into his own. Machine-gun blasts of raw pain, alternately broadcasting at full volume and then complete silence. Each shriek that made it through was like a fishhook in Ben's mind that pierced and yanked. He felt like his skull would explode with Diego's misery. Alarms were now sounding in the observation room, sirens and strobe lights accentuating the throbbing terror and agony pounding in Ben's mind. Ben clutched his head and slumped against a wall, incapacitated and overwhelmed.

Dr. Ying elbowed one of the techs out of the way and cycled through the procedural log with a flick on the touchscreen, her fingers dancing as everyone else froze. The malfunction was immediately apparent. She swore in Mandarin and turned to an American technician standing, dumbfounded and terrified, by another console in the corner.

"Activate the incinerator," she ordered.

"Wha, what?" he replied.

"You heard me. Now."

Ben heard enough of this exchange to open his eyes and face Dr. Ying. "What are you doing?"

"Some kind of malfunction in the arm. It delayed the injection by a second or two and some of the nanoparticles reactivated and reverted to their original programmed state. Others did not. Now the two batches are at war with each other inside Petty Officer Marquez's body. He will not survive."

She didn't look up as she entered the command codes to activate the incineration process.

The screaming in Ben's head was louder now. He tried to reach out to Diego to steady him, offer something, anything. But like a drowning man consumed with panic will thrash and strike even his rescuers, Diego's mind was overwhelmed and terrified. It lashed out like a bullwhip, and Ben could not reach him.

"Maybe he'll fight this off?"

"No. His body is being consumed by the battle. It is destroying him. We must activate the incinerators, for his protection and ours."

On the screen, everyone could see that Diego's body appeared to be melting. His skin was torn open and peeled back, and rivers of green and gray fluid oozed and spattered out. Some of the fissures closed, as one group of nanobots tried to repair his body, but new wounds appeared faster than the previous ones could be sewn shut. Larger canyons now opened in his torso; thick red blood, almost black, bubbled out. A silver metallic tentacle snaked through the gore, trying to vacuum it up and return it to his body, but a larger green worm rolled over the silver thread and devoured it.

Ben tried to speak, but the assault on his senses was overpowering. He sank to his knees.

"Activate the incinerator!" Dr. Ying yelled, her composure slipping. The technician, who had to enter his code before the process could activate, glanced at Ben, who wanted to protest, but could only groan in mental anguish. "Now!"

The terrified technician keyed in the instructions, his fingers mistyping, and the incinerator remained cold. The nanobots were now pouring out of Diego's body, consuming the restraints and table. They were enlisting reinforcements, converting any nearby matter to additional nanomachines, just as their cousins had done at Saint Petersburg. They were eating, rebuilding, and reprogramming the atoms and molecules of the table, restraints, and anything else they could touch—even the air in the room—into more nanobots. The temperature in the chamber soared 20 degrees in 10 seconds, then 20 degrees more, the molecular reactions releasing a torrent of heat, miniature weapons factories cranking at maximum production. The clumsy tech hadn't recognized his error and was babbling about a clogged fuel line. Dr. Ying shoved him aside and reached under her collar and yanked out a chain with a red metal key. She flipped up a plastic shield covering a key slot on the wall and inserted the key.

"Stop. Please, stop," Ben said, struggling to his feet, one hand holding the wall and the other his head. "Please."

Without a word, Dr. Ying turned the key, activating a final failsafe. On the video screen, Diego's physical form was almost unrecognizable, a lumpen, writhing mass that had all but liquefied. The table was disintegrating beneath him, and puddles of steaming material were eating through the floor as thick black clouds of smoke filled the space. The temperature gauge read 153 degrees Fahrenheit and rising. The audible cries had ceased—Diego had no functioning mouth anymore—but the mental siren continued, shrieking at uneven intervals, ricocheting through Ben's mind like a terrified bullet. Ben pounded on the metal door, his hardened fist denting the thick steel with each strike. The collisions rang through the room like a bell.

The ceiling in Diego's room seemed to collapse as seven funnels of what looked like reddish-brown dirt poured into the room. Ben recognized it immediately. Thermate. A military-grade incendiary compound that burned at more than 4,500 degrees, one of the hottest man-made burns short of a nuclear bomb. A combination of iron oxide, aluminum, and other chemicals, it was fierce enough to turn the steel room into molten goo and, presumably, incinerate the raging nanomachines. A white-hot magnesium rod shot into the room, the ignition source for the material, which the nanobots were already trying to eat.

All became one giant flame.

The material didn't burn. It rioted. Fire stormed through the room like a caged demon, raw heat obliterating the man-made sensors and cameras, liquefying and then vaporizing everything it touched in incandescent fury. The monitors in the observation room went dark, bereft of data. But Ben's senses endured. He could feel the fleeting terror, pain, and then agonizing relief that flooded through the remnants of Diego's mind in the split second before his remaining physical form was turned to ash. With a final scream, both man and machines were extinguished in the furnace. The chemical reaction had to take its course. Even if the room were flooded with water, the substance would burn unimpeded as it generated its own oxygen.

So the bodies burned.

And burned.

And burned.

The technicians and Dr. Ying had backed to the far side of the observation room, as heat was radiating even through the two-foot-thick walls. Ben didn't move. The silence was, if anything, even more excruciating. The flames in the injection room were finally settling down, but Ben knew the temperatures had permanently sealed the facility, melting the door into its frame. It was now a sarcophagus, buried in the mountain, sealed more effectively and eternally than any pharaoh. Diego was in there; all the particles that had once been a man now twisted and embedded into the remains of an alien technology that had been designed for Ben. Ben had killed his friend. He had poisoned him with the nanomachines, inflicted on Diego inhuman suffering, and then mutilated his remains. There would be no burial. No final goodbye with family or visitations with the body. There would be only this sealed room, both empty and full, locked and dark and unvisited as long as the world itself existed. Ben had killed his friend. He felt like his body would collapse under the pressure, praying it would.

He wept openly, the grief too much to bear, and he wished that this room, too, would be filled with fire and finality.

Then a small sensation coursed through his mind like a soft breeze. Eddie and Nick, no less aware of Diego's death, reached out to Ben in the dark and gave what comfort they had. There were no words, no persuasion. Just comradery. Knowledge that Ben was not alone. That, whatever else, he did not have to shoulder the burden alone. And the sealed room wasn't the end of their journey. Diego would have insisted they go on, and would have expected nothing less. Their silent companionship wasn't much. It was certainly no match for the sealed room, but it was enough . . . for now.

Ben raised his head. Fear, shame, horror, and sympathy were etched in varying amounts on the faces of the technicians in the room, but he ignored them. Dr. Ying, though, was calm, almost expressionless. She approached Ben, but stopped a few feet away, offering neither comfort nor despair, only acknowledgment.

"The three of you, for now, must carry on. You are the only hope the world has, for now. We will construct a new facility. In the meantime, you and your comrades should train with your new abilities. It is important. Nothing else matters."

He nodded.

"This could happen again."

"Yes, it's possible," she said. "We'll analyze what went wrong and fix it. But there are no guarantees." Her gaze finally faltered. "Your actions in Shanghai spared me and my family great pain. I owe you everything that matters to me. I am here to repay that debt. So far I have only added to your anguish."

"No, it's okay, I understand. I . . ."

She put her hand on his shoulder.

"You deserve better from us, Lieutenant. From me. Our enemies bring enough sorrow for us all. Go. Do what you need to do, and we will, too."

The exit door opened and Nick and Eddie walked in. Their faces were grim, but steady. They were ready, too. Ben wiped his eyes and straightened up. He let go of the now-sealed door to the former injection room, heat fading from his fingertips. He faced his men, his friends.

"It's time to go to work," he said.

17

ick looked out at the Moroccan desert, shielding his eyes from the swirling grit, squinting at the mountains in the distance, shimmering in the heat, and turned to Ben and Eddie.

"We're a long way from Coronado."

Eddie grunted. "Yeah, but we're still gonna get sand in our damn undies."

Ben even smiled a little.

"You wanna quit, maggot?" he sneered, echoing the instructor they'd had many years ago at the Naval training center on the California coast. "You can ring the bell anytime you want."

The highlight of the first training stage for prospective SEALs was "Hell Week," a five-and-half-day nonstop marathon of running, swimming, paddling, pushups, sit-ups, log-carries, and verbal abuse. You were lucky to get four hours of sleep over that time. It was the ultimate test of sheer desire, to determine which recruits would rather die than give up. It was an early stage in the long process of the construction of a SEAL. Many of the recruits who survived the grueling slog would still wash out in future training segments, but Hell Week survivors were forever bonded by the experience. And none ever again set foot in so much as their kids' sandbox without remembering the sadistic grins of their instructors as they shoveled piles of cold, wet sand down the backs of recruits struggling through one more set of pushups in the frigid midnight surf. For those who couldn't bear the onslaught, quitting required only walking over to a bell and ringing it three times. Do that, and you could take a shower, hit your bunk, and return to your life. Many did. Those who gutted it out, like Ben, Nick, and Eddie, pitied the quitters, but also envied them.

The shared memory went unspoken among the three men, but they really didn't need to speak at all anymore, at least when communicating with each other. They were connected telepathically now, radios inside their bodies connected to each other in a way the scientists still didn't understand.

"Y'all ever been to Disneyland?" Nick said out loud, startling the other two men.

"I thought this was it," Eddie said, surveying the endless sand dunes around them. "Looks like I need to kick my travel agent's ass."

Ben chuckled, but Nick just continued staring out into the distance.

"We went when I was a boy. Drove, because my dad was a construction worker and couldn't afford airfare. But still, we saved and saved, and off we went. We finally got to our hotel in Anaheim at like midnight, and everyone just crashed in their beds. But I remember looking out the window. I could see the Magic Kingdom, all lit up. We were so close."

He picked up a handful of sand and watched it slip through his fingers. Ben checked his rifle and Eddie flopped down on his back, pulling the tan kerchief around his neck up over his eyes.

"It felt like the next day would never get there. Just waited all night. Think I slept about two hours. Next morning, we're all up, bouncing like fleas, ready to go, and my dad gets a call from his boss, tells him he needs him back ASAP for a rush job because three other guys called in sick. Vacation canceled. Couldn't say no. They fire you or leave you off the next job. So, we all packed in the car—me, my two sisters, Mom, Dad—and drove back to Bakersfield. You can probably imagine. I watched out the rear window until I couldn't see Disneyland anymore. Kinda feels like that now."

Nick caught the puzzled looks of the other two men.

"What I mean is, we're close to something. I just hope we make it all the way."

They were quiet for a few minutes. Eddie pulled his kerchief down and gazed thoughtfully out into the blank landscape.

"I took a trip to Vegas once," he said softly. "Got crabs."

They all laughed.

"All right, enough woolgathering, you dirt bags," Ben said. "Back to work."

He hoisted his sleek black rifle to his shoulder and walked off into the swirling sea of hot sand.

•

Nick wasn't sure where his sudden bout of introspection had come from. He was usually reserved and quiet. He loved his job and the guys he worked with. Just wasn't much of a talker, especially about his past. This new job, this new *body*, though . . . *I'm literally a different person than I was three days ago.*

Did the alien technology in their bodies also change their psychology? It had to, even if just by accident, right? No way could you completely transform someone's biology without changing how they felt about themselves and their place in the world.

The moment he'd walked into the injection chamber, Nick had known he was stepping into uncharted territory. Even Ben hadn't known how the mental links between them would work, since he'd been flying solo up until then. Part of the change was simply a physical transformation. Nick never thought much about his looks. Pretty average black dude was how his online dating profile read. Not a line that tended to get a lot of attention from women, but it was just how he saw himself. He'd tried a goatee for a while, but shaved it off after a couple weeks. Physically, as a SEAL, he was in top condition. Had to be. He was fast, fit, and a crack shot. But he didn't have the bulging muscles a lot of the other guys on the team had. At 5-foot-10, he was usually in the middle row for family photos. He loved his job and could keep up with anyone. When he was out with his teammates, hitting the bars or playing golf, he was happy blending into the background.

Those days were over. Whatever happened, he was now one of the most noticeable people in the world. His gray skin was a darker shade than Ben's and Eddie's, a link to who he'd been before, or at least a reminder. He was something more than human now, though. Strangely, it made him feel connected to the rest of humanity in a way he never had before. The world, all of mankind, was counting on them. He wasn't fighting just for his country or his commanders or his president, he was fighting for everyone. In a way, he was carrying everyone inside of him, inside this superpowered alien body. He'd been through a fire and come out a different man. Eddie had, too. Nick could also feel it.

Ben's transformation was harder to map. Somehow, he kept his mental and emotional walls up. Nick could still sense his presence and could communicate with him telepathically whenever he needed to. But Ben was holding something back, keeping something closed off, or at least draped in shadows. Nick sensed he could force his way in if he really wanted; blast a floodlight on the darkened corner. He trusted Ben completely, though. Whatever he needed to work through, he deserved to do it on his own terms. Intruding on that would be a complete obliteration of the unspoken trust they'd developed as SEALs and were strengthening as . . . whatever they were now.

Besides, there was work to do.

Nick and Eddie spread out at tangents to Ben, each tracking the other two on a mental radar. Out in the Saharan desert, the most remote place the US military could find away from the frantic, rabid eyes of the press and public, a virtual armada of drone tanks and aircrafts waited. Behind the three men, a handful of temporary observation towers had been erected for the brass to track their performance. Behind the towers were dozens of semi-hardened tents and other hastily constructed structures interspersed with portable air conditioning units, supply trucks, satellite dishes, armed patrols, armored personnel carriers, Apache attack helicopters, antiaircraft missile batteries, you name it. Even further out, a runway had been laid in the shifting sand, the tarmac requiring nonstop maintenance and clearing to keep it from being swallowed by the elements. A pair of V-22 tiltrotors were being dragged into a metal hangar, while a C-130J Super Hercules transport aircraft was landing, its four ferocious turboprops adding to the chaos. The Pentagon never left a light footprint.

Out ahead in the virtual battlefield, the desert was unblemished and smooth, ever-shifting but always the same. Treacherous, but also simple and peaceful. An easy place to die and a good place to train.

Ben and his squad could easily see through the heat haze and the dust devils, their upgraded eyes filtering out the noise, tracking heat signatures and other bits of electromagnetic radiation. The three men could have found a TV remote buried under two feet of sand within a few seconds. But the equipment they were tracking had been disguised specifically to foil their superhuman senses. And they weren't here to just blow stuff up, although they intended to do plenty of that. They were primarily here to test and develop their mental connection, to learn how to work not just together, but as one. Rickert and Dr. Ying, after poring through the data on their initial testing, had discussed with the three men on the flight over their theory that the communication link between them was more than just a silent radio. It was possible, the two scientists thought, that the link could enable something closer to a psychic bond; a sharing of physical senses, thoughts, and emotions. That each man could inhabit, and perhaps even control, the others' bodies. A "hive mind," to use the sci-fi term, although "remote control" might perhaps have been a closer term to what they had in mind.

Eddie and Nick were skeptical, but Ben suspected this was accurate, or at least mostly so. He remembered his initial belief that the technology in his body had been incomplete, like a jigsaw puzzle with a handful of pieces missing. It felt like they'd found at least one of the pieces, and Ben suspected the nanomachines had always been designed to operate as a link in a chain, the fuel for an army that could move, think, and fight as one. Not really a remote control, not commandeering another's body against their will or control. A shared link, heightened perception and coordination. As time went by, each man found it harder to distinguish his own thoughts from the other two. They all seemed to see, hear, touch, and react in tandem.

What one saw, they all saw. What one felt, they all felt.

The wind was picking up. Ben tugged a tan kerchief over his mouth and pulled a pair of bulky goggles over his eyes. Eddie and Nick did likewise. Superpowers or no, a grain of sand in the eye still hurt like a mother. The three men hadn't spoken to each other much since that last day under the mountain, instead experimenting with their mental connection, learning to not just finish each other's thoughts but anticipate them. Ben could almost see thoughts and impulses forming in his friends' minds, as they could his.

They had not yet spent any time testing that connection in combat situations, however. Between the tests and the travel and the briefings with government and military officials over the last week, they felt more lab rats than warriors. *Warrior rats*, Ben thought at one point, and the other two had laughed from across the room, startling technicians.

Dr. Ying was building another injection chamber, but the brass had clamped down on any further human trials until she could guarantee there wouldn't be a repeat of Diego's death—not that it was Diego's death that really worried them. If the nanobots had leaked out of the room, everything could have been destroyed. Which, of course, she could not guarantee. She and Rickert had railed against the restriction, imploring the president personally to intervene. Ben had lent his support as well. He knew the clock was ticking. While his horror at Diego's death remained fresh, and probably always would, he knew there was no turning back. The leadership had frozen. Rickert raged at their timidity, but Ben suspected they were just as afraid of him as they were of the mrill. A recruit dying during training was not unheard of, particularly among the Special Forces community. This was something else, though.

Diego's agony had highlighted the truly alien nature of the technology that coursed through the three men. It was destructive and mysterious. Ben could essentially put his body on autopilot, surrender control of his warrior abilities to the inhuman technology embedded in his very DNA, as he had with the first mrill soldier he had encountered in the New Mexican desert. Some of the generals were whispering that perhaps the mrill or some other race might be able to tap into that system as well. To turn these fighters against their own kind. Ben could only do so much to counter that argument. Perhaps they were right. Still, the mrill were coming. Ben knew that, too.

The generals and the admirals and the politicians thought they could hold the line with conventional weapons. They were wrong. He'd struggled to take down just one of their machines in Shanghai. Tanks and helicopters didn't stand a chance. Not alone, anyway. Ben and his men had to be able to take the fight to the enemy.

So here they were in the desert, an eager and nervous army watching their progress from afar.

LT, three o'clock. Nick's thought pierced the rolling heat like an ice-tipped arrow. And even as he thought it, all three men were already spinning and rolling right, rifles coming up to their shoulders. Ben felt his technology tugging for control. Battle senses fully engaged. He did not fight it. The sensors in the rifle were now feeding data directly to the nerves in his right arm, identifying the target and firing before Ben's brain could even verify what he was shooting at. A machine-gun turret was lifting from the sand and before he could even consciously recognize it, it was pelted with laser fire from all three rifles. As the shrapnel was still whistling through the air, Ben was spinning, as were Nick and Eddie. The initial attack had been a diversion, of course, but the follow-up assault was also destroyed before it could even begin. All three men were now operating like a three-headed beast, firing in all directions as new threats emerged, still moving in a coordinated swarm toward their objective a kilometer or so away. This "capture the flag" mission was fairly straightforward, but the odds were heavily stacked in favor of the defenders. In theory, anyway.

The three men flowed through the storm, covering each other, moving, ducking, crouching, swiveling in a spontaneous ballet that no strictly human squad ever could perform. They didn't speak at all, fighting in silence, but in constant communication. While Ben's brain was disconnected from his own actions, it could still serve a purpose. He tapped directly into the vision stream of his companions, his augmented brain cataloging the data, sharing it with the rest of his body. As Nick turned to fire at a flying drone coming over a hill, he spied at the corner of his vision an armored vehicle trundling around a bend. While Nick's body continued turning to attack the drone, Ben calculated range to the small tank and fed the information to his body. Already turning to cover Eddie, Ben blew the tank apart in the blink of an eye. The three men cut a path through the armor like a tornado through a trailer park, leaving only a long smear of smoking debris.

The "battle" was over in minutes. The three reached the flag—literally a plastic pole with a red triangular flag planted in the hub of a tire from an old Humvee—ripped it down and knelt in defensive positions.

Ben surveyed the landscape one last time, toggling his mic. "Base, objective achieved. Please advise."

Silence, then a soft chuckle crackled over the radio. It was Rickert.

"Roger, Cerberus. We read that. We were going to send a second wave, but it looks like you boys killed that, too. Stand by for extraction."

Nick glanced over at his buddies. *Cerberus? The three-headed dog? I was kind of hoping for the Three Musketeers.*

Ben laughed. *Shit, could be worse. I suggested the Three Stooges.*

●

The team drilled day and night. The mission planners threw everything they had at them, from amphibious assaults and defense skirmishes along Morocco's Atlantic coast to fast-rope missions out the rear door of a helicopter to antiaircraft assaults against waves of incoming drones and cruise missiles. The three men deflected and defeated everything that came their way. Most of the time, the technicians remote-controlling the opposition force couldn't even see them coming, in some cases literally.

Ben, Nick, and Eddie now wore combat suits that could mimic the invisibility effect their bodies could perform. Dr. Ying had cracked that particular code based on research that had actually been well underway before the aliens had landed. The trick had been getting the suits to respond as quickly as the three men's skin, but she and her team had done it. They had not, as of yet, been able to duplicate their other properties, such as instant armor hardening. But at least the three soldiers didn't have to worry about going into battle nude anymore.

On the fifth day of the training missions, surrounded by the burned-out husks of several attack helicopters, Ben, Nick, and Eddie sat down, awaiting pickup from an armored personnel carrier. The men normally would have used this time to clean their weapons and check their ammo, but the nano-powered weapons were self-cleaning and self-loading.

The rifles were essentially miniature versions of the ion cannons in the defense satellites. While slightly less powerful, they carried more than enough of a punch to destroy tanks and planes, much less individual troops. The weapons could pull in the hydrogen atoms they needed from the surrounding atmosphere, and their electrical charge was generated by a small thermoelectric generator. It was basically a miniature nuclear reactor with equipment that converted the heat given off by the pellet of plutonium-238 directly into electricity. Add an electron to the vacuumed hydrogen atoms, apply negatively charged electricity to the negatively charged hydrogen ions, and the ions shot out the barrel at nearly the speed of light. The soldiers grasped the science only at the most basic level, but had a deep appreciation for any weapon that could function for a decade without needing to be loaded or cleaned. It was also deadly as hell.

Even so, Ben itched for a good, sharp knife he could strap to his thigh.

Old habits die hard, man, Eddie thought. Ben grunted.

The solar system had been quiet since the drone assault. No signals yet. It was a lot noisier down on Earth. Russia had erupted in civil war. A rebel force was coalescing in the south of the country, inching north toward Moscow. General Gretchenko already had his hands full with the humanitarian disaster around what was left of Saint Petersburg. Russia's nukes were still secure—for now, anyway. No one was sure what the rebels wanted. Its leadership was murky and most of the world's surveillance capabilities were now directed away from the planet. There was just too much to watch.

You know, the funny part is that we're now the perfect spies to get into the Russian rebel camp, Nick thought. *We're literally invisible. If we didn't have to fight off a damn alien invasion, we could sneak into any organization or building in the world.*

Yeah, but if we didn't have to fight a damn alien invasion, Russia wouldn't be in this mess in the first place, Ben replied.

The three men shouldered their weapons as the retrieving APC rumbled into view, and they headed back to the base.

Even outside of Russia, public opinion was turning bitter. The Chinese blackout around the attack in Shanghai was complete. Their leadership had gone into a protective crouch, cutting off almost all internet access to the outside world. The flood of amateur videos of the robot attack that Rickert and others had counted on to galvanize a global response? It never materialized. While the Chinese remained a key contributor of technical expertise to the military buildup, the White House had so far failed to convince them of the value of a media response. Ben pleaded regularly with Dr. Ying in video calls and emails to make the case to her superiors, but she invariably deflected or ignored the requests. After a particularly frustrating chat, Ben slapped his laptop shut, paused, then snapped the machine in half over his knee. It whined its disapproval, the hard drive still spinning and sputtering. Ben hurled the debris out a window, where it landed in the sand. Ben had brought his emotions back under control, or at least held them at bay.

Rickert understood the anger, even shared some of it. His age and experience provided him a bit more perspective, though.

"I think she's doing the best she can. She's ready to go as soon as she's given the word. Look, Ben, you've got to understand where she's coming from. The Chinese government doesn't have a much stronger grasp on its citizens right now than the Russians do. From the bits and pieces I've gathered talking to Chinese generals, the attack in Shanghai was a hell of a disturbance. Blackout or not, the Chinese people pretty much know what happened, and they feel vulnerable."

"Tom, we're *all* vulnerable."

"Yeah, but that's not how most Chinese were raised. The oldest remember World War II and the Japanese invasion. For most of them, their entire life has been lived in a propaganda bubble. Whether they fully believed the BS they were fed or not, it's one thing to suspect the world isn't as simple as you've been led to believe and quite another to have a damn alien robot crash land in the middle of your richest city and kick your army square in the nuts. Being saved by an American super soldier only makes all that tougher to swallow."

"They'll come around. They aren't stupid."

"No, they're not, and that's the problem. That sort of system shock has repercussions. You start getting angry. And you get enough angry citizens together and they become revolutionaries. Hell, that's the history of China. And the leadership knows it."

"So even if the whole world ends, at least they'll have saved their jobs for a few weeks. Fucking idiots."

Rickert shrugged. "Maybe. Would you rather hang today or hang next month? Look what's happening in Russia."

"So we do nothing?"

Rickert smiled. "Oh, I wouldn't say that. C'mon, I think you guys are done here. We've got a flight to catch."

"Where are we going?"

"Ever been to Israel?"

"Well, I flew over it a couple times, I think, when I was flying my spaceship, shooting down invading alien robots. But that was, like, a whole month ago and I haven't done anything really weird since, like, lunch. So yeah, sure, let me grab my toothbrush."

Rickert sighed.

"Just grab your team and load up."

18

Goldberg could tell the three gray-skinned guys thought these ships were the same as the last one. He couldn't wait to tell them how wrong they were.

"The Chinese salvaged some of the mrill ship that crashed over there, and we've actually been able to reverse-engineer some of it to upgrade your ship," Goldberg said as he strolled around the craft, wiping the mustard off his hands from the two hot dogs he'd just devoured. "We've increased the power output of the MPD thrusters 74 percent by expanding the capacity of the reactor to 200 megawatts, which should give you much better acceleration and three-dimensional thrust vectoring. We've also added an auxiliary power unit should the main generator be knocked offline, and made a few minor tweaks to the external fuselage, such as adding rear-facing cannons and fiddling with the targeting algorithms."

Ben stopped walking after hearing that last claim.

"Oh, I know," Goldberg said with a flap of his hand. "I gave them holy hell about even thinking about that. The hardware here is complex and advanced, but not light years ahead of us. I mean, the brin knew we'd have to be able to manufacture this stuff ourselves and wouldn't have time to cram four hundred years of advances in optical lithography, metallurgy, and propulsion systems into a couple months. But to compensate for the primitive hardware, they obviously sent us some pretty fantastic software. I mean, this is just hardcore, kick-ass stuff. Not my specialty, but guys I trust made it clear how insane it was. So when the software guys told me they had some modifications in mind, my first reaction was to tell them to cram it up their ass."

Goldberg laughed at his own wit. Ben smiled politely and waited.

"Anyway," he continued, "there was a team from Stanford, these computer science and applied mathematics nerds, and they showed me some demos and hell, you'll be impressed. So anyway, continuing our tour . . ."

Goldberg dragged the three men along in his wake. They probably couldn't understand most of what he said, but he was still enjoying the audience. He liked to talk, and being unemployed for three months had mostly left him with no one to talk to but his dog. Berta didn't care for shop talk.

He wasn't sure what to make of these three, though. The gray skin didn't freak him out like it did most folks. The inside was what mattered; true with radios, true with people. They were hard to read, though. Quiet. Barely spoke. Occasionally Bert would look over and they'd all seem to be nodding at each other or grinning at some private joke, which was weird. Bert had heard a little about their supposed mental connection or something. He guessed that's what they were doing, chatting with their brains.

It was hard to get to know people who almost never talked. He'd never really thought about it before, but Bert realized now that the way you mostly got to know people was by talking to them. How people talked was supposed to show how people thought. Maybe that's why politicians talked all the time. These guys, though, were like three walking rocks. Good luck rallying the planet with that attitude. On the other hand, they did have more immediate concerns.

Ben, Nick, and Eddie, for their part, were almost completely oblivious of their garrulous tour guide.

Part of it was that the engineering jargon was mostly incomprehensible. More importantly, though, was that they didn't need it. Their onboard computers had begun communicating with the ships about five miles before they'd even reached the disguised hangar, the electronic link providing in an instant a full technical readout to each man. It was a two-way connection, with each man's nanomachines providing a readout to the ships so each craft could tailor itself to the particular neural pathways of the different pilots. The walkaround was superfluous.

Well, superfluous to *them*. Rickert had impressed on Ben the importance of the moment. Goldberg was a gifted engineer, a savant, really, but his promotion had made many of his more accomplished peers considerably envious. President Lockerman had gathered some of the most brilliant technical minds in academia and industry; men and women who commanded thousands of employees, ran prestigious departments, and had patents, awards, and accolades piled on their résumés. "Ambitious" was an understatement. Watching the crass, flabby Bert Goldberg saunter in from the unemployment line to lead the whole operation had generated enough resentment that Rickert only half-jokingly suggested to him that he hire someone to check his meals for poison. Even at the world's end, you still had to worry about who got lead credit in the scientific journals.

Ben had shaken his head at this nonsense. What a waste of time. But if he needed to do a photo op with Goldberg to make sure everyone knew their place, so be it.

". . . and that's pretty much it," Goldberg said. "Any questions?"

Nick and Eddie had been unable to contain their boredom and drifted off a bit to check out the ships themselves. If the technobabble left them cold, the beauty of the war machines they would soon be piloting did not. It was a professional interest, but also something personal. They were about to become space fighter pilots. Even though their first mission was probably a suicide run, it was still thrilling, and Ben could sense their concealed excitement.

Been there, done that, Ben thought, and turned back to Goldberg.

"What do you think?" Ben said.

"About what?"

"Can we win? With these?"

Goldberg frowned and scratched his head, leaving a small smear of mustard on his temple.

"Win? I don't know. They'll do what we built them to do. They're as close to magic as I think I'll ever see. You boys are in good hands."

"That's not what I meant. You mentioned that the brin had to dumb down their tech so that we could build it. We're driving last year's model. What do you think the mrill are going to come with?"

Goldberg sighed.

"It's a problem, and we're working on it. We've got guys cranking on stuff you wouldn't believe. Hell, *they* don't believe what they're doing. For now, though, the truth is, you're gonna be outgunned. That first wave of unmanned drones was amateur hour. They were hoping to catch us with our pants down and our wangs in the wind, and they sent their most basic stuff our way. They probably weren't ready for a full invasion at that point. The mrill did us a real favor. I'd guess they're assembling one hell of an armada now, their best. Can you win? I honestly don't know."

Ben nodded, reflective. Goldberg was silent, too, for a change.

"Invasions follow a pattern, you know," Ben said as he ran his hand over the surface of one of the ships. To him, it felt alive, a glistening race horse with a thumping heart, eager to run.

"The invader almost always has the advantage of surprise, of technology, of organization and momentum. That's why you invade. The defender has advantages, too. Shorter supply lines, knowledge of the terrain, reinforcements arrive faster. And desperation. That counts for a lot."

Ben turned to Goldberg, who was obviously flummoxed. Ben suppressed a laugh as he realized his speech to Goldberg had been as pointless as Goldberg's to him.

"Stay busy, Bert. Build as fast as you can. We're gonna take a beating. The world doesn't know what's coming. Saint Petersburg was just the start. And we're going to lose a lot more than we win, at least for a while. We won't quit. My men and me, and whoever comes after us, we'll fight until we're dead."

"I'd rather you fight until you win."

"Me too. To do that, we must be able to take the battle to them, and we can only do that if we're properly armed. Keep your assembly lines running."

"Rosie the Riveter. That's us. Don't worry, we got this."

Ben opened his mouth to speak. At that moment, an alarm went off, a red klaxon. The early warning sensor.

The armada was on its way.

19

Rickert felt like shit.

"You look like shit," Ben said as he walked into the room.

He waved Ben and his team to their seats in the briefing room with a grunt. Rickert's stomach was on fire, a grumpy volcano of corrosive acid sputtering and belching up his throat. Empty bottles of Tums and Pepto filled a trashcan near his feet. He wasn't sure if the ulcers were due to the stress, the fact that he was basically getting all of his calories now from vending machines, or an alien parasite the mrill had dropped during their last attack. *If we win the war but they infect us with some kind of intergalactic diarrhea, man, that would be a bummer,* he thought. He shook his head. *Focus.*

"The long-range sensors picked it up," he said, trying to ignore the knot in his gut. "So far, nothing from the close-range scanners, so we think we have 24 hours, maybe less, before they pop into our solar system. At that point, we're looking at about an hour or so until contact, assuming they cut in the same place they did last time. No guarantees, though."

"The interceptors are ready," Nick said. "We just checked 'em out, and they're ready to fly. So are we."

"I'm not worried about that," Rickert said. "The real issue is the defensive satellites. We've gotten most of the replacements into orbit. We're still short a few satellites, and not all of the ground-based antiaircraft systems are operational. If any of the mrill get past you guys and the orbital defenses, a lot of our cities are as exposed as Lady Godiva."

"What, sir?" Eddie asked.

"The lost art of the classical education," Rickert said. "I need some more Tums."

"They won't get past us," Nick said. "We've got this. Is the injection chamber ready to crank out some new recruits?"

A pained look drifted over Rickert's face and refused to move along.

"No," he said at last. "Another 36 hours and maybe the answer would be yes. I think we're close to getting everyone to sign off. Going as fast as they can. The equipment is so complex, and we're designing this one from scratch to avoid . . . a repeat of last time. And this is our design. Not the brin's. No blueprint for this."

Rickert could tell they were all concerned and relieved; concerned that they wouldn't have backup and relieved they wouldn't have to worry about seeing another volunteer get torn apart in the injection process. Not just yet, anyway.

Ben shifted in his seat.

"Something on your mind, sailor?" Rickert asked.

"How many ships did the sensors pick up? Any indication of what's coming our way?"

Rickert shuffled through some papers on the table. He rubbed his stomach.

"Nothing definitive. Analysts at the National Reconnaissance Office say the cluster looks to be much bigger than the first attack. Whether that means a couple hundred small ships or a dozen huge ones, they aren't sure. Probably a mix of both. And there could be more coming behind, but they apparently detected our scanners and took them out, so we don't know for sure. And given that they know we *have* long-range scanners, they know we'll be ready."

"And we know that they know that we know, which means they know we know they know we know, which means . . ."

"Jesus, Eddie, can you shut the fuck up for three seconds?" Nick said. They both laughed.

Ben glanced at Rickert, obviously curious if the general would blow up at the seemingly pointless and time-wasting banter. Despite his stress and lack of battlefield experience, Rickert knew to let this moment play out a bit. It was Combat Psych 101; that even the fiercest warriors had to find a way to release tension before battle. Those who tried to bite down and swallow it generally had a much more difficult time operating under the stressors of combat. Tighten a string and it could play a hell of a tune, but pull too hard and it would inevitably snap.

"We're moving your interceptors to the launch pad here in Florida. Worked well enough last time. We've built redundant mission control centers in Houston, Alaska, and Australia. It's possible the mrill will aim for our command and control capabilities, so we've dispersed as much of it as possible."

"What about evacuating the cities?" Ben asked.

"It's under way, but we just don't have anywhere to send everyone," Rickert replied, shaking his head. "With a hurricane or earthquake, you can relocate a small region temporarily. This . . . I don't know. We've got temporary camps set up around a dozen major cities. Can't hold everyone, and not everyone wants to go. Those that do evac, though, will be out of range of a defensive nuclear strike . . . should that prove necessary."

Everyone in the room felt those words fall like a hammer. If the nanomachines were unleashed again, America would be forced to burn its own cities, just like the Russians had.

"What kind of warning are we giving people?" Nick asked.

"A calming one, hopefully," Rickert said, meeting the eyes of everyone in the room. "The president is making an address"—he checked his watch—"uh, 10 minutes ago. Urging people in the big cities to follow evacuation procedures. If they want to remain with their homes, stockpile as much food and water as possible. Truth is, any city that gets hit probably gets wiped out. Can't say that, though."

"Why not?" Eddie said. "Tell people what they're up against. Let 'em make up their own minds."

"The global economy is already in shambles," Rickert shot back, a hint of anger creeping into his voice. "We're probably not too far from some kind of worldwide food crisis. People have enough to deal with."

The government had essentially nationalized food and energy production and distribution in the US. No one had wanted to do that, but the commodities and shipping industries had been paralyzed after the attacks on Russian and China. Everyone was in a defensive crouch. The US Army Corps of Engineers was now driving or accompanying trucks and trains full of corn and wheat and oil all over the country to try and keep everyone from starving. The US, with its massive farmlands, oil reserves, and highways and railroads, could be self-sufficient for a while. Other countries that relied heavily on imports were in much worse shape. You put the entire world on a war footing against an alien invasion, and your GDP goes all to hell.

Nick began to protest, but Rickert cut him off.

"My team actually made these predictions back before this all started. We gamed this thing out a hundred times. Not that anyone bothered to act on anything we suggested—even stuff like hardening our electric grid, which would have helped against terrorist attacks. Everyone up the chain who even knew my team existed thought we were a joke. You think anyone wanted to requisition $6 billion to prepare evac plans in case of extraterrestrial assault?"

The anger drained from Rickert. He was too tired for a longer burn.

"And so now we're exactly where we thought we would be. Now we have all the money in the world, but no time to spend it. So, a little more panic is the last thing we need right now. As it is, we've got revolutions and civil wars popping up in Eastern Europe, the Philippines, Pakistan, India, and South Africa. And that's only the worst of it. There have been protests pretty much everywhere, from Los Angeles to Lagos."

"Protesting what, exactly?" Eddie said.

"Anything. Everything," Rickert said, waving his hands around like a helicopter. "It's fear and paranoia mostly. But it's hard to reason with a conspiracy nut when the 'reasonable' explanation is an alien invasion and human super soldiers augmented with nanotechnology and the deliberate nuclear destruction of a major city. We went through the looking glass and then blew it up."

Ben glanced at Nick and Eddie. They all shared the same quick thought. Even if they won the coming battle, the upheaval and destruction on Earth would be devastating. And if they lost, it would be complete.

"Let's go check the interceptors," Ben said. "I want to be ready to lift off at a moment's notice. We can't be late for this dance."

20

After thirteen separate assassination attempts, President Lockerman had finally evacuated the White House. Even with the eight hundred or so Marines and Sailors of the 2nd Battalion, 6th Marines deployed on the White House lawn in defensive formation and Air Force F-35s blanketing the air space above, the barrage of attacks continued almost daily. Truck bombs. Lone gunmen. One kook with a fire axe. It was a carnival of crazy. The attackers ignored the warning shouts and shots and advanced. While they were all cut down before doing any serious damage, the fear was growing that eventually one of the attackers would arrive with a weapon big enough to inflict real harm. His wife was beyond freaked out.

"Also, not great for national morale for Pennsylvania Avenue to be covered in bomb craters and blood," President Lockerman had said to Dan Henning, his chief of staff, as they worked out of the secure bunker beneath the White House. "And I haven't seen the sun in two weeks. We're leaving. Have the Joint Chiefs draw up some alternatives."

Henning glanced at Jeff Goldman, the president's national security advisor, who looked equally nervous.

"Sir, I'm not sure that's wise," Henning said. "You're going to be a target anywhere you go, and this is as safe a place as any."

"Dan's right, Mr. President," Goldman said. "We can keep you secure from everything but a direct nuclear attack strike here."

"Yeah?" Lockerman said. "And what if that's exactly what the mrill have planned for this place? Look, I'm not worried about the crazies rushing the gate out there. I'm worried about the alien army that's about to drop out of the sky. And I'd bet Washington is pretty high on their strike list."

"Well, we don't know that, sir," Goldman said. "The truth is, they've so far had very limited contact with Earth, and their grasp of our political and military structures is likely minimal."

"You're assuming they haven't been here before," Lockerman said.

Both men looked taken aback.

"Oh, relax. I'm not talking Roswell or Area 51, but the universe is obviously a lot more crowded than we ever knew. Is it really so unlikely that the mrill or some other species has visited us previously and kept it quiet? You're assuming they only know of us what they've seen in the two skirmishes we've had thus far, but I'm not sure I'd bet money on that."

Lockerman looked around the cramped room, packed with monitors and communications gear and the stale smell of too many stressed people surrounded by too few air filters.

"While I am damned tired of this bunker, I also think there's a good military reason to evacuate as well," he said. "This place just doesn't feel safe to me, so we're leaving. We'll make an announcement that we're relocating to a secure, undisclosed location—we won't be able to hide that from the press, anyway—and set up camp at a hardened fallout shelter in Nevada or Idaho or something. Maybe NORAD again, but God, that coal mine is even deeper than this one. Besides, if these nut jobs are going to continue to come at me, we might as well draw them away from DC. This place is getting trashed, and we might want to come back someday."

"Someday, sir?" Henning said.

Lockerman was quiet for a moment, rolling a pencil on the desk in front of him.

"C'mon, Dan, I know what the odds are on this thing," Lockerman said. "Shepherd and Rickert and their guys might think they can win this, but I think we'll be lucky if anyone survives. We're sending three guys out to fight an army. Even the Spartans sent 300, and they knew that was a suicide mission."

Henning and Goldman didn't say anything.

An aide accompanied by a Secret Service agent—they shadowed every staff member within 30 feet of the president now—stepped into the room.

"Mr. President, the Royal address is starting."

Lockerman picked up a TV remote and flipped through news channels. Most of the protests in the US were still peaceful, but there were thousands camped out in open-air spaces in Seattle, Boston, and Los Angeles. He thought it was a mistake to allow those, but the mayors were reluctant to stir up more trouble than they had to, and most of the police and military were busy with evacuation efforts. New York and DC were mostly clear of those protest camps, as the soldiers and first responders had commandeered almost every public space for their own needs. True to his word, Locker-man had not declared martial law, but the National Guard was everywhere, and regular military had deployed outside almost every major city to set up defensive, surface-to-space batteries and guard them from sabotage. The situation was much more volatile and violent in other cities around the world.

Most world leaders had fled their capitals for military bunkers or naval ships. More than a few had been quietly flown to the US. The British royal family and prime minister had refused to budge, which Lockerman admired, but now the king was making a public address from the balcony on the East Front of Buckingham Palace.

"This is a bad idea," Lockerman muttered. He turned the remote over and over in his hands while leaning forward. He'd pleaded with the Brits to forgo the public proclamation. Appear live on television, write a letter to the paper, post a damn tweet. But going out in public made no sense. It was like dangling raw meat in front of a pack of wild dogs.

King Henry appeared on the balcony, surrounded by a dozen bodyguards. Even the notoriously fat monarch looked much thinner these days. No one was eating right or getting enough sleep. The king's security detail had dropped all pretense of subtlety or camouflage, and they were cradling rifles in their arms as they scanned the massive crowd below. A handful of armored personnel carriers were stationed in the square, with soldiers manning the machine-gun turrets and swiveling to try and keep an eye on everyone. Lockerman knew there were also snipers on the roof and drones high above running facial recognition software to try and spot known troublemakers. No helicopters, though, as the sound would have drowned out his speech.

"My fellow countrymen . . ." the king began. The network covering the speech switched to a wide-angle camera, capturing the 20,000-plus who had filled the square. It was an unruly gathering, with various protest banners held high as different factions screamed at the king, the cops, and each other. The protesters were ragged, mostly young men and a few women. No families, but plenty of the sort of rough-and-tumble youths that always showed up to protest economic summits and political conventions. Those who weren't there to protest stood in sullen silence, shoulders hunched against the cold and damp. A light drizzle was falling, but umbrellas had been banned, which gave the police and military at least one less headache to deal with.

Lockerman knew the British prime minister and her team were just as unhappy with the king's appearance as the US government was, but the old man was convinced he was somehow the reincarnation of King George VI and could rally the nation much as that monarch had during World War II.

"This might actually do some good," Henning said, waving at the screen.

Lockerman opened his mouth to reply when a flicker of movement in the crowd caught his eye.

One of the banners dropped. Lockerman squinted to try and see the person in the crowd who had been holding it but the cameraman, oblivious, had swiveled away.

"Did you catch that?" Lockerman said to no one in particular. Without warning, two of the armored vehicles exploded, flattening the people standing nearby. The camera jerked around to center on the blast, and now Lockerman could see the man who had dropped the banner. He lifted up a long, slender device with a bulbous tip and pointed it at the balcony.

"Oh, Christ," Lockerman said as everyone in the room with him surged forward to see the screen.

The rocket-propelled grenade was unmistakable on the massive TV screen as it streaked over the heads of the frothing crowd. The camera operator, presumably acting on pure instinct, tracked it perfectly. The king's bodyguards tried to drag the monarch back inside, but the warhead was faster. It hit slightly to the left of the balcony and punched a hole in the building, flames and smoke and shards of masonry and body parts flying in every direction. Snipers tore the attacker apart, the high-caliber shots echoing through the square, and now the crowd became a panicked mob, fleeing in all directions. The camera swiveled wildly, uncertain where to focus. Lockerman noticed through the stampede that a handful of figures seemed to be running in unison toward the palace. The half dozen or so men were pulling objects from their coats. Lockerman realized they were hand grenades and Molotov cocktails. Snipers cut most of them down, the explosives detonating where they fell, adding to the chaos. Two of the men made it to the front of the building and hurled their bombs, which detonated with concussive force. The attackers didn't live long enough to even see the debris hit the ground, but the damage was done.

Pandemonium. The crowd was trampling itself, hurtling around and through the burning hulks of the sabotaged armored vehicles. Buckingham Palace was on fire. Several people were also on fire. Soldiers streamed through the crowd, shooting at anyone who grabbed them. Lockerman suspected most of the clawing bystanders were looking for aid, but at this point it was total chaos and he couldn't blame the soldiers for assuming everything was a threat. The destroyed balcony was sagging toward the ground, covered in blood and soot, although the king—or what remained of him—had finally been pulled inside. The TV announcer was jabbering frantically, clearly on the verge of all-out hysterics. It was a war zone.

The camera was yanked around, and a Royal Marine was demanding, *screaming* that it be turned off. The sweaty marine's eyes were bulging like they were about to pop out of his head. The cameraman argued and the marine's rifle came up. The picture went dead.

Lockerman hit mute as the rattled studio hosts came back on, at a loss for words. They looked terrified. Lockerman turned off the TV before they could replay the video of what had just happened—he didn't need to see that again—and looked around at his staff.

"It's getting out of control," he said.

The Brits had a critical role in the defensive installations in Europe, and the prime minister, the true head of government, was secure. Well, presumably secure.

"Dan, we need to get the State Department on the phone with the UK. I know it's probably a total cluster over there right now, but we need to know that the PM is still safe and in charge. And I know they had considered relocating to their military base at, uh, Tidworth, right, Jeff?"

"Ye—yes, Mr. President," Goldman said with a slight stammer, dragging his eyes from the TV screen. "The Brits have their 1st Mechanized Brigade headquartered there, along with several other units. It's an ideal spot, about 80 miles from London."

"Good, yeah. Dan, make it clear that we strongly suggest they evacuate to Tidworth. This is not the time to go down with the ship."

"Yes, sir." Henning rose and left the room with his aide.

Lockerman paced around the room. "Can we hold this thing together long enough, Jeff?"

Goldman gave a nervous shrug. Lockerman noticed for the first time that Goldman's clothes were hanging off him like pillowcases. The man seemed to have lost 20 pounds in the last month. Lockerman thought of the king and wondered how the rest of his staff was dealing with the stress.

"One way or another, yes."

"What does that mean?"

"Well, look, we, the US, yes, we can control the situation here at home, although who knows what sort of chain reaction this attack might set off. We've got enough troops in enough places and a population that trusts you just enough that we can finish the work on surface-to-space defenses. Once the battle is engaged, who knows how it will go. But the prep phase? Yeah, I . . . I think we can manage that. I don't know about the rest of the world. We've still got small military detachments in most allied countries, but they're reporting that a lot of the local officials are disappearing."

"What, they're being attacked?"

"Some, maybe, but most are just fleeing, going into hiding with their families, or just running away. They're scared, and they're not using the secure comms channels we've provided."

"Idiots."

"Maybe, but human psychology doesn't change just because of an alien invasion, Mr. President. And what just happened there"—he waved at the screen—"isn't going to make things easier. Desertion is becoming a major problem in the countries that we still have some communication with. Russia, India, most of the Middle East, who knows what's going on there. Satellite surveillance shows some work being done at the proposed defensive sites. We can only hope they'll be operational when the mrill arrive."

Lockerman knew that sabotage and civil unrest might shut down even the stations that were functional. They'd already been over the scenarios. Russia was the biggest unknown. The rebel forces were still on the move. Gretchenko didn't want to nuke them, to send up even more mushroom clouds over his own soil. Not everyone agreed with that stance, even on Lockerman's staff. Lockerman agreed with Gretchenko on this one, but he was in no position to offer any kind of aid.

He'd recalled almost all US forces from overseas: Japan, South Korea, etc. Others had pleaded against that; it pained him to do it, and North Korean troops were already massing at the border of South Korea. The NorKs remained as volatile as ever, and they probably were on the verge of invasion. China, preoccupied and silent, wasn't doing anything to calm the situation. A lot of people were about to die on the Korean peninsula. They were on their own. US troops were needed at home. North Korea at least didn't have much food or gas to sustain a lengthy campaign. A conventional invasion would be fierce but short, and the North's nuclear stockpile was tiny, no more than a couple of low-yield warheads. The defensive satellites orbiting over Asia could shoot down any incoming missiles, just as long as they weren't busy shooting up at incoming mrill attack ships. Russia was definitely a much bigger problem.

If Russia went over the brink, it was impossible to predict who else might get dragged along. Not to mention the thousands of Russian nuclear warheads up for grabs. That country was being pulled apart, like a man chained to trains headed in opposite directions. The mrill might arrive to find they'd already won the battle without firing another shot.

Lockerman's stomach churned, and he wondered how much weight *he'd* lost in the last several weeks.

"Damn, Jeff, sounds like we should be praying the mrill attack sooner rather than later."

"Mr. President, that is my most fervent hope."

21

As the British were trying to recover their fallen king, Yuri Leonov hopped down from a T-90 tank parked on the shoulder of the M6 highway leading into the Russian city of Volgograd. His boots sank into the mud. Most everything around here was mud, but that was the least of his concerns. Same for his men. The flurry of activity made him proud. These were his countrymen, his comrades, his brothers, both by blood and by allegiance, and they were fueled by purpose.

A young captain with an AK-47 slung over his shoulder hurried up, snapping a salute that Leonov returned. The junior officer was thin and his dirty, battered fatigues hung off his frame, but he was alert and energetic.

"Colonel Leonov, our forces are in position around the city. Shall we advance?"

Leonov could sense the captain's enthusiasm, his revolutionary spirit. It came off him in waves, like a fever. Leonov's own enthusiasm was tempered by his battlefield experience, but he shared the urge to move forward. He wondered if this was what it felt like in 1917. Nevertheless, he knew the General was counting on him to lead these men with wisdom and passion.

"Well done, Captain Ilyushin." Leonov could see the man's slender chest swell a bit with pride. "But we'll wait until dawn. It's getting dark and the men are tired from their march today. The southern approach is secured. Besides, our camps and fires will serve as a beacon for other men who wish to join our cause. Tomorrow we'll take the city. We'll enter under the light, on parade. Not thieves sneaking in the night."

"Yes, colonel."

A column of BTR-80 armored personnel carriers roared by on the M6, setting up a defensive perimeter to the north. The soldiers in the machine-gun turrets saluted as they passed.

His army was getting bigger. Every day, a hundred or so soldiers arrived, abandoning their old units, looking to join this burgeoning movement. Not all of the new arrivals were fit to serve. Not yet. They bore the hallmarks of the old Russia. Many were overweight, poorly equipped, lacking necessities like clean, dry socks—trench foot was endemic—and ammunition. When they arrived, they had their names, ranks, and skills recorded, were issued equipment by the quartermaster and his squad, and reassigned in the 2nd Red Army.

The 2nd Red Army now numbered some 15,000 men, fully equipped with tanks, helicopters, food, and fuel. They still lacked jets and other major weapons systems, a deficiency which Leonov had been sure would doom his force to a quick and violent death at the hands of the Russian army. The General had assured him he had other methods for dealing with those threats. Whatever those methods were, they were working. Other than the occasional reconnaissance flight, Leonov's force had not seen a single Russian aircraft overhead. Still, he would be nervous until he had his own air support. His men saw Volgograd—once, Stalingrad—as a key objective. Leonov was eager to push on to capture the air base at Lebyazhye, about 170 kilometers to the north, where the General had assured him a sizable force of jets and bombers was waiting to be commandeered. First there was work to be done in Volgograd.

"Captain, deploy your scout teams to the surface-to-space site and report back by 1930 hours. Reconnaissance only. Do not engage any sentries or enter the facility, or even approach closer than 100 meters. If the government forces have left any defense or booby-trapped the facility, we must know. That is our priority."

The young officer snapped another salute and departed.

Leonov looked toward the city. Although every Russian knew Volgograd's history as the turning point in the Great Patriotic War against Germany, Leonov had little use for the city's heritage. Stalin had been a fool and a tyrant, and the blood of more than a million Russian heroes had soaked this land because the paranoid schemer had been too busy consolidating power internally to notice the Nazi threat creeping toward his doorstep. Indeed, blind greed had too often cost Russia the greatness that was its due. No more.

Leonov walked toward the command tent that had been hastily erected in the grass near the highway, next to an overpass that rose over a train track. "Highway" was too generous a term for this two-lane strip of asphalt with dirt shoulders, but then most Russian highways were similarly glorified country roads. Leonov felt both contempt and shame at the degraded condition of his country.

For all its boasting and wealth, Russia in many ways was a third-world nation. And this business about "alien invasion" had only siphoned off more of its treasures, while the treacherous destruction of Saint Petersburg had annihilated much of the nation's spirit. That decline must be reversed. There was a sleeping giant in this land waiting to be awakened. He felt it in his soul, if there was such a thing.

The sun was sinking as Leonov reached the tent. To the east, the massive Volga River reflected the last glittering embers of the fading sun. While he felt no emotional connection to this place, its military history certainly fascinated him. More than a million Russians had been killed or injured defending this city, and the brutality of the war and the incompetence of Stalin had ensured that many of the dead, both German and Russian, had never been recovered from the battlefield. Ancient, decayed bodies and military equipment were still being found to this day in the countryside surrounding the city. Leonov thought there was a good chance that, even now, he was standing over the shallow grave of some German private still clutching a rifle. No matter. Eventually, everyone died. You could only hope to die fighting for something great.

Aides were plugging in computers and communications equipment as Leonov stepped into the command center.

Lieutenant Colonel Ivan Rodchenko stepped forward with two steaming mugs of tea, handing one to Leonov. Leonov knew without asking—and was thankful without saying—that each contained a splash of vodka.

The two men silently tipped their cups toward each other and drank.

"Good progress today, Vanya," he said to his old friend with a smile. "The city shall be ours tomorrow, and then on to the airfield at Lebyazhye."

"Indeed," said Rodchenko, sipping his tea.

"Spit it out. I'm too tired to guess at your troubles."

"My trouble is the lack of trouble. No one's fired a shot at us in nearly a week. What's going on? The Federation troops have all but disappeared. And our air defenses are almost depleted, as they must know."

Leonov shrugged.

"The General assured me he would take care of the jets and bombers, and he's been true to his word."

"But how, Yuri?" Rodchenko said softly, so no one else would overhear his question. "We've made our intentions clear. We're marching on Moscow. Why would the government not defend itself?"

"They are cowards. They think the Americans can save them." Leonov couldn't have kept the sneer from his voice if he'd wanted to. "Cowards and weaklings. The Americans ordered them to burn Saint Petersburg and they obeyed like that." He snapped his fingers. "This will be easy. Moscow is nothing but old women. Hell, worse than old women. My grandmother could overthrow this government."

Rodchenko nodded absently.

"These so-called 'surface-to-space' defensive installations are interesting, yes? Have you seen one up close yet?"

Leonov waved his hand dismissively.

"Vanya, these are crude distractions. Don't you see? There is no . . . alien invasion." He spat the words, angry that he even had to say such childish things. "What evidence have we seen? Fuzzy telescope images of explosions in space and vague reports of some attack in Shanghai?"

"The Chinese certainly seem to be taking it seriously."

"The Chinese can do as they please," Leonov said, taking another sip. He wished his friend could see what they were building; how the American lies were just an attempt to thwart Russia's deserved greatness. "Perhaps we will turn our attention to them later, in a year or two, once we've finished with our efforts here. Tomorrow we'll take this installation outside Volgograd and you'll see it's just some American technological toy designed to slow us down. It will be a minor delay, and then we'll press onward and finish the job."

Rodchenko finished his tea.

"I'm sure you are right, comrade. Soon we will have set things right."

Rodchenko seemed satisfied. Leonov nodded.

"That's more like it. Now, let's review tomorrow's movements. We should be ready just in case there are a few stubborn malcontents remaining in the Federation army."

Outside, the sun had gone down and the crescent moon was rising over the river, casting a silver reflection over the water like a blade.

●

An hour later, tactical briefings over the next day's plans were finalized and Leonov headed off to his tent. He hadn't been lying to his friend. He was tired. He couldn't show it while still out in public, in front of his men. Although it was late and most of the soldiers were exhausted, many were still awake, huddled around fires, talking and laughing, playing cards or clutching their own mugs. Leonov stopped at each group on his way back to his tent, offering a few words of encouragement, deferring the offered vodka from his officers. He would not have minded a sip or two, but if he took a drink at every opportunity, he would be drunk before he made it halfway to his quarters. He had work still to do.

He was also still unsettled by his friend's doubts. Rodchenko's loyalty was beyond question. At the same time, he clearly was not completely satisfied with Leonov's answers to his questions. In truth, Leonov himself wasn't sure what was happening. Things were moving so fast. Lies or not, this business about aliens had been a spark in a pool of gasoline. Flames were everywhere. Had the Americans outsmarted themselves? Started a wildfire they thought they could control, only to see it leap over their firewalls? Perhaps, but why?

A pair of guards stood watch at his drab green tent, men who had served under him in Chechnya. Men he trusted with his life.

That had been the beginning of his military career. Horrible place. You had to watch your back everywhere you went, no matter how many houses you burned or terrorists you killed. Leonov had wanted to be a soldier ever since he was a boy. Chechnya had made him reconsider. Then he'd met The General, who had counseled patience.

He didn't fear for his life here. The guards at his tent were watching over the contents inside, the laptop and its secure satellite connection. Leonov dismissed the men and ordered them to get some rest, and then went inside.

The machine sat on a plain folding table, in front of an equally plain folding chair. A cot and small footlocker were set up to the side of the room, by a small mirror hanging on pegs over a minuscule sink. An electric lamp hanging from the center of the canvas ceiling was the only illumination. The tent and its modest contents had been set up in minutes and would be torn down just as quickly in the morning when the army broke camp.

Leonov looked at the mirror, noting that stubble with flecks of gray were coming in, even though he'd shaved that morning. He shaved every morning. No gray in his close-cropped hair. Not yet. His nose was as long and slender as it had been since he'd hit puberty. Dark circles under his eyes, the shadows appearing even deeper in this paltry light. His nose was strong and his cheekbones sharp. A bit of a status symbol in this rotten age, when the faces of many men his age had already started to turn pink and mushy from too much vodka. His body was fit, too. He was a field commander, not a desk rider. He still ran five kilometers every morning.

He splashed some water on his face from a canteen dangling next to the mirror and wiped it with a rough towel.

The screen on the laptop was dark, but the blue and orange lights along the edge indicated it was powered up. Leonov stared at it a moment, then pulled a bottle of vodka and a single shot glass from his personal trunk. He poured himself a drink, but only one. He needed to be able to focus for these conversations, no matter how tired he was. Leonov took a sip, sat down, and moved the glass out of visible range of the camera embedded in the laptop. He rubbed his finger over the touchpad to wake the machine, and the screen came to life. Leonov activated the secure link, the satellite dish on the roof reaching out for a signal.

ESTABLISHING CONNECTION>>>
>>>
>>>
CONNECTION ESTABLISHED>>>
CREDENTIALS REQUIRED>>>

Leonov pressed his thumb against the scanner connected to the laptop through a USB connection and leaned closer so the camera could scan his retina.

CREDENTIALS CONFIRMED>>>

The screen was dark for a moment, and Leonov squinted, looking for movement in the inky blackness. Then The General's face appeared. It was lined, but not old. The beard was still mostly dark brown. The scar on his forehead stood out even on the grainy computer image. Leonov had been there when he got that scar. Leonov knew his name, of course, but still thought of him mostly as The General.

"Good evening, Colonel Leonov," The General said.

"General."

"So, are you in position?"

"Yes, General, we will move into Volgograd tomorrow and secure the facility. I shall leave a company behind to guard it, and then take the rest of the regiment on to Lebyazhye. We'll then begin preparations to move on to Moscow."

"Excellent. Contact me once you've taken the facility."

"Will you be joining us at the air base?"

"Perhaps. I am still working to convince some of my colleagues to join our campaign. Our victory is inevitable, and I would prefer to ride into Moscow with fresh troops, but it is possible there will be holdouts. You may be forced to suppress some of the more reluctant elements of the Federation Army—in particular, the 20th Guards Army out of Voronezh seems to be mobilizing to confront your force."

Leonov quickly did the math in his head. A couple tank divisions and missile brigades, along with some other auxiliary forces.

"We should be able to handle that."

"True, Colonel, but they may have supplemented their original forces. There are still many who fear a renewed Russia."

Leonov shrugged.

"We are supplementing our forces, too. By the time we reach Moscow, we'll be 50,000 strong, at the minimum. When we complete our political takeover, the rest of the military will fall in line. I am concerned, though, with the Americans. Have you received any indication of a possible response from them?"

"Bah. They are all engaged with this foolish alien invasion business. They have withdrawn most of their forces from Europe and the Pacific in a vain attempt to subdue their own population. And the Europeans are in disarray. We have a free hand."

Leonov was silent.

"Yes, comrade?"

"General, I don't understand. What is America's endgame? What do they gain by spreading this fiction?"

"Confusion and deception, Yuri. Their economy is weak and they are losing their standing in the modern world. This is nothing more than a desperate attempt to reclaim power and destabilize the rest of the world. Who knows who they are conspiring with? I'm sure the lie will be exposed soon enough, and they will admit their cover-up. In the meantime, we must not relent. We must not forget Saint Petersburg. Our dead demand justice."

Leonov nodded.

"Indeed, General. You are surely correct. I will be in contact tomorrow as soon as the facility is secured."

"Excellent, Colonel Leonov. Sleep well."

The screen went dark. Leonov stared silently into the darkness for some time. Eventually, he drained his vodka and rose to find his bed.

●

The battle the next morning turned out to be far fiercer than Leonov expected. Indeed, he hadn't expected any battle at all. Volgograd had been completely abandoned by the Russian army, and he had no reason to expect the defensive facility to be any different. Captain Ilyushin had taken a company of 160 men in armored personnel carriers and a couple of T-90 tanks on the A-260 highway heading west out of Volgograd to the facility while Leonov was establishing a headquarters at the oblast Duma, the regional legislative building in the center of the city. Another company under Rodchenko's command was establishing a post at the Volgograd International Airport. There were only useless civilian aircraft, but the airstrip might be helpful later when they did have military planes under their control.

Leonov had observed Ilyushin's movements through a live video feed from a camera mounted on the exterior of the captain's lead vehicle. Many civilians used them to guard against insurance fraud by other drivers. Most importantly, the technology behind them was cheap, effective, and reliable. A thousand times better than anything the military had ever produced.

So, while Leonov busied himself with setting up his temporary headquarters, he also kept an eye on the video feed on his laptop. He expected no resistance, but he was restless. For the first 15 minutes, it was uneventful, as the vehicles trundled along the two-lane road through flat countryside, mingled with the occasional spruce tree. Leonov could barely contain himself, though, popping out of his seat, barking at his lieutenants, tapping his fingers on the side of the laptop. Finally, he stood up, scooped up the laptop, and had a sergeant drive him out to the airport. The two men hopped in a light truck, a freshly washed UAZ Hunter, and sped off. Leonov focused on his laptop while the vehicle bounced through the streets of Volgograd. Most of the residents seemed to be indoors, watching through curtains at the military vehicles crisscrossing the city. A few people were out and about, but most of the stores were shuttered, with nothing left to sell. There were a lot of beggars. They were impossible to miss, even as he focused on the screen in front of him.

He watched as Ilyushin's column rolled through the village of Gorkovskiy and turned right on a rural road just west of the town. There were no markings or signs on this road, much less any kind of indication that it led to a high-tech military installation. The trees were thicker, thanks to a nearby river. But The General had given Leonov precise directions, and he had no doubt they were accurate.

Sure enough, two minutes later, a series of increasingly dire warning signs appeared along the side of the road, first instructing drivers to turn back and then indicating that they were in imminent danger of being shot. The company pressed on. A massive concrete wall soon loomed out of the scraggly trees and brush. The barrier was at least 15 feet high and stretched off in both directions, gradually curving away into a circle. The road ended before an equally high iron gate embedded in the wall. There was no guard shack or secondary entrance. A pair of security cameras on either side of the gate pointed down at the road. Ilyushin brought his column to a halt about 100 feet away from the gate. Leonov leaned in even closer to the laptop screen. He keyed open his radio and confirmed that Captain Ilyushin could hear him.

"Yes, Colonel, I read you."

"Good. It appears our scouting report was correct. Place the charges."

"Yes, Colonel."

Leonov had considered dispatching his pair of Mi-24 helicopter gunships to support the ground assault, and in any normal military campaign would have done so without a moment's hesitation. He'd hesitated because of his meager supply of jet fuel. The installation was supposedly undefended, so he'd opted not to send the massive gunships as backup. They were prepped and fueled on the runway of the Volgograd airport, with the crews on standby, just in case. He was headed to the airport now to accompany the helicopters should they be needed. From the time he gave the order, the helicopters could be at Ilyushin's location in less than five minutes.

Leonov struggled to suppress his concerns. He felt unusually indecisive. From a military standpoint, the airfield at Lebyazhye was the far more critical target, and Leonov wanted the air support from the Mi-24s when he arrived there. And for that, he needed them to have full gas tanks. He knew he'd made the correct tactical move, but was still bothered. Should he have sent them with Ilyushin? Something didn't feel right. He hunched even closer to the video screen.

Leonov watched as a handful of Ilyushin's men planted explosive charges around the gate. The tanks could have just used their cannons to blast through, but the shaped charges were far more precise and would throw less shrapnel and leave a cleaner opening. The soldiers hustled back to the cover of their armored personnel carriers and Ilyushin radioed Leonov that they were in position and ready to detonate.

"Go," Leonov said.

Four coordinated explosions blew the gate inward, the heavy metal no match for the expertly placed munitions. Leonov could briefly see the gate shoved forward into the compound, and then a cloud of smoke and dust obscured his view.

"Captain, wait for the smoke to clear, and then proceed inside."

"Yes, Colonel."

Leonov nearly warned him to be careful, then caught himself. Ilyushin was a professional soldier in a war zone. Additional caution would sound like a mother telling her children to bundle up in the snow.

The cloud had finally started to settle and Ilyushin ordered his men into the compound. Unfortunately, Leonov did not have a map of the interior of the facility, and the compound was too new to show up in commercial satellite imagery. The General, however, had assured him there would be a main central building, a tower, surrounded by smaller support buildings and barracks. They would be abandoned. The plan was to send the tanks in first, followed by the armored vehicles. They would park in a semicircle, and the ground troops would fan out from there, sweeping the buildings and converging on the central building to plant additional charges. Leonov drummed his fingers nervously on his laptop. The airport was just ahead.

The moment the first tank passed through the demolished gate, a loud snap filled the air and a red filament lanced into the 50-ton vehicle from somewhere within the compound. The massive tank glowed like a light bulb and then flew apart in a cloud of metallic vapor. The shockwave tossed men to the ground, and even the other tanks and APCs rocked slightly.

"Shit," Leonov muttered.

Ilyushin and his men were well-trained and barely hesitated. The tanks and APCs opened fire into the haze. The second tank began blasting the concrete walls to form additional entry points, while ground troops poured out of the carriers to present a larger number of dispersed targets. Additional bolts sizzled out of the compound, annihilating the vehicles and slicing apart any of Ilyushin's men who happened to be in the way. The beams snapped and whined. It sounded like no weapon Leonov had ever heard.

Leonov thumbed his radio and ordered the helicopter pilots to prepare for immediate liftoff. Leonov's truck was pulling into the airfield now, and he could see the pilots and gunners scrambling to the hulking predators. He could hear Ilyushin ordering all his men into the compound.

Leonov considered ordering Ilyushin to fall back and wait for the air support, but half of the strike force was already through the gates. He watched on the screen as the red beam continued to obliterate men and machines with a single touch. The ground force was pressing forward regardless, laying down heavy fire. Now explosions were coming from the compound, as the bullets and rockets slammed into the buildings and vehicles inside. The red beam continued to rake the attackers, firing in five-second intervals. Leonov couldn't see any enemy troops, just the beam, and he guessed it was some sort of automated defensive system. It seemed to be coming from the middle of the compound.

"Captain, concentrate your fire on the central building," Leonov yelled into his radio, hopping from his truck and running for the lead helicopter, whose rotor blades were starting to spin. Ilyushin didn't waste time responding but directed all his men to concentrate their fire on the main building now visible through the haze.

Leonov scrambled into the side troop compartment of the lead helicopter as both machines came to full power, the massive titanium blades convulsing the air. He pulled the heavy armored door shut as the pilot was already lifting off. Leonov leaned in the cockpit door so he could see through the bubble canopy. "How long?" he said as he pulled his bulky headset on.

"Two minutes, Colonel," the pilot responded without looking back.

Leonov tightened his grip on the bulkhead as the gunship roared through the sky. The pilot was at full throttle, guzzling precious fuel. Still, Leonov willed the gunship to go faster. The compound came into view through the curve of the glass. The red blasts were indeed emanating from a cluster of odd-looking equipment poking out of the roof of the central building. Fireballs were erupting around the machinery as Ilyushin's men fired on it, but so far none of them seemed to do any damage.

Leonov pressed the microphone closer and ordered both helicopters to fire on the central building.

"Sir, do we not want to take the building intact?" the gunner in the other helicopter asked over the radio.

"Fire," Leonov demanded.

Without another word, both attack helicopters swooped in.

The Mi-24 was a masterpiece of ground-support airborne weaponry. It bristled with rockets, missiles, and a 30 mm cannon in the nose. A terror during the Soviet campaign in Afghanistan and the later Russian offensive in Chechnya, the helicopter was essentially a flying tank. The heavy armor, hulking profile, and stubby wings gave it the appearance of being slow and clumsy, but the machine was surprisingly agile and fast, thanks to its powerful turbine engine and deceptive aerodynamics. These two helicopters were, at the moment, the jewel of Leonov's burgeoning army. He did wonder briefly at the wisdom of personally accompanying the machines into battle, then tossed the thought aside. Those were his men dying down there. He was a soldier, first and foremost.

The pilots of the two helicopters instinctively separated, approaching the compound at a 90-degree angle to make themselves a harder target for whatever was shooting from inside the compound.

Leonov could see a weapon on the main building swiveling to follow the two helicopters. The gunners, seated in front of and below the pilots, saw it too and squeezed their triggers. Both machines unleashed a barrage of 57 mm rockets from the pods under their wings, raking vertically up the sides of the buildings. The cannon in the tower intercepted several of them, and they burst with a *pop-pop-pop*. Some made it through, slamming into the structure and blowing it open. It wasn't enough damage to destroy the tower, though, and the machine kept up its barrage.

The gunners in the helicopters pressed their attack, opening up with their 30 mm cannons. With the defensive cannon now occupied with the helicopters, the ground forces were also finding their target. Tank shells blasted the building, as did shoulder-mounted missiles used by the infantry. The building was slowly coming apart.

Leonov watched as the other helicopter juked sideways just as one last blast from the tower sizzled through the air, clipping its tail rotor. The tail disintegrated instantly, and the smoking gunship shuddered as the pilot tried to wrestle it to the ground without crashing. It was now vulnerable to a final kill shot.

Leonov fired at the tower using the heavy machine gun mounted to the side of his helicopter, tracer rounds pinging at the odd machinery, ripping out fistfuls of metal. At the same time, the gunner in the cockpit unleashed a final salvo of anti-tank missiles. The support beams inside the tower were obliterated, and the whole structure began to keel over. As it tumbled to the ground, the odd weapon itself began to glow red, crimson filaments crawling across the structure like the tentacles of an ancient sea monster swallowing a sailing ship. It exploded in a shriek of shrapnel. The shockwave brushed Leonov's helicopter sideways toward a clump of trees. As the pilot struggled to recover and avoid the looming branches, Leonov saw the other helicopter crunch into the ground. The aircraft seemed to be intact and did not catch fire. Leonov couldn't see much more as his own pilot fought to stabilize his aircraft and swung it around to avoid slamming into the compound's wall. At last he had it under control and asked Leonov if he wanted to land or return to base.

"Drop me off, pick up any wounded, and then return to the airfield. Begin any repairs immediately."

Leonov popped open the passenger compartment door as soon as they touched down and ran to the tank and remaining APCs winding their way into the compound. Ilyushin waved him over. He tried not to think about the fact that his chopper would be running on fumes by the time it got back, and the other would likely never get off the ground again.

Ilyushin snapped off a harried salute, which Leonov crisply returned. He had noticed long ago that the more bloody and frantic the situation, the more the ancient ritual helped men calm themselves and think a bit more clearly. The young captain looked shaken, but was holding together.

"Well done, Captain," Leonov said. "We have taken the compound and destroyed the enemy defense system. What are your casualties?"

"I, I'm not sure, Colonel," Ilyushin stuttered back. He spun around and did a quick survey of his force, now fully inside the compound. Leonov could see him doing a mental tally of the missing.

"It looks like one tank and four APCs. Perhaps thirty or forty men injured or dead. I did not expect this . . . sir, what was that?"

"I'm not sure, Captain. Most likely some American gadget. Regardless, it has been neutralized and we have won the day. Our fallen will be memorialized as heroes of the new revolution. Do a full tally and send me the names. Have your men search the compound, seize any computers or files, and return to base. Load the wounded onto my helicopter and I'll return with you in the convoy."

"Yes, sir," Ilyushin said, offering a sturdier salute. His composure was coming back. *Good man.* Ilyushin marched off to organize his men.

Leonov walked over to the smoking ruins of the central building, curious to investigate. He kept his eyes fixed on the wreckage, wondering if some final booby trap remained. Despite what he'd said to Ilyushin about the Americans being behind the cannon, he wasn't sure. Energy weapons weren't unheard of, and he knew the Russians, Americans, and others had all been investigating such capabilities for years. But this device had been accurate and lethal and *fast* beyond anything that seemed possible. It was . . . alien.

Leonov drew his pistol as he approached the tower.

The entrance, once secured with an impressive metal door, had been torn open in the battle. Leonov climbed through the mangled gate and squeezed into the damaged entryway beyond. Security cameras hung limp and inert from the walls, and a guard station was empty and dark. Debris crunched under Leonov's boots as he stepped into a hallway and holstered his weapon. This place was dead.

On the right side, shattered glass panels gave a view to the interior of the building: an open concrete space with a thick metal scaffolding reaching up to where the top of the tower had once been, with the gun mounted to the top of the steel structure. He could see bits of the clear blue sky through the twisted wreckage. The nature of the explosion had been such that it had extinguished or prevented any fires. While there were charred streaks running down from the top of the tower, everything inside was essentially intact. Computer panels were set up at the base of the scaffold, and several massive cables ran up from the metal grate of the floor to the roof. Some of the cables, severed during the attack, now hung back down the scaffold, spitting occasional sparks. The red emergency lights were still working, splattering a crimson kaleidoscope across the walls. Holes punched in the tower by tank shells and rockets let in shafts of more serene sunlight.

Leonov pulled open a heavy door leading down into that main room. The facility seemed completely abandoned. The technicians and military personnel had apparently fled either out of fear of Leonov's advancing force or as part of the broader panic that seemed to be engulfing Russia. He didn't care either way. The whole world seemed to be falling apart, the basic fabric of civilization stretching and tearing. It wasn't a new order coming, but an older one. A world of strength and will, rather than law and bureaucracy. Weak and decadent economies, military shocks, the destruction of Saint Petersburg, this alien invasion hoax, it was all too much. Chaos threatened to engulf everything, and only force could push it back. No room for the weakness that had led to this fantastic weapon being abandoned like a flat tire by the side of the road.

Leonov walked down a short flight of metal steps to the control room floor, his feet clanging on the grating. A body, the only he had seen so far in the building, was crumpled on the ground. He turned it over with his boot. Bullet holes riddled the suit-and-tie-clad corpse. The man's face also appeared to have been bludgeoned.

"Yegorov," he read out softly from the name badge.

Yegorov had obviously been killed some time before Leonov and his men had arrived. The body was already a bit stiff. Other soldiers were now making their way into the building, cataloging their findings and retrieving anything of value. Leonov nodded at them and left the dead man, walking over to the laptops plugged into the base of the metal scaffold. Diagnostic and targeting systems, presumably. Perhaps the technicians would be able to make something of it.

He saw another laptop on a table near the wall, unconnected to the weapon and obviously more of a standard workstation. Leonov righted a chair that had been knocked over and sat down. The activity lights were illuminated along the front edge, so he scribbled on the touchpad with his finger to wake up the machine, expecting to see a password screen. Instead, the laptop opened to the home screen.

Leonov shook his head at the lax security, even as he was thankful for it. He opened the email account and began to scroll through. Standard stuff, mostly. Communications between the troops, workplace directives, purchase orders. On a hunch, Leonov scrolled all the way to the bottom, to the very first email received.

FROM: Aerospace Defence Forces Command
TO: XB-7 installations
RE: operational status

Comrades,

We have very little time, and I trust the urgency of our mission was duly impressed upon you by Captain Obukhov during your orientation. Our directive is clear, and the enemy is coming. All you require to construct the machine has been provided. You MUST have the facility operational within two weeks. You are also expected to hold fast against the traitorous elements advancing from the south. Rest assured, reinforcements are en route, and will arrive within the week. In the meantime, make all possible haste. The attack on Saint Petersburg was but a prelude, and your family, friends, and countrymen depend on your speed and courage. Lt. Yegorov has been assigned to facilitate and monitor your progress and provide daily reports back to me. I trust you will extend him all due courtesy and grant him full access to your operations so that we might gather a full briefing for the General of the Army Stepanov.

Make haste.

General Arkady Pishchalnikov

"Well, comrade Yegorov, it seems you were indeed extended all due courtesy," Leonov said to the corpse with a chuckle.

Political officers had always been seen as loathsome carbuncles attached to the military body. At best, they were annoying, useless blemishes—dead weight in actual combat. At worst, they were curdled, poisonous men constantly threatening to scurry to their masters with the least bit of incriminating gossip on the field officers to whom they were attached. Why even send your warriors into battle if you had so little trust in their judgement and abilities? Still, Leonov had never seen a political officer murdered. Presumably the silly bastard had threatened to squeal on the soldiers deserting their posts, and the men had turned on him.

Leonov stood up and wiped his hands on his pants. Rats killing rats. Good riddance.

Still, the tone of the email nagged at him. The machine these men had been assigned to build remained a mystery; a technology he had never seen. And the email itself seemed straightforward and earnest. Pishchalnikov, at least, had believed in the alien invasion story. Captain Ilyushin stepped into the room as his soldiers headed out carrying papers and laptops. Leonov stood up from the laptop as Ilyushin approached.

"Take everything, Captain," Leonov said, gesturing around the room. "This technology is indeed unusual, but perhaps we can replicate some of it. This weapon would be a worthwhile addition to our arsenal."

"It does not appear to have been powerful enough to prevent desertion, though," Ilyushin said, looking around at the abandoned space.

"True. But apparently these workers had been promised reinforcements that never arrived. This was most likely a scientific and technical detachment, with no real combat capability. It was a deployment done exceedingly poorly, although the *botan* seem to have done their jobs before fleeing."

The *botan*, or nerds, had been cowards, yes, and their weapon had killed many of his men. Leonov was tempted to let his mind chase this riddle a bit longer, but Ilyushin shuffled a bit, waiting for further orders. Leonov refocused.

"Captain, continue the recovery efforts. Salvage everything you can. I want a full report tomorrow morning from the engineers. I'm returning to base to oversee our efforts there. We will hold a ceremony for our fallen comrades this evening."

Ilyushin saluted. Leonov returned it and walked out of the room, deep in thought.

●

Leonov sat in a conference room in the oblast Duma, his muddy boots propped on the polished oak table as he turned over a chunk of the destroyed weapon from the base in his hands. Rodchenko sat nearby, but otherwise the room was empty. Leonov tossed the twisted wreckage onto the table, dislodging flakes of scorched carbon, and rubbed the back of his neck. God, he wanted a cigarette and a drink.

"Vanya, what is this?"

Rodchenko frowned and picked up the damaged section.

"The reports so far are inconclusive, Yuri. The materials are all familiar. Steel and plastic and other elements. But the construction is . . . sophisticated. Incomprehensible, really."

"You watched the video of the attack?"

"Yes. And I'm as perplexed as you. What I saw on that video is not something we could've made, or the Chinese or, I think, even the Americans. Or perhaps they have some, how do they call it, 'skunk works' project for this."

"Come on, Vanya, you don't believe that. Speak freely. We're alone in here."

Rodchenko shifted in his chair. Leonov could tell his friend was just as eager as he was for nicotine or alcohol.

"Colonel, I know of only one explanation for the source of this technology, but that explanation contains . . . complications . . . for us."

"Indeed it does, friend," Leonov said. "The alien invasion. This is alien technology. There is nowhere else this could have come from. I believe The General has been misinformed."

Rodchenko went even paler than he already was.

"What does this mean for us?"

Leonov looked at Rodchenko, dropped his feet, and leaned forward.

"What does this mean? What do you think it means?! It means there is another player at the poker table, Vanya. Another hand has been dealt. But we're still in the game. These facilities seem to be entirely automated. So, we bypass them. Leave them to their work. We continue on to Moscow. The Russian government is still weak. Even with this fancy tech, they still fled before us. They're not worthy of this country. This new enemy, though, that's something else. The Americans, if their story is true, will be occupied for a while. We have some time to gather our forces and finish our mission."

"But Yuri, if this . . . this alien threat is real, it's as much a threat to us as to them, no?"

Leonov picked up the shredded alien technology again and ran his fingers across the jagged edges, as if looking for a button or latch that might unlock its secrets.

"Perhaps. Or perhaps they might look for an ally down here. It's a big world, Vanya. Perhaps we will share it. For a while, anyway."

Rodchenko was silent for a moment.

"What does The General say?"

Leonov paused, seeming not to have heard his friend. He could tell Rodchenko was uneasy. They'd all known this rebellion was dangerous. Death in battle was always a possibility. At least they'd been going in with a clear sense of their adversary . . . or so they'd thought. Rodchenko shuffled his feet, the boots scraping on the rough wood floor.

"He concurs with me," Leonov said at last, appearing to have settled some question in his mind. "As we speak, he is working to establish communication with the alien invaders. Our job, for now, is to continue as planned. Moscow still beckons, Vanya. Come, let us speak for our dead, and then find a drink."

Rodchenko couldn't help himself.

"Yuri, I don't like this. We're not prepared for this. Our men are not trained for this. The General was . . . mistaken? Misled? Should we reconsider?"

Leonov knew that Rodchenko would have spoken like this with no other officer, and even now would be nervous at saying those words. They were close to treasonous. *Treason on top of the treason we've already committed. No going back now.*

"Vanya, I do not . . . I think our course must hold," Leonov said, still looking into the distance. "Was The General wrong? Perhaps. Or perhaps he kept secrets we don't yet know, or do not need to know. Perhaps he knew more than he was willing to reveal. Our course is set. If we turn away, what is left? Not for us, but for Russia? For our men? No," Leonov said, shaking his head, purpose returning to his eyes. "The only way is forward. Everything else is death."

Rodchenko watched as Leonov continued to idly turn the blackened chunk of metal in his hands.

"Everything else is death."

22

"Are you sure?" Rickert asked as he walked.

"Yeah, we're sure," said the rumpled CIA analyst, hustling alongside him down the hallway. He smelled like coffee and cigarettes. "Well, as sure as we can be of anything these days. We don't have any human assets on the ground. Nor do the Russians. Beacon at the Volgograd location went dark, and the satellite overpass shows the entire facility covered in smoke. It's gone. The 2nd Red Army—that's what they call themselves—was camped in Volgograd and presumably headed for the air base at Lebyazhye. That's where we hoped they were headed, anyway. Somehow they knew about the installation at Gorkovskiy. Looks like they made a damn beeline right to it."

"A mole from our side?"

The analyst shrugged.

"Maybe. Or theirs. Or something else. Maybe some local villagers tipped them off. We warned the Russians about keeping the location a secret, but who knows. Everything has been slapdash and half-assed on their side since Saint Petersburg."

Rickert nodded. "What about the other Russian sites? Are they still online?"

"Yeah, and they're far enough away that they shouldn't be overrun anytime soon. But who knows? It's a shitty situation."

"The president has been briefed?"

"Yeah, the team's with him now."

Rickert stepped into the control room. There were a few people inside, but it was mostly quiet. Again, they were basically just observers. The other countries involved in Earth's defense had complained just as the

American generals had the first time around. Nothing anyone could do about it.

Mankind is going to war with an army of three soldiers and about fifteen computer nerds, Rickert realized. *Jesus.*

The analyst seemed shocked, too.

"Where's the rest?" he said.

"There is no 'rest,'" Rickert said. "This is it."

The analyst fished out his pack of cigarettes, realized it was empty, and grimaced as he crumpled and flicked it into an overflowing trash can.

"You can't smoke in here, anyway," Rickert said. "Government building."

The analyst snorted.

"Yeah, well, hopefully that stops the aliens from turning this place into a smoking crater. I doubt they'd survive the lawsuits."

The analyst started dialing his phone and plopped into a chair as Rickert pushed open a door leading out to the floor of the vehicle assembly building. The humidity wrapped him in a damp hug as he headed toward the three ships in the middle of the room, but at least it smelled better out here.

Outside the hangar door, a lazy breeze fiddled with the tall grasses around the building. Farther off, sunlight sparkled off the Atlantic Ocean. It was a day for tourists to gather on the beach, drink cold beer, get sunburned, and yell at their kids not to swim out too far. There are sharks out there, ya know? But the beaches were empty.

The Army had locked down this stretch of Florida for 50 miles in every direction. They needn't have bothered. Every beach and holiday spot was essentially abandoned. Disney World was a ghost town, Times Square was so empty you could pitch a tent and take a nap, and everyone seemed to have forgotten the Alamo. Rickert didn't understand that mentality. *If I was a civilian, I'd be out on that beach right now with the biggest damn piña colada I could find. Hell, maybe I oughta be doing that anyway.*

Ben, Nick, and Eddie were moving around the ships, completing their final preparations. They all looked up as Rickert approached, his forehead soaked in sweat and his armpits not far behind.

"It's time to go," Ben said. "They're here."

"Yeah, but we've got a problem," Rickert said.

"We know," Eddie replied. "The Russian installation near Volgograd is gone."

"What? Christ, is it on the news? How did you hear?"

Nick tapped the side of his head. "Nah, each facility shows up on our internal networks. They're all linked together through the satellites, and we can tap into that."

Rickert sighed. "I guess I should have known. Still, the destruction of that facility is not a good sign. Things in Russia are falling apart. Even if we can hold off the mrill, you guys might come home to World War III."

"We'll worry about that later," Ben said. "Right now, our scanners are showing the mrill fleet coming around Venus. They're slowing down, but they'll be here soon. It's time to go."

Rickert felt nervous and flustered. "Yeah, good luck. We'll do what we can from here, but unless they land, you guys are mostly on your own."

"We know," Nick said. "Just stay out of our way."

"How about Project X?" Ben asked.

"They're working as fast as possible," Rickert said. "I don't know. Maybe. I don't know."

Ben nodded.

"Well, we'll just have to make do without."

Rickert held out his hand to the three soldiers. "Good luck."

Each man shook it, Ben last. Both men looked strained.

"Don't die," Rickert said.

"Don't get killed," Ben replied.

●

As the three men headed for their ships, Rickert retreated to the air-conditioned control room. He tugged on a radio headset, shivering a bit as his sweat seemed to freeze on his body. The analyst was still on his phone, reporting back to Langley. He nodded perfunctorily at Rickert. The pale blue illumination from the monitors made the spy look like a damp corpse, Rickert thought. Then he realized he probably looked the same. This wasn't a control room. It was a morgue.

"All systems green from our end," Rickert said into the mic.

"Roger that," Ben replied. "We're good to go."

"Godspeed," Rickert said.

Without another word, all three ships spun to life with a deep hum and then shot straight up into the air, leaving a cloud of startled technicians in their wake and Rickert rocking back and forth in his chair.

●

Liftoff was just as exhilarating the second time around. The ground sank away, and Ben felt Nick and Eddie's exhilaration at taking to the air like a flock of birds. Again, it wasn't like piloting a ship. Man and machine were one entity.

Ben had felt this connection on his first flight, but for Nick and Eddie, it was novel. It didn't take them more than a few seconds to adapt, but Ben felt their initial confusion at suddenly realizing their bodies now didn't end at their fingers and toes, but at gleaming metal hulls, massive engines, and lethal cannons.

"Whoa," Nick said.

"Once you're done looking down, you should look up," Ben said.

The ground was falling away, and overhead the sky was turning from pale blue to navy to deep purple to black as the ships rose through the atmosphere and bounded toward space. It was hard to tell the difference between heading out into space and sinking down into the sea. The farther you went, the darker it got. People weren't meant to survive in this crushing blackness.

The last filaments of terrestrial gasses and gravity slipped away, and the three were now in the final layer of the atmosphere, the exosphere, the last leap from Earth to everything else. Ben tried to seal his dread in a deep compartment in his mind. At the same time, he felt surprise and something like joy spread out from his teammates across their mental link.

Eddie laughed with delight.

"My life has not gone as planned," he said.

"You never wanted to be an astronaut?" Ben said.

"Nah. When I was a kid, I thought I was going to be a movie star."

"Hasn't humanity suffered enough?" Nick quipped back.

The approaching mrill spacecraft popped up on their short-range scanners.

"Apparently not," Ben said.

Eddie sighed.

"Well, we may not be movie stars, but I'm guessing we make the six o'clock news," he said.

"Let's just make sure there's a six o'clock news to go home to," Ben said.

The three men accelerated toward the confrontation as the sun rose over the Earth behind them, a white spear in the dark. Their plan was to engage the mrill as far from the planet as possible, minimizing collateral damage on the ground. Ben would have preferred to attack even farther out, but the ships the three men were in weren't long-range crafts. So far, in all the blueprints and schematics they'd seen, there were no long-range ships. That had puzzled the scientists. It worried Ben. Why hadn't the brin provided those capabilities? No time to consider it now.

Ben felt his conscious mind decoupling from control of his ship, and sensed Nick and Eddie going through a similar disengagement. The machines in their bodies and the machines around their bodies would do most of the fighting. Ben had warned them about this, explained the inhuman sensation of being unplugged from yourself. But he had also explained that they remained in ultimate control, and that they should assert that control as needed.

Ben's electronic vision filled with dozens of mrill warships coming around the moon. Then hundreds. He counted 237 in total.

"Draw them in," he said. "We have to use the satellites. Drop your mines."

One of the capabilities of the antigravity technology on their ships was to generate small gravitational fields on command. This allowed the ships to make sweeping, banking turns otherwise only possible in the gravitational confines of a planet, moon, or other large body. It felt more natural to the three men who had no experience with zero G flight. As the three ships arced over the Earth, they each deployed half a dozen black, featureless orbs from their bellies. The stealthy bombs drifted apart in a loose cloud toward the oncoming mrill force.

Ben didn't know if the enemy ships could detect the mines. They were so small that they didn't show up on his own sensors, and they emitted no signals of any kind. They were unpowered, essentially inert space junk, activated and powered by energy emitted by passing ships. The downside was that they were the ultimate "dumb" bombs, incapable of tracking or following their targets if they changed course. Still, a nifty piece of hardware.

Ben felt increasingly nervous about the technology on the other side of the battlefield. There was so much they still didn't know, and that either the brin hadn't told them or also hadn't known. On the other hand, Ben forced himself to remember: there was also much the mrill didn't know. About Earth, about Ben, Nick, and Eddie, and who knew what else. Ben knew, from training and experience, how easy it was to see an enemy as omnipotent and omniscient, while despairing over your own flaws. You never saw the blunders and miscalculations and uncertainties on the other side of the line. You only saw the glint of his weapons and the mass of his army, while every scrap of arrogance and cowardice on your own side scraped like broken glass in an open wound. The truth was that everyone made mistakes in combat. No army, no general, no soldier planned and performed perfectly. Everyone was human. Hopefully even the aliens.

The mrill ships began to spread out as they approached. Ben calculated that they were traveling at a bit over 150,000 kilometers per hour, more than 40 kilometers every second, closing the gap between Moon and Earth at terrifying speed. Despite his fear, Ben was fascinated by the approaching machinery. The small ships were identical to the drones he'd previously faced and the single-man fighter he'd seen in the New Mexico desert. But there were larger ships as well. There were green, bulbous crafts bristling with what had to be weapons, and long smooth cylinders that he suspected were troop transports. Behind those ships and swathed in a protective phalanx of drones and fighters were three large cruisers that had to be the command vessels. They were large gray spheres, with long thin stalks protruding from the front and ending in a cluster of smaller spheres. Ben thought they looked like lollipops with a clump of soap bubbles on the end. They were now less than 30 seconds away from intersecting with the mines, and Ben held his breath. As the men sped back toward Earth, each could almost feel the mrill ships straining to reach them before they could reach the protective cocoon of the defensive satellites. Ben prayed their eagerness made them blind.

They could now also feel the connections between the mrill ships and soldiers, the same sort of invisible thread that linked the three men. Both sides were networked together, seeing and feeling and working as one. Then another one of those closed-off portions of Ben's internal computer, one of the secrets he had suspected still lurked within him, came to life.

He felt a part of himself reaching out to the mrill web, trying to establish a link, to connect the two networks together. Panic spilled over Ben. *What the hell was this?*

Nick and Eddie similarly recoiled, unable to stop whatever was happening. Then the connection was established. White noise poured out of the three men, out of the computers in their cells and their blood, flooding the mrill link. A jamming signal of some sort. A last trick the brin had hidden up their sleeve, concealed even from their human hosts.

The mrill fleet hesitated, uncertain.

Ben realized instantly why the brin had kept this ability locked away. They knew the humans, in a panic, would have used the jamming capability against the smaller scout force. Probably would have worked. Saint Petersburg might still be standing. Winning that battle could have lost the war, though. The mrill would have had time to adjust before their larger fleet arrived. They would have figured out how to deflect the jamming signal. It was a one-shot weapon. Had to save it for the pivotal moment.

Now the mrill had to either flee and regroup and let the guardians dig in further or press their numerical advantage and hope it was enough.

Ben knew they would fight. It was what he would have done. He wondered how many other secrets the brin had locked away in his body. What other surprises would pop out when that dead alien race deemed it appropriate? God damn all of this.

What's that saying about gift horses and mouths? Eddie said in thought, his delight piercing Ben's shadows.

"The bad guys are flying blind now," Eddie said out loud with a whoop. "We're gonna play chess while these fools are playing checkers."

"You know how to play chess?" Nick chided.

"You can't see it, but I'm giving you the finger right now," Eddie said. "Checkmate."

The first mrill ships were close to the cloud of mines, their confused sensors not registering the mines as anything more than random space debris. The antimatter bombs would only be in the center of the mrill force for a moment, though. If the ships accelerated or changed course, the bombs might not have enough time to gather the electromagnetic energy pulsing from the ships and detonate.

The guns on the mrill drones unfolded from their fuselages. In the millisecond it took for their weapons to charge, the mines siphoned off a tiny fraction of that energy and detonated. Red antimatter slapped across the mrill fleet, dozens of ships destroyed instantly. Damaged fighters smoked and burned. Some of the wounds were fatal, and the burning spacecraft exploded like fireworks, green and yellow fireflies spiraling out into the darkness. The shrapnel was a secondary assault, raking more mrill crafts. The large command ships, traveling at the rear of the convoy, had avoided the mines, but were now pelted with chunks of the exploded ships ahead of them. They seemed to shrug off the smaller pieces, but one massive, spinning hunk of metal slammed directly into the main sphere on one of the command ships.

A flame flickered briefly in the jagged crater and was then extinguished in the vacuum. The ship was crippled, and it drifted off slowly at an angle away from the battlespace. Secondary explosions from other damaged ships sent additional debris flying in every direction.

The men shared a brief surge of hope. Maybe they could pull this off. They were still outnumbered thirty or forty to one, but they now knew the mrill could bleed. The trail of wreckage was a twisted road to victory, or at least the possibility of victory. Now the mrill fighters were closing in, but the men were within range of the satellites orbiting Earth. As the mrill powered up their guns, the three men did a tight loop back toward the attackers as a dozen satellites began tracking the enemy ships.

Ben thought briefly of all the famous battlefields on the planet below: the muddy, rocky fields where cowards and heroes and everyone in between had crashed into each other, from Thermopylae to Gettysburg to Normandy. Once the bodies were piled high enough and the blood soaked deep enough, the ground was consecrated and hallowed. Whether driven by guilt or pride, if you piled enough dead in one spot, it forced people to remember. Those forests and fields were marked with bronze plaques set in stone, a clearing where you could assemble the survivors for a speech on green grass on a sunny day, visit with your children long after the survivors had died of old age.

Not this time. This battle, perhaps the last battle, would be fought in a cold, empty void. Win or lose, there would be no commemoration here. Laser fire would vaporize the blood and bodies, gravity would carry off the remains, and the surviving machines would proceed to the next mission. Once this battle was over, there would be nothing left.

Eddie, reading his thoughts, spoke out loud as everyone prepared to fire.

"Maybe we won't get a parade up here, but I'm going on a hell of a bender once we get back down there."

Across a thousand kilometers of emptiness, as sunrise poured over the edge of the Earth, the two armies opened fire. Bolts of neon energy filled the darkness, stabbing at their targets, while the ships danced and dodged the assaults. Ben, Nick, and Eddie hurled clusters of mines at the oncoming mrill ships while the satellites behind them tossed thunderbolts of ionized hydrogen. Ahead of them, the mrill ships dumped a wall of fire, hoping to simply overwhelm the defenders. The command ships held back while the fighters pressed in. The mrill were now avoiding the spots where the three men were dropping mines or trying to blast them apart from a distance. Some still slipped through and created mini sunrises of their own, destroying more ships.

Ben and his team held back, not advancing too deep into the mrill swarm, letting long-range cannons on the satellites do their work. *Swoop in and out, but don't linger.* A mrill bolt scraped across the edge of Ben's ship, cutting a crease through the fuselage, and he felt it like a knife cutting across his own skin. Warning messages popped up in his vision, and he scanned the damage report. Nothing major, but the mrill were closing in.

You okay, boss? A mental ping from Nick.

Just a flesh wound.

His bigger concern was that the mrill seemed to be herding themselves away from the satellites. Ben fired a burst from his cannons, sensing the explosion rather than seeing it as he maneuvered to avoid another ship coming in from behind. Staccato blasts of green skimmed past his cockpit, missing by no more than a dozen feet. Nick obliterated the chasing ship with a brief blast, but was then chased off himself. Ships seemed to be corkscrewing in random directions; the cumulative effect was to send Ben and his team banking deeper into space each time, a bit closer to the main fleet and out of reach of the satellites.

Stay tight, Ben flashed. *Don't let them push us too far out.*

Keeping close to Earth, though, was like fighting in a school of fish. The mrill were everywhere. The mines were useless now, as everyone was too close and missiles were too slow. The satellites were firing at their maximum rate, picking off the disjointed invaders, but the mrill were now turning their attention to those devices.

One exploded, then another. The mrill were down to about fifty fighters. The drones were effective but predictable and relatively easy to target. But there were so many of them, too many of them, and the three men, despite their best efforts, found themselves edging farther from·the remaining satellites.

Another satellite exploded. Several troop transports zoomed into the opening, preparing to stab at the planet below.

Ben was about to order his team to chase the troop ship when Rickert spoke over his secure radio.

"Bad news and good news, gentlemen. Bad first. Mrill reinforcements are here. Looks like this was just the first wave. You've got about a dozen of those larger ships incoming, surrounded by a few hundred drones. Enemy fighters coming your way. And there's something even bigger coming in behind them. Possibly a command ship?"

"I hope the good news is *really* goddamn good," Eddie said as he downed two more mrill drones and swerved around three more, letting Nick pick them off. "Is Nick finally getting his fucking season pass to Disneyland?"

"Better," Rickert said. "Project X inbound."

Nick laughed. "And hey, the sun's coming up. It's gonna be a good day."

Ben glanced over to the horizon and caught a glimpse of the sun spilling again over the edge of the planet. Beneath the brilliant white light racing across the Atlantic Ocean, two dozen silver drones, reinforcements, were darting up through the atmosphere.

"The cavalry is here," Nick said.

"I didn't think the team was going to be able to pull it off," Ben said. "Much obliged, General. And say thanks to Bert for me."

"Will do, and good luck."

Ben was about to respond when another volley of enemy fire lanced past his ship, several of them grazing the surface and causing the craft to shudder before stabilizing. Again, he felt the damage as his own pain. A satellite hovering over Africa blasted two of Ben's pursuers. Several mrill drones broke off to attack the offending satellite.

Now the human drones were here. As they came into range, the internal computers inside the three men took over their navigation and targeting. While the drones had been outfitted with basic guidance systems and could be remote-controlled from the ground, those connections were primitive compared to the computers embedded in their bodies. Ben sensed that his team's jamming signal was still active, keeping the mrill from working in coordination. They were still lethal, but were forced to rely on basic, crude tactics in the absence of their wireless link. The drone battle was lopsided in terms of numbers but evenly matched in terms of results, as the humans and their drones outmaneuvered their alien foes. Fire filled the sky as enemy ships ruptured and spilled open.

The second wave of mrill fighters poured in. There were so many of them that they simply couldn't attack all at once without being caught in their own crossfire.

"They're heading for Earth. The transports are heading for Earth," Eddie said.

"Take them out," Ben shot back. "We can't let them get on the ground. I'll cover you."

"We're on it," Nick said.

Nick and Eddie peeled off, chasing the troop ships down toward the nighttime side of Earth, near Siberia. As the mrill scuttled above Asia, the cannons on the ground opened fire.

They blasted several of the drones, creating small, temporary suns in the darkness. Two of the fifteen troop transports were also destroyed. Two more were wounded, and they went into uncontrolled spins. As they slammed through the atmosphere, they began to heat up, then glow, compressing the air in front of them into incandescent plasma. They whipped around like pinwheel fireworks, debris and sparks screaming in every direction. As they neared the ground, one of the ships finally came apart, exploding across the desolation of Mongolia and eastern Russia. Day turned to night. The other ship stayed intact long enough to spear directly into the dark water of Lake Baikal at over 600 meters per second, nearly twice the speed of sound. The catastrophic impact gouged a temporary hole in the liquid and sent a roaring wall of water out in every direction. A small band of Buryat tribesmen camped along the shore had woken with the lights and now scrambled for cover. Before they could even begin to flee, the waves devoured them and washed their camp away like it had never existed.

The other transports changed course, streaking west, and Nick and Eddie realized they were aiming for the hole left by the destruction of the cannon in Volgograd.

"Wait, how do they know?" Eddie said.

"Maybe they're the ones who tipped off the Red Army guys," Nick said.

"Oh, man, they've got a presence on the ground already, somehow," Eddie said. "No bueno."

He fired off a burst at another approaching ship, tearing it apart in the thin upper atmosphere, and was then chased off by a handful of drones. Nick followed in pursuit, blasting the drones as more ships descended.

"It's getting crowded down here," Nick said. "I don't think we can hold them off."

"Have a little faith, brother," Eddie said. His pendant was tucked safely beneath his shirt, and the metal nudged him with every maneuver. He made a tight turn, destroyed the last of his pursuers, and pulled up off Nick's left. They both bore down on a transport fleeing for the open plains and shredded it with their weapons. The ship disintegrated as it fell. A gaping hole opened in its side, and dozens of robotic foot soldiers, copies of the machine Ben had fought in China, were ripped out of the wound. Nick and Eddie picked them off as they tumbled down, not taking any chances. The last fragment of the ship slammed into the side of a mountain and exploded with a crack of thunder.

"Let's go check on our boy," Eddie said.

"We're going to have to come back," Nick said. "There's a hole in our defenses here big enough to drive a planet through. They're all going to be aiming for Russia."

"Yeah, but we'll have better luck plugging it from above than below," Eddie said.

The two fighters rose back into the sky, headed toward the pulsing glow of battle.

23

"hat am I looking at here?" Lockerman asked.

"Mr. President, the Russian perimeter is barely holding up. The loss of the installation at Volgograd created a small gap in our defensive shield, and the mrill are attempting to exploit it. As you know, we have almost no control over the defensive satellites. They are either automated or controlled by Lieutenant Shepherd and his men. Any attempt to reposition them would take hours and probably take them out of the fight for the duration."

"Can our drones handle the extra load?"

The technician chewed his lip as he studied the numbers on his monitor. "Maybe. We're not sure."

Lockerman hated it here in the Cheyenne Mountain facility—the cramped rooms and stale air were the least of it. The most oppressive element was simply the millions of tons of rock and dirt piled above. You could almost taste the crushing weight suspended above and all around. He hadn't seen natural sunlight in three days. He thought of the stories of Victorian-era aristocrats who were buried with a string leading up to a bell at their grave markers, so that if they had accidentally been buried alive, they could ring the bell and summon someone with a shovel. Probably bullshit. But down here, he could see the appeal. The only problem was that there was no one to call for help if he got smothered alive in this pile. The Secret Service and all his staff had nixed the idea of staying mobile in Air Force One, and no other facility in the US was hardened like the NORAD headquarters. The mountain had been outfitted with brin cannons, but it would only be used in case of a direct attack, to keep the mrill from targeting it as part of their general assault. So the president had gone underground. And this portion of the facility was buried even further underground than the main command room.

Lockerman looked over at Goldman, his national security adviser, and gestured at the large monitors in the center of the room pouring out video and other data of the battle above.

"How are we doing, Jeff?"

"Well, not horribly, all things considered. Lieutenant Shepherd and his men, plus the drones, seem to be fighting the mrill to more or less a standstill. The troop ships keep trying to break through, but so far our defenses are holding."

"The surface-to-air lasers are doing their jobs? And yes, I know they're not really lasers."

"Yes, sir. They seem to be. The gap in the Russian net is a problem, but the drones seem to be filling it for now. I don't think the mrill expected that."

"Are the mrill responsible for the Russian cannon being destroyed? How would they have done that?"

"We just don't know, Mr. President," Goldman said. "We don't have any hard data. It's difficult to see how they could have been responsible. But who knows. We're getting almost no communication from the Russian government."

Lockerman had ordered troops, tanks, and gunships around all of the American cannons, and as many of the overseas installations as possible. The European sites were pretty well locked down. The governments in Brazil, Venezuela, Argentina, South Africa, Nigeria, Tanzania, Algeria, and Egypt were doing their best, with varying levels of support from US Special Forces and the Marine Corps. He didn't know how helpful they would be—they were spread thinner than anyone preferred—but at least they gave him eyes and ears on the ground. The Chinese, Australians, and Japanese were on their own, but Lockerman felt comfortable that they could handle their own security. Well, as comfortable as he felt about anything these days.

"Jeff, do you think it's weird that they haven't even tried to communicate with us? No demands, no terms, no 'Take me to your leader' stuff?"

"I don't know, Mr. President. General Rickert and his team gamed out some scenarios, and most of the hostile scenarios followed almost exactly what we're seeing. No point in negotiating an extermination. The signal guys at the National Security Agency and the National Reconnaissance Office haven't detected any attempt to communicate. Lieutenant Shepherd and his team haven't reported anything, either."

Lockerman grunted. "Yeah, I guess they've made their intentions pretty clear."

"True, Mr. President. Given the initial encounters Lieutenant Shepherd had, I see no reason to think that the mrill are anything but hostile. Even so . . ."

"Yes?"

"I'd really like to talk to them, Mr. President. We have almost no sense of their psychology, or if that word is even appropriate. We're fighting purely on the basis of hardware and tactics. But we don't have a clue what their true weak points are, what pressures or incentives they might respond to, how we might deceive or delay them. We might hold them off here, for now, but we have no idea if they'll consider that a setback, a defeat, or merely time to plot their next move."

Lockerman thought about that for a moment.

"We do know something about them, though," he said. "They don't negotiate."

"Perhaps," Goldman replied. "Or maybe they do and we're completely misinterpreting the signs. But if this truly is a colonization mission, then there's probably not much to negotiate about. It's a zero-sum game."

"We're just fishing in the dark here, aren't we?"

Goldman had no reply, and they turned back to the monitors.

24

Ben blasted two more mrill drones apart as he dodged three on his tail. Scattered energy blasts crisscrossed the darkness, a constantly shifting 3D maze that only his internal computers could navigate. His human brain saw only a maelstrom.

The troop ships had pulled back after their failed initial charges. They were now gathered about 60,000 kilometers above Earth, waiting, as the drones continued to probe for openings. The three men and their own drone army were holding their own, backed up by the defensive satellites. Most of the action continued to be over Russia, as the mrill charged repeatedly at the gap left by the destruction of the ground cannon. They were probing other areas as well. The twenty-two remaining human drones were engaging the thirty or so mrill drones around the world. As Earth rotated to dip the American hemisphere into night, a fiery battle raged overhead. Ben suspected anyone on the ground with even a modest telescope or pair of binoculars was getting a hell of a show. So far, though, Ben and his team had been able to keep the fight up in the skies.

Three mrill drones came straight toward Ben. He accelerated to attack, expecting them to break formation and try to get behind him, as others had done. Instead, they kept coming. He was about to fire when he realized Nick was engaged with another group directly behind them. If Ben fired, he might hit Nick. A defensive satellite on Ben's port side, at a nearly 90-degree angle to the oncoming mrill drones, shattered one of them. The other two continued their rush, spinning a complex spiral to evade the satellite's targeting system. Ben searched quickly for an alternate attack route, but before he could change course, he noticed a brief blip on his sensors as the charging mrill opened their weapons bays for just a moment. Several mines flew out, hurtling toward Ben like shotgun pellets.

Too far away to hit me, he thought. *What the hell are they trying at?* The mines exploded, but there was almost no fireball. Miniature EMP bombs meant not to destroy, but disable. A wave of electromagnetic energy washed over his ship, and his view went black as the ship's systems were overwhelmed by the power surge. He was now drifting along at close to 2,000 kilometers per hour, on a collision course with Earth.

The more immediate danger, though, were the two drones swooping in for the kill. Several more, having noticed his crippled state, were scuttling in behind them. Eddie, farther off, had seen the EMP attack and zipped in, ripping open one of the incoming drones, but was chased off by three more before he could help any further. Ben could sense a small army of his ship's onboard nanobots streaming out to repair the short-circuited systems, but for the moment he was, if not a sitting duck, then at least a flightless one.

The mrill drones swarmed. Eddie and Nick picked off as many as they could, and the surrounding satellites sent beam after beam of plasma energy through the attacking ships. The mrill were pouring in, far more than there had been a moment ago, and Ben realized they were now streaming out of one of the larger ships. The Project X drones were still busy over Russia. As he skidded toward Earth, he wondered if he'd get shot before he had a chance to crash. His nanobots were finally beginning to repair the damaged electrical systems, and the first equipment to come back online was the basic radio equipment used to communicate with Rickert and the ground team. Static popped and crackled in his head.

"Ben, you there? Ben?"

"Still here, sir. For the moment."

"There are more mrill ships inbound. Looks like this one is the mothership. You okay? Do you still have control of your ship? You look like you're drifting."

Ben's scanners flickered back to life; a moment later, so did his guns. He destroyed a mrill drone that had slipped through, as the sensors plotted range and trajectory even though he couldn't see it. His viewscreen came back to life, and it was full of Earth as he continued to sink toward the planet. The gravitational pull wasn't the problem; that effect was fairly mild. Rather, he was a victim of his previous acceleration, of Newton's first law, a body in motion staying in motion unless acted upon. At this point, the only force preparing to act on the ship was the eastern seaboard of the United States, about 160 kilometers below.

All this weird alien shit, and I'm about to die from the most fundamental physical law in the universe. I would really like my engines back.

The nanobots seemed to be struggling with that one. His hull was heating up, singeing his metal skin. As he reentered the atmosphere, aerodynamics became a problem. The thickening air began to tug and shove at the contours of his ship. He was spinning. Spinning and shaking, like a yo-yo in an earthquake. And still no thrusters. Warning indicators flashed in his vision. He wasn't worried about the heat or vibration—the ship could easily take it. The confrontation with the ground, on the other hand, would be much less survivable.

Twenty-five kilometers. Thirty seconds to impact.

He could hear Rickert calling his name over the radio, but he ignored it. Instead, he opened a secure channel to Eddie and Nick, whom he could see engaging his pursuers.

"Break off, break off," he ordered. "Do not follow me down. Continue to engage the incoming mrill. It looks like more drop ships and attack cruisers are cutting into the solar system, and we need you boys back above on the battlefield."

"But . . ." Nick began.

"No. That's an order. My machines are still working on repairs. I'll make it. And if I don't, you do not have time to waste on me."

These were easy orders for Ben. He'd never had trouble going into harm's way solo. There was nothing they could do to help him, and they would probably be safer fighting on their own than trying to watch his back. And maybe they'd take a few of the mrill with them.

Sixteen klicks. Fifteen seconds to impact.

Virginia loomed below. Washington, DC, in fact.

Ben hoped he wasn't about to pancake into the White House. Maybe the mrill would put up a plaque for that, and their kids, if they had any, would come and laugh at the idiot human in the decades to come.

He and his ship punctured the clouds, guns blazing, and the mrill drones followed. His ship whistled as air flooded every crevice and channel at nearly supersonic speed. He was actually slowing down, the thick cushion of air acting like a brake. Eddie and Nick broke off and headed back to the upper atmosphere. Three mrill attack ships chased after them, leaving just two on Ben's tail. But a new signal swooped in from the west, a mrill troopship. The defensive cannons clustered around Washington, DC, couldn't fire, given how Ben and the mrill ships were bunched together, and the mrill were using the cover to send in their dropship to establish a beachhead.

Five klicks. A shade over 15,000 feet.

"Now would be a good time," Ben yelled to his mindless, oblivious nano-bots. "You little bastards are going to die with me if you don't hurry up."

The troopship disappeared from view as it decelerated for landing. Ben tried to shoot it, but the mrill drones crisscrossed in front him, serving as a protective shield for the drop ship. He tried to blast them away, like batting at a swarm of gnats, but the vibration and spin was so fierce that most of his shots streamed wildly off into the air.

Five seconds to impact.

He was still traveling far too fast to survive. This was it. *I would have liked to have seen how this all ended*, Ben thought.

His engines came to life, and Ben threw the throttle open. The volcanic roar rattled his teeth, but it wasn't nearly enough to stop his descent. Traveling almost two hundred and fifty kilometers per hour, he slammed into a small pond.

The water was cement at that speed, and the ship shattered around him. The hull cracked open like an egg and he was ripped from his chair. The violent separation, the severing of the connection between man and machine, felt like his brain was being torn from his skull. His body slammed down against the floor of the cockpit, snapping his arms and legs at obscene angles. His head bounced against a panel and his vision turned fuzzy as cold water rushed in.

He tried to escape, to just move, but nothing was working the way it was supposed to, and he wasn't sure which way was up.

He was back on his father's boat. The squall had become a storm, and everything was falling apart. The swirl of water was like a blindfold, and all the old familiar surfaces were now alien territory. Cries for help seemed to come from both just beyond reach and a million miles away. Ben thrashed in the gloom. How many times could a man die in one lifetime? One last stab of light from the setting sun through the splintered hull and then muddy water covered everything. Even as he sank, the machines in his body were already working, emergency response crews tirelessly sewing him up, dragging him back, again, from the edge of darkness. No rest. Not yet.

The ship gurgled deeper into the cold murk. His nanobots could store enough oxygen to allow him to nearly take a nap beneath the waves if he wanted. His body would take care of itself. His memories were still broken. Ben wrestled with his mind, pushing the old visions away to let his training take over.

The eight weeks of training as an aspiring frogman at the Naval Special Warfare Training Center in Coronado, on the California coast, had been all about retraining the body and mind to deal with, then ignore, then finally embrace physical suffering. Floating on your back in water so cold that it cut like a blade, arms locked with those of his fellow classmen, shivering and chattering through exhaustion and lurking hypothermia while a grinning instructor bellowed through a bullhorn. Water, water everywhere, and more than a few puked as nature tried to force them to drink. Most quit. Everyone considered it. After that first shock, though, Ben felt himself enjoying it in a perverse way.

Maybe part of it was just the primordial tether that all life had to the ocean. It had once been home for every living organism. Listen closely enough and you could hear it calling you back. That was part of it. Ben had eventually decided that part of the draw was also the raw physical challenge, something most Americans no longer had to deal with in a world of heated seats and push-button convenience. Some people just need to push themselves, to test themselves. That was what he told himself. That was the reason he refused to quit. And maybe that was true. Partly, anyway. But as he felt the frigid muck of this small pond settle on him like buzzards, he now realized there was more to it. He'd gone back to the water as a man because he'd never really come out of the water as a child on his father's boat. If he couldn't rescue his dad from the deep, he'd rescue everyone else from it . . . or die trying.

Ben waited as his superhuman bones were knitted back together, tears and cuts in his skin and organs and tendons stitched up. His ship fully sank beneath the surface of the water, burping one last bubble of air, but still he waited. When he could finally move, he tested his limbs. *Back in the fight.*

The wreckage of the ship landed gently on the floor of the lake and settled into the mud. Instead of swimming out, he pulled himself to the crunched stern of the ship, his augmented eyes seeing through the murky haze. The weapons locker was jammed shut and would not respond to his electronic commands. Ben braced his feet against the wall, shoved his fingertips into a small gap that had opened in the locker, and pulled. The metal groaned, then finally gave way, sliding up. He grabbed a pistol and a long, bulky rifle. He shoved the pistol into a holster on the side of his leg and strapped the rifle over his back, where it attached itself magnetically. His senses were deciphering the chemical contents of the muddy water. Ben mentally shoved the useless data to the side. *Time to leave.*

Wriggling back through the gloom, searching for the tear in the hull. More mud had oozed into the space in just the last few seconds, and even his upgraded eyes were now useless. The darkened, twisted interior felt truly alien for the first time. Nothing was where it was supposed to be. Ben ran through a mental checklist of alternative sensory options. He smiled in the cold water. Then he yelled.

The sound waves bounced around the interior and then back to his ears. His computers translated the crashing acoustics, forming an image, a map. Sonar. There was the hole. He kicked and felt the muddy water swirl around him. Everything was buried under a thick layer of sludge. He found the jagged opening and used his superhuman strength to wrench the shards out so he could squeeze through. He swam upward and toward a hazy light filtering down from above. A few feet below the surface, he realized the light wasn't the steady glow of the setting sun, but a pulsing strobe, accompanied by an irregular thumping sound, the concussive rhythm of battle.

Ben broke the surface of the water and emerged into chaos.

25

Artillery shells and rockets bounded across the darkening sky as mrill drones buzzed overhead. The mrill troop ship had landed about half a kilometer away, near the shore, and robots and mrill soldiers were spreading out, firing at the American soldiers charging through the city streets from the south. What they lacked in coordination they made up for in raw firepower.

A quick check of his internal compass told Ben he'd landed in the McMillan Reservoir, just a few kilometers away from the White House. There were American soldiers, tanks, and helicopters everywhere. None of that bothered the mrill. The invaders had landed on the south edge of the reservoir and were continuing in that direction—through the Howard University campus—to meet the oncoming elements of the 2nd Battalion, 6th Marines, the infantry unit that had been deployed near the White House. A dozen or so M1A1 tanks from the Army's 77th Armor Regiment were also clattering into the fight. Apache helicopters and F-35 and F-16 fighter jets screamed overhead as they engaged the mrill drones. It was a massive force, yet the mrill were kicking it aside like a pile of dried leaves.

Missiles and tracer rounds whipped through the air from the advancing human troops, gouging and ripping chunks from everything but the mrill. Flashes of plasma sparked out from the far more sophisticated mrill weapons. All the dying was happening on the human side. The sun had almost vanished in the west, but the red glare of the rockets was enough illumination to show that the humans were being chewed up as fast as they arrived on the scene. Tanks rumbled forward, yet most were destroyed before ever firing a shot. An F-16 Fighting Falcon roared overhead, pursued by two drones. The drones pulverized the fleeing jet, raining fiery debris down on an apartment building, then split up to continue their hunt. The chatter of machine-gun fire and the snap of mrill energy cannons filled the night, punctuated only by men, vehicles, and buildings detonating in the dark, momentarily turning the night to day.

A dozen or so terrified civilians stumbled out of a building just as a squad of marines ran around the corner. The two groups, heading in opposite directions, got tangled up, and the soldiers struggled to redirect the hysterical civilians while trying to establish a firing position behind some parked construction equipment.

Before the marines could aim and fire, a squad of mrill robots homed in on the confused gaggle of warriors and civilians, killing them all where they stood. Screams of pain were short-lived, as the robots fired repeatedly into the position.

Two army snipers on the roof of a nearby parking garage opened up on the mrill robots with powerful Barrett M107 rifles. The .50 caliber slugs slammed into the machines, tearing off chunks of metal and sending a couple robots to the ground. From behind the snipers, a third soldier launched an FGM-148 Javelin anti-tank missile at a cluster of robots. The missile popped free of its launcher and soared up into the sky to punch down into the enemy grouping—it never had a chance. While two of the robots dumped green energy blasts into the building, destroying a handful of cars along with the three-man fire team, a third pointed up in the air and fired at the descending missile. It detonated like an asteroid hitting the atmosphere, the boom briefly overpowering the noise around it. In all, the mrill had killed twenty-seven people in the space of less than six seconds.

Rage bubbled up through Ben's cold computer senses, a useless emotion that would only get him killed if he gave into it. He pushed down his fury and kicked hard through the cold water. At the shore, he paused for a moment to calculate his attack. He'd emerged on the southwest shore of the reservoir, about a hundred meters from where the mrill had landed and were pushing further southwest toward the Capitol and the White House. Military infantry and vehicles continued to stream from that direction, trying to stop the mrill assault. They were being steadily pushed back and Ben could hear in the background of his mind the chaotic radio chatter passing between the soldiers charging into their deaths.

Ben knew the president had been evacuated, but there was also one of the surface-to-space guns installed on the White House lawn, and it was vital to keep it operating. As Ben prepared to move, the cannon fired in the distance, a bright red lance charging up into the sky. Ben reached out to Eddie and Nick, who responded by connecting him with their visual sensors, and for a few moments he watched the space battle raging through their eyes. More mrill ships were cutting in, and the situation was getting more difficult to contain. Nick and Eddie wouldn't be able to help down here.

Ben switched to a radio connection to Rickert.

"General? Do you read?" he whispered.

"Ben? Holy hell, where are you?"

"On the ground in DC, about two klicks from the White House. We've got about two hundred mrill foot soldiers and a handful of drones pushing southwest from the McMillan Reservoir. Our guys are being chewed up. I'm about to engage the mrill from the rear and I need you to patch me in to whoever is in charge on the ground to let them know I'll be linking up with them in about 45 seconds. We're also gonna need a hell of a lot more air support."

"I'm working on it. In the meantime, don't die."

Ben shouldered his rifle and slipped out of the water. A quick glance showed him he probably could have cartwheeled out of the water and not been noticed. The mrill were focused on the tanks and soldiers and hadn't secured their flank, assuming all the defenders were in front of them.

A second mrill force emerged from the troop ship. In addition to foot soldiers, there were a handful of hovering platforms. On each platform were four mrill soldiers, operating what looked to be massive cannons. Mobile artillery. These levitating weapon platforms skimmed above the asphalt, avoiding jagged debris and rubble. Each cannon sizzled and snapped for a moment before firing, sending a thunderbolt into the human ranks. This second squad wasn't bothering with scouts or perimeter security either. Why should they? As far as they knew, Ben was dead and nothing else on the ground was a serious threat.

Ben dropped prone behind a dirt embankment, looking through the wreckage of two cars. He mentally toggled his rifle to fire timed explosives and felt his brain surrendering active control of his nano computers. While many of his fellow soldiers had spoken of an odd, Zen-like calm that fell over them before going into battle, Ben had never experienced such a sensation. Combat had always been a visceral, hyperreal experience for him, with every sense operating in overdrive. He'd spent years learning to throttle down that engine, to keep it from overheating and burning out mid-race. He could let the nanobots handle that now. Was that an upgrade? Was there a long-term price for having a literal off switch for some parts of his brain? *Problem for another day*, he thought.

The switch flipped, and Ben fired off half a dozen timed charges into the mrill troop ship, onto two of the hovering weapons platforms, and onto the ground near the advancing mrill infantry. Two of them looked down at the glob of explosive gel and tried to warn their fellow troops just as the bombs exploded. All six explosives detonated simultaneously, tearing apart the troops and vehicles.

Ben was already moving, engaging his high-tech camouflage, an invisible wraith flitting through the fiery night. A dozen mrill turned to fire at the apparent source of the explosives, but he was already gone. He fired as he ran around their right side, picking off several more. Ben disappeared behind the burning wreckage of the drop ship and spotted a cluster of marines huddled behind the corner of a building. He could "see" the stream of radio signals pouring forth from their comms devices, and mentally hacked into them. Half a dozen more tanks rumbled into the intersection behind Ben, firing as they moved, doing some damage to the distracted mrill. As the mrill returned fire, the Apaches that Ben had sensed earlier roared into view, rockets belching out of their weapons pods as their rotors sent up a riot of smoke, dust, and glowing embers. The mrill were already regrouping, and Ben could sense the airborne drones coming back for a second attack run. He was almost to the group of marines.

"This is Lieutenant Ben Shepherd. I'm coming up at your three o'clock position. You're going to see me in about two seconds. Do not shoot me."

The bewildered soldiers managed to hold their fire as Ben appeared out of thin air, skidding to a halt in front of them. He spotted the three upward chevrons on the sleeves of one of the men and glanced at his name patch.

"Sergeant Daniels, is this your squad?"

They were all sweaty, confused, and nervous, but the sergeant relaxed a bit as he noticed Ben's gray skin and realized who he was.

"Yes, sir. What's left of it. I've lost one fire team and most of a second. We're about to engage the enemy."

Ben glanced back, saw the mrill moving away from his location.

"No, you're not," Ben said. "I'm about to engage the enemy, and you're going to wait for my signal."

Ben didn't need his heightened senses to read the anger on the soldiers' faces.

"Don't worry, marines. You'll get your shot in a minute. I just want to give you the opportunity to make it count."

Ben noticed a claymore bag slung over the shoulder of a young Lance Corporal.

"Any left?" Ben said, gesturing at the bag.

The marine smiled.

"Been waiting all day to use these, sir," he said, handing over the bag.

Ben lifted the strap over his head.

"When you hear these go up, attack their flank."

"Where will you be?" Sergeant Daniels asked.

"I'll be firing from their three o'clock position. When these babies start cooking, you come running."

The marines nodded, eager to join the fight.

"It doesn't take these guys long to regroup, so you'll only have a few seconds to take advantage of their confusion. If for whatever reason the claymores don't detonate, rally point is . . ." Ben consulted his internal map. "Northwest corner of Georgia Street and Bryant Avenue. Meet there and we'll try again. These assholes are going for the cannon near the mall. If they destroy it, it gives them an open highway to send in their full ground assault and establish a beachhead. We're not going to let that happen."

Ben stood to leave. He tried not to be crushed by the weight of the responsibility he had just assumed. Whatever happened to these men, it would be under his orders. They knew who he was and they trusted him to see a path forward that they couldn't. Ben knew that wasn't the case. He was acting on his best instincts, but had no guarantees. He saw the battlefield with only a bit more clarity than they did. Even Ben's augmented senses could only see so deeply though the smoke and the fire and the noise. His electronic sensors strained for data, but the jamming signal that he, Eddie, and Nick were broadcasting was straining the capabilities of their own internal computers. Ben knew there were cameras scattered in parking garages, storefronts, police and military vehicles all around him.

Normally, he could have tapped into those cameras with just a thought and looked at the entire city at once through their glass eyes. But his machines were maxed out. For all he knew, he was sending these men straight to their deaths. In fact, that was very likely the case. His plan gave them a better chance than the suicidal frontal charge they'd been on the verge of attempting. But in the end, it was war.

Ben lifted his weapon, activated his cloaking, and advanced into the chaos.

26

"Mr. President, we have to at least consider it."

Lockerman glanced up from the thin paper folder he'd been scanning. All his briefing documents had gotten thinner over the last couple weeks. Crises were developing too rapidly for his staff to prepare extensive background materials. Decisions were being made on the fly, with minimal data. His aides and generals were tormented at the lack of paperwork and protocol, but Lockerman was quietly relieved. The endless summaries and briefs generally boiled down to little more than he could have gleaned from the news, but with endless caveats and ass-covering. Most decisions didn't get easier past a certain data threshold. On the contrary, they only got harder, as the "on the one hand, on the other" debates progressed to the point where only an octopus could have tracked all the equivocating.

That wasn't to say the choice in front of him was easy. Just simple. And Lockerman had made up his mind as soon as he understood the choice. He decided to let his team hash it out a bit more before he spoke. They were all tense and nervous, jittery about the combat playing out on the TV screens and satellite feeds that they were largely helpless to influence.

Hawthorne, Lockerman's science adviser, was fed up.

"John, it's stupid and pointless," she said, not bothering to hide her disdain. "First, a nuclear strike will kill hundreds of thousands of people on the ground. Good job on that. Second, you'll blow up our own surface-to-space weapon, giving the mrill a green light to send along another wave. All your fucking nuke will do is give them a nice, flat parking lot to land on."

John Hall, the secretary of defense, leaned forward on the conference room table.

"Sir, we might already have lost DC. And if the mrill seize control of the cannon and start targeting our satellites and ships in space, it will be worse than if we simply destroyed it."

Lockerman waved his hand to indicate he was ready to end the debate.

"How far are the B-2s from DC?"

Hall tapped an app on his tablet, bringing a display up on the massive monitors on the wall of the conference room. A dozen blue dots were moving across the western portion of West Virginia, headed toward DC.

"Fifteen minutes, Mr. President," Hall said. "Ten of the planes have a conventional load of CBU-87 and CBU-97 cluster bombs, as well as AGM-158 cruise missiles. The other two are armed with low-yield B83 nuclear bombs."

"No sign that the mrill have spotted the bombers?"

"Not that we can see, sir. Lieutenant Shepherd's men have almost all the spacecrafts engaged in space, and the handful in the atmosphere are concentrating on providing ground support for the infantry they've landed in the area. I don't know how long we have, but for now the B-2s seem to be avoiding detection."

There were nine bombers still parked at Whiteman Air Force Base in Missouri—fueled, armed, and ready to launch within seconds. Lockerman had ordered them to remain prepped. As critical as the situation was in DC, they had to keep something in reserve should the mrill break through their orbital defenses elsewhere. Likewise, there were ground troops and fighter jets stationed across the country, and he didn't want to flood the capital with those assets unless it was absolutely necessary. At the same time, losing DC could very well be the single opening the mrill needed to win the entire war. Let them squeeze through one door and the entire house might be lost. In that case, holding those troops and weapons in reserve could end up being the final act of the last American president. Lockerman had replayed the debate in his head a dozen times. It had been a long time since an American president had to seriously contemplate defending his home turf from a hostile enemy.

"Hold the nuclear-equipped B-2s, but keep them on station," Lockerman said. "We're proceeding with the conventional strike. Do we have a clear target on the ground?"

Hall swallowed his disagreement.

"Semi-clear, Mr. President. The mrill have destroyed all our surveillance satellites, so we're improvising. We're getting visual feeds from traffic and security cameras on the streets in DC, and our reconnaissance team is mapping those feeds to a map overlay to send strike coordinates to the pilots. We have a decent strike map, but I think we're only going to get one pass at this, Mr. President. Once our bombers reveal themselves, we expect the mrill response to be severe."

"You don't expect the bombers to survive the attack?" Lockerman asked.

Hall paused. "Sir, I do not."

Lockerman nodded. He glanced around the other members of his team at the table. No one disagreed with Hall's assessment. "I understand. I want to talk to them."

"Mr. President?"

"You said they've still got 15 minutes to target? I want to speak to them."

"Yes, sir."

While Hall spoke to a pair of technicians in the room, Jeff Goldman, Lockerman's national security adviser, leaned close to the president.

"Mr. President, we'll be securing your transmission as thoroughly as possible. But the fact is you will be broadcasting a radio signal, and there could be a security risk. I doubt those bombers are going to go unnoticed for much longer, and the mrill might trace the transmission back to here."

"Is that even possible?"

"Not with any technology on this planet, sir, but . . ." Goldman trailed off.

Lockerman thought for a moment.

"Do your best. I have a feeling this is going to be over soon, anyway. We either hold them off or they break through and everything changes."

One of the technicians approached Lockerman.

"It's ready, Mr. President. We're patched in to all the pilots. Just tap the 'unmute' button on the speakerphone when you're ready."

Lockerman took a deep breath.

•

Some 50,000 feet over the West Virginia countryside, the B-2 bombers cruised through the night. The V-winged aircrafts were virtually undetectable to any man-made technology. The black planes embraced the black sky, nearly as invisible to the naked eye as they were to radar. Thanks to some of the technology provided by the brin, engineers had made additional modifications to the aircraft, improving their stealth capabilities. No one knew for sure how effective the upgrades would be. All the crews knew they could be destroyed at any moment by the almost supernatural collection of enemy spacecraft and ground weaponry arrayed against them. On top of that, their mission was to bomb their own country, their capital, against the first enemy army to successfully land in DC since the War of 1812. The pilots flew in silence, running through their checklists, trying not to think about their target or their odds of survival.

Major Stephanie Williams of the 393rd squadron, 509th Bomb Wing, pilot of the B-2 *Spirit of Missouri*, glanced over at her mission commander, 1st Lieutenant Shawn Jones, as the radio announced the commander in chief wanted to talk to them. His anxiety and exasperation were easily visible in the green glow of the instrument panels. Jones said nothing, but Williams sighed. Damn politicians always loved to talk when it was time to act.

"Stand by for POTUS."

The radio crackled.

"Airmen, I'll be brief, since I know I'm probably the last person you want to hear from right now. I understand that your mission briefing indicated a high probability that this mission will not be survivable, and it's hard for me put into words my admiration for your courage. You are the best of America, and we—I—do not send you on this mission lightly. It is vital."

Ahead through the cockpit window Williams could see the faint orange glow of the capital on fire.

"We cannot allow a single breach in our defenses," Lockerman continued. "And we're going to need you to do this again. Your aircraft might be obsolete after tonight, but you're not. No matter what happens, you are ordered to return home. This is not a suicide mission. I expect to welcome all of you back. Okay, that's it. Godspeed and happy hunting."

The radio went silent again. They flew in silence for a moment.

"I ever tell you about my first job?" Williams said. Jones, a small smile curling one corner of his mouth, shook his head.

"Sophomore year of high school," Williams said, shifting in her seat and glancing at the instrument panel, the orange glow in the distance growing brighter and closer. "I applied to work at McDonald's. I loved cheeseburgers and had horrible taste. Anyway, I send in my application, and the manager schedules an interview. I come in, and we're sitting in those hard plastic chairs, and I'm all excited because I'm imagining all the free burgers and fries I can eat."

Jones chuckled.

"But I'm nervous as hell, too, because it's my first job, so I tell him what a responsible babysitter I was, and he's just sitting there nodding and writing with this stubby pencil, and every time he nods and bends over to write something, I notice his toupee is slipping a little farther down his head. He doesn't notice it, and I'm worried the damn thing is going to plop right down on the table. Quarter Pounder with hair. Finally, he wraps it up, doesn't give me a clue how the interview went, but says they've got a bunch of other candidates and he'll call me back. Okay. I go home, and next day, no call. So I call him, get voicemail, leave a message, nothing. This goes on for a week."

"You waited a week to hear about a job at McDonald's?" Jones asked.

"Shut up and let me finish. So, my parents think I blew the interview. *I* think I blew the interview. I'm bummed out. I mean, who blows an interview to work the deep fryer at fucking McDonald's, right? A syphilitic monkey with a criminal record could get that gig. My dreams of free apple pies are toast. But two weeks later, I get a letter from the manager. I tear it open, and you know what it says?"

"Mayor McCheese didn't like the cut of your jib?"

"I'm fired."

Jones snorted into his face mask.

"I shit you not," Williams said. "They hired me without telling me, held orientation and my first day on the job without telling me, and then fired me without telling me."

"That's the most inspirational speech I've ever heard," Jones said.

"Up yours. The point is, at least this time we know what the boss man wants us to do before it's time to do it."

"Your parents pissed you screwed up that job?" Jones asked.

"Nah, I just got a job at the Burger King instead," Williams said with a laugh. "I was a chubby kid."

The navigation system beeped to indicate the bombers were crossing into the combat zone. Williams pushed a button on the console marked PEN, for penetration. The few antennas protruding from the B-2's sleek skin retracted, external communication links were shut off to minimize electronic detection, and the aircraft was now in full stealth mode. She knew the other pilots in her formation were doing the same. She checked the fuel gauge again. The B-2 could easily make the round trip from Missouri to DC and back without needing to refuel, but it was a reflex born of training and habit she could no more control than she could the beating of her heart. Jones was running through weapons diagnostics, equally obedient to his years of simulator repetitions and live-fire combat runs. You checked and checked and checked so you could count on the machine to perform when you no longer had time to check.

"Okay," she said. "Let's go blow up Washington."

27

Eddie pulverized a mrill ship with a barrage from his cannon and the white-hot debris sprayed another mrill ship unfortunate enough to cross its path at that moment.

"Two for the price of one," Eddie whooped.

"Easy there, Walmart shoppers," Nick replied. "We've still got plenty of crazy deals inbound."

They were holding the mrill at a standstill. They were plugging the gap over DC whenever dropships or fighters tried to sneak through, and the other satellites and ground installations were holding up. Russia so far was equally protected. The mrill had apparently not counted on the extent of the human defensive systems as they repeatedly plunged toward the planet, only to be destroyed by a barrage of intersecting energy beams. They were still buzzing like a swarm of enraged bees, but were now holding back for the most part, out of range, only sending in the occasional attacker to probe Earth's defenses.

"I don't like it," Nick said. "It's like they're waiting for something."

The mrill ships were weaving in what looked like a random formation. Eddie could sense Nick's tension across their telepathic link. The mesmerizing movement was almost hypnotic. Eddie wasn't sure what to do. Charge? Just as he was about to wade in, the mrill ships spat out clusters of what looked like small gray rocks. The enemy still couldn't communicate with each other thanks to the jamming signal, but apparently this was something they'd planned in advance. Nick and Eddie scanned the projectiles. Each nondescript lump was a delivery vehicle for the same sort of voracious nanomachines that had devoured Saint Petersburg. Only instead of one such warhead, Nick and Eddie were facing about fifty.

"Shit, they're too small for the satellites. They don't see them," Nick said.

"Can we take them out individually?" Eddie asked.

"Take them out and hold off the other ships? I don't know." Nick shot back. "I think we have to fight fire with fire. Time to let old painless out of the bag."

Nick could sense Eddie's fierce grin.

"Mind if I do the honors?" he asked.

"By all means," Nick said. "I've got your six."

Eddie toggled open the missile bay on his ship, an addition that had not been part of the original brin specifications. He'd argued that they might need some brute force eventually, and the engineers had eventually worked out a way to make that happen. Inside the belly of his ship, a missile pod rotated out and Eddie fired off a modified, nuclear-tipped BGM-109A Tomahawk missile. The cruise missile's solid-fuel rocket booster kicked in and the weapon streaked through the void toward the projectiles. Even moving at roughly 1,000 kilometers per hour, the missile seemed to be barely inching across the 200-kilometer gap between defenders and attackers. The mrill could see the slow-moving missile, and their attack ships and larger cruisers maneuvered into position to fire their energy weapons at it before it could reach their wall of nano bombs. Just as they unloaded, though, just as the cascade of antimatter and ion streams spread out across the heavens, Eddie activated the crude cut drive on the missile and said a silent prayer.

His Saint Michael the Archangel pendant clinked softly as he banked hard to dodge the wayward mrill bolts. The medallion was nicked and scratched. It had been dragged over and through mountains, deserts, and oceans. It had been bloodied, dirtied, and banged up on almost every continent on Earth.

The pendant had been a gift from Father Kowalski, the parish priest at St. Gabriel's Church in Prairie du Chien, the small Wisconsin town nestled along the Mississippi River on the Iowa border where Eddie had grown up. He'd been an altar boy at the old limestone and stained-glass church, which dated to 1839. "Almost as old as I am," the priest liked to say with a cackle to every first-time parishioner.

The tour of duty as altar boy definitely hadn't been Eddie's idea. His parents had "volunteered" him to the crusty padre his senior year after a schoolyard fight over a winking girl named Maria. The other boy, Frank

Mintner, ended up spitting out a cracked, bloody tooth and Eddie was packed off to find God. Eddie had shown up on a Saturday in late September at the doorway of the double-towered church. It was unseasonably hot, and the face that greeted him when the door opened had been equally grumpy, if considerably more wrinkled. The first thing Father Kowalski had made the kid do was mop the church floor. It was cool and dark inside the building, the illuminated windows and exposed ceiling trusses giving an air not of gloom, but of serenity. Eddie hadn't really grasped those concepts at the time. It was just a quiet, soothing place, and his anger started to seep away.

When he had finished nearly two hours after he started, had cleaned and emptied his bucket and stowed his mop in the closet in the small sacristy behind the altar, Eddie had found the priest looking down on him quietly from the choir loft at the back of the church. The old man disappeared, and Eddie heard his heavy feet clumping down the stairs.

"Got another job for you," he growled when he emerged from the small stairway.

Before Eddie could fire off a retort, the priest tossed a silver key to the boy.

"You want me to wash your car?" Eddie said.

"Not quite."

Eddie followed the priest out to a small garage behind the rectory. Father Kowalski lifted up the rusty, squeaking door, and Eddie expected to see a small, drab hatchback. Instead, a gleaming blue convertible '67 Mustang crouched in the space. It was so clean and polished it almost glowed.

"I wash it myself," the priest said, watching Eddie closely. "What I need, according to my eye doctor, is a driver. Think you can handle that?"

Thirty minutes later they were doing 75 down Highway 18, heading west, crossing the river, wind whipping Eddie's thick mop of hair and the priest's gray fringe, both of them laughing and cackling.

Several months later, the day after his high school graduation, Eddie came to see the old man for the last time, not sure what to say even as he knocked on the door of his small rectory. He shuffled his feet as he heard the heavy footsteps approaching the door. Kowalski opened the door and looked Eddie over. Eddie didn't know what to say, but the old man seemed to have been preparing for this moment.

"Don't go applying to the seminary. They'll kick your trouble-making keister out before you've had time to unpack your underwear. Anyway, I believe the Lord has a different purpose for you. I don't know what that is, but I have something to help guide you on the journey."

The priest handed him a small black cardboard box. Eddie opened it, spotted the chain, and assumed it was a pendant of Saint Gabriel the Archangel, the namesake of the parish. God's messenger. He flipped the medallion over and was surprised to see Saint Michael the Archangel. God's warrior.

"Probably the closest thing to sacrilege an old coot like me can get up to," said Father Kowalski, his eyes gleaming beneath his bushy brows. "But this fellow seemed more appropriate for a boisterous soul like yours. Go do something useful with all that energy. Okay, get out of here, and don't forget your rosary, you hooligan. I'll be seeing your parents here on Sunday."

Years later, sweating through his SEAL training, Eddie realized Father Kowalski must have seen deeper into Eddie's soul than he ever had. He'd recognized an unusual spirit who needed both rigid structure and wild freedom to thrive. The old man, who had passed away before Eddie enlisted, probably wouldn't have been surprised at all by the young man's career.

Although I'd bet 50 bucks he didn't see this chapter coming. An enemy energy beam sizzled past his cockpit.

Eddie wondered briefly if the mrill or the brin had any kind of religion; if any of the creatures out there were flying with their own pendants tucked next to their skin, beseeching their gods for victory.

Pray harder. The command floated through Eddie's mind, a message from Nick, who had sensed Eddie's memories as if they were his own. *And ask Him to keep an eye on that missile.*

Bert Goldberg, the rotund engineer with the perpetually sweaty brow, had made it clear that the missile was going to be far from a precision machine. He and his team had rigged up what they were pretty sure was a functional equivalent of the star drives the mrill and brin used to jump across interstellar distances without being shackled by the propulsion constraints of traditional physics.

"The problem with traveling at speeds higher than five or six percent of the speed of light," Goldberg had said, ignoring Eddie's befuddled look, "is that your mass starts to increase to an unmanageable level."

He cupped his hands together and then pulled them apart slowly, like a balloon being inflated.

"And the more force you apply to try to continue accelerating, the greater your mass becomes, requiring more force, and eventually you get stuck in this loop. Then, before you know it, you're using more energy than is contained in the entire galaxy just to accelerate by the smallest amount. And even if you could somehow get a ship moving at the speed of light, that doesn't do you much good in a universe where stars are dozens or hundreds of light years away. Then you've got the relativistic effects of time dilation, where events for the lightspeed traveler would seem to occur at normal rates, but much more time would have passed for everyone else."

Eddie had made a "hurry up" spinning motion with his index finger.

"Okay, look, never mind. Just remember that lightspeed travel is bunk for anything but visible light and radio waves. If you're going to be traveling long distances, you need something else. That's what the cut drive does. Even our best eggheads aren't sure how it works, but it probably opens some type of artificial wormhole . . . a tunnel between two different points in space." Goldberg made two circles with the thumb and index finger on each of his hands, holding them a foot apart and then bringing them together. "And you pass through instantly from your point of origin to your destination. It's really cool. Captain Kirk never had something this bad-ass. Unfortunately, we don't have a very good handle yet on how to pinpoint the arrival location."

Goldberg had sighed and looked at the circle he'd formed with his right hand, still suspended in the air. "We can get within shouting distance. But if you fire off this missile with a programmed arrival portal . . . well, you're looking at about a 75 percent confidence level that it will pop out within 50 miles of your intended target. Probably good enough for government work."

Out in space, Eddie held his breath as the missile disappeared and prayed again that 50 miles was close enough. For the briefest of moments, the missile's electronic signature disappeared from Eddie's internal sensors. *What the hell is actually inside that wormhole—*

The thought wasn't even fully formed before the missile reappeared on his scanners, barely two miles from the oncoming cluster of nano warheads. The proximity detectors on the mrill bombs sensed the missile and dispersed their cargo to consume it, but it was already too late. Eddie gave the mental command to detonate, and the encrypted signal traveled across the gap in an instant. The missile became a star. A perfectly symmetrical sphere of light bloomed outward, completely unlike the mushroom cloud Eddie associated with nuclear explosions from every video they'd ever seen, as the lack of gravity and ground resistance sent the fury of light and energy in every direction at once. The nano devices were consumed in fire, obliterated before the mrill had time to attempt any kind of evasion. The mrill fighters and drop ships frantically accelerated away from the growing fireball, but almost half were incinerated.

"Yeah, welcome to the barbecue," Nick said. "Hope you bastards like your meat well done."

The remaining mrill pulled back, waiting, widely dispersed against a second such attack. Nick and Eddie waited too, not sure what to expect next. The mrill were out of range of all their weapons but the cut-equipped nukes.

Nick prepared to fire his nuke—he and Eddie only had one each—but Eddie stopped him with a mental request. They'd lost the element of surprise, and the mrill were spread far enough apart that a single nuke couldn't take them all out. If they fired another barrage of nano warheads, Eddie wasn't sure they could take them all out individually. They might need that last nuke. And the mrill weren't retreating. They seemed to be regrouping, preparing . . . *but for what?* Nick thought.

Something else. Something we haven't seen yet, Eddie replied.

Then a cut portal opened—a portal that seemed as big as the moon, directly behind the remnants of the mrill fleet. It seemed to be full of all colors and none, a brilliant darkness spinning in every direction. At the other end of this vortex, at the other end of the galaxy, they could see a planet and a ship. The planet was a dusty green. The ship was immense and soon blotted out the planet as it moved through the opening. The ship was far larger than all the other mrill vessels combined, easily a kilometer tall and just as wide. The main structure was rectangular and at the stern, four massive arms branched out perpendicularly—forming a cross. Jagged structures pointed forward from each arm of the cross, running parallel to the ship. The furious dance of color and darkness undulated across its surface briefly. Then it was through. The doorway closed and the ship opened up, vomiting thousands of mrill attack ships that streamed toward the two men and their depleted forces.

Well, crap.

28

en planted the last of his claymore mines in a jumble of rubble in the middle of the street and covered them with loose dirt and crumbled concrete. The chatter of machine-gun fire echoed everywhere, and tracers seemed to tap out endless Morse code across the sky. It was still night, but the air was filled with a dirty orange hue from the fires and explosions. Missiles and rockets from the human defenders streaked out from between burning buildings, few of which found their targets. The mrill were organized, thorough, and merciless. Here on the ground, shoulder to shoulder, their lack of electronic communication was less of a hurdle, as they could turn and talk to each other or simply point to targets. Every tank and helicopter that got too close was destroyed.

The US military was now trying to engage the enemy from farther off, but the thick cluster of buildings made it difficult to target the mrill, and most of their ordnance was crashing into apartments, offices, and parking lots. The only battle mankind was winning right now was against its own creations.

Ben arrived at the northeast corner of Logan Circle, barely a kilometer from the White House lawn. Two separate mrill detachments were moving southwest down Vermont Avenue and Rhode Island Avenue, inadvertently converging on his location.

He was safe for the moment, though, and ordered his ragged squad to take cover behind a white duplex along the southwest edge of the Circle. They were alive. Many others weren't. Ben estimated military and civilian dead and wounded numbered somewhere close to 10,000, with the tally ticking up like digits on a gas pump. Most of those casualties were fatalities. The mrill didn't leave many wounded.

Thousands of civilians were hunkered down all around him. He could sense them, even if he couldn't see them. They were frantically trying to make calls and send texts on the overloaded network. And the body heat generated by their fear stood out clearly through the walls of their apartments and homes. The mrill knew they were there. They didn't target the civilians specifically, but they bulldozed any building in their way, cutting jagged tunnels through concrete and steel. Dead bodies and screaming people tumbled out of the wreckage.

It drove Ben nearly insane not to leap to their defense, but he couldn't risk it. Couldn't stand it. A block and a half away, dozens of refugees were packed in the Hotel Helix, too terrified to make a run. The building was directly in the path of the advancing mrill. It was as good a spot as any for the next ambush. One claymore and seven marines wouldn't be enough to stop the mrill, but maybe it would slow them down long enough for a nearby squad to clear the hotel. The old weight was compressing his chest. It felt harder to breathe. He knew he wasn't choking. Still felt like it, though, the invisible weight of the dead and soon-to-die lying across his throat.

He was running back to take cover with the marines when his sensors detected the incoming B-2s. He smiled, and the invisible vise eased just a bit. Maybe this would be enough.

Ben opened a secure voice channel with the B-2 squadron.

"This is Lieutenant Shepherd. Nice of you boys to show up."

"It ain't just the boys, Lieutenant," a voice drawled back over his internal radio. "Major Stephanie Williams, 509th Bomb Wing, reporting for asskicking duty. We'll review your gender sensitivity training materials later."

Ben laughed despite himself.

"Yes, ma'am. Looking forward to it. In the meantime, I've accessed your targeting systems and you should see markers indicated on your screens. If you would ever so kindly be disposed to bomb the ever-loving shit out of those positions, us leathernecks and frogmen would be much obliged."

"I'm not going to ask how you just bypassed a dozen security systems to hack into our targeting and comms systems. You can explain that one after you've been socially enlightened. In the meantime, ETA is two minutes. Activate your transponders so we can see your team and avoid friendly fire."

"Negative on that front, I'm afraid," Ben said. "The mrill might see those signals and would be on us in two seconds. This channel is secure, but the transponders are not. I'm jamming most of their comms, but just barely. You do what you have to do, and we'll make sure to not be in the way."

"I hope so, Lieutenant. We brought the big iron, and I'd damn sure regret it if we couldn't bring you home in one piece for your political reeducation."

"That makes two of us, Major. Good luck."

"You too, caveman. See you on the other side."

Ben looked up at Sergeant Daniels and the seven marines huddled with him. Beyond the duplex loomed another building.

"Change of plans," he said. "We've got a flight of B-2s inbound, ETA one minute forty-five seconds. We've got about sixty mrill foot soldiers and combat robots headed our way, one claymore planted in the circle. No partridge in a pear tree, but improvise, adapt, and overcome, oorah?"

"Oorah."

Most of the exhausted, grimy foot soldiers managed to smile, slightly refreshed at hearing their traditional battle cry. They were on the edge of exhaustion but still in one piece. Still in the fight.

"We have to give those bombers as much cover as we can before they strike," Ben said. "The mrill haven't detected them yet, and I suspect that's because their air cover has been blown to hell and I'm still able to keep most of their sensors jammed. Once those bombers are within line of sight, I wouldn't be surprised if the mrill ground units spot them, stealth or no stealth. So we're going to take positions on the rooftops overlooking the circle. Now here's the tricky part."

"Shit," one of the marines let slip out.

"Yeah, I know. We can't fire and give away our positions too soon. I'll be passively monitoring their comms channels, and if I get a hint that they've detected the bombers you'll get my signal. Gotta be Johnny on the spot. Engage for no more than 10 seconds, fast-rope off your building, and regroup at Thomas Circle two blocks southwest down Vermont. Nobody plays hero. We might need to do this a couple times. Got it? Go."

Four marines darted in through the back of the building they were taking cover against on the west side of Vermont and headed up the stairs. Daniels and the other three sprinted across the street to the east side and kicked in the door of an office. Ben reactivated his cloaking technology and waited. He wasn't sure why the mrill weren't using their own cloaking tech. He suspected the robots were seen as expendable and didn't have the capability, while the mrill soldiers simply didn't see the need. While Ben had done some damage, their force was still largely intact, and the human weapons they'd encountered thus far posed almost no threat. The hulks of smoking tanks scattered across the streets behind them were testament enough to that.

Ben thought they kept themselves visible for the psychological edge as well. Seeing enemy troops march down the streets of your capital was intimidating. *If that's why they're staying visible, then their psychology maybe isn't so different from ours.* If so, if they understood fear, then maybe they were susceptible to it, too. Ben sent a quick mental note to Nick and Eddie, a piece of intel that might prove helpful in this battle or a future one, if they lived to see it.

Ben shouldered his rifle, mentally counting down to the arrival of the B-2s. *Just a few more seconds.* A new signal popped up on his internal sensors. An army force was approaching the circle from P Street to the west. They were about to stumble right into the bombers' target zone.

It appeared to be an entire infantry company, some 200 soldiers in total, going by the electromagnetic froth swirling around them like an invisible dust cloud. He glanced back to the Circle, spotting the vanguard of mrill forces moving into the clearing from Vermont and Rhode Island Avenues. The unit was marching into a slaughter from above and below.

It looked like three rifle platoons up front and a heavy weapons platoon in the rear, armed with powerful recoilless rifles. The human fighters poured into the circle and the mrill opened fire. A sizable force, but in the wrong place at the wrong time. Streaks of energy screamed across the once-tranquil park, tearing apart man and machine. The soldiers returned fire, the big recoilless guns thundering over the heads of the infantry, who darted from cover to cover, firing their rifles. None of it was having much effect against the responsive, adaptable mrill armor. Ben itched to engage but knew the B-2s were only moments away from striking. He needed the mrill bunched up here. If he signaled to the company to retreat, it would give away his position. He raged as he watched men die, some in agony, others instantly. He felt the nanobots trying to take over his senses, to cool his fury and transform him into the cold machine he needed to be. He resisted.

His anger rose in him like magma, a caldera filling up that would annihilate everything around it. His mind refused to relinquish his body to his alien companions. Ben hated them, too. All of these creatures that had come to this planet, invaders and would-be saviors alike, had brought only death.

The bombers overhead began dropping their bombs, their payload plummeting to the ground. Ben finally surrendered to the pestering machines in his body. Hatred would have to wait. As he did, he squeezed the remote trigger for the claymore mine planted across the circle, behind the mrill who had marched right past the hidden and inert lump of metal. The mine roared and hurled a wall of energy and shrapnel at the aliens, knocking them off their feet. At the same time, Ben opened fire, as did the marines on the rooftops a moment later. The army infantry troops who could still stand and fight did the same, and the mrill were momentarily stunned.

It wouldn't last long. While his rifle was capable of hurting and killing the mrill, most of the human weapons were not. One of the marines on the roof was pumping explosive rounds from his grenade launcher, and that weapon at least had some effect on the alien force. But the standard-issue M4 carbines might as well have been BB guns and slingshots against the armored, reactive skin of the mrill and the thick shielding of their mobile cannons. The mrill were already regrouping.

Then the bombs began to hit.

29

"This is one hell of a weird war, John."

"Mr. President?"

"The whole world is at war, and we've basically got three guys fighting it for us. If we make it through this battle, we need to get more troops on the front line. Those guys are going to be overwhelmed sooner rather than later."

Hall tried to keep a blank face. He'd never been comfortable with the "super soldier" program, as everyone had taken to calling it, like it was some kind of damn comic book. It trivialized a life-and-death situation. Worse, he resented how Shepherd and his men were operating outside the normal chain of command. These guys weren't really soldiers in the traditional sense, with superior officers and specific orders. Technically, they answered directly to the president. In truth, though, they were acting on their own out there. Special operations troops were always something of a wild card. You gave them a mission objective and left it up to them to improvise in the field and make it happen. Shepherd, Dworsky, and Parson were beyond even that loose chain of command, operating almost as an independent army. Invincible mercenaries, not too put too fine a point to it. How did you control that? How did you, if necessary, defend against that?

"Cat got your tongue, John?" Lockerman asked.

Hawthorne ignored the conversation as she cycled through various video feeds from Washington, DC, on her laptop.

Hall sighed. He did trust the president, even if he didn't always agree with him.

"No, Mr. President. And you're right, this is the damn strangest war I've ever been part of. I just hope I live to see the next one."

"I . . ."

A display on the president's touchscreen monitor on his desk flashed red and beeped.

"Yes?"

A dozen Secret Service agents barged into the room. They hadn't drawn their weapons, but their faces were strained.

"Mr. President, we must evacuate to the bunker. There's an incoming threat."

Lockerman scooped up his tablet, motioned to Hawthorne, Hall, and the rest of his skeleton staff to follow, and moved out the door. A squad of marines stationed outside the room went with them. They'd been working in the main NORAD facilities in Cheyenne Mountain. Everyone was more comfortable there, even if none of them talked about it. The mountain squatted over you, but the road out was straight ahead. If they opened all the blast doors, you could even see a bit of sunlight at the end of the tunnel. Down below, the feeling of living in your own tomb was overwhelming. Hall hated it down there. Everyone did.

But at this moment, the Secret Service agents didn't care about anyone's anxieties. They hustled everyone toward the already-opened granite elevator. Lockerman turned to speak to Hall, but at that moment, one of the agents pressed his finger against his ear, listened for a moment, and yelled "Move!"

The agents all but lifted Lockerman from his feet and started running for the open elevator. Hall and the rest of the startled entourage of a dozen or so hustled to keep up. The marines moved like a ballet troop in perfect coordination, sweeping every corner with their weapons, knowing where each teammate was and would be without needing to look or speak. Only a few key cabinet members and advisers were there, so the mrill couldn't eliminate the government with a single strike. This entourage was expendable in the eyes of the Secret Service. Slip out of this protective bubble and you were on your own.

The last few flustered staff members tumbled into the elevator as it started to descend, before the granite door had even begun to close.

A gargantuan explosion rocked the mountain and a storm of light and noise hurtled down the long entrance tunnel from the outside. Flames licked the elevator entrance just as the stone and steel barrier shut with a hiss. The mountain continued to shake from a series of smaller impacts. The lights flickered and a cloud of dust drifted down from the receding ceiling above, but the lights steadied themselves and the elevator kept moving. A series of steel firewalls closed overhead as the platform clanked deeper into the heart of the mountain. Clanging alarms and pulsing yellow lights throbbed in the enclosed space. The elevator passengers could do nothing but huddle as the machinery carried them down.

Hall knew there were several defensive cannons hidden in camouflaged positions around the mountain that weren't wired into the rest of the surface-to-space batteries. They were there only if the mountain itself came under attack. Keep this place as inconspicuous as possible. *So much for that.* He could feel these ion cannons opening up now, a deep hum and then a receding vibration, less cataclysmic than the mrill artillery raining down from the sky.

The elevator reached the bottom of the shaft. At that moment, the most violent explosion yet hammered the mountain. It was strong enough to tumble most of the people in the elevator off their feet like bowling pins. One of the agents was shouting into the mic in his sleeve, trying to contact anyone on the upper levels. There was no response. Hall knew it had all been destroyed, but the agent persisted. The elevator door slid open and the agents popped out with Lockerman in a protective bubble. The marines, in their bulky gear, exited with the same effortless grace as before while the rest of the group struggled to keep up. The elevator doors were rumbling shut as another explosion rocked the facility while car-sized boulders and twisted knots of steel tumbled down the elevator shaft as the door closed for the last time.

The lights on the lower level ran off a separate power supply and were holding steady. The group moved into the conference room, with the marines setting up a defensive position outside. Hall walked into the adjoining communications room to get an update.

Lockerman plopped down in a chair and tried to collect his thoughts.

He hadn't expected this attack. How had the mrill found them? His 30-second call to the B-2 pilots? Something else? Some*one* else? He shook his head. *Worry about that later.*

"Miranda, take as many of the staff as you can to the evac shuttle and get to the airfield," Lockerman said.

"What? No. I . . ."

"That's an order. There's not enough room for everyone to go in one trip. And you're a civilian, not a soldier. You're no use here right now. I'm sorry, but you need to get going . . . and send the shuttle back as soon as you're there."

She snapped her mouth shut and left. Lockerman knew she was pissed, but also know that he was right, or she'd have kept arguing.

Lockerman tapped open the video conferencing app on his tablet. The drawn, exhausted faces of the Joint Chiefs of Staff popped up on the screen, and they all let out a collective sigh upon seeing his face.

"Mr. President, thank God," said General David Winston, the chairman of the JCS. "What's happening there?"

"General, I was hoping you'd be able to tell me," Lockerman replied. "Give me a status report on DC."

As they rattled off what they knew, another explosion rocked the mountain. The tremor was less violent down below, but unsettling nonetheless. Lockerman opened another app with a video feed of the exterior of the mountain complex. There were nine cameras positioned around the main entrance, as well as at concealed locations around the property. The defensive guns were placed on the east and west slopes. The western gun was intact and firing constantly, trying to track the attacking ships. Lockerman switched to a camera view from the main parking lot, including a view of the energy cannon. Maybe the cannon could take out the attackers, if there weren't too many of them. The view switched just in time to show a dozen mrill ships swoop in and obliterate the overmatched weapon. The facility, even hundreds of feet below the surface, shook again. Lockerman glanced at a bottle of water on the table and watched it ripple and vibrate.

"We're not safe here either," he said. "We have to leave."

At that moment, Hall hurried back in from the comms room, a pinched look on his face. "Time to go. Defenses are compromised. The mrill just sent reinforcements, including some type of interstellar aircraft carrier. We're looking at close to 2,000 mrill ships in orbit and looks like they've pinpointed our location. We're moving to the fallback location."

The Secret Service agents were on the move again. Four of them surrounded Lockerman as he stood and headed for the door, while the rest yanked open closets and scooped up laptops, files, and communications gear. They also donned body armor and grabbed assault rifles and hand grenades out of a separate locker. The mountain continued to tremble, and Lockerman wondered if the mrill plan was to simply turn it to dust. Just then, the explosions stopped. Lockerman opened the video app on his tablet again, but all he saw was static. The mrill assault must have destroyed the cameras, or at least their connections.

"Thirty seconds," one of the agents announced. Normally, the agents would have escorted the president out immediately, but they wanted to be as heavily armed as possible before leaving the room. One man would not be leaving the room. One of the nuclear-defense operators, the last surviving "angel of death," would be locked in a small alcove concealed behind the armory, in front of the last hardwired switch to detonate the six nuclear bombs buried throughout the mountain. Should mrill foot soldiers enter the facility and overwhelm the defenses, it would be this man's job to destroy the complex, kill the invaders, and protect the fleeing president.

While the agents strapped on their vests, weapons, and extra ammo, Lockerman stepped over to the bomb operator, who was gathering a few papers in a folder. Detonation codes. He glanced at the name badge on the young Air Force major's breast pocket. KHALAF.

"What's your first name, son?" Lockerman said.

"Yacoub, sir," the major said without missing a beat as he snapped the folder shut.

Lockerman searched his brain for an appropriate comment. He opened and shut his mouth.

Khalaf stood up.

"No worries, sir. I knew the mission when I signed up. It's an honor, sir." Khalaf saluted, then paused for a moment and extended his hand. Lockerman shook it, still unsure what to say.

"Time to go," one of the agents said. It wasn't a request. Lockerman nodded at Khalaf, who was already turning to leave for the trigger room.

The agents formed a tight perimeter around the president and moved into the hall. The squad of marines formed a second ring around that group, and the few remaining staff members and advisers followed.

One of the Secret Service agents, Jonah Sykes, ran ahead and tapped a panel on the wall, and a palm and iris scanner slid out.

"Mr. President," Sykes said, motioning toward the machine as the rest of the group caught up. Lockerman pressed his hand down against the plate and leaned forward into the iris scanner. The machine beeped and a door slid open, revealing a small electric tram that looked like a shuttle at an airport. Hawthorne and her group had come this way a few minutes earlier and sent the shuttle back. The door to the tram slid open. As the group started to move forward, the stone and steel doors to the elevator were blown open in a deafening explosion.

"Go!" one of the marines yelled as the squad started firing blindly into the dust cloud billowing out of the elevator shaft. They knew they couldn't afford to wait to see their targets. The barrage of fire was immense, including two marines who opened up with M249 machine guns on tripods on the floor. Two more were pumping grenades down the hallway. The mrill were already coming through, the explosives and bullets providing only minimal resistance. They fired their ion rifles as they came, the thin streams vaporizing anything and anyone they touched.

The agents shoved Lockerman into the tram even as several of them were vaporized by the mrill weapon. Most of the civilian aides and advisers were killed, too, their screams cut short as the alien technology ripped their bodies apart, turning them into dust clouds.

"C'mon!" Lockerman yelled to Hall.

Hall turned to leap into the tram, but a mrill rifle found him just as Lockerman extended his hand. For an instant, Hall's entire body glowed a deep red, and Lockerman could actually see the shadow of Hall's skeleton inside his body and the look of utter confusion on his face. Then his entire body, bones and all, vaporized. Lockerman tripped and fell backward in shock and fear, banging his head on the corner of one of the plastic seats. Slick blood coursed down his face and he stumbled, trying to climb to his feet.

The marines who remained targeted their grenades at a support beam and blew it apart, bringing a slab of the ceiling down with a crash. The blockade wouldn't last more than a few seconds. The lead agent ordered Sykes into the tram, and he obeyed without a word of protest despite his urge to stay and fight with his comrades. The door to the tram slid shut and Sykes punched the accelerator just as the first mrill pushed a hole through the rubble and fired. The remaining soldiers and agents opened fire again as the battle disappeared from Sykes's view, the tram speeding away. Sykes hit another button on the control panel and explosive charges began sealing the tunnel behind them, collapsing it with debris, creating an effective blockade. This was a one-way trip.

Lockerman looked over at Sykes, who was covered in sweat and dirt. Lockerman realized the dirt was actually the residue of the ash clouds from the dead. Lockerman realized he must be carrying the same caul, the cremated remains of the men and women who had protected him and saved him. If he was saved. He staggered to his feet and slumped into one of the six seats. Sykes tore off a strip from his tattered shirt, shook off the ash, and held the rag out to the president, nodding at the gash on his head. Lockerman took it and stared at the other empty seats, replaying in his mind the vision of Hall, his longtime aide and close friend, being annihilated just inches from escape.

Sykes was checking his M4 carbine, popping out the magazine to check for dust or other debris that might clog the mechanism. Lockerman felt his head begin to clear a bit. It also hurt like a sonofabitch. Stitches. He'd need stitches. He kept the bit of Sykes's shirt pressed against his wound, sagging in his seat. There was no navigation or guidance system to control in the tiny train. It was completely automated, and the trip would be brief, just over a mile on a gradual incline to a small cave with a concealed airfield extending out and a jet waiting to ferry the president to a safe house—assuming there was any such thing left in the world.

The two agents who had gone ahead should be waiting there with Hawthorne and a small flight crew. Lockerman wasn't sure if they'd have a fighter jet escort. From the scattered info he'd been able to gather in the last 20 minutes, the mrill fleet was now encircling the globe. The nation's entire defense was likely engaged, if not already defeated. The mountain continued to vibrate from the aerial attack. He was waiting for the full implosion of the mountain from the nuclear self-destruct charges.

Lockerman looked up.

"Khalaf should've blown the place by now."

●

Khalaf huddled in his small, sweltering alcove, watching on his display as the tram inched to the marker for minimum safe distance. The motionless air was so thick he felt like he nearly had to swallow it rather than breathe it. The mrill were finishing off the last of the military guardians out in the passageway, their dying screams quickly cut off. That wasn't Khalaf's assignment, and he ignored the sounds as best he could. They didn't last long. The mrill then tried blasting their way through the clogged tram tunnel. The explosive charges had sealed that route, though. Even for the mrill, digging out that tunnel would be nearly impossible. That meant Khalaf was also trapped down here. No matter what happened, he was never leaving this place. He tried to ignore that thought as well.

The mrill had apparently recognized the futility of any excavation and stormed into the conference room outside Khalaf's alcove. He watched them on his screen moving through the room, not speaking. Even if they had been talking, there were no speakers in here. Nothing that could generate a sound, even accidentally. The young major was a bit disappointed he wouldn't get to hear an actual alien language, and then amused at his disappointment. As an intelligence analyst earlier in his career, he'd spent a decade translating Farsi, Pashto, Persian, and Arabic intercepts. He'd been seventeen when his parents brought him and his sister out of Baghdad in late 2004. He'd become an American citizen, then an American soldier. He'd seen what the tyrants and terrorists were like back home. His new country wasn't perfect. But demons stalked his homeland, corrupting his faith. A gift for language became his weapon against them.

Ten years mastering tongues and dialects, detecting and deciphering the most minute vocal inflections and intonations, learning to distinguish one voice from another through a static hiss beamed from the other side of the world. A career of service built on sound. And now here he was, about to do his final duty in the quietest room he'd ever been in. It was almost funny.

There were no wireless receivers or transmitters in this room, no electromagnetic clues to lead the mrill to his location. The handful of cables running to the monitor and the trigger were insulated with multiple layers of metal mesh and plastic to smother the low-level magnetic and electrostatic fields that all electrical wires emitted. They ran deep into the rock before branching up and out to the various surveillance systems and ultimately to the nuclear explosives carved into the mountain. The room had no air conditioning, and only a small duct leading to a corner of the larger comms room adjacent to the main conference room. The little room was invisible to any human sensor equipment. It was also sauna-level hot. Sweat ran in rivers down Khalaf's body. He tried to move as little as possible, but had to wipe his eyes with his sleeve to keep his vision clear.

The frenzy of mrill activity in the room outside suddenly stopped. Khalaf looked down at the monitor. Ten more seconds before the president's tram would be outside the blast zone. A dozen or more energy blasts tore the steel door open, knocking him out of his seat and slamming him against the steel wall, crunching his outstretched right arm. He looked down and a chunk of splintered bone was poking through the skin. Didn't hurt much, adrenaline already pumping through his body. He looked up to see three mrill clawing their way through the jagged opening.

Khalaf pulled himself to his knees, nearly slipping in his own blood.

The president wouldn't be clear for another three seconds according to the screen. Khalaf prayed it was close enough. He prayed he'd done enough.

One of the aliens grabbed his leg, and he turned the key.

●

The terminus came into Lockerman's view just as a thunderclap ripped apart the world. The train, the tunnel, the track, and the mountain were shredded like eggshells in a blender. Sparks and shards of metal and plastic exploded through the small cabin, and the only reason the president and his bodyguard weren't impaled on the jagged wreckage at the front of the capsule was because the capsule, too, was hurled forward toward the small pin of light Lockerman had spotted a moment ago. The light winked out, and then the tram was crushed under rocks and dust and Lockerman had only a fragment of time to think that his own light was about to go out, too. Then, everything was just . . . soft darkness.

30

Arturo Vargas peeked out the damaged front door of his apartment building near the corner of N Street and Vermont Avenue in Washington, DC. The crazy sounds—explosions and roaring helicopters and buzzing spaceships and screaming and the *thump-thump* of machine guns—were getting closer and he had decided it was time to get his family out. He cursed himself for having ignored the evacuation requests and convincing his wife to stay. None of it had seemed real. He'd hunkered down to watch the news, and now the news had come to him.

There didn't seem to be any immediate danger on the street outside their apartment, although the mishmash of cars jammed and crashed at every angle made it hard to see very far. And smoke was starting to drift through their neighborhood from the north.

"Is Mrs. Salinas coming?" he hissed at his wife, Nona, who hovered over their two young children, Miguel and Esmeralda.

The old woman was a nuisance, always yelling at his kids to pipe down. Her hearing was apparently her only bodily function that hadn't broken down over the four years they'd shared a building. Vargas had lugged oxygen tanks, a wheelchair, a motorized hospital bed, and other equipment up her stairs at various times. She was as surly as a Teamster whenever Vargas finished these sweaty expeditions, complaining that he'd banged the wall too many times. Who was gonna clean those scuff marks? Vargas patiently assured her he'd do it, and tried to keep his mumbled curses to a minimum after she retreated back into her apartment.

"I tried. She says it's safer here. She says that's what you told her yesterday."

"I know. But I was wrong. Did you tell her that?"

"Yes, but she won't budge."

He opened his mouth to yell up the stairway to the second floor where the old woman lived. Just then an explosion, the closest yet, ripped through the night. The children screamed.

"Jesus, that sounded like just the next block over," he said to his wife. "If she's not coming, we can't wait. Go!"

They'd mapped out a zigzagging route to the White House, trying to stay on the side streets. That would be safer, right? His brother, a congressional aide, had said on the phone 20 minutes ago (before the lines went dead) that there was apparently a civilian evacuation zone there, with buses ferrying people out of the city. Better than trying to make it on their own. He and his wife had hastily scribbled out their route on a pair of paper maps, along with backup meeting spots, in case they got separated. Each of their cell phones was fully charged, but neither could get a signal. The cell towers were either destroyed or simply overwhelmed with traffic. Probably both.

One last look around, and he led his family out in a tight cluster. The thick smoke was getting closer, like a giant gray worm swallowing the block. They were no more than 20 feet down the street when a high-pitched, almost hysterical voice called out.

"Arturo! Wait! Take me with you. Arturooooooo!" The wail pierced even the battlefield din that was rapidly approaching.

He looked back and Mrs. Salinas was leaning out her second-floor window, oxygen tubes dangling around her neck. Even at the short distance, she was clouded in haze. He was tempted to turn away and keep moving, but his wife looked at him with pleading eyes.

He turned with a sigh and yelled, "Okay, Mrs. Salinas, hold on, I'm . . ."

The building erupted outward, as if kicked in by a giant. The fireball swallowed Mrs. Salinas, and the shockwave knocked the Vargas family backward and drove them into the ground. Arturo cried out as his shoulder slammed into the edge of the concrete curb. He staggered to his feet, clutching his arm, and looked for his family. They had been blown into a thick hedge and seemed scratched and dirty but otherwise unharmed. He rushed over and knelt down to check on the kids, who were looking around, stunned.

Arturo was about to speak when his wife went rigid, looking back at the smoldering wreckage of their apartment building. He turned around just in time to see an armor-plated robot with red glowing eyes stomp through the rubble. It looked up and down the street, raising its rifle the moment it spotted the battered family. Arturo, overwhelmed, could do no more than raise his one good arm to try to shield his children. He knew it was pointless and cursed himself again for having waited so long to leave.

The barrel of the robot's rifle began to light up when a blur of *something* rushed in from Arturo's left. The robot paused and swiveled its rifle to track the object. Suddenly the blur was a man—well, it looked like a man—rolling in a somersault and coming up with a weapon, still moving.

The robot and man fired at the same time. The beam from the robot's rifle snapped through the air and vaporized a dusty red Chevy Impala and the corner of a florist shop. Arturo gaped as brilliant rhododendrons, chrysanthemums, tulips, and roses sprayed out of Fanny's Flowers through the gray smoke. The moving man's blast was more accurate. The left half of the robot was fried away. It hopped for a moment on its one remaining leg and then fell over. The man was nowhere to be seen. The machine sat up and raised its rifle again and strafed the street. The staccato yellow beam cut through the building in a horizontal line toward Arturo and his family, still huddled near the mangled bushes. At the last moment, the blur leaped from the top of the building behind Arturo. He only knew that was what had happened because the robot looked up and tried to raise its rifle. Before it could, a single explosive round burrowed into the robot's chest and exploded, transforming the machine into a ticker tape parade of glittering metal shards.

The blurred man landed lightly on his feet, no longer a blur. Arturo staggered to his feet, wiping dirt and sweat from his face, holding his damaged arm against his side. The man's gray skin glistened in the firelight.

"You folks okay?"

Arturo struggled to speak, just nodding.

Esmeralda, only eight years old, was the first to speak.

"Are you the one on the news? The Army man?"

The man laughed.

"I guess so. But I'm a lieutenant. In the Navy. You all seem to be in one piece, from what I can tell. Your baby is fine, too, ma'am," he said, pointing at Nona's flat belly.

Now Arturo found his voice and turned to his wife.

"What? You're . . . what?"

The gray-skinned man laughed again. His skin seemed to match the tone of this now drab and pulverized world. His laugh, though, filled the air and somehow seemed stronger than the gloom.

"I'll leave you folks to sort this out. But I very strongly suggest moving south as fast you can. That one"—the gray man pointed to small crater where the last remnants of the robot were scattered—"was a bit ahead of the rest of the mrill force, but more are coming. I've got to get back. And you need to get out of here."

Without another word, the man became a blur again and disappeared back into the storm of smoke and fire.

Arturo pulled his son to his feet and looked at his wife. He tried to think of something to say, then just wrapped her in a hug. She squeezed back for a moment, then broke the embrace.

"I love you. But we've got to go. Now."

He nodded and got his family moving.

"You know," he said as they hustled off, "I forgot to thank him."

"I bet you aren't the only one," his wife said.

As they walked off, Arturo scooped up a white carnation that had somehow emerged unscathed from the flower shop. He tucked it behind his daughter's ear. She smiled, and they kept moving.

31

The bombs from the B-2s had been more effective than Ben had dared to hope. The heavy explosives had fallen like a storm, overwhelming the mrill attempts to blast them out of the sky. The bombs had taken out thirty-four of the mrill infantry and robots, leaving eleven of them still fighting. Plenty lethal, but no longer overwhelming. After destroying the robot on Vermont Street, Ben had instructed his small squad of marines to fall back and rejoin the main defenses at the space cannon, rearmed with grenades and missiles, and regroup on the south side of McPherson Square on K Street. This was a winnable fight, but the only way the American forces could prevail was by firing and falling back. Any toe-to-toe skirmish was an instant slaughter. Even the guerilla tactics resulted in heavy losses, but it was at least a manageable strategy. And Ben had also instructed the marines, once they reached the command center, to relay the coordinates of McPherson to the USS *Anzio*, a guided missile cruiser parked in the Chesapeake Bay. One more combined aerial and ground attack might be enough to finish this off.

Ben's internal communications systems lit up, pinged simultaneously by Nick and Rickert. He fired three quick blasts and sprinted from behind the jumble of mangled concrete and rebar to the smoking wreckage of a carved-out tank.

He connected Eddie, Nick, and Rickert to a joint audio session over his internal network.

"Hey team. How we doing?" Ben asked.

"The mrill just sent in more than 2,000 additional ships and they've got one big-ass mother of a ship parked in orbit," Nick said.

"The mrill somehow discovered Cheyenne Mountain and attacked it, and we've lost contact with the president," Rickert said.

Ben sagged against the scorched tank. He accessed Nick's visual feed and watched remotely as Nick and Eddie hopped and dodged and fired, while the defensive satellites, ground-based cannons, and human drones fired at an almost continuous rate against the incoming swarm. The defenders were outnumbered 100 to 1, and it was only a matter of time before they were overwhelmed.

Ben didn't need to see through Rickert's eyes to feel his despair.

"Did the defensive nukes detonate? Are the mrill inside the mountain, or did the explosion simply knock out our comms?" Ben asked.

"It looks like the nukes were detonated, but there's no sign of the president's escape plane. We're sending a team in from Peterson Air Force Base, but who knows if they'll be able to make it in, given the reinforcements the mrill just put in orbit. The rest of the government has gone dark. No one wants to communicate electronically for fear of giving away their position. The VP is holed up in California, and we've got the rest of the cabinet scattered at different sites. The SecDef was with the president, though, so his status is also unknown. We don't really have a functional government right now. I . . . hold on, getting a call on my secure line."

Ben felt his brief hope flickering out, a candle thrust into a tornado. Two fireballs bloomed on the horizon to the east, and Ben knew before the sound wave hit that it was the *Anzio* being destroyed by the mrill drones. With their numbers, the mrill didn't even need to engage with Nick and Eddie in orbit. Just leave enough drones up there to keep them busy and send the rest down to the surface to wipe out the other defenses. Despair curled its clammy fingers around Ben's mind and stepped on his chest as he wondered who was now in charge of the American government, and how soon they would start lobbing nukes at everything that moved in the sky. At least a dozen people had the launch codes. Someone would undoubtedly come up for air just long enough to use them. Nukes wouldn't win the war. All they'd do was kill a lot of people. But the brass would get desperate as defeat loomed, and the end felt very near. A squirming, plummeting sense of panic twisted his gut. He was eleven again, helpless in the heaving storm, his grip slipping no matter how hard he held on.

Two mrill drop ships whooshed down about a block away and vomited out two squads of robot infantry. Ben looked up and could see mrill drone fighters and drop ships now crisscrossing the sky and, farther up, the blink and pop of the battle above the planet. A squadron of F-22 fighter jets were screaming in from Andrews Air Force Base, but Ben wanted to call them off. The moment they engaged the mrill, they were dead.

Rickert came back on.

"You guys will want to hear this."

Ben was surprised to hear the voice of Ying Lai, the Chinese doctor who had overseen the initial nanobot transfusions.

"I have good news," she said. "The Chinese government has completed its first drone fleet based on the specifications from the brin your team provided, and they are being launched as we speak."

"Yeah?" Eddie said without much hope in his voice. "Well, we're looking at nearly 2,000 mrill ships up here, but I guess if you've got a couple drones, send 'em our way. We'll delay the inevitable as long as possible."

"We have 543 drones inbound to your position," Ying said.

There was silence for a moment, then Eddie chortled and whooped.

"Well, damn, let's do this."

"How the hell did you have time to build 543 drones?" Rickert asked.

"All of our major consumer electronics assembly plants shut down when the global economy stopped," Ying said. "We had 400,000 workers with nothing to do. We provided the brin blueprints, retooled the assembly lines, and put them back to work. It was efficient."

"I bet," Ben said.

"The technology was quite challenging, but the concepts were straight-forward. There was . . . considerable debate over whether to enable the machines to be remote-controlled by you and your team, Lt. Shepherd. But I was able to prevail, saying that it was necessary to enable this functional-ity to ensure our survival."

"You pushed for that?"

"Simple logic, Lieutenant. You and your men are by far the most advanced weapons in the human arsenal. Even with these drones, we'll face a tremen-dous challenge to overcome the enemy. Why cripple our chances further? Plus, your actions in Shanghai were not forgotten."

Ben, Nick, and Eddie felt 543 connection points suddenly open them-selves to their minds as the Chinese drones rose into the sky. The team quickly divvied up the reinforcements, with most rocketing toward Nick and Eddie, who were now battling in the skies over South America. Thirty of the ships veered off to Ben's location in DC. Then he reconsidered.

"General, I'm sending five of the drones to Cheyenne Mountain, or what's left of it. Alert the rescue team from Peterson that they're going to be getting some company, and not to shoot at it. The drones will provide cover for the rescue team. Dr. Ying, do the drones have any passenger capabilities?"

"I'm afraid not. They are purely weapons platforms."

"Well, if the president is still alive, hopefully the runway and jet are still useable. Okay, let's go."

Rickert signed off from his bunker in the foothills of South Dakota, but Ben kept his connection open with Nick and Eddie a bit longer. Through their eyes, he could see them fighting through the cloud of mrill ships. A bolt of enemy fire carved a precise, black streak down the edge of Nick's ship. Then the cavalry arrived, cutting in from the east like a silver hailstorm. There were too many for Nick and Eddie to control directly, so their internal computers instantly distributed a series of orders and guidelines, turning the drones loose as autonomous weapons. Nick and Eddie kept a handful to fly a protective formation around their own ships, and with that, the largest vehicular battle in human history was underway.

Ben pushed the feed to the background of his mind but didn't cut it off. He needed to deal with the mushrooming mrill presence down on the ground, though he had a feeling he would be needing backup soon and in some form. The twenty-five drones he'd commandeered would be there in five minutes, but he had to hold the fort until they arrived.

At that moment, Sergeant Daniels and his marines came into view. Daniels whistled softly, unable to see Ben, who was still cloaked. Ben ducked down behind the wreckage of the tank and deactivated his invisibility cloak. The marines, weighed down with missile launchers and various explosives, hustled over, weapons and ammo clinking softly, and squeezed up against the twisted metal.

"What's the situation, sir?" Daniels said.

"A bit more complicated since you left, but nothing we can't handle," Ben said. "We've got two squads of mrill robots half a block away, and they've got a hell of a lot more air cover now thanks to some reinforcements that just parked themselves about 500 miles above our heads. And unless I'm very much mistaken, they just took out the USS *Anzio*, so no missile support."

Every man in the squad glanced up involuntarily and muttered a soft curse.

"Good news is we've got some reinforcements of our own inbound. Made in China, and I think they commandeered every manufacturing site in the country, so I hope y'all aren't planning on buying a new phone anytime soon. More than 500 drones to call our own. Most of them are dispatched to help with the orbital battle, but we've got twenty-five inbound to provide us some air support. And we're mostly facing mrill robots down here, not foot soldiers. The robots are tough, but they're a damn sight dumber and slower than the mrill themselves, so we've got a fighting chance."

"How's the rest of the world doing, sir?" one of the soldiers asked. "Is there anything left out there?"

Ben decided not to say anything about Lockerman.

"We'll find out once we kick these shitheads off Earth," he said. "So, same drill as before. I'll draw their attention, you plant claymores at the intersection to the south and set up missile teams on the roof. I'll draw them in, you'll cut them apart. Things go pear-shaped, rendezvous point is the White House lawn. We're running out of real estate to retreat to, and we've still got to protect that cannon. Drone ETA 45 seconds."

As if to offer a reminder of its existence, the cannon fired three times into the sky. They were close enough now that they could feel the jolt in both the ground and the air. The mrill robots and handful of remaining infantry were clawing closer to the weapon, bulldozing their way through the city. The marines dispersed to set up their explosives and move to the rooftops of the adjacent buildings. Ben suspected the mrill would be wise to the maneuver this time, but they would definitely not be expecting the drone attack from above. The marines were moving silently up the fire escape of one of the buildings when one of them, Private Robert Black, slipped and clattered down a few steps. He caught himself quickly, but it was enough to attract the attention of the mrill force, which swiveled as one toward the sound. The marines were caught, exposed in an indefensible position, their heavy weapons useless in the tight, confined, twisting space of the staircase.

Five blips streaked into DC airspace.

The only one who noticed was Ben, who had been tracking the signals from the Chinese fighters on his internal feed. Now it was a party. The five drones, designed in a distant star system by a dead race, assembled on the other side of the world, guided by a man who was no longer certain whether he still qualified as human or not, responded to a thought and opened fire on the alien invaders.

Crackling darts of energy sawed through the mrill robots and soldiers, drilling deep craters in the surrounding streets and buildings. The mrill drones were already responding to the attack, flying in from the east, presumably the same drones that had taken out the *Anzio*. Ben sent the Chinese drones around for another pass, moving well over the speed of sound to avoid the return fire from the forces on the ground. A clutch of sonic booms rattled the few windows that were still intact. At the same time, the marines reached the rooftops and unleashed their missiles and rockets. Though less lethal than the ion guns on the drones, the conventional explosives found their marks. It was nearing 3 a.m. now, but the glow of battle and trail of fire extending back to the original mrill insertion point made it look like feeble dawn.

Four mrill drones arrived just as the Chinese drones began their second attack run.

Two of the drones were picked off as they strafed the mrill position. Ben turned his drones to engage the enemy ships. Despite the hundreds of reinforcements engaging the mrill fleet in orbit, Nick, Eddie, and their machines were still outnumbered nearly four to one. The ground defenses had to hold.

Ben and the remaining military forces on the surface would have to deal with the mrill ground forces directly. Even as his nanomachines took over his body, his mind was already mourning the deaths to come. In his previous life, the chaos of combat had required him to focus both his mind and body on the task at hand. Now the machines in his body handled the fighting, leaving his mind to agonize even as the battle still unfolded. He was still unclear if this was an improvement or not.

From the rooftops, missiles and rocket-propelled grenades whistled and hissed. Beautiful red, orange, and yellow fireballs blossomed where ordnance was planted: in the ground, on top of buildings, inside shattered vehicles. As the mrill struggled to pivot from the air attack to this new ground assault, Ben wondered again if they felt any emotions at all. Did they question and hesitate? Did they mourn? Fear?

It didn't matter. They would.

32

As thousands of starships skittered and skirmished around him, crisscrossing on chaotic vectors, pairing up, splitting up, regrouping, some exploding into temporary starbursts, others withdrawing, charging, and circling back to do it all again, Eddie observed and recorded it all with some detachment. Even amusement. The human brain really wasn't meant for this sort of thing.

It was enough to make you crazy if you thought it about it too much. Eddie had a brief flashback to his childhood struggles with basic algebra and geometry and how he'd had to sweat through the underwater mapping and distance calculations early in his SEAL training. Through raw sweat and will, he'd figured it out, but it had never been anything close to second nature. The brin technology had changed his nature. So here he was commanding a fleet of spaceships whirring through a three-dimensional battlefield and his heart rate was as steady as a metronome and his brow was a dry as a desert.

Well, I've still got blood and tears to give. At least I'm still human enough for that. He picked off three mrill ships, trailing the third so closely that as he rocketed through the wreckage, he could hear pieces ping off the hull of his own ship. He knew Nick was similarly bemused and horrified at what he'd become. Ben's connection was more distant, but Eddie wasn't sure if that was simply due to physical distance or if Ben kept his emotions on a tighter leash.

Eddie knew Ben had hoped to be rid of fighting, to be left alone. He also knew there was no one better at the art of war, and no one he'd rather follow into it. And if Eddie was being completely honest, there was nowhere he'd rather be. A failure in everything but soldiering, civilian life held only debt, failed relationships, and boredom. Eddie was a Navy lifer. *Am I still in the Navy? We might need to think of a new branch of the military for what we are. Space Rangers?* He could sense Nick chuckling.

Three more shots. Three more kills.

What really bothered Eddie was the total lack of fear he felt. Prior to his transformation, every firefight, every demolition mission, recon assignment, and protective detail had been fueled by a cocktail of unequal parts fear, adrenaline, and pride. It had probably been that way since the first caveman picked up a stick to fight off the neighboring clan. SEALs were, by nature and training, better able to control those emotions, but the fear was always there. The experience of seeing your friends and comrades ripped apart in combat was never something you got used to. There was no way of preparing for the things you might see. The things you might become.

No longer. Whatever electrochemical reaction in the brain that was responsible for fear had been erased by the brin nanobots—or at least suppressed. Eddie reflected that this was probably the most sought-after weapon in all of human history: the ability to send men to battle who would obey any order, advance on any position, and throw themselves against any defense, regardless of the cost.

A wall of mrill drones swept into view, firing as they came, a flying battering ram. Nick directed a detachment of his own drones to meet the assault, and the two forces slammed into each other. The mrill drones flung their nano bombs and the Chinese drones destroyed them—except one. The lone shot sped through the green blasts and burst open like a pregnant spider. The gray blob of miniature robots coated one of the Chinese drones and began eating it. They devoured the outer armor, exposing the bones of the unmanned craft, which was still dodging and firing as it was disrobed. Then the nanobots began to chew through the powerful support structures under the skin. The glow of the guns and engines pulsed through the drone's exposed skeleton. The growing gray swarm of nanobots moved over the ship like an infection. Mrill drones kept firing at the limping Chinese drone, which had all but disappeared inside the blob. Occasionally flashes of light escaped, like lightning from a thundercloud.

The nanobots started chomping on the central computer system of the craft. Nick, who had been watching the entire cannibalistic ordeal as he fought his own battles, suspected the nanobots were trying to break into the drone's communication system to hack into the secure network connecting the humans and the machines. *Not happening.* He ordered the wounded drone to self-destruct. The craft immolated itself in a green and yellow fireball, consuming the ravenous nanobots and one mrill drone that had gotten too close.

Nick knew the mrill were happy to make that trade. The drone reinforcements had only slowed the pace of mankind's defeat. The supply of mrill ships seemed endless, as wave after wave poured out of the mothership and broke against the human defenses. Each wave consumed a handful of defenders. Nick had a vision of a sand castle, slopped together with plastic pails and shovels, erected in a panic as the only line of a defense against a tsunami. It was a cruel joke. So be it. If sandcastles in a storm were their last, best line of defense, then they'd shovel until the water washed them away.

Nick ordered a hundred of the drones to form up in two wedges and attack the mothership. "We've been playing defense too damn long," he said out loud to Eddie. "If we're going to do any damage, we've got to turn this thing around."

"Copy that," Eddie said. "I'll take this group from the bottom, and you run the top. Godspeed, man. Let's kick some alien ass . . . or whatever they sit on."

Nick laughed, cranked his engines up to full thrust, and charged.

33

Leonov watched the television with growing alarm, although he kept it well hidden. The 2nd Red Army was still camped in Volgograd. He had planned to continue their march to Moscow that morning, but the assault playing out on the TV was impossible to ignore. There wasn't much to see of the space battle. But the ground war was playing out live to the world, as a few reporters were still broadcasting scattered, confused coverage from Washington. It was impossible to tell propaganda from truth. Maybe it always had been. He doubted anyone could track everything that was happening right now.

His own spies reported that the cannon in Moscow was firing nonstop, apparently targeting the alien ships up above the planet. The General had gone dark for the moment. Leonov's men remained loyal and obedient. No desertions. They were waiting for orders. For guidance. He knew he couldn't remain glued to the TV or wait around for his laptop to buzz much longer. He suddenly realized the satellite that provided the computer's connection might have been destroyed. Rodchenko and a few others were in the room, and their gaze was locked on the flickering, fiery images, just as Leonov's was. They didn't have the burden of command. They didn't have to make decisions.

Deciphering the correct next move was difficult, given the destruction unfolding on the TV screen. The reporters and their cameras were having a hard time grasping the flow of the battle on the ground. Part of it was that they were afraid to get too close to the firefight. Several reporters had already been killed in the crossfire, live on the air. It was like nothing Leonov had ever seen. One idiot reporter, decked out in military-style cargo pants and a blue bulletproof vest, had accompanied a squad of soldiers directly to the front. The journalist had been incinerated where he stood when a group of alien soldiers materialized out of thin air and launched a flurry of green fire at the American detachment. Leonov suspected the unsecured wireless transmission from the camera back to the studio had drawn the enemy fire, but it was impossible to know. At any rate, he couldn't believe the United States military would allow reporters into battle, and broadcasting live!

Still, he had to admit he could not tear his eyes from the calamity unfolding on the screen before him.

It should have been a rout. The Americans were obviously outgunned. They were nevertheless fighting an effective, orderly retreat, inflicting heavy losses as they fell back in formation. Their weapons were clearly primitive compared to those of the enemy. And yet, every time the smoke cleared on a skirmish, alien bodies and shattered alien weaponry were nearly as numerous as American casualties. The American military wasn't *that* good. The human with the alien machines in his body must be among the defenders. There were glimpses of a shape flitting through the chaos, quick fire directed toward the aliens and then a second volley from hundreds of meters away just seconds later. It was far too fast for any human infantryman to move.

Leonov couldn't get a clear look. The reporters and camera operators obviously had no idea what was happening. All they saw in the retreat was defeat. They couldn't grasp the tactical brilliance of the maneuver or the heavy toll it was taking on the mrill. The media then babbled their gibbering ignorance out to the world. Still, even the TV idiots understood where the mrill were going. The cameras occasionally cut to shots of the defensive cannon sending thunder and lighting up into the night sky, another security violation that Leonov found both bizarre and enlightening. It looked like the mrill didn't have enough troops to make it before the last of them were destroyed. This American soldier with the alien technology was obviously good at his job.

Leonov looked down at the chunk of debris he had rescued from the destroyed station in Gorkovskiy. He was an intelligent man, educated and well-traveled. The technology at play here was slipping beyond the grasp of human understanding. He wondered if even the Americans were truly comfortable with the weapons and tools they had been given. What was that saying? Any sufficiently advanced technology is indistinguishable from magic?

"Arthur C. Clarke," Rodchenko said, and Leonov was startled from his reverie, thinking for a moment his friend had read his mind. "That quote is from the science fiction writer Arthur C. Clarke."

Leonov realized he must have muttered the phrase quietly as it had run through his head.

"I didn't know you read such decadent literature, Vanya," Leonov said with a friendly smile.

Rodchenko shrugged, not looking away from the TV.

"It always seemed a bit ridiculous to me . . . apparently I was wrong."

They were quiet for a moment. On the table, two cups of long-ignored tea had gone cold. Leonov absently picked up one of the cups, sipped, and grimaced at the taste.

"There must have been truth to the reports," Rodchenko added, nodding toward the screen. "The Americans should have been defeated otherwise."

He handed Leonov a flask without looking away from the TV, and the older man poured a splash into the tea cup. A sip, then a sigh, and he set it back down. Later.

"And they must have more than one of these guardians," he said. "We cannot see the space combat, but if the Americans have engaged the aliens up there as well, then they must have a similar force piloting their space craft."

He thought for a moment.

"But they must not have many of these men. Otherwise, we would see more of them on the ground in Washington. They're fighting an effective tactical retreat, but they are losing many lives. Americans are always eager to send technology to do a soldier's job when possible. If they're sending the soldiers instead, then the technology must be spread very thin."

Rodchenko nodded.

"Very soon, I would expect these aliens to concentrate all their fire on these upgraded men. They're the only real threat, no?"

"And if they're defeated, the Americans will have no choice but to turn their nuclear weapons on their own cities. Although perhaps the aliens will have countermeasures for that, as well," Leonov replied.

Rodchenko, uncertainty etched on his face, leaned forward so only Leonov could hear him.

"Yuri, are we fighting the wrong enemy? We can still take Moscow and overthrow the bureaucrats, but we cannot stand against *that*," he said, gesturing at the TV. "Maybe we should form an alliance with the United States?"

Leonov stared at the screen for a long moment.

"No, Vanya, I think we stick to our plan. You're right. I don't think we can defeat this force. But maybe the Americans can. We let them exhaust themselves against this foe, and we step into the vacuum. Russia still needs saving. We must be on our way soon."

"And if the aliens win?" Rodchenko asked.

The light from the fierce battle on the TV flickered across Leonov's face, leaving reflections of orange flame in his eyes.

"Then, Vanya, we die for the Motherland."

●

Ben couldn't believe how close the news reporters were getting to the battle. He tried to protect them as well as he could, but the mrill separated their forces every time he did, sending the larger detachment on to attack the cannon near the White House, which Ben had to pursue. The hapless reporters were soon destroyed. Ben got on his own secure line to Rickert and yelled at him to keep the media back.

"We're trying," Rickert said. "Things are falling apart. There's major panic all through the New York, Boston, DC region, and we've had to deploy National Guard, Army, Marines, everything, just to prevent 30 million people from stampeding in every goddamn direction."

"And the reason they're panicking is because these TV news idiots are covering everything we're doing," Ben said. "Of course they're panicking! I'm sure it looks like a fiasco on TV. You've got to cut that shit off."

"Even if I could, it wouldn't matter," Rickert said. "The news crews are just a tiny part of it. You've got maybe a thousand people with cellphone cameras broadcasting all over the internet—at least the parts of it that are still working. There are even a couple guys flying personal drones, the two-hundred-, three-hundred-dollar jobs out over the battlefield, live streaming from their onboard cameras. Or they were, anyway. Apparently they got taken out in the bombing run by the B-2s."

"Those guys make it back to base safely?"

"Yeah, most of them. Looks like the mrill managed to shoot one down.

We're not sure if the crew was able to eject. I'm like that damn Dutch kid trying to plug a million leaks with his fingers and toes."

"Who?"

"Never mind. What's your status?"

Ben fired three shots from his rifle, toggled over to a timed explosive round that he launched into the side of a building near a mrill squad, and sprinted down the street, hurtling over wreckage and sliding to a stop beneath the jagged roots of an overturned tree. Hot shards of shrapnel embedded in the tree, surrounding cars, and concrete smoked and smoldered.

"We're holding a quarter mile from the White House, and I think I can stop them here."

The timed explosive round detonated. The force of the blast shoved one of the concealed mrill out into the street, and Ben blew it apart with two quick shots. It fired wildly into the air as it tumbled to the ground. The mrill didn't seem interested in even rudimentary battlefield tactics. They didn't bother to establish overwatch or sniper teams to protect their main force. No advance scouts. They just massed and charged, like some seventeenth-century European army blundering across an open field. *All that's missing are the drums and fifes.* Not that it mattered against most of the defenders. The military forces simply couldn't touch their technology. Ben, on the other hand, was dancing around them like a wasp around a bear. It had obviously been a long time since the mrill had faced anything like an equal foe. Even the brin had been overmatched.

The mrill's arrogance was the most effective tool in Ben's arsenal. Even with their signal jammed, they still assumed their numbers and better guns would overwhelm the defenders. He thought about how the US had stomped into Iraq and Afghanistan. Night vision and motion detectors and body armor and drones and satellite surveillance against malnourished mountain men wrapped in raggedy gowns and clutching AK-47s older than some of the soldiers they were trying to shoot. Turkey shoot. Cakewalk. Some fifteen years later, and the US had staggered out in some kind of bloody-nosed, ill-defined draw. You didn't need technological parity to defeat your enemy. Sometimes, close enough was close enough.

A pair of A-10 "Warthog" jets rumbled in low over the horizon for an attack run. Ben found their radio link through the tangle of wireless communication threads nearly choking the sky overhead. He sliced through the relatively primitive encryption around their signal. There was no time for pleasantries.

"US ground force to approaching A-10s, this is Lieutenant Ben Shepherd. I'm on the ground engaging the enemy. You're also patched in to US Army General Tom Rickert. I need you to listen very closely and quickly. You're about twelve seconds out from the enemy position. I'll mark target with smoke. If you waste time with questions, you'll probably be shot down. Out."

He didn't wait for a response, ordering the marines who'd gathered near him to pop smoke grenades on the mrill position while he provided cover fire. Everyone moved without question. They were too tired to do anything but obey at this point. As the smoke grenades arced through the air and Ben fired and ran, he noted briefly that this smelled unlike any battle he'd ever been a part of.

The flames and smoke were familiar, though other elements were radically different. The smell of gunpowder lingered in the background, the result of the conventional weapons fired by the military units; the old black brew of sulfur, charcoal, and potassium nitrate that had been the hallmark of every battlefield Ben had ever known. But his own weapon and those of the mrill forces produced an odor, or really a lack of odor, that Ben could only think of as alien. Even though he knew the basics of the hydrogen ionization process that formed the heart of his rifle, the total lack of noticeable smell was still jarring. Goldberg, the excitable engineer, had explained that hydrogen was odorless, and his weapon would not produce any kind of trackable smell when fired. That chubby savant had assured him that was a good thing, as it was one fewer way for mrill sensors to detect Ben's movements. It was also more proof how much everything had changed.

Ben noted almost subconsciously that the humans were winning, at least down here. There were three mrill fighters and one robot left. They were still doing heavy damage to everything around them, but their pace had slowed. Ben could hear the regular pulse of the cannon behind him, now no more than a thousand yards or so, and a blanket of red light fell over everything each time it fired. *These bastards are going to die within sight of their objective*, Ben thought with savage satisfaction.

And then the A-10s arrived.

Each opened their massive, nose-mounted 30 mm "Avenger" Gatling guns. The cannons burped and delivered a mix of armor-piercing and incendiary rounds, aluminum slugs wrapped around a depleted uranium core. The supersonic shells landed before the sound even reached the ground, screaming through the yellow smoke.

The banana-sized bullets ripped through the mrill position, obliterating the robot and one of the mrill troops.

The A-10s peeled off. One of the remaining mrill troops fired at the receding aircraft, catching the tail of one of them. The aircraft broke apart and spiraled into the ground, but not before the pilot ejected. A ragged cheer went up from the US ground forces closing in on the mrill position. Two Abrams tanks clattered into view from an adjacent street, firing as they came, while Ben directed two of the Chinese drones that had just shot down a pair of mrill drones to circle back and engage as well. This would be over in moments. And the sun was rising, Ben noticed. *We're winning*, he thought.

Ben felt Nick opening his internal communication link.

"Shit, watch out below, boss. Major incoming. And we've got our hands full up here."

Ben looked up just in time to see forty mrill drones escorting three mrill drop ships punch through the orange-tinged clouds. The drones rained green fire in every direction, emerald beams sending up yellow and orange fireballs—all of it reflecting off the low-slung clouds. Even as he was mentally rallying the Chinese drones and readying his own rifle, Ben thought it was the most beautiful thing he'd ever seen.

34

e're losing, Eddie thought.

There were so many of them. For every mrill ship they destroyed, two seemed to take its place. Eddie understood how Ben found the battle oddly captivating. Thousands of exotic machines twirled around him, spitting green darts through the darkness of space, while the endless stars shone brighter out here than he had ever seen them on Earth. The sun rose and fell endlessly as the battle migrated around the planet. Eddie's mind was transfixed every time the spike of white light sliced across the dark surface, even as his transformed body kept fighting.

There was no way humankind could prepare for this kind of war. It was too . . . alien. You just wanted to stare at everything. Forget the frenzied, technicolor battle. Even just seeing the Earth from this vantage point was enough to send your mind reeling. The universe was huge. Everything was huge. There was so much out here. There was a whole new frontier out here to explore.

"And these assholes want to kill us all, just as we get a chance to do some sightseeing," he said out loud.

"Yeah, these aliens are trash," Nick agreed. "I bet we'd have even been willing to rent them some space down here while we went exploring. But no, had to make a ruckus."

A mrill shot nicked the hull of his ship. The vessel shuddered and kept going. But the damage was piling up. The repair systems were chugging along, patching up holes, reconnecting circuits, keeping the weapons firing. The repairs were taking longer with each hit, though, as a handful of the tiny repair droids were lost each time.

Nick and Eddie had noticed the same lack of tactical imagination among the mrill pilots that Ben had seen among their infantry. Without their mental link, each individual mrill soldier or drone fell back on brute-force tactics, massing and charging, falling back and regrouping. Of course, sheer numerical superiority was its own tactical advantage. They just kept coming and coming. Even if each wave was predictable, another and another and another would eventually wear down even the most skilled pilot. The drones were the only thing keeping Nick and Eddie alive. Once they were all gone, the conclusion would be inevitable.

"I don't suppose anyone else is sending up a few hundred more drones to support the cause?" Nick asked. "No chance that France or, uh, Uruguay has been holding out on us?"

Eddie grunted as he yanked his ship into a sharp turn, fired three times, destroying another mrill drone, and skimmed beneath a cloud of wreckage.

"That's a negatory, sailor," Eddie finally replied.

Both men could see that they had 134 Chinese drones left, versus 627 mrill ships. And the mothership still lurked in the background. It hadn't fired a shot after disgorging its initial fleet.

"You think that thing is spent, or just biding its time?" Nick wondered, directing a squadron of drones to break formation and circle back to obliterate four mrill ships he'd managed to lure away from the main force.

"I think we're going to have to find out," Eddie replied. "We're playing a sucker's game. We can't keep up this slap-and-tickle forever. It's time to take the fight to the enemy."

The two men instantly shared a battle plan through their mental link, swapping and refining it in moments. Their ships converged, as did one hundred of the remaining drones. The drones formed themselves into a wedge, with Eddie and Nick trailing behind. Before the mrill could regroup, Eddie ordered the formation to speed toward the mrill command ship, firing in all directions, a battering ram of ionized energy.

The first, disorganized line of defenders was pulverized in moments. The mrill simply weren't expecting a frontal attack. But they reformed quickly. The second line of defense was also defeated, but now the mrill were finally trying a new tactic. Scores of ships swooped around behind the attacking wedge. They had recognized that Eddie and Nick were the literal brains behind Earth defenses. Kill them, and the rest of the fleet would be, if not sitting ducks, then at least unimaginative ducks.

Eddie ordered the remaining Chinese drones that hadn't formed the tip of the spear to circle around and cover the rear of the formation, essentially forming a protective three-dimensional shell around the two pilots. He then ordered the drones at the rear to turn around and fly backward, their guns facing out to intercept the approaching mrill. The entire formation now resembled a spiny porcupine, quills extended in all directions. It was an ancient maneuver. The Roman army had called it the "Testudo Formation," when legionaries would march with their shields interlocked on all sides and above to protect against incoming enemy arrows. It looked impressive as hell, but it wasn't invincible. The formation depended on everyone moving as one. If one spear carrier fell half a step behind, the entire enterprise could collapse in seconds. Still, it felt like their only shot at getting close enough to the alien command ship to stab the fuckers in the heart.

"Charge of the friggin' Light Brigade," he muttered. "Let's get it on."

●

Ben stumbled as an explosion hit nearby. A second, closer detonation knocked him over completely. Chunks of the building and street rained down on him as he clambered back to his feet. The reinforced mrill assault was shaking the city like an earthquake. The surviving A-10 jet had tried to circle around for a second attack run, but the mrill had blown it apart before it could fire a single missile. No parachute this time, as the plane spiraled directly into the Washington Monument, slicing it in half.

The remaining drones were having slightly better luck, the handful that remained. Ben struggled to maintain his communication link with them, but the mrill seemed to have finally brought some of their own jamming tech to bear. Ben's internal computers were trying to route around it while keeping his own jamming signal active. Keeping track of everything happening in the sky overhead while also leading the leathernecks and soldiers on the ground was straining even his superhuman senses.

More than a hundred mrill troops were now advancing through the streets. A company of fourteen M1A3 Abrams tanks was converging on McPherson Square, just a block from the White House. The heavy armor rolled into the grassy opening and the mrill shots destroyed them like a finger through aluminum foil. Infantry died even quicker. Wide energy beams swept out from the mrill rifles and cut down dozens of men at a time. Ben fought with everything he had.

The mrill were moving faster now, their objective in sight. The cannon had taken out more than half of this assault group before it had reached the ground. Once the cannon was gone, the mrill would be able to land with impunity and that would be that. Maybe Ben could take out this bunch before they reached the cannon. Maybe.

The feeble morning sun was momentarily obscured by a plume of ash and dust as another building collapsed. Everything seemed to be on fire. A restaurant on the northeast corner of the square burst outward in a ball of flame as glass shards covered the entire area.

Ben's small squad of marines had pulled back, on his orders. The ones who were still alive were almost out of ammo and nearly drunk with exhaustion, staggering, and swaying on their feet. But if Ben had given the order, they would have charged immediately. The stew of adrenaline and fatigue had nearly turned them into robots themselves. Ben had seen it before, had *felt* it before. At some point, your brain slipped into neutral while your body kept going, not even realizing how clumsy it had become. Maybe the brin had just figured out a way to weaponize that feeling. Turn a person into a fearless, tireless weapon and set him loose. Whatever the brin had done, though, they hadn't figured out how to erase guilt. Sending these shambling men back into the fight would have been a death sentence, and Ben already carried too many of those with him. He'd ordered them back to the command center on the White House lawn.

Not that they were much safer there. The mrill were still advancing, and drones continue to drop in from the outer atmosphere, strafing the city as long as they could. The defensive cannon and the Chinese drones had picked them all off so far, like fleas on a dog. But more were undoubtedly coming. For whatever reason, the mrill had chosen this as their landing spot; the point on the anvil where the hammer would fall. Ben doubted the mrill had any interest in taking prisoners or keeping slaves. Mankind was of no use to them. They simply wanted a ready-made planet on which to settle. Even if their combat tactics were almost insultingly rudimentary, they'd know, as they'd learned from the brin, that you couldn't leave a single native behind to get up to mischief. They'd scrape the planet clean of people, flatten the cities, and then start over so that no sign would remain that mankind had ever built a civilization on this planet or even walked its surface.

Ben realized with a jolt that if the mrill won, the only proof of man's existence might be the Voyager spacecraft, launched in 1977 and now cruising out of the solar system. The primitive machines carried gold plates embedded with basic data about the human race. Should, by an astronomically tiny chance, another alien civilization ten thousand years from now scoop up the spindly probes, they'd discover the brief history of an extinct species etched on these tombstones sent hurtling through the dark.

The Abrams tanks were firing wildly as they entered the square, desperate to at least do some damage before getting destroyed. The 120 mm cannons and .50 caliber machine guns roared and barked as the tanks bounced into the square, careening over sidewalks and cars, most of the shots going wild. The weapons tore into storefronts, trees, park benches, and the still-smoldering hulks of the cars and trucks the mrill had destroyed during their advance. Everything seemed to be exploding at once, and Ben used the chaos as cover for his own, more effective attack. The mrill were concentrating their fire on the tanks, which exploded like sealed food cans shoved into camp fires. Ben saw the mrill aiming at one of the tanks trying to circle around the burning, popping wreckage of another Abrams. Before they could fire, Ben snapped off a volley of shots, killing two of the mrill and sending the third tumbling backward. The tank roared into a clearing in the square, lowered its turret to aim at the cluster of mrill, and fired one shot before it was torn apart by another squad of troops . . . but it was a magnificent shot.

The General Dynamics M1028 round was more like a massive shotgun shell than a traditional tank round, packed with tiny tungsten balls to shred infantry or punch holes into concrete or cinderblock walls. The 1,098 hardened spheres, each 9.5 millimeters across, screamed out of the barrel at more than 1,400 meters per second.

Even the mrill didn't move that fast.

The pellets, moving at roughly four times the speed of sound, mulched a small plot of trees in the square and then plowed through a cluster of mrill troops, turning them to mulch as well. Two mrill soldiers simply ceased to exist in any visible form. Their rifles exploded, sending wild bolts of electricity arcing in every direction.

The air now stank of electricity and explosives. The mounting human losses were staggering. There were at least 60,000 dead, both military and civilian. It was hard for any mind, even Ben's augmented brain, to grasp that number. The piles of shattered hardware were also overwhelming. He'd never seen so much military equipment destroyed in such a short time. Tanks, planes, helicopters, ships, trucks. Crushed and stomped by the thousands. The nation's capital was on fire. What wasn't on fire had simply been turned to dust, for miles in every direction. Even if the mrill disappeared right now, this would go down as one of the costliest wars in history.

A jagged landscape of ruined, blackened tanks now blocked the streets heading out of McPherson Square, so the mrill started bombarding the wreckage, carving a canyon through the ruins. A few wounded soldiers were killed in this secondary assault, and Ben felt his hatred threaten to overwhelm him again. It was all he could do not to charge head-on at the mrill force. The writhing, impotent rage had no outlet, and he felt it would consume him; that he would die of bitter guilt before the mrill could kill him.

A dozen artillery shells, arcing in from the southwest, slammed into the mrill position without warning. A handful burst in midair, while the rest slammed into the ground. The staccato explosions reverberated through the battered square, gouging the concrete, puncturing the few remaining windows, and excavating craters in the ground. Several of the mrill were knocked to the ground, and Ben fired and fired and fired.

An Air Force AC-130J "Ghostrider" gunship was also coming on station. The massive airplane, bristling with a 30 mm cannon, bombs, and missiles, was built to slowly circle ground targets and grind them into powder. It was a devastating and demoralizing weapon—at least against human enemies. Ben had worked with them multiple times in his previous life. The gunships were tasked to Special Operations Command, and often served as angels on the shoulders of SEALs, Rangers, and other SpecOps boots on the ground. The ships were outfitted with a mix of weapons, and these new Ghostrider units were outfitted with the most sophisticated sensors and tracking technology known to man. Ben knew that the sixty or so mrill cutting a swath through downtown DC possessed technology about which man knew almost nothing, and they would destroy the lumbering aircraft as easily as they had the massive Abrams tanks.

"Ghostrider, acknowledge, this is US Navy Lieutenant Benjamin Shepherd. Acknowledge immediately. Yes, I can hack into your secure connection. You probably have about five seconds to acknowledge my communication and break off before the enemy zeroes you in."

To his credit, the pilot barely hesitated before responding.

"Copy that. Breaking off and awaiting instruction. Damn glad you're still with us, sir. Let us know what you need."

"Sit tight, pilot. I'm gonna conference you in with the artillery units positioned half a klick south of here. You're going to need the distraction, but it's gotta be timed perfectly. You'll probably get half a full pass before you'll need to withdraw and maybe we can get a second shot. No hero bullshit. There will be Klondike bars in hell before the mrill drop their guard for more than a couple seconds."

"Roger that," the pilot said and chuckled. "I never liked Klondike bars, anyway."

Ben scanned through the thicket of radio transmissions pouring in and out of the defensive emplacements near the White House. It was a tangled mess back there, and the snippets of conversation he intercepted contained an undercurrent of panic beneath the river of military jargon. He found the command frequency and dialed in.

"All US military forces stationed at the White House, this is Lieutenant Ben Shepherd, United States Navy. I am engaged with the enemy at the southwest corner of McPherson Square. I need an artillery barrage in the northeast corner of the square in sixty seconds to provide a diversion for an inbound Air Force AC-130 gunship. Strike coordinates are 38 degrees, 54 minutes, 8.5 seconds north, 77 degrees, 2 minutes, 1.8 seconds west. We've got sixty-some tangoes advancing on the White House, and this is our shot to clear their ranks a bit before its close quarters combat on the White House lawn. Acknowledge."

There was a moment's silence, then garbled conversation as multiple voices tried to jump in to respond. A deep southern accent cut through the jumble.

"Goddammit, radio discipline. This is Colonel Hank White, 1st Battalion, 201st Field Artillery. I've still got thirty-five M109A6 Paladin artillery units functional. I'm tasking them all to your strike coordinates. Mark sixty seconds . . . now. Good luck, son."

"Aye aye, sir," Ben said. "AC-130 captain, do you copy that?"

"This is Captain Tim Hackwell, and I damn well copy. Inbound in fifty-six seconds."

35

Colonel White ordered his artillery units, scattered across Arlington National Cemetery in defensive positions near the Pentagon, to prepare to fire. The heavy machines clanked as they repositioned to face northeast. The motorized 155-mm howitzers could deliver an artillery shell at a distance of more than 24 kilometers with pinpoint accuracy. They'd need that accuracy now.

The thirty-five Paladin units had left a trail of shredded grass and dirt behind them through the manicured mall, like fingers raked through the ground. They were stationary now as each four-man crew slammed home their shells. Each unit could fire as many as three rounds in fifteen seconds. White, parked a few dozen feet behind the cluster of Paladins in an armored Humvee, wondered if they'd get fifteen seconds before the mrill drones returned. The aliens had destroyed more than a dozen of his units in a strafing run minutes earlier; thankfully a handful of the Chinese drones had chased them off. The smoking, splintered hulks still dotted the landscape like fresh gravestones.

Medical units had poured out of the Pentagon to search for survivors, though the mrill weaponry had ensured that there were none. The medics were pulling what was left of the bodies from the vehicles and laying them on the churned meadow of the cemetery, the dead above resting on the dead below. Surprisingly, the mrill seemed not to have recognized the significance of the Pentagon itself, and the massive building stayed untouched.

"Twenty-four seconds to mark," White said into his headset, trying to ignore the procession of bodies being laid out behind his diminished unit.

The men had been well drilled and most were veterans of the recent campaigns in Afghanistan and Iraq. Whatever the nature of the enemy they were facing and the friends they had already lost and were likely still to lose, they knew their jobs. The "First West Virginia," as the National Guard unit was known, had a history dating back to the American Revolution and was the ancestor of parts of the Maryland and Virginia Rifle Regiment.

The fire teams plugged in the coordinates and White scanned the sky for a last check of incoming mrill drones. Radar just seemed to draw them in, so it had been shut down. For all the technology packed into the Paladin, the team was mostly driving and shooting blind. He hoped the coordinates were accurate.

"Four seconds to mark," White said into his mic.

Three mrill drones dropped out of the clouds about half a mile away and raced toward the artillery team. White gripped the dashboard, and the driver next to him tensed.

"Fire!"

The thirty-five barrels erupted in a drumroll, rocking each machine back on its treads.

White knew the men were reloading already, but the drones were here, and their green bolts walked up the green grass, pulling it apart, then ripping open the heavily armored Paladins. Four were obliterated instantly. A pair of antiaircraft guns, modified Phalanx 20 mm Gatling guns, hastily deployed in the Pentagon parking lot, opened fire, sending a stream of shells into the sky to bring down the drones. The military had been forced to shelve its surface-to-air missiles, as they simply could not get a radar lock or track a heat signature from the alien ships. That meant the soldiers were firing the massive Phalanx machine guns manually, tracking the drones visually on a high-resolution camera and firing the gun using a joystick control in a small shed hardwired to the gun emplacements about fifty feet away.

The Phalanx guns, originally designed to track and destroy incoming anti-ship missiles for the navy, packed a massive punch. Visually tracking the mrill drones was an almost impossible task, though, and the fire teams could only hope to distract the mrill long enough for the Paladins to fire off another volley or two.

One of the Phalanx guns raked directly across the hull of a mrill drone in a fantastically lucky hit. The explosive rounds tap-danced across the exotic armor, unable to penetrate the hull, but knocking the ship off course. Now all three drones turned toward the Phalanx guns. The Paladins fired another volley, a rolling thunderclap. One of the drones swooped across the field of fire at that exact moment and was hit by an artillery shells. This round, a 155 mm, high-explosive shell designed for tearing apart tanks, buildings, and infantry packed more than enough force to puncture the ship. A blinding explosion filled the sky, putting the still-struggling sun to shame, and the drone was yanked sideways. A jagged hunk was torn from its hull, and the wounded machine spiraled into the ground, furrowing into the soft dirt. The other drones, ignoring their downed companion, methodically raked the Phalanx emplacements, destroying them in moments.

But they'd done their job. The Paladin artillery units rocked on their heels one more time, hurling explosive shells at the mrill forces on the ground for a third time. White ordered the units to disperse. He harbored no illusions about escaping, but knew the additional time it took the drones to hunt them down represented a few more seconds that Shepherd could use to attack the mrill infantry. Maybe just enough time.

The drones, hovering in midair and glistening in the full sun, spun on their axis like no earthly aircraft White had ever seen. Their gun barrels hung low, and the bellies of the ships glowed a faint blue through the crisscrossing metallic structure. At least White thought it looked metallic. *Just one more mystery to take to my grave*, he thought without bitterness as the weapons swung to target his vehicle.

Then a massive sound, like a giant stomping his foot, filled the air. *Crump, crump, crump.* The AC-130 had arrived and was pounding the mrill infantry. White could see the fireballs and mushrooms of smoke to the northeast. He could feel the vibrations through the ground. The drones hesitated for a moment, then rose and zoomed off to the confrontation. Before they could rise thirty feet off the ground, a pair of green bolts sizzled through the sky from the south and lanced the two drones, blowing them apart. Two of the Chinese drones whistled through the air, their supersonic booms doing nothing to subdue the wild, ragged cheers of the soldiers on the ground.

White grinned, then roared.

"Keep firing, dammit. Everything you've got."

The artillery crews turned back to their work with savage joy.

White turned to his lieutenant.

"Don't know if we'll make it to supper, but we'll make damn sure these bastards don't either."

Lieutenant Daniel Fish smiled.

"I'm still full from breakfast, sir. I'd rather be working."

●

McPherson Square had almost literally been turned upside down.

The small plot, less than two acres of formerly tranquil grass and trees, park benches, and a statue of its Civil War namesake, looked now like the tortured surface of some volcanic, primordial planet. Jagged craters were formed, destroyed, and reformed as explosives and artillery mingled with the electric green crackle of mrill and brin weaponry. The air was a choking brew of dust, ash, and smoke, and splotches of fire dotted the uneven terrain. The buildings surrounding the square looked like the shattered faces of drunken barflies who'd somehow ended up in a ring with a heavyweight boxer. Chunks of masonry dripped from the mangled structures and shattered on the ground, adding to the noise, haze, and chaos. Soldiers fired haphazardly from the rubble on the south side of the square at the scattered mrill, the space too choked for any kind of vehicle to enter, while the AC-130 gunship above pounded the enemy infantry with bombs and 30 mm shells.

Ben slipped through the whirlwind, continuing to fire. He danced across the precarious rubble and bounded over the jagged craters in the ground. A building loomed ahead, and he scaled it in three giant vertical leaps, his feet and hands finding purchase on window ledges and fire escapes. He poured green fire into the shrinking body of the mrill force, picking them off one by one.

The three remaining mrill ground troops and the two remaining robots had been bunched up, concentrating their fire to plow through the last cluster of buildings between them and the cannon on the White House lawn. The battering ram had disintegrated as their numbers dwindled. The enemy troops and robots dispersed, fanning out like arms on a rake. The soldiers in the square tried to keep them in their sights, but the mrill troops vanished, activating their cloaking systems.

Ben's jamming signal had originally disabled their cloaking tech, but the mrill on the ground had finally managed to overpower his signal—at least for a moment. He knew they couldn't fire while invisible, as nearly all the nanomachines in their bodies had to be retasked to maintaining the visual illusion. The mrill would disappear, move to a new position, reappear for a second or two to fire, and then move on. The robots weren't equipped with the cloaking technology and weren't quite as mobile as the mrill foot soldiers, though what they lacked in stealth they made up for in armor, and bullets zinged harmlessly off their hides as they marched forward, red eyes glowing.

The AC-130 gunship overhead went silent. The robots were getting too close to the soldiers' positions. The robots seemed impenetrable and the mrill troops were impossible to track.

But Ben *could* see the mrill, or could at least see the heat signatures of their rifles.

He spotted the infrared blur of one of the weapons racing up the side of a crumpled building, where the mrill fighter would have an open line of fire into a squad of soldiers. He ordered his own nanobots to direct most of their resources to reestablishing the jamming signal. It meant losing his own ability to turn invisible, but he had no choice. He couldn't let those soldiers die while he could do something about it.

He turned and slung his rifle onto the roof of the building across the street, a 55-foot shot put. The clattering sound of it landing on the cement roof was lost in the roar of the battle, and he needed to be as nimble as possible. Even before the rifle landed, he launched himself up the side of the building. He bounded dozens of feet at a time, his feet finding slim edges, his hands growing thin adhesive pads similar to those on a gecko's toes. He couldn't dangle from a flat wall by just his hands, but the sticky pads allowed him to momentarily cling to the rough surface as his feet found purchase and propelled him further. It was, despite the furor, exhilarating.

Ben hauled himself over the cornice and landed on the balls of his feet on the dirty roof. He retrieved his rifle and crept to the edge of the rooftop. The scene below almost defied belief. A jagged ravine ran from the northeast, where the mrill had originally landed, down to the square. The charred, blackened trench was littered with bodies, mostly human, some mrill, as well as chunks of crushed and shredded civilian and military vehicles. The scar cut straight through buildings, and mangled wires spit sparks through the tangles of crumbled masonry, twisted steel rebar, and mutilated furniture that sagged out from the vivisected structures. Fires burned everywhere. A blackened fire truck, torn in half, its red and blue strobe lights still spinning lazily, had been abandoned at one street corner. No firefighters were in sight. *Can't blame them.* It was an active battlefield and the mrill would kill them as promptly as they did the soldiers. Maybe they already had.

To the southwest, now just a stone's throw away, the White House was still pristine, but the lawn was stuffed with soldiers and marines. The defensive cannon bathed them in crimson light every time it fired, making them look like scurrying ants in a puddle of blood. The stench of burning plastic and flesh filled the air. Ben was momentarily paralyzed at the horror of it all. *If this isn't what hell looks like, then the devil needs to take some notes.*

Ben could see a ring of troops and armor closing in from a few miles away. They wouldn't get here in time to engage the last few mrill before they reached the White House lawn. Fighter jets streaked across the sky, pursued by the last few mrill drones over the city. He knew the bulk of the force was still above the planet, tangling with Eddie and Nick. The cannon, less than half a mile away, continued to pump out concussive bolts of energy. Ben sensed that the battle above was slipping away.

He ingested all this information in less than half a second. His jamming signal took over, the remaining mrill became visible, and Ben fired. Two of the three remaining mrill soldiers went down before the last zeroed in on his position and returned fire, along with the two robots. He tumbled back from the edge of the roof as their shots punched into the building, ripping out concrete. Even with Ben out of visual range, they continued to fire into the wounded building and he realized they intended to demolish it and crush him in the debris.

He rolled backward, away from the edge of the disintegrating building, as wads of masonry hurtled in all directions. The structure was collapsing beneath him. He swung his left hand out to grab onto an exposed girder while his right hand flipped his rifle onto his back, where his internal nanomachines grabbed it in a magnetic embrace. The building looked like Swiss cheese, with more holes being punched open every second. The floors below were collapsing into a growing bonfire fueled by chairs, papers, and desks, while the bitter smell of burnt plastic filled the air. A "Hang in there, baby!" motivational poster of a cat dangling from a rope swung on its hook, came loose, and somersaulted down into the flames.

"Sorry, kitty," Ben said, feeling the girder in his hand begin to come loose.

He started to pull himself up until one of the energy blasts sliced across his left shoulder. He cried out and lost his grip, falling. He landed with a thud on the sharp edge of a desk perched on a chunk of the floor below that was still intact and felt several thick shards of glass puncture his back. He rolled to the floor, groaning, trying to move to the rear of the building as it continued to collapse around him. Had to get out of here. He staggered to his feet just as another energy blast cut through his right thigh. He fell again, and a massive section of ceiling slammed into his head, driving him to the floor. His body was already repairing itself, but there was no time to wait.

Off the ground, dazed, leaving a thick trail of blood. Almost to the window, his right leg dragging. Flames engulfed him from the rear, the heat burning his skin. He threw himself at the window with all his strength, feeling the damaged muscles in his leg and shoulder tear further.

He struck the glass at the same moment as the fireball. He was only three stories off the ground, but it gave him enough time to realize he was going to land on a small iron fence on the ground below. As the firelight twinkled through the fragments of spinning glass, Ben tried to twist his body to avoid impaling his head on the iron spikes. His lower body crashed into the fence, his nanomachines trying to harden his skin against the impact even as they struggled to repair his other wounds. The spikes didn't completely penetrate his body, but Ben felt them slice deep. The building finally gave up, like a dizzy child wobbling off a merry-go-round, and came down with a *whoosh*. Gray air and gnarled fragments of debris sprayed out like a shotgun blast. A chunk of meat was ripped from the back of Ben's right leg, the protective nanomachines overwhelmed, and he stifled a scream while smaller fragments peppered his back and shoulder. He pulled himself to his feet using the last remaining fragments of the fence that were still standing. His vision dimmed and he slipped to one knee, forcing himself back up.

Ben hopped on his good left leg as he turned and pulled his rifle from his back, which seemed undamaged. He sensed the last soldier and two robots working their way through the rubble. He was suddenly back in New Mexico, on that absurd moonlit night when this had all started. He was back in Pakistan. He was back in Afghanistan, Iraq, and every other warzone he'd ever gone to. He was back in boot camp. Nothing ever changed. There was always another war, another battle, another fight. What was it Santayana had said? *Only the dead have seen the end of war.* Ben wasn't so sure. If there was a hell, or at least a place more hellish than Earth, then surely the eternal punishment for all dead soldiers was eternal war, a never-ending battlefield where the dead were endlessly stitched up, resurrected, and shoved back into combat.

He could sense, in the brief lull, the waning struggle above the atmosphere. Nick and Eddie were not doing well. The enemy's numbers were simply too great. Their last charge had almost failed, and the Chinese drones were being plucked like feathers on a goose.

The trooper and robots rushed over the rubble of the collapsed building, firing as they charged. Ben, his leg already knitting up, rolled sideways, returning fire, his machines uninterested in his despair. One of the robots slipped in the loose debris and a concrete slab shifted and slid down onto its leg. The slab pinned the robot down for just a moment, long enough for Ben to draw a bead and fire, obliterating its upper body. The explosion knocked the other robot sideways, but it recovered in midair and landed neatly on the side of an exposed segment of shredded concrete and steel rebar, clinging to the mangled metal with its metallic claws, its eyes glowing red. But again, that was just enough time for Ben, who fired two shots into its body. The machine blew apart like Legos.

The last mrill soldier had momentarily disappeared in the dust, but Ben spotted it with his upgraded eyes. The mrill still seemed to not fully appreciate that this human was as capable as they were. The arrogance struck him again, and Ben wondered if they had never truly encountered a similarly advanced and equally warlike species. He looked for one last shot to end this battle.

Just as his finger curled around the trigger, the briefest flicker of a gray dart plunged into the thirty feet of jagged terrain between Ben and the mrill soldier and exploded. In the fraction of a second before both combatants were hurled from their feet, Ben realized that the AC-130 must have dropped a GBU-39 bomb out of an excess of enthusiasm. Known as a "Small Diameter Bomb," the weapon was designed to focus the destruction in a limited area and minimize collateral damage. That was not much consolation if you were inside the impact area of the 206-pound warhead, he realized in that moment. The light from the blast was the first thing to hit Ben, he noticed in almost slow motion. The shockwave and debris then hit next, almost simultaneously, at the speed of sound. Ben felt his eyeballs flatten under the pressure and his skin quivered and flapped before the nanomachines were able to link together and harden. Even with the protection, the force of the detonation still lifted the human and mrill off their feet with ease, like dandelion seeds in the breeze.

As Ben looped through the air, his mind slowing down, he realized he was traveling in a predictable and calculable arc. Simple Newtonian physics.

And he still had his rifle.

Particles of concrete, fragments of steel, bits of paper, dirt, and a thousand other unidentifiable pieces of debris all moved through the air with him like dancers at a waltz. They slid and spun as the universe demanded, the already diminishing force of the explosion and the relentless tug of gravity prescribing their paths with precision. Ben knew he was being driven back toward the spikes of the iron fence and wondered if his tiring body would be able to fully protect him. Probably not.

He brought his rifle to his shoulder, his body about fifteen off the ground, flying backward at about thirty feet per second. He sighted down the barrel, between his feet, waiting for a spinning planetoid of asphalt to clear his view. Time barely seemed to exist anymore, and his senses felt amped even beyond what they'd been before. If he concentrated hard enough, Ben felt like he could count the molecules in the air. The chunk of what had previously been a parking space rotated as it moved through its brief trajectory, ancient clots of gum dotting its surface. A quarter was embedded in one of the pink blobs, and George Washington seemed to nod as he spun, unable to tell a lie.

A thousandth of a second later, the pavement and the former president slid out of the way, and Ben finally had a clear line of sight to his enemy.

The mrill soldier had apparently noticed the same opportunity and was bringing its weapon up as well. Through a thin corridor in the dust and the flame, the two faced each other down the long barrels of their guns. Ben smiled. For one of them, this battle was blessedly over. The faintest puzzled look passed over the face of the mrill soldier at the sight of Ben's smirk, and they both fired. The beams crossed in the thick cloud of dust and smoke, vaporizing particles of concrete and debris. As the bursts of energy passed within inches of each other, they interacted briefly; sizzling bolts of electricity arcing from one beam to the other for the barest fraction of a second. The two beams went their separate ways, leaving swirls of superheated gas behind them. Each fighter was struck by the other's shot and, with that, time seemed to notice the two soldiers again and sent them crashing down out of their slow dances and slamming them into the ground.

Ben landed in a jumble on the ground and cried out, a deep cut burning the side of his torso. Instinctively, he tried to sit up to examine the wound, but his nanomachines had immobilized him from the neck down to minimize additional injury so they could try and seal the gash. He sensed it wasn't a sure thing. The beam had gone deep. He turned his head to the right, the only movement he could make, and saw the mrill spread on the ground. Ben's shot had hit him directly in the chest, punching a hole straight through. Green blood trickled from the alien's mouth. It looked over at Ben, its fingers twitched, and then it was still.

Ben looked up and realized thick, heavy clouds had moved in. The sun was gone. He could hear fires raging everywhere. There were sirens in every direction. Hundreds, if not thousands, of American soldiers were dead.

But it wasn't over.

"Ben, you still there?" Rickert's voice filled his head.

"For the moment," Ben replied. "We got 'em all on the ground, but . . ."

"But what?"

"Hold on."

Ben, who had been following only peripherally the battle above the planet, connected fully to Nick's and Eddie's internal computer systems. The gloom from the gathering rain clouds was replaced by the black of space and the pinprick of a million stars and the fury of the alien armada.

Nick and Eddie sensed the link, and Ben could feel their relentless determination but also their quiet acknowledgment that they were fighting a battle they could not win.

"Hey boss, welcome to the main event," Eddie chirped.

"Yeah, we've got them right where we want them," Nick said, racing beneath the tangled structure of the mrill mothership, firing at anything that looked like critical machinery. A small swarm of Chinese drones covered his attack run, but the mrill drones and defensive weapons on their ship picked them off methodically. Plus, the shots on the mothership seemed to have no effect. Nick and Eddie's scanners couldn't penetrate the shielding around the ship, so they had no idea where they should be targeting their attack. They were essentially firing blind.

"We've hit it at least two dozen times, from every angle, but they're fixing it as fast as we tear it apart, and we're not sure where the weak points are or even if there *are* any weak points," Eddie said. "Our drone fleet is about gone. We've seen them launch seven additional troop dropships, and so far we've managed to destroy them before they get past us. But I—wait, hold on"—Eddie took three quick shots—"I get the feeling they're just waiting to finish smearing us before sending in the *real* reinforcements."

Ben grunted in pain as his nanobots pulled another piece of his torn flesh together.

"We got all the ones down here, but just barely. And if they land anywhere else, where I can't help out, we're done," Ben said. "And not sure how much help I'd be if they landed five feet away right now. I'm leaking pretty good."

A Chinese drone on Nick's starboard side blew apart and he angled off to avoid being vaporized himself.

"I don't suppose the Chinese are sending us any more presents," he wondered.

"Afraid not," Ben said. "General, you got any good news we don't know about?"

Rickert sighed.

"No. We still don't know if the president and SecDef survived the attack on NORAD. We've got no reinforcements to send up. Comms are spotty, but it looks like most of the world is in various stages of either civil unrest or complete social collapse. Half the world seems to be fleeing from the cities and the other half fleeing *into* them. Just . . . just chaos. It's not surprising, but we couldn't send in more ground reinforcements to DC because every highway is clogged. We're airlifting in a marine battalion to the area, but it's just messy as hell. I'm not sure what they'll do when they get there, but everyone's flying off half-cocked. The VP has disappeared. Don't know if he's been killed or just in hiding. I guess I'm pretty much in charge, for whatever that's worth."

Ben felt his nanomachines return some control to his muscles as his body began to heal. He pushed himself up on one elbow as it began to rain. Soldiers—*human* soldiers—were now picking their way forward through the rubble, rifles raised. He sat up completely and waved them over. Their rifles swiveled to face him, then lowered as the men recognized him and began running over.

Ben turned his attention back to the skies above, the smoking, subdued streets of DC disappearing from his vision, replaced by the fury of battle at all angles. Attacks and retreats unfolded above and below, at every speed, the ships firing and dodging and regrouping too fast for any normal human brain to grasp, much less direct.

Any purely human technology guided by a purely human pilot would have been destroyed in an instant. This was the last line of defense now . . . and Ben knew what had to happen.

He'd known for a while, suspected since the first moment he'd stood in the cold New Mexican desert and understood what the invaders wanted. A sacrifice was required—a blood sacrifice. But not his own. Ben's punishment would be the fulfillment of Abraham's nightmare, murdering the one closest to him at the command of a mysterious, otherworldly entity. Unlike Isaac, though, there would be no reprieve. The vision would become the reality. He had not been able to save his father. That failure, that weakness, had now led him inexorably to this moment where he must cast his brother over the side, as well, into the uncaring void.

Nick and Eddie sensed the situation before Ben could articulate it. Their wireless link made it almost impossible for one to conceal anything from the other two.

"You don't need to give the order, boss," Nick said. "We'll take care of it."

"Yes, I do," Ben responded without hesitation.

"What order?" Rickert asked. "What's going on?"

Ben calculated in a moment which of the two men was in a better position to carry out the final strike.

"Nick," Ben said. He could feel raindrops pattering his face while his eyes stared into the beautiful vacuum two hundred thousand miles above. "I need you to fly your ship into the mrill mothership and activate your self-destruct and detonate your nuke. I'd tell you to fire your Tomahawk, but it's simply not precise enough."

"Aye aye, Lieutenant," Nick said without hesitation.

"Eddie, withdraw about two hundred klicks and observe. If they shoot Nick down before he can get close enough, it will be up to you," Ben continued.

"Copy that."

"Wait," Rickert said. "Don't the drones have self-destruct mechanisms?"

"Yes, but they're not powerful enough. We need to blow the warhead on the Tomahawk as well, and the drones aren't armed with those."

Ben and Eddie linked their minds to Nick. From here on out, whatever he felt, they'd feel. Whatever he thought, they'd share. They were all one mind from this point forward.

Nick could finally see all the things Ben had been holding back. All the memories—a lifetime of them—filled him in a momentary flash. Over all of them lurked the memory of the struggle on the boat. Nick thought he could see it clearer than perhaps Ben ever had, without the tangled knot of guilt and fear and deep shame that had wrapped itself around Ben's mind.

The water is smooth as liquid glass as they leave the harbor. No clouds. No birds. Just sea and sky and a rising red sun at their backs. Such a setting was perhaps more ominous in the days of sailing ships, but it is perfect weather for a diesel-powered craft. The catch is plentiful, and the ship soon is slung low on the water, weighted down by good fortune. They eat fistfuls of hard biscuits and crumbly cheddar as fast as they can, enjoying the hard and simple work beneath the warm sun. As they putter through the dark blue water, the father shows his son how to mend the nets, read the sonar, work the pumps. Only when the last slip of land slinks from view behind them does the flat air begin to fold. A small breeze and a gray cloud chugging over the western horizon, slow and fat. Plenty of time to finish the catch.

"Should we go back now, Dad?"

The man seems unsure, perhaps weighing the racing clouds against the responsibilities and debts the child can barely understand. He pulls his tattered Giants cap, the orange SF logo now faded, up and down on his head, sweat glinting in the retreating sun.

"One more catch. Hold is almost full. Easiest hunt we've had in months."

They drop the nets one more time, as the tall and deep cumulonimbus clouds get faster and blacker. The boy sees the man whip his gaze back and forth between sea and sky, a jittery cigarette sending up a jagged distress signal.

"Okay, that's enough. Pull up the lines."

The whine of the electric motor as the full, squirming nets are brought up, the last load of yellowfins are dumped in the hold. A rumble of thunder from no more than a mile or two to the west, Neptune clearing his throat. The man races to the cabin and pulls on the throttle. As they turn the boat back to the east, to home, the engine stalls; a clog in the fuel line.

A minor thing on any other day. The storm, almost sensing the handicap, rushes in, boxing its fists around the crippled ship. It spins and rolls on the growing waves. The boy can hear the dead-eyed, slippery tuna shifting and sloshing in the hold as he struggles with his lifejacket. The father lets go of his handhold to help the boy. The ship is now just debris carried at the whim of the frothing water. A mountainous wave crashes down, nearly rolling the ship, and the father tumbles overboard, twisted in a heavy fishing net. The boy cries out as the father grabs the wood railing with his one free arm, the other bound in the net. The boy skids and stumbles across the lurching deck, slamming hard against the railing. He bounces up, grabs his father's arm, and pulls with all his strength, green rubber boots squeaking for purchase. He leans back, pitting his slender body against the entire amused weight of the ocean. He can't even see his father's face. His grip is slipping. His boots are inching forward. A metal cleat is just inches away. If he can get his father's hand around that, then maybe attach the hook from the electric winch to the twisted net, he could . . .

The water surges and heaves, a bull tossing its rider, and his father is gone without a sound, slipping away.

The boy screams, crunches again against the railing, and yells for his father. The thick nets are an anchor, though, and there is nothing to see but a faded cap swirling in a small whirlpool. The ocean spray slaps at the boy's face—he can taste the salt—and the rain washes it away. He keeps yelling, but the storm drowns him out. When the sea finally quiets down, the boy is too hoarse to make a sound. He tries to fix the fuel line, but salt water has soaked the engine. *Constance* drifts and bakes in the hot sun in the emptied sky. The dead fish in the hold stink. The entire ship is a floating coffin, with one small boy stubbornly still alive. He sips from a bottle of water and devours the few biscuits that weren't liquidated. He does not touch the fish.

Eventually, he is found, if not saved.

Nick felt all this in an instant.

That was an accident, Nick sent back. *And what I'm doing now is a choice. My choice. You are not responsible for what happened then, or what's happening now. I am choosing this path. This is not your guilt to carry.*

For a moment, Ben resisted the offer. But it wasn't really an offer. It was a command, a revelation, and it would not be denied. His emotional defenses, a fortress of ice, dissolved beneath the blazing heat and light of Nick's words. Ben felt brief panic at releasing so much, surrendering so much of what he had become. If he was no longer bound by this grief, this guilt, what was he?

Then relief.

He was free.

Free to do what needed to be done, and to save all those he still could. Maybe not everyone. But he would save all he could, mourn the ones he could not, and keep moving. Those who died protecting and serving the ones they loved would no longer be his burden. They would be his inspiration.

Nick felt these revelations wash over Ben as completely as if they had been his own. Ben deserved this peace. But Nick didn't have any time left to sit around discussing. Not if he wanted to make his own choice count.

Nick swirled the remaining drones around him like a cloak. They criss-crossed around him, firing as they moved, trying to distract and confuse the mrill fighters. The swarm rushed the mrill ship. Drones were picked off, the fifty or so ships diminishing quickly. Nick closed fast on the mothership, programming his craft to initiate the self-immolation moments before it struck the hull. Once the four-second countdown was started, there would be no turning back, no maneuvering. It was a one-shot opportunity.

Nick thought back on his childhood, peaceful and happy. No major traumas, only the standard pains and regrets. His final year of high school, when he'd mentioned that he was thinking of joining the Navy and trying out for the SEALs, his dad had taken him out for a drive in their old but well-maintained pickup truck. They'd wandered aimlessly for an hour or so, Nick, always quiet and pensive, letting his dad take his time. He finally told Nick that his mother was probably going to cry a bit, hell, that he might cry a bit, too. But not to let that stop him. That wasn't why they were crying. They were proud of him. That Nick was about to grow up fast, faster than most men his age, who seemed determined to stay boys as long as possible. Most people ran away from the world, and Nick was running toward it. That was good, something to be proud of. Just be careful. Now let's stop and get gas before it goes up another nickel because your dad spent a week running his mouth.

Nick watched the swirl of color outside his cockpit and realized he'd known himself for a long time. He was ready. He hoped his parents wouldn't cry too much again. He accelerated toward the mothership.

I'll carry your memories for you, Ben said in a mental telegram. *I'll keep those alive for you.*

Thank you, my friend. You can shut down our link, if you'd like, he replied to Ben.

No. I'm with you all the way.

Me too, Eddie thought.

Without another word, Nick charged in with Ben and Eddie looking over his shoulder. The Chinese drones huddled tight, firing straight ahead, cutting a path straight toward the spiky mrill ship. Six seconds out.

Nick took a deep breath and let out all his regret. Everything else he'd envisioned for his life, he let it go.

Ben felt those dreams fall on his shoulders. The girl Nick had loved privately, Trisha, a short girl with long braids, who told jokes and loved spicy food and midnight movies. A half-repaired motorcycle, parts strewn in a garage around tools and oil spots and tattered user manuals. A not-yet-conceived child, the hope of a child, a fierce love waiting to be unleashed, a boy or girl to be introduced to Grampa and Gramma. Nick let it all fall away and Ben picked it up, feeling his friend's memories as if they were his own. Not guilt. Just the memories and dreams of a friend who did not deserve death but had chosen it so that others might live.

Four seconds out. Nick activated the self-destruct and long tendrils of pure energy snaked out of the ship's engine; the vessel began to vibrate with the impending reaction. The cockpit filled with light, and he watched as the mothership loomed ahead. All of its guns were now firing at his ship, but it was still shielded by the last of the ally drones. The mrill drones had also converged on his position. Shots rained down from every direction and began to pick through the gaps in the drone shield around his ship, but the blasts were now absorbed by the energy bubble growing around the ship. Ben felt the ion blasts and the raindrops pelt him simultaneously. The storm was everywhere. Nick, connected to Ben across two hundred thousand miles, felt it too. A bolt of lightning and cannon blast of thunder filled the skies over Washington as Nick's ship reached its crescendo.

Everything was white.

Everything was destroyed.

His ship erupted like a like a new star being born, a furious sphere that engulfed everything in its path. The reaction fed on the mrill ship, growing and expanding. Ben felt his connection with Nick snap. He almost cried out with the pain as the explosive reaction continued, indifferent to his anguish.

The mothership tried to fire its engines, to open a cut in space and escape. Ben, through Eddie, saw a gaping, jagged portal open, and through it glimpsed for a moment a yellow, stormy planet, a random escape point somewhere in the universe that the desperate mrill had punched in. The ship tried to move toward the portal, but the explosion from Nick's ship had done too much damage. The mothership's engine tore itself apart, sending a flash of purple flames darting out into the vacuum. The stern of the ship disintegrated, and with that the portal collapsed. The ship was wrenched in half and Ben could now hear the pained, panicked screams of the mrill crew spilling over across frequencies. For a moment, the sound was everywhere, although another signal, impossible to decipher, seemed to be hidden in the cacophony. Then the ship bulged outward and detonated, a shockwave expanding in all directions that obliterated the last of the mrill drones and attack ships. All the voices were silenced.

Eddie, who had cruised out of range of the explosion, sat steady in the void.

Then he slowly turned his ship around and headed back toward Earth.

36

"**S**ir, are you okay? Sir?"

Ben blinked, and he was back on the ground in Washington, DC. It was still raining, and he blinked again, pushing the water from his eyes. Above him stood a bloodied marine, rifle still at the ready. When Ben moved, he yelled for a medic.

Ben sat up and ran his hand along his side, then his leg. The wounds were gone. His body had expelled various pieces of metal and other shrapnel, and they lay on the ground around his body in an outline. No scars. None you could see, anyway.

"Don't bother, Sergeant. I'm good. It's over."

"Sir?"

"We got 'em. Both the ground force and the mothership are destroyed. It's time to look for wounded and regroup."

The marine opened his mouth, glanced again at Ben's gray skin and steady gaze, closed his mouth and moved off, ordering his men to organize search and rescue teams.

"General, you there?"

"I'm here, Ben," Rickert replied. "I'm glad you're there, too. I guess thank you doesn't begin to cover it, but thank you."

Ben looked up as he sensed Eddie's ship descending through the rain clouds. The soldiers on the ground cried out as it emerged from the gloom, thinking it another mrill ship.

Ben stood and waved them off, assuring them it was one of the good guys.

He walked toward the ship as it settled in a small clearing in the wreckage.

"You know, all of this, all of the sacrifice, all it did was buy us some time," Ben said to Rickert and Eddie over his connection. "The mrill sent their expeditionary force because they thought they could catch us with our pants down, or at least only halfway up. They thought they'd get lucky—they almost did. But this wasn't their full strength. I don't know how long we've got. A year or more, hopefully, while they assemble a complete invasion force and cross the galaxy. We'll have to be better next time. We'll need more like us."

Eddie stepped down the ramp of his ship, quiet and thoughtful.

"We need to restart the nano injection process," Ben said. "We need an army. The three of us barely held them back, and now there's only two of us."

"I know," Rickert said.

"And I think the mrill sent one last signal down here at the very end."

"Yeah, I felt it too," Eddie said. "I don't know what it was, but they broadcast something toward Earth. I don't know. Something . . . a sleeper agent maybe?"

"Yeah, we might be fighting a two-front war before we know it," Ben said. "Any word on the president?"

"They're still digging. I don't know. I hope so. I'm trying to get a command system up and running. Someone needs to address the country soon. The TV anchors have basically been crapping their pants, and I don't think anyone else smells much better. If we're going to regroup, we need to do it soon."

"Copy that. I'll be there soon, sir," Ben said.

"Copy that. And . . . heck of a job out there. A lot of people are going to have a hard time saying that. There will be some that will blame you for what happened. Don't listen to any of that. You, Eddie, Nick, you guys are heroes."

"Thank you, sir. See you soon."

Ben sighed. Eddie walked up to him and was silent for a moment. He dug into his pocket.

"You know, I heard you liked these," he said as he pulled out two cigars.

Ben laughed in the rain. Eddie waved at one of the marines combing through the wreckage nearby.

"Hey, kid, got a light?"

The marine, a Lance Corporal with O'MALLEY stitched above his heart, approached slowly, picking his way through the concrete and steel, stun bling occasionally. He fumbled through his pockets, unable to keep his eyes off the two men and their gray skin. He finally produced a battered lighter and held it out to Eddie.

Eddie took it, flicked the cap open, and spun the wheel.

Click.

Ben leaned in to the fragile flame, blocking out the rain. He took a deep pull, letting the smoke fill him as his nanomachines filtered out the toxins. He exhaled, watching the smoke drift off. Eddie tossed the lighter back to the marine, who stared for another moment before his sergeant yelled for him to get back in formation. As the troops moved on, Ben and Eddie stood without speaking or thinking, surveying the destruction that stretched off to the northeast.

"So, you think you could have broken some more shit down here? I see a flower pot over there you forgot to nuke," Eddie said, finally breaking the silence.

Ben laughed again. It seemed right. Earned. The rain was passing, and he felt cleansed, if not yet healed.

"Seriously, it's like Godzilla used the city as his own personal ball scratcher. I'll be damned if I'm gonna get stuck for the tab on this one."

"Next time Godzilla has itchy nuts, I'll be sure to call you first," Ben said.

They both smiled and smoked as the clouds began to turn from gray to a soft white.

After a few minutes, Ben ground his cigar under his foot. He almost left it there, then bent down, picked it up, and flung it into a nearby trashcan that was almost miraculously unscathed. He lifted an eyebrow toward Eddie, who shrugged.

"Well, it's a start. Ready to go?"

Ben nodded, his smile fading.

"Yeah, something I've got to do first."

"What's that?"

"I need to go see Nick's parents. Diego's, too."

The sky coughed one last spat of rain, then fell into sullen silence as the weather system trudged east, out to sea.

The sun wasn't out yet. Ben thought it might rain again, but the sun would emerge before the day was done.

"I'll come with you," Eddie said.

EPILOGUE

The Russian stood and stretched in his gray apartment. Out the window, the dishwater sky seemed to lack the conviction to promise rain, only to suggest it. The Russian rubbed the scar on his forehead and looked back at his now-dark laptop on the table in the corner.

This had not gone as planned. As promised.

He'd done his part. The invaders had not. He'd watched on the television as the tide of the battle shifted back and forth. He'd also had access to a video stream on his laptop that the Americans quite literally would have killed for; a vantage point in space that no one else on the planet had. That had gone dark when the Americans launched their final kamikaze attack.

It had gone dark, and then a last blip of data had arrived, and then contact had stopped altogether.

That blip contained a new world, though. Or, at least, blueprints for a new world. The invaders would return. Not immediately. They needed to regroup. But they would come. The Russian knew the blip meant he was expected to facilitate that effort. He considered that.

The invaders had been desperate. They had sent him much—perhaps too much for their own good.

The Russian had never been more than a general. A man who took orders. Perhaps it was time to start giving them.

ACKNOWLEDGMENTS

Thank you to my agent, Mike Hoogland, for faith, enthusiasm, advice, and insight into where I needed to add and where I needed to subtract, as well as prompt replies to my anxious emails.

Thank you to my editor, Jason Katzman, for saving me from myself multiple times and helping me see the way ahead.

Thank you to my wife, Sarah, and our kids, for letting me run off for hours on end to write, rewrite, and pretend to write.

Thank you to Mom and Dad, for believing all this was possible, and for reading first drafts that were far too rough.

Thank you, Gramma, for making me rewrite that essay in high school a dozen times until it was just right. You prepared me for the last seven years.

Thank you, reader, for reading.